HEART OF DARKNESS

AND TALES OF UNREST

HEART OF DARKNESS
AND TALES OF UNREST

JOSEPH CONRAD

This edition published in 2018 by Arcturus Publishing Limited
26/27 Bickels Yard, 151–153 Bermondsey Street,
London SE1 3HA

Introduction by Brian Busby
Typesetting by Palimpsest Book Production Limited

Cover design: Peter Ridley
Cover illustration: Peter Gray
Design: Beatriz Custodio

AD001540UK

Printed in the UK

Contents

Introduction

Joseph Conrad was born Józef Teodor Konrad Korzeniowski on 3 December 1857. The son of Polish parents, his birthplace was the small Ukrainian city of Berdyczów, then part of the Russian Empire. Conrad's father, Apollo Korzeniowski, was a playwright and translator whose political activism eventually forced the family into exile. Orphaned at the age of eleven, Conrad was cared for by an uncle. Five years later, he was allowed to embark on a 21-year career as a mariner. While Conrad's adventures would come to inspire his fiction, it was not until he left the sea behind that he began to write with any seriousness. Conrad's first novel, *Almayer's Folly* (1896), was a critical success, but achieved nowhere near the sales he needed to support himself. He was still struggling when, in 1899, *Heart of Darkness* appeared as a three-part series in *Blackwood's Magazine*. An autobiographical tale, it was inspired by a six-month voyage up the Congo River that Conrad had made some nine years earlier. While it has come to be considered one of the greatest works in English literature, reception at the time was more muted; it was not until 1902 that the novel appeared in book form. Other classic works followed – *Lord Jim* (1900), *Nostromo* (1904), and *The Secret Agent* (1907) – but these, too, attracted little more than respectable sales.

In addition to his novels, Conrad was a prolific writer of short stories. The earliest collection of these was *Tales of Unrest* (1898), which set the tone for much of Conrad's later, and more acclaimed, literary work.

Conrad's financial fortunes changed with the 1913 publication of his fourteenth book, *Chance*. During the decade that followed, in much more comfortable circumstances, he completed five more novels, including *Victory* (1915).

Conrad died on 3 August 1924.

HEART OF DARKNESS

I

The _Nellie_, a cruising yawl, swung to her anchor without a flutter of the sails, and was at rest. The flood had made, the wind was nearly calm, and being bound down the river, the only thing for it was to come to and wait for the turn of the tide.

The sea-reach of the Thames stretched before us like the beginning of an interminable waterway. In the offing the sea and the sky were welded together without a joint, and in the luminous space the tanned sails of the barges drifting up with the tide seemed to stand still in red clusters of canvas sharply peaked, with gleams of varnished sprits. A haze rested on the low shores that ran out to sea in vanishing flatness. The air was dark above Gravesend, and farther back still seemed condensed into a mournful gloom, brooding motionless over the biggest, and the greatest, town on earth.

The Director of Companies was our captain and our host. We four affectionately watched his back as he stood in the bows looking to seaward. On the whole river there was nothing that looked half so nautical. He resembled a pilot, which to a seaman is trustworthiness personified. It was difficult to realize his work was not out there in the luminous estuary, but behind him, within the brooding gloom.

Between us there was, as I have already said somewhere, the bond of the sea. Besides holding our hearts together through long periods of separation, it had the effect of making us tolerant of each other's yarns – and even convictions. The Lawyer – the best of old fellows – had, because of his many years and many virtues, the only cushion on deck, and was lying on the only rug. The Accountant had brought out already a box of dominoes, and was toying architecturally with the bones. Marlow sat cross-legged right aft, leaning against the mizzen-mast. He had sunken cheeks, a yellow complexion, a straight back, an ascetic aspect, and, with his arms dropped, the palms of hands outwards, resembled an idol. The Director, satisfied the anchor had good hold, made his way aft and sat down amongst us. We exchanged a few words lazily. Afterwards there was silence on board the yacht. For some reason or other we did not begin that game of dominoes. We felt meditative, and fit for nothing but placid staring. The day was ending in a serenity of still and exquisite brilliance.

The water shone pacifically; the sky, without a speck, was a benign immensity of unstained light; the very mist on the Essex marshes was like a gauzy and radiant fabric, hung from the wooded rises inland, and draping the low shores in diaphanous folds. Only the gloom to the west, brooding over the upper reaches, became more sombre every minute, as if angered by the approach of the sun.

And at last, in its curved and imperceptible fall, the sun sank low, and from glowing white changed to a dull red without rays and without heat, as if about to go out suddenly, stricken to death by the touch of that gloom brooding over a crowd of men.

Forthwith a change came over the waters, and the serenity became less brilliant but more profound. The old river in its broad reach rested unruffled at the decline of day, after ages of good service done to the race that peopled its banks, spread out in the tranquil dignity of a waterway leading to the uttermost ends of the earth. We looked at the venerable stream not in the vivid flush of a short day that comes and departs for ever, but in the august light of abiding memories. And indeed nothing is easier for a man who has, as the phrase goes, 'followed the sea' with reverence and affection than to evoke the great spirit of the past upon the lower reaches of the Thames. The tidal current runs to and fro in its unceasing service, crowded with memories of men and ships it had borne to the rest of home or to the battles of the sea. It had known and served all the men of whom the nation is proud, from Sir Francis Drake to Sir John Franklin, knights all, titled and untitled – the great knights-errant of the sea. It had borne all the ships whose names are like jewels flashing in the night of time, from the *Golden Hind* returning with her round flanks full of treasure, to be visited by the Queen's Highness and thus pass out of the gigantic tale, to the *Erebus* and *Terror*, bound on other conquests – and that never returned. It had known the ships and the men. They had sailed from Deptford, from Greenwich, from Erith – the adventurers and the settlers; kings' ships and the ships of men on 'Change; captains, admirals, the dark 'interlopers' of the Eastern trade, and the commissioned 'generals' of East India fleets. Hunters for gold or pursuers of fame, they all had gone out on that stream, bearing the sword, and often the torch, messengers of the might within the land, bearers of a spark from the sacred fire. What greatness had not floated on the ebb of that river into the mystery of an unknown earth!... The dreams of men, the seed of commonwealths, the germs of empires.

The sun set; the dusk fell on the stream, and lights began to appear along the shore. The Chapman lighthouse, a three-legged thing erect on a mudflat, shone strongly. Lights of ships moved in the fairway – a great stir of lights going up and going down. And farther west on the upper reaches the place of the monstrous town was still marked ominously on the sky, a brooding gloom in sunshine, a lurid glare under the stars.

'And this also,' said Marlow suddenly, 'has been one of the dark places of the earth.'

He was the only man of us who still 'followed the sea.' The worst that could be said of him was that he did not represent his class. He was a seaman, but he was a wanderer too, while most seamen lead, if one may so express it, a sedentary life. Their minds are of the stay-at-home order, and their home is always with them – the ship; and so is their country – the sea. One ship is very much like another, and the sea is always the same. In the immutability of their surroundings the foreign shores, the foreign faces, the changing immensity of life, glide past, veiled not by a sense of mystery but by a slightly disdainful ignorance; for there is nothing mysterious to a seaman unless it be the sea itself, which is the mistress of his existence and as inscrutable as Destiny. For the rest, after his hours of work, a casual stroll or a casual spree on shore suffices to unfold for him the secret of a whole continent, and generally he finds the secret not worth knowing. The yarns of seamen have a direct simplicity, the whole meaning of which lies within the shell of a cracked nut. But Marlow was not typical (if his propensity to spin yarns be excepted), and to him the meaning of an episode was not inside like a kernel but outside, enveloping the tale which brought it out only as a glow brings out a haze, in the likeness of one of these misty halos that sometimes are made visible by the spectral illumination of moonshine.

His remark did not seem at all surprising. It was just like Marlow. It was accepted in silence. No one took the trouble to grunt even; and presently he said, very slow – 'I was thinking of very old times, when the Romans first came here, nineteen hundred years ago – the other day... Light came out of this river since – you say Knights? Yes; but it is like a running blaze on a plain, like a flash of lightning in the clouds.

We live in the flicker – may it last as long as the old earth keeps rolling! But darkness was here yesterday. Imagine the feelings of a commander of a fine – what d'ye call 'em? – trireme in the Mediterranean, ordered suddenly to the north; run overland across the Gauls in a hurry; put in charge of one of these craft the legionaries – a wonderful lot of handy men they must have been too – used to build, apparently by the hundred, in a month or two, if we may believe what we read. Imagine him here – the very end of the world, a sea the colour of lead, a sky the colour of smoke, a kind of ship about as rigid as a concertina – and going up this river with stores, or orders, or what you like. Sandbanks, marshes, forests, savages – precious little to eat fit for a civilized man, nothing but Thames water to drink. No Falernian wine here, no going ashore. Here and there a military camp lost in a wilderness, like a needle in a bundle of hay – cold, fog, tempests, disease, exile, and death – death skulking in the air, in the water, in the bush. They must have been dying like flies here. Oh yes – he did it. Did it very well, too, no doubt, and without thinking much about it either, except afterwards to brag of what he had gone through in his time, perhaps. They were men enough to face the darkness. And perhaps he was cheered by keeping his eye on a chance of promotion to the fleet at Ravenna by-and-by, if he had good friends in Rome and survived the awful climate. Or think of a decent young citizen in a toga – perhaps too much dice, you know – coming out here in the train of some prefect, or tax-gatherer, or trader, even, to mend his fortunes. Land in a swamp, march through the woods, and in some inland post feel the savagery, the utter savagery, had closed round him – all that mysterious life of the wilderness that stirs in the forest, in the jungles, in the hearts of wild men. There's no initiation either into such mysteries. He has to live in the midst of the incomprehensible, which is also detestable. And it has a fascination, too, that goes to work upon him. The fascination of the abomination – you know, imagine the growing regrets, the longing to escape, the powerless disgust, the surrender, the hate.'

He paused.

'Mind,' he began again, lifting one arm from the elbow, the palm of the hand outwards, so that, with his legs folded before him, he had the pose of a Buddha preaching in European clothes and without a lotus-flower – 'Mind, none of us would feel exactly like this. What saves us is efficiency – the devotion to efficiency. But these chaps were not much account, really. They were no colonists; their administration was merely a squeeze, and nothing more, I suspect. They were conquerors, and for that you want only brute force – nothing to boast of, when you have it, since your strength is just an accident arising from the weakness of others. They grabbed what they could get for the sake of what was to be got. It was just robbery with violence, aggravated murder on a great scale, and men going at it blind – as is very proper for those who tackle a darkness. The conquest of the earth, which mostly means the taking it away from those who have a different complexion or slightly flatter noses than ourselves, is not a pretty thing when you look into it too much. What redeems it is the idea only. An idea at the back of it; not a sentimental pretence but an idea; and an unselfish belief in the idea – something you can set up, and bow down before, and offer a sacrifice to . . .'

He broke off. Flames glided in the river, small green flames, red flames, white flames, pursuing, overtaking, joining, crossing each other – then separating slowly or hastily. The traffic of the great city went on in the deepening night upon the sleepless river. We looked on, waiting patiently – there was nothing else to do till the end of the flood; but it was only after a long silence, when he said, in a hesitating voice, 'I suppose you fellows remember I did once turn fresh-water sailor for a bit,' that we knew we were fated, before the ebb began to run, to hear about one of Marlow's inconclusive experiences.

'I don't want to bother you much with what happened to me personally,' he began, showing in this remark the weakness of many tellers of tales who seem so often unaware of what their audience would like best to hear; 'yet to understand the effect of it on me you ought to know how I got out there, what I saw, how I went up that river to the place where I first met the poor chap. It was the farthest point of navigation and the culminating point of my experience. It seemed somehow to throw a kind of light on everything about me – and into my thoughts. It was sombre enough too – and pitiful – not extraordinary in any way – not very clear either. No, not very clear. And yet it seemed to throw a kind of light.

'I had then, as you remember, just returned to London after a lot of Indian Ocean, Pacific, China Seas – a regular dose of the East – six years or so; and I was loafing about, hindering you fellows in your work and invading your homes, just as though I had got a heavenly mission to civilize you. It was very fine for a time, but after a bit I did get tired of resting. Then I began to look for a ship – I should think the hardest work on earth. But the ships wouldn't even look at me. And I got tired of that game too.

'Now when I was a little chap I had a passion for maps. I would look for hours at South America, or Africa, or Australia, and lose myself in all the glories of exploration. At that time there were many blank spaces on the earth, and when I saw one that looked particularly inviting on a map (but they all look that) I would put my finger on it and say, "When I grow up I will go there." The North Pole was one of these places, I remember. Well, I haven't been there yet, and shall not try now. The glamour's off. Other places were scattered about the two hemispheres. I have been in some of them, and . . . well, we won't talk about that. But there was one yet – the biggest, the most blank, so to speak – that I had a hankering after.

'True, by this time it was not a blank space any more. It had got filled since my boyhood with rivers and lakes and names. It had ceased to be a blank space of delightful mystery – a white patch for a boy to dream gloriously over. It had become a place of darkness. But there was in it one river especially, a mighty big river, that you could see on the map, resembling an immense snake uncoiled, with its head in the sea, its body at rest curving afar over a vast country, and its tail lost in the depths of the land. And as I looked at the map of it in a shop-window, it fascinated me as a snake would a bird – a silly little bird. Then I remembered there was a big concern, a Company for trade on that river. Dash it all! I thought to myself, they can't trade without using some kind of craft on that lot of fresh water – steamboats! Why shouldn't I try to get charge of one? I went on along Fleet Street, but could not shake off the idea. The snake had charmed me.

'You understand it was a Continental concern, that Trading society; but I have a lot of relations living on the Continent, because it's cheap and not so nasty as it looks, they say.

'I am sorry to own I began to worry them. This was already a fresh departure for me. I was not used to get things that way, you know. I always went my own road and on my own legs where I had a mind to go. I wouldn't have believed it of myself; but, then – you see – I felt somehow I must get there by hook or by crook. So I worried them. The men said "My dear fellow," and did nothing. Then – would you believe it? – I tried the women. I, Charlie Marlow, set the women to work – to get a job. Heavens! Well, you see, the notion drove me. I had an aunt, a dear enthusiastic soul. She wrote: "It will be delightful. I am ready to do anything, anything for you. It is a glorious idea. I know the wife of a very high personage in the Administration, and also a man who has lots of influence with," etc., etc. She was determined to make no end of fuss to get me appointed skipper of a river steamboat, if such was my fancy.

'I got my appointment – of course; and I got it very quick. It appears the Company had received news that one of their captains had been killed in a scuffle with the natives. This was my chance, and it made me the more anxious to go. It was only months and months afterwards, when I made the attempt to recover what was left of the body, that I heard the original quarrel arose from a misunderstanding about some hens. Yes, two black hens. Fresleven – that was the fellow's name, a Dane – thought himself wronged somehow in the bargain, so he went ashore and started to hammer the chief of the village with a stick. Oh, it didn't surprise me in the least to hear this, and at the same time to be told that Fresleven was the gentlest, quietest creature that ever walked on two legs. No doubt he was; but he had been a couple of years already out there engaged in the noble cause, you know, and he probably felt the need at last of asserting his self-respect in some way. Therefore he whacked the old nigger mercilessly, while a big crowd of his people watched him, thunderstruck, till some man – I was told the chief's son – in desperation at hearing the old chap yell, made a tentative jab with a spear at the white man – and of course it went quite easy between the shoulder-blades. Then the whole population cleared into the forest, expecting all kinds of calamities to happen, while, on the other hand, the steamer Fresleven commanded left also in a bad panic, in charge of the engineer, I believe. Afterwards nobody seemed to trouble much about Fresleven's remains, till I got out and stepped into his shoes. I couldn't let it rest, though; but when an opportunity offered at last to meet my predecessor, the grass growing through his ribs was tall enough to hide his bones. They were all there. The supernatural being had not been touched after he fell. And the village was deserted, the huts gaped black, rotting, all askew within the fallen enclosures. A calamity had come to it, sure enough. The people had vanished. Mad terror had scattered them, men, women, and children, through the bush, and they had never returned. What became of the hens I don't know either. I should think the cause of progress got them, anyhow. However, through this glorious affair I got my appointment, before I had fairly begun to hope for it.

'I flew around like mad to get ready, and before forty-eight hours I was crossing the Channel to show myself to my employers, and sign the contract. In a very few hours I arrived in a city that always makes me think of a whited sepulchre. Prejudice no doubt. I had no difficulty in finding the Company's offices. It was the biggest thing in the town, and everybody I met was full of it. They were going to run an over-sea empire, and make no end of coin by trade.

'A narrow and deserted street in deep shadow, high houses, innumerable windows with venetian blinds, a dead silence, grass sprouting between the stones, imposing carriage archways right and left, immense double doors standing ponderously ajar. I slipped through one of these cracks, went up a swept and ungarnished staircase, as arid as a desert, and opened the first door I came to. Two women, one fat and the other slim, sat on straw-bottomed chairs, knitting black wool. The slim one got up and walked straight at me – still knitting with downcast eyes – and only just as I began to think of getting out of her way, as you would for a somnambulist, stood still, and looked up. Her dress was as plain as an umbrella-cover, and she turned round without a word and preceded me into a waiting-room. I gave my name, and looked about. Deal table in the middle, plain chairs all round the walls, on one end a large shining map, marked with all the colours of a rainbow. There was a vast amount of red – good to see at any time, because one knows that some real work is done in there, a deuce of a lot of blue, a little green, smears of orange, and, on the East Coast, a purple patch, to show where the jolly pioneers of progress drink the jolly lager-beer. However, I wasn't going into any of these. I was going into the yellow. Dead in the centre. And the river was there – fascinating – deadly – like a snake. Ough! A door opened, a white-haired secretarial head, but wearing a compassionate expression, appeared, and a skinny forefinger beckoned me into the sanctuary. Its light was dim, and a heavy writing-desk squatted in the middle. From behind that structure came out an impression of pale plumpness in a frock-coat. The great man himself. He was five feet six, I should judge, and had his grip on the handle-end of ever so many millions. He shook hands, I fancy, murmured vaguely, was satisfied with my French. *Bon voyage*.

'In about forty-five seconds I found myself again in the waiting-room with the compassionate secretary, who, full of desolation and sympathy, made me sign some document. I believe I undertook amongst other things not to disclose any trade secrets. Well, I am not going to.

'I began to feel slightly uneasy. You know I am not used to such ceremonies, and there was something ominous in the atmosphere. It was just as though I had been let into some conspiracy – I don't know – something not quite right; and I was glad to get out. In the outer room the two women knitted black wool feverishly. People were arriving, and the younger one was walking back and forth introducing them. The old one sat on her chair. Her flat cloth slippers were propped up on a foot-warmer, and a cat reposed on her lap. She wore a starched white affair on her head, had a wart on one cheek, and silver-rimmed spectacles hung on the tip of her nose. She glanced at me above the glasses. The swift and indifferent placidity of that look troubled me. Two youths with foolish and cheery countenances were being piloted over, and she threw at them the same quick glance of unconcerned wisdom. She seemed to know all about them and about me too. An eerie feeling came over me. She seemed uncanny and fateful. Often far away there I thought of these two, guarding the door of Darkness, knitting black wool as for a warm pall, one introducing, introducing continuously to the unknown, the other scrutinizing the cheery and foolish faces with unconcerned old eyes. *Ave!* Old knitter of black wool. *Morituri te salutant*. Not many of those she looked at ever saw her again – not half, by a long way.

'There was yet a visit to the doctor. "A simple formality," assured me the secretary, with an air of taking an immense part in all my sorrows. Accordingly a young chap wearing his hat over the left eyebrow, some clerk I suppose – there must have been clerks in the business, though the house was as still as a house in a city of the dead – came from somewhere upstairs, and led me forth. He was shabby and careless, with ink-stains on the sleeves of his jacket, and his cravat was large and billowy, under a chin shaped like the toe of an old boot. It was a little too early for the doctor, so I proposed a drink, and thereupon he developed a vein of joviality. As we sat over our vermouths he glorified the Company's business, and by-and-by I expressed casually my surprise at him not going out there. He became very cool and collected all at once. "I am not such a fool as I look, quoth Plato to his disciples," he said sententiously, emptied his glass with great resolution, and we rose.

'The old doctor felt my pulse, evidently thinking of something else the while. "Good, good for there," he mumbled, and then with a certain eagerness asked me whether I would let him measure my head. Rather surprised, I said Yes, when he produced a thing like calipers and got the dimensions back and front and every way, taking notes carefully. He was an unshaven little man in a threadbare coat like a gaberdine, with his feet in slippers, and I thought him a harmless fool. "I always ask leave, in the interests of science, to measure the crania of those going out there," he said. "And when they come back, too?" I asked. "Oh, I never see them," he remarked; "and, moreover, the changes take place inside, you know." He smiled, as if at some quiet joke. "So you are going out there. Famous. Interesting, too." He gave me a searching glance, and made another note. "Ever any madness in your family?" he asked, in a matter-of-fact tone. I felt very annoyed. "Is that question in the interests of science, too?" "It would be," he said, without taking notice of my irritation, "interesting for science to watch the mental changes of individuals, on the spot, but ..." "Are you an alienist?" I interrupted. "Every doctor should be – a little," answered that original, imperturbably. "I have a little theory which you Messieurs who go out there must help me to prove. This is my share in the advantages my country shall reap from the possession of such a magnificent dependency. The mere wealth I leave to others. Pardon my questions, but you are the first Englishman coming under my observation..." I hastened to assure him I was not in the least typical. "If I were," said I, "I wouldn't be talking like this with you." "What you say is rather profound, and probably erroneous," he said, with a laugh. "Avoid irritation more than exposure to the sun. Adieu. How do you English say, eh? Goodbye. Ah! Goodbye. Adieu. In the tropics one must before everything keep calm." ...He lifted a warning forefinger... "*Du calme, du calme. Adieu.*"

'One thing more remained to do – say goodbye to my excellent aunt. I found her triumphant. I had a cup of tea – the last decent cup of tea for many days – and in a room that most soothingly looked just as you would expect a lady's drawing-room to look, we had a long quiet chat by the fireside. In the course of these confidences it became quite plain to me I had been represented to the wife of the high dignitary, and goodness knows to how many more people besides, as an exceptional and gifted creature – a piece of good fortune for the Company – a man you don't get hold of every day. Good heavens! and I was going to take charge of a twopenny-halfpenny river-steamboat with a penny whistle attached! It appeared, however, I was also one of the Workers, with a capital – you know. Something like an emissary of light, something like a lower sort of apostle. There had been a lot of such rot let loose in print and talk just about that time, and the excellent woman, living right in the rush of all that humbug, got carried off her feet. She talked about "weaning those ignorant millions from their horrid ways," till, upon my word, she made me quite uncomfortable. I ventured to hint that the Company was run for profit.

'"You forget, dear Charlie, that the labourer is worthy of his hire," she said, brightly. It's queer how out of touch with truth women are. They live in a world of their own, and there has never been anything like it, and never can be. It is too beautiful altogether, and if they were to set it up it would go to pieces before the first sunset. Some confounded fact we men have been living contentedly with ever since the day of creation would start up and knock the whole thing over.

'After this I got embraced, told to wear flannel, be sure to write often, and so on – and I left. In the street – I don't know why – a queer feeling came to me that I was an imposter. Odd thing that I, who used to clear out for any part of the world at twenty-four hours' notice, with less thought than most men give to the crossing of a street, had a moment – I won't say of hesitation, but of startled pause, before this commonplace affair. The best way I can explain it to you is by saying that, for a second or two, I felt as though, instead of going to the centre of a continent, I were about to set off for the centre of the earth.

'I left in a French steamer, and she called in every blamed port they have out there, for, as far as I could see, the sole purpose of landing soldiers and custom-house officers. I watched the coast. Watching a coast as it slips by the ship is like thinking about an enigma. There it is before you – smiling, frowning, inviting, grand, mean, insipid, or savage, and always mute with an air of whispering, "Come and find out." This one was almost featureless, as if still in the making, with an aspect of monotonous grimness. The edge of a colossal jungle, so dark-green as to be almost black, fringed with white surf, ran straight, like a ruled line, far, far away along a blue sea whose glitter was blurred by a creeping mist. The sun was fierce, the land seemed to glisten and drip with steam. Here and there greyish-whitish specks showed up clustered inside the white surf, with a

flag flying above them perhaps. Settlements some centuries old, and still
no bigger than pin-heads on the untouched expanse of their background.
We pounded along, stopped, landed soldiers; went on, landed custom-
house clerks to levy toll in what looked like a God-forsaken wilderness,
with a tin shed and a flagpole lost in it; landed more soldiers – to take
care of the custom-house clerks, presumably. Some, I heard, got drowned
in the surf; but whether they did or not, nobody seemed particularly to
care. They were just flung out there, and on we went. Every day the coast
looked the same, as though we had not moved; but we passed various
places – trading places – with names like Gran' Bassam, Little Popo;
names that seemed to belong to some sordid farce acted in front of a
sinister back cloth. The idleness of a passenger, my isolation amongst
all these men with whom I had no point of contact, the oily and languid
sea, the uniform sombreness of the coast, seemed to keep me away from
the truth of things, within the toil of a mournful and senseless delusion.
The voice of the surf heard now and then was a positive pleasure, like the
speech of a brother. It was something natural, that had its reason, that had
a meaning. Now and then a boat from the shore gave one a momentary
contact with reality. It was paddled by black fellows. You could see from
afar the white of their eyeballs glistening. They shouted, sang; their bodies
streamed with perspiration; they had faces like grotesque masks – these
chaps; but they had bone, muscle, a wild vitality, an intense energy of
movement, that was as natural and true as the surf along their coast. They
wanted no excuse for being there. They were a great comfort to look at.
For a time I would feel I belonged still to a world of straightforward facts;
but the feeling would not last long. Something would turn up to scare it
away. Once, I remember, we came upon a man-of-war anchored off the
coast. There wasn't even a shed there, and she was shelling the bush. It
appears the French had one of their wars going on thereabouts. Her ensign
dropped limp like a rag; the muzzles of the long six-inch guns stuck out
all over the low hull; the greasy, slimy swell swung her up lazily and
let her down, swaying her thin masts. In the empty immensity of earth,
sky, and water, there she was, incomprehensible, firing into a continent.
Pop, would go one of the six-inch guns; a small flame would dart and
vanish, a little white smoke would disappear, a tiny projectile would give
a feeble screech – and nothing happened. Nothing could happen. There
was a touch of insanity in the proceeding, a sense of lugubrious drollery

in the sight; and it was not dissipated by somebody on board assuring me earnestly there was a camp of natives – he called them enemies! – hidden out of sight somewhere.

'We gave her her letters (I heard the men in that lonely ship were dying of fever at the rate of three a day) and went on. We called at some more places with farcical names, where the merry dance of death and trade goes on in a still and earthy atmosphere as of an overheated catacomb; all along the formless coast bordered by dangerous surf, as if Nature herself had tried to ward off intruders; in and out of rivers, streams of death in life, whose banks were rotting into mud, whose waters, thickened into slime, invaded the contorted mangroves, that seemed to writhe at us in the extremity of an impotent despair. Nowhere did we stop long enough to get a particularized impression, but the general sense of vague and oppressive wonder grew upon me. It was like a weary pilgrimage amongst hints for nightmares.

'It was upward of thirty days before I saw the mouth of the big river. We anchored off the seat of the government. But my work would not begin till some two hundred miles farther on. So as soon as I could I made a start for a place thirty miles higher up.

'I had my passage on a little sea-going steamer. Her captain was a Swede, and knowing me for a seaman, invited me on the bridge. He was a young man, lean, fair, and morose, with lanky hair and a shuffling gait. As we left the miserable little wharf, he tossed his head contemptuously at the shore. "Been living there?" he asked. I said, "Yes." "Fine lot these government chaps – are they not?" he went on, speaking English with great precision and considerable bitterness. "It is funny what some people will do for a few francs a month. I wonder what becomes of that kind when it goes up country?" I said to him I expected to see that soon. "So–o–o!" he exclaimed. He shuffled athwart, keeping one eye ahead vigilantly. "Don't be too sure," he continued. "The other day I took up a man who hanged himself on the road. He was a Swede, too." "Hanged himself! Why, in God's name?" I cried. He kept on looking out watchfully. "Who knows? The sun too much for him, or the country perhaps."

'At last we opened a reach. A rocky cliff appeared, mounds of turned-up earth by the shore, houses on a hill, others with iron roofs, amongst a waste of excavations, or hanging to the declivity. A continuous noise of the rapids above hovered over this scene of inhabited devastation.

A lot of people, mostly black and naked, moved about like ants. A jetty projected into the river. A blinding sunlight drowned all this at times in a sudden recrudescence of glare. "There's your Company's station," said the Swede, pointing to three wooden barrack-like structures on the rocky slope. "I will send your things up. Four boxes did you say? So. Farewell."

'I came upon a boiler wallowing in the grass, then found a path leading up the hill. It turned aside for the boulders, and also for an undersized railway-truck lying there on its back with its wheels in the air. One was off. The thing looked as dead as the carcass of some animal. I came upon more pieces of decaying machinery, a stack of rusty rails. To the left a clump of trees made a shady spot, where dark things seemed to stir feebly. I blinked, the path was steep. A horn tooted to the right, and I saw the black people run. A heavy and dull detonation shook the ground, a puff of smoke came out of the cliff, and that was all. No change appeared on the face of the rock. They were building a railway. The cliff was not in the way or anything; but this objectless blasting was all the work going on.

'A slight clinking behind me made me turn my head. Six black men advanced in a file, toiling up the path. They walked erect and slow, balancing small baskets full of earth on their heads, and the clink kept time with their footsteps. Black rags were wound round their loins, and the short ends behind waggled to and fro like tails. I could see every rib, the joints of their limbs were like knots in a rope; each had an iron collar on his neck, and all were connected together with a chain whose bights swung between them, rhythmically clinking. Another report from the cliff made me think suddenly of that ship of war I had seen firing into a continent. It was the same kind of ominous voice; but these men could by no stretch of imagination be called enemies. They were called criminals, and the outraged law, like the bursting shells, had come to them, an insoluble mystery from the sea. All their meagre breasts panted together, the violently dilated nostrils quivered, the eyes stared stonily uphill. They passed me within six inches, without a glance, with that complete, deathlike indifference of unhappy savages. Behind this raw matter one of the reclaimed, the product of the new forces at work, strolled despondently, carrying a rifle by its middle. He had a uniform jacket with one button off, and seeing a white man on the path, hoisted his weapon to his shoulder with alacrity. This was simple prudence, white men being so much alike at a distance that he could not tell who I might be. He was speedily reassured, and with a large, white, rascally grin, and a glance at his charge, seemed to take me into partnership in his exalted trust. After all, I also was a part of the great cause of these high and just proceedings.

'Instead of going up, I turned and descended to the left. My idea was to let that chain-gang get out of sight before I climbed the hill. You know I am not particularly tender; I've had to strike and to fend off. I've had to resist and to attack sometimes – that's only one way of resisting – without counting the exact cost, according to the demands of such sort of life as I had blundered into. I've seen the devil of violence, and the devil of greed, and the devil of hot desire; but by all the stars! these were strong, lusty, red-eyed devils, that swayed and drove men – men, I tell you. But as I stood on this hillside, I foresaw that in the blinding sunshine of that land I would become acquainted with a flabby, pretending, weak-eyed devil of a rapacious and pitiless folly. How insidious he could be, too, I was only to find out several months later and a thousand miles farther. For a moment I stood appalled, as though by a warning. Finally I descended the hill, obliquely, towards the trees I had seen.

'I avoided a vast artificial hole somebody had been digging on the slope, the purpose of which I found it impossible to divine. It wasn't a quarry or a sandpit, anyhow. It was just a hole. It might have been connected with the philanthropic desire of giving the criminals something to do. I don't know. Then I nearly fell into a very narrow ravine, almost no more than a scar in the hillside. I discovered that a lot of imported drainage-pipes for the settlement had been tumbled in there. There wasn't one that was not broken. It was a wanton smash-up. At last I got under the trees. My purpose was to stroll into the shade for a moment; but no sooner within than it seemed to me I had stepped into the gloomy circle of some Inferno. The rapids were near, and an uninterrupted, uniform, headlong, rushing noise filled the mournful stillness of the grove, where not a breath stirred, not a leaf moved, with a mysterious sound – as though the tearing pace of the launched earth had suddenly become audible.

'Black shapes crouched, lay, sat between the trees leaning against the trunks, clinging to the earth, half coming out, half effaced within the dim light, in all the attitudes of pain, abandonment, and despair. Another mine on the cliff went off, followed by a slight shudder of the soil under

my feet. The work was going on. The work! And this was the place where
some of the helpers had withdrawn to die.

'They were dying slowly – it was very clear. They were not enemies,
they were not criminals, they were nothing earthly now – nothing but
black shadows of disease and starvation, lying confusedly in the greenish
gloom. Brought from all the recesses of the coast in all the legality of time
contracts, lost in uncongenial surroundings, fed on unfamiliar food, they
sickened, became inefficient, and were then allowed to crawl away and
rest. These moribund shapes were free as air – and nearly as thin. I began
to distinguish the gleam of the eyes under the trees. Then, glancing down,
I saw a face near my hand. The black bones reclined at full length with
one shoulder against the tree, and slowly the eyelids rose and the sunken
eyes looked up at me, enormous and vacant, a kind of blind, white flicker
in the depths of the orbs, which died out slowly. The man seemed young
– almost a boy – but you know with them it's hard to tell. I found nothing
else to do but to offer him one of my good Swede's ship's biscuits I had in
my pocket. The fingers closed slowly on it and held – there was no other
movement and no other glance. He had tied a bit of white worsted round
his neck – Why? Where did he get it? Was it a badge – an ornament – a
charm – a propitiatory act? Was there any idea at all connected with it?
It looked startling round his black neck, this bit of white thread from
beyond the seas.

'Near the same tree two more bundles of acute angles sat with their
legs drawn up. One, with his chin propped on his knees, stared at nothing,
in an intolerable and appalling manner: his brother phantom rested its
forehead, as if overcome with a great weariness; and all about others
were scattered in every pose of contorted collapse, as in some picture
of a massacre or a pestilence. While I stood horror-struck, one of these
creatures rose to his hands and knees, and went off on all-fours towards
the river to drink. He lapped out of his hand, then sat up in the sunlight,
crossing his shins in front of him, and after a time let his woolly head fall
on his breastbone.

'I didn't want any more loitering in the shade, and I made haste
towards the station. When near the buildings I met a white man, in such
an unexpected elegance of get-up that in the first moment I took him for
a sort of vision. I saw a high starched collar, white cuffs, a light alpaca
jacket, snowy trousers, a clean necktie, and varnished boots. No hat.

Hair parted, brushed, oiled, under a green-lined parasol held in a big white hand. He was amazing, and had a penholder behind his ear.

'I shook hands with this miracle, and I learned he was the Company's chief accountant, and that all the book-keeping was done at this station. He had come out for a moment, he said, "to get a breath of fresh air." The expression sounded wonderfully odd, with its suggestion of sedentary desk-life. I wouldn't have mentioned the fellow to you at all, only it was from his lips that I first heard the name of the man who is so indissolubly connected with the memories of that time. Moreover, I respected the fellow. Yes; I respected his collars, his vast cuffs, his brushed hair. His appearance was certainly that of a hairdresser's dummy; but in the great demoralization of the land he kept up his appearance. That's backbone. His starched collars and got-up shirt-fronts were achievements of character. He had been out nearly three years; and, later, I could not help asking him how he managed to sport such linen. He had just the faintest blush, and said modestly, "I've been teaching one of the native women about the station. It was difficult. She had a distaste for the work." Thus this man had verily accomplished something. And he was devoted to his books, which were in apple–pie order.

'Everything else in the station was in a muddle – heads, things, buildings. Strings of dusty niggers with splay feet arrived and departed; a stream of manufactured goods, rubbishy cottons, beads, and brass-wire set into the depths of darkness, and in return came a precious trickle of ivory.

'I had to wait in the station for ten days – an eternity. I lived in a hut in the yard, but to be out of the chaos I would sometimes get into the accountant's office. It was built of horizontal planks, and so badly put together that, as he bent over his high desk, he was barred from neck to heels with narrow strips of sunlight. There was no need to open the big shutter to see. It was hot there, too; big flies buzzed fiendishly, and did not sting, but stabbed. I sat generally on the floor, while, of faultless appearance (and even slightly scented), perching on a high stool, he wrote, he wrote. Sometimes he stood up for exercise. When a truckle-bed with a sick man (some invalid agent from up country) was put in there, he exhibited a gentle annoyance. "The groans of this sick person," he said, "distract my attention. And without that it is extremely difficult to guard against clerical errors in this climate."

'One day he remarked, without lifting his head, "In the interior you will

no doubt meet Mr Kurtz." On my asking who Mr Kurtz was, he said he
was a first-class agent; and seeing my disappointment at this information,
he added slowly, laying down his pen, "He is a very remarkable person."
Further questions elicited from him that Mr Kurtz was at present in
charge of a trading-post, a very important one, in the true ivory-country,
at "the very bottom of there. Sends in as much ivory as all the others put
together . . ." He began to write again. The sick man was too ill to groan.
The flies buzzed in a great peace.

'Suddenly there was a growing murmur of voices and a great tramping
of feet. A caravan had come in. A violent babble of uncouth sounds burst
out on the other side of the planks. All the carriers were speaking together,
and in the midst of the uproar the lamentable voice of the chief agent
was heard "giving it up" tearfully for the twentieth time that day… He
rose slowly. "What a frightful row," he said. He crossed the room gently
to look at the sick man, and returning, said to me, "He does not hear."
"What! Dead?" I asked, startled. "No, not yet," he answered, with great
composure. Then, alluding with a toss of the head to the tumult in the
station-yard, "When one has got to make correct entries, one comes to
hate those savages – hate them to the death." He remained thoughtful for
a moment. "When you see Mr Kurtz," he went on, "tell him from me that
everything here" – he glanced at the deck – "is very satisfactory. I don't
like to write to him – with those messengers of ours you never know who
may get hold of your letter – at that Central Station." He stared at me for
a moment with his mild, bulging eyes. "Oh, he will go far, very far," he
began again. "He will be a somebody in the Administration before long.
They, above – the Council in Europe, you know – mean him to be."

'He turned to his work. The noise outside had ceased, and presently in
going out I stopped at the door. In the steady buzz of flies the homeward-
bound agent was lying flushed and insensible; the other, bent over his
books, was making correct entries of perfectly correct transactions; and
fifty feet below the doorstep I could see the still treetops of the grove of
death.

'Next day I left that station at last, with a caravan of sixty men, for
a two-hundred-mile tramp.

'No use telling you much about that. Paths, paths, everywhere; a
stamped-in network of paths spreading over the empty land, through long
grass, through burnt grass, through thickets, down and up chilly ravines,

up and down stony hills ablaze with heat; and a solitude, a solitude, nobody, not a hut. The population had cleared out a long time ago. Well, if a lot of mysterious niggers armed with all kinds of fearful weapons suddenly took to travelling on the road between Deal and Gravesend, catching the yokels right and left to carry heavy loads for them, I fancy every farm and cottage thereabouts would get empty very soon. Only here the dwellings were gone, too. Still I passed through several abandoned villages. There's something pathetically childish in the ruins of grass walls. Day after day, with the stamp and shuffle of sixty pairs of bare feet behind me, each pair under a 60-lb load. Camp, cook, sleep, strike camp, march. Now and then a carrier dead in harness, at rest in the long grass near the path, with an empty water-gourd and his long staff lying by his side. A great silence around and above. Perhaps on some quiet night the tremor of far-off drums, sinking, swelling, a tremor vast, faint; a sound weird, appealing, suggestive, and wild – and perhaps with as profound a meaning as the sound of bells in a Christian country. Once a white man in an unbuttoned uniform, camping on the path with an armed escort of lank Zanzibaris, very hospitable and festive – not to say drunk. Was looking after the upkeep of the road, he declared. Can't say I saw any road or any upkeep, unless the body of a middle-aged negro, with a bullet-hole in the forehead, upon which I absolutely stumbled three miles farther on, may be considered as a permanent improvement. I had a white companion, too, not a bad chap, but rather too fleshy and with the exasperating habit of fainting on the hot hillsides, miles away from the least bit of shade and water. Annoying, you know, to hold your own coat like a parasol over a man's head while he is coming to. I couldn't help asking him once what he meant by coming there at all. "To make money, of course. What do you think?" he said, scornfully. Then he got fever, and had to be carried in a hammock slung under a pole. As he weighed sixteen stone I had no end of rows with the carriers. They jibbed, ran away, sneaked off with their loads in the night – quite a mutiny. So, one evening, I made a speech in English with gestures, not one of which was lost to the sixty pairs of eyes before me, and the next morning I started the hammock off in front all right. An hour afterwards I came upon the whole concern wrecked in a bush – man, hammock, groans, blankets, horrors. The heavy pole had skinned his poor nose. He was very anxious for me to kill somebody, but there wasn't the shadow of a carrier near. I remembered the old doctor – "It would be interesting for science to watch the mental changes of individuals, on the spot." I felt I was becoming scientifically interesting. However, all that is to no purpose. On the fifteenth day I came in sight of the big river again, and hobbled into the Central Station. It was on a back-water surrounded by scrub and forest, with a pretty border of smelly mud on one side, and on the three others enclosed by a crazy fence of rushes. A neglected gap was all the gate it had, and the first glance at the place was enough to let you see the flabby devil was running that show. White men with long staves in their hands appeared languidly from amongst the buildings, strolling up to take a look at me, and then retired out of sight somewhere. One of them, a stout, excitable chap with black moustaches, informed me with great volubility and many digressions, as soon as I told him who I was, that my steamer was at the bottom of the river. I was thunderstruck. What, how, why? Oh, it was "all right." The "manager himself" was there. All quite correct. "Everybody had behaved splendidly! splendidly!" – "You must," he said in agitation, "go and see the general manager at once. He is waiting!"

'I did not see the real significance of that wreck at once. I fancy I see it now, but I am not sure – not at all. Certainly the affair was too stupid – when I think of it – to be altogether natural. Still… But at the moment it presented itself simply as a confounded nuisance. The steamer was sunk. They had started two days before in a sudden hurry up the river with the manager on board, in charge of some volunteer skipper, and before they had been out three hours they tore the bottom out of her on stones, and she sank near the south bank. I asked myself what I was to do there, now my boat was lost. As a matter of fact, I had plenty to do in fishing my command out of the river. I had to set about it the very next day. That, and the repairs when I brought the pieces to the station, took some months.

'My first interview with the manager was curious. He did not ask me to sit down after my twenty-mile walk that morning. He was commonplace in complexion, in features, in manners, and in voice. He was of middle size and of ordinary build. His eyes, of the usual blue, were perhaps remarkably cold, and he certainly could make his glance fall on one as trenchant and heavy as an axe. But even at these times the rest of his person seemed to disclaim the intention. Otherwise there was only an indefinable, faint expression of his lips, something stealthy – a smile – not a smile – I remember it, but I can't explain. It was unconscious, this smile was, though just after he had said something it got intensified for an instant. It came at the end of his speeches like a seal applied on the words to make the meaning of the commonest phrase appear absolutely inscrutable. He was a common trader, from his youth up employed in these parts – nothing more. He was obeyed, yet he inspired neither love nor fear, nor even respect. He inspired uneasiness. That was it! Uneasiness. Not a definite mistrust – just uneasiness – nothing more. You have no idea how effective such a... a... faculty can be. He had no genius for organizing, for initiative, or for order even. That was evident in such things as the deplorable state of the station. He had no learning, and no intelligence. His position had come to him – why? Perhaps because he was never ill... He had served three terms of three years out there... Because triumphant health in the general rout of constitutions is a kind of power in itself. When he went home on leave he rioted on a large scale – pompously. Jack ashore – with a difference – in externals only. This one could gather from his casual talk. He originated nothing, he could keep the routine going – that's all. But he was great. He was great by this little thing that it was impossible to tell what could control such a man. He never gave that secret away. Perhaps there was nothing within him. Such a suspicion made one pause – for out there there were no external checks. Once when various tropical diseases had laid low almost every "agent" in the station, he was heard to say, "Men who come out here should have no entrails." He sealed the utterance with that smile of his, as though it had been a door opening into a darkness he had in his keeping. You fancied you had seen things – but the seal was on. When annoyed at meal-times by the constant quarrels of the white men about precedence, he ordered an immense round table to be made, for which a special house had to be built. This was the station's mess-room. Where he sat was the first place – the rest were nowhere. One felt this to be his unalterable conviction. He was neither civil nor uncivil. He was quiet. He allowed his "boy" – an overfed young negro from the coast – to treat the white men, under his very eyes, with provoking insolence.

'He began to speak as soon as he saw me. I had been very long on the road. He could not wait. Had to start without me. The up-river stations had to be relieved. There had been so many delays already that he did not know who was dead and who was alive, and how they got on – and so on, and so on. He paid no attention to my explanations, and, playing with a stick of sealing-wax, repeated several times that the situation was "very grave, very grave." There were rumours that a very important station was in jeopardy, and its chief, Mr Kurtz, was ill. Hoped it was not true. Mr Kurtz was… I felt weary and irritable. Hang Kurtz, I thought. I interrupted him by saying I had heard of Mr Kurtz on the coast. "Ah! So they talk of him down there," he murmured to himself. Then he began again, assuring me Mr Kurtz was the best agent he had, an exceptional man, of the greatest importance to the Company; therefore I could understand his anxiety. He was, he said, "very, very uneasy." Certainly he fidgeted on his chair a good deal, exclaimed, "Ah, Mr Kurtz!" broke the stick of sealing-wax and seemed dumfounded by the accident. Next thing he wanted to know "how long it would take to"… I interrupted him again. Being hungry, you know, and kept on my feet too. I was getting savage. "How could I tell?" I said. "I hadn't even seen the wreck yet – some months, no doubt." All this talk seemed to me so futile. "Some months," he said. "Well, let us say three months before we can make a start. Yes. That ought to do the affair." I flung out of his hut (he lived all alone in a clay hut with a sort of verandah) muttering to myself my opinion of him. He was a chattering idiot. Afterwards I took it back when it was borne in upon me startlingly with what extreme nicety he had estimated the time requisite for the "affair."

'I went to work the next day, turning, so to speak, my back on that station. In that way only it seemed to me I could keep my hold on the redeeming facts of life. Still, one must look about sometimes; and then I saw this station, these men strolling aimlessly about in the sunshine of the yard. I asked myself sometimes what it all meant. They wandered here and there with their absurd long staves in their hands, like a lot of faithless pilgrims bewitched inside a rotten fence. The word "ivory" rang in the air, was whispered, was sighed. You would think they were praying to it. A taint of imbecile rapacity blew through it all, like a whiff from some corpse. By Jove! I've never seen anything so unreal in my life. And outside, the silent wilderness surrounding this cleared speck on the earth struck me as something great and invincible, like evil or truth, waiting patiently for the passing away of this fantastic invasion.

'Oh, these months! Well, never mind. Various things happened. One evening a grass shed full of calico, cotton prints, beads, and I don't know what else, burst into a blaze so suddenly that you would have thought the earth had opened to let an avenging fire consume all that trash. I was smoking my pipe quietly by my dismantled steamer, and saw them all cutting capers in the light, with their arms lifted high, when the stout man with moustaches came tearing down to the river, a tin pail in his hand, assured me that everybody was "behaving splendidly, splendidly," dipped about a quart of water and tore back again. I noticed there was a hole in the bottom of his pail.

'I strolled up. There was no hurry. You see the thing had gone off like a box of matches. It had been hopeless from the very first. The flame had leaped high, driven everybody back, lighted up everything – and collapsed. The shed was already a heap of embers glowing fiercely. A nigger was being beaten near by. They said he had caused the fire in some way; be that as it may, he was screeching most horribly. I saw him, later, for several days, sitting in a bit of shade looking very sick and trying to recover himself; afterwards he arose and went out – and the wilderness without a sound took him into its bosom again. As I approached the glow from the dark I found myself at the back of two men, talking. I heard the name of Kurtz pronounced, then the words, "take advantage of this unfortunate accident." One of the men was the manager. I wished him a good evening. "Did you ever see anything like it – eh? it is incredible," he said, and walked off. The other man remained. He was a first-class agent, young, gentlemanly, a bit reserved, with a forked little beard and a hooked nose. He was stand-offish with the other agents, and they on their side said he was the manager's spy upon them. As to me, I had hardly ever spoken to him before. We got into talk, and by-and-by we strolled away from the hissing ruins. Then he asked me to his room, which was in the main building of the station. He struck a match, and I perceived that this young aristocrat had not only a silver-mounted dressing-case but also a whole candle all to himself. Just at that time the manager was the only man supposed to have any right to candles. Native mats covered the clay walls; a collection of spears, assegais, shields, knives was hung up in trophies. The business entrusted to this fellow was the making of bricks – so I had been informed; but there wasn't a fragment of a brick anywhere in the station, and he had been there more than a year – waiting. It seems he could not make bricks without something, I don't know what – straw maybe. Anyways, it could not be found there, and as it was not likely to be sent from Europe, it did not appear clear to me what he was waiting

for. An act of special creation perhaps. However, they were all waiting –
all the sixteen or twenty pilgrims of them – for something; and upon my
word it did not seem an uncongenial occupation, from the way they took
it, though the only thing that ever came to them was disease – as far as I
could see. They beguiled the time by back biting and intriguing against
each other in a foolish kind of way. There was an air of plotting about that
station, but nothing came of it, of course. It was as unreal as everything
else – as the philanthropic pretence of the whole concern, as their talk,
as their government, as their show of work. The only real feeling was
a desire to get appointed to a trading-post where ivory was to be had,
so that they could earn percentages. They intrigued and slandered and
hated each other only on that account – but as to effectually lifting a little
finger – oh, no. By heavens! there is something after all in the world
allowing one man to steal a horse while another must not look at a halter.
Steal a horse straight out. Very well. He has done it. Perhaps he can ride.
But there is a way of looking at a halter that would provoke the most
charitable of saints into a kick.

'I had no idea why he wanted to be sociable, but as we chatted in there
it suddenly occurred to me the fellow was trying to get at something – in
fact, pumping me. He alluded constantly to Europe, to the people I was
supposed to know there – putting leading questions as to my acquaintances
in the sepulchral city, and so on. His little eyes glittered like mica discs
– with curiosity – though he tried to keep up a bit of superciliousness.
At first I was astonished, but very soon I became awfully curious to see
what he would find out from me. I couldn't possibly imagine what I
had in me to make it worth his while. It was very pretty to see how he
baffled himself, for in truth my body was full only of chills, and my head
had nothing in it but that wretched steamboat business. It was evident he
took me for a perfectly shameless prevaricator. At last he got angry, and,
to conceal a movement of furious annoyance, he yawned. I rose. Then I
noticed a small sketch in oils, on a panel, representing a woman, draped
and blindfolded, carrying a lighted torch. The background was sombre –
almost black. The movement of the woman was stately, and the effect of
the torchlight on the face was sinister.

'It arrested me, and he stood by civilly, holding an empty half-pint
champagne bottle (medical comforts) with the candle stuck in it. To my
question he said Mr Kurtz had painted this – in this very station more than

a year ago – while waiting for means to go to his trading-post. "Tell me, pray," said I, "who is this Mr Kurtz?"

'"The chief of the Inner Station," he answered in a short tone, looking away. "Much obliged," I said, laughing. "And you are the brickmaker of the Central Station. Every one knows that." He was silent for a while. "He is a prodigy," he said at last. "He is an emissary of pity, and science, and progress, and devil knows what else. We want," he began to declaim suddenly, "for the guidance of the cause entrusted to us by Europe, so to speak, higher intelligence, wide sympathies, a singleness of purpose." "Who says that?" I asked. "Lots of them," he replied. "Some even write that; and so *he* comes here, a special being, as you ought to know." "Why ought I to know?" I interrupted, really surprised. He paid no attention. "Yes. Today he is chief of the best station, next year he will be assistant-manager, two years more and… but I daresay you know what he will be in two years' time. You are of the new gang – the gang of virtue. The same people who sent him specially also recommended you. Oh, don't say no. I've my own eyes to trust." Light dawned upon me. My dear aunt's influential acquaintances were producing an unexpected effect upon that young man. I nearly burst into a laugh. "Do you read the Company's confidential correspondence?" I asked. He hadn't a word to say. It was great fun. "When Mr Kurtz," I continued, severely, "is General Manager, you won't have the opportunity."

'He blew the candle out suddenly, and we went outside. The moon had risen. Black figures strolled about listlessly, pouring water on the glow, whence proceeded a sound of hissing; steam ascended in the moonlight, the beaten nigger groaned somewhere. "What a row the brute makes!" said the indefatigable man with the moustaches, appearing near us. "Serve him right. Transgression – punishment – bang! Pitiless, pitiless. That's the only way. This will prevent all conflagrations for the future. I was just telling the manager…" He noticed my companion, and became crestfallen all at once. "Not in bed yet," he said, with a kind of servile heartiness; "it's so natural. Ha! Danger – agitation." He vanished. I went on to the riverside, and the other followed me. I heard a scathing murmur at my ear, "Heap of muffs – go to." The pilgrims could be seen in knots gesticulating, discussing. Several had still their staves in their hands. I verily believe they took these sticks to bed with them. Beyond the fence the forest stood up spectrally in the moonlight, and through that dim stir, through the faint sounds of that lamentable courtyard, the silence of the land went home to one's very heart – its mystery, its greatness, the amazing reality of its concealed life. The hurt nigger moaned feebly somewhere near by, and then fetched a deep sigh that made me mend my pace away from there. I felt a hand introducing itself under my arm. "My dear sir," said the fellow, "I don't want to be misunderstood, and especially by you, who will see Mr Kurtz long before I can have that pleasure. I wouldn't like him to get a false idea of my disposition…"

'I let him run on, this papier-mâché Mephistopheles, and it seemed to me that if I tried I could poke my forefinger through him, and would find nothing inside but a little loose dirt, maybe. He, don't you see, had been planning to be assistant-manager by-and-by under the present man, and I could see that the coming of that Kurtz had upset them both not a little. He talked precipitately, and I did not try to stop him. I had my shoulders against the wreck of my steamer, hauled up on the slope like a carcass of some big river animal. The smell of mud, of primeval mud, by Jove! was in my nostrils, the high stillness of primeval forest was before my eyes; there were shiny patches on the black creek. The moon had spread over everything a thin layer of silver – over the rank grass, over the mud, upon the wall of matted vegetation standing higher than the wall of a temple, over the great river I could see through a sombre gap glittering, glittering, as it flowed broadly by without a murmur. All this was great, expectant, mute, while the man jabbered about himself. I wondered whether the stillness on the face of the immensity looking at us two were meant as an appeal or as a menace. What were we who had strayed in here? Could we handle that dumb thing, or would it handle us? I felt how big, how confoundedly big, was that thing that couldn't talk, and perhaps was deaf as well. What was in there? I could see a little ivory coming out from there, and I had heard Mr Kurtz was in there. I had heard enough about it, too – God knows! Yet somehow it didn't bring any image with it – no more than if I had been told an angel or a fiend was in there. I believed it in the same way one of you might believe there are inhabitants in the planet Mars. I knew once a Scotch sailmaker who was certain, dead sure, there were people in Mars. If you asked him for some idea how they looked and behaved, he would get shy and mutter something about "walking on all-fours." If you as much as smiled, he would – though a man of sixty – offer to fight you. I would not have gone so far as to fight for Kurtz, but I went for him near enough to a lie. You know I hate, detest, and can't bear a lie, not because I am straighter than the rest of us, but simply because it appalls me. There is a taint of death, a flavour of mortality in lies – which is exactly what I hate and detest in the world – what I want to forget. It makes me miserable and sick, like biting something rotten would do. Temperament, I suppose. Well, I went near enough to it by letting the young fool there believe anything he liked to imagine as to my influence in Europe. I became in an instant as much of a pretence as the rest of the bewitched pilgrims. This simply because I had a notion it somehow would be of help to that Kurtz whom at the time I did not see – you understand. He was just a word for me. I did not see the man in the name any more than you do. Do you see him? Do you see the story? Do you see anything? It seems to me I am trying to tell you a dream – making a vain attempt, because no relation of a dream can convey the dream-sensation, that commingling of absurdity, surprise, and bewilderment in a tremor of struggling revolt, that notion of being captured by the incredible which is of the very essence of dreams…'

He was silent for a while. FINALLY

'…No, it is impossible; it is impossible to convey the life-sensation of any given epoch of one's existence – that which makes its truth, its meaning – its subtle and penetrating essence. It is impossible. We live, as we dream – alone…'

He paused again as if reflecting, then added –

'Of course in this you fellows see more than I could then. You see me, whom you know…'

It had become so pitch dark that we listeners could hardly see one another. For a long time already he, sitting apart, had been no more to us than a voice. There was not a word from anybody. The others might have been asleep, but I was awake. I listened, I listened on the watch for the sentence, for the word, that would give me the clue to the faint uneasiness inspired by this narrative that seemed to shape itself without human lips in the heavy night-air of the river.

'…Yes – I let him run on,' Marlow began again, 'and think what he pleased about the powers that were behind me. I did! And there was nothing behind me! There was nothing but that wretched, old, mangled steamboat I was leaning against, while he talked fluently about "the necessity for every man to get on". "And when one comes out here, you conceive, it is not to gaze at the moon." Mr Kurtz was a "universal genius", but even a genius would find it easier to work with "adequate tools – intelligent men." He did not make bricks – why, there was a physical impossibility in the way – as I was well aware; and if he did secretarial work for the manager, it was because "no sensible man rejects wantonly the confidence of his superiors." Did I see it? I saw it. What more did I want? What I really wanted was rivets, by heaven! Rivets. To get on with the work – to stop the hole. Rivets I wanted. There were cases of them down at the coast – cases – piled up – burst – split! You kicked a loose rivet at every second step in that stationyard on the hillside. Rivets had rolled into the grove of death. You could fill your pockets with rivets for the trouble of stooping down – and there wasn't one rivet to be found where it was wanted. We had plates that would do, but nothing to fasten them with. And every week the messenger, a long negro, letter-bag on shoulder and staff in hand, left our station for the coast. And several times a week a coast caravan came in with trade goods – ghastly glazed calico that made you shudder only to look at it, glass beads value about a penny a quart, confounded spotted cotton handkerchiefs. And no rivets. Three carriers could have brought all that was wanted to set that steamboat afloat.

'He was becoming confidential now, but I fancy my unresponsive attitude must have exasperated him at last, for he judged it necessary to inform me he feared neither God nor devil, let alone any mere man. I said I could see that very well, but what I wanted was a certain quantity of rivets – and rivets were what really Mr Kurtz wanted, if he had only known it. Now letters went to the coast every week… "My dear sir," he cried, "I write from dictation." I demanded rivets. There was a way – for an intelligent man. He changed his manner; became very cold, and suddenly began to talk about a hippopotamus; wondered whether sleeping on board the steamer (I stuck to my salvage night and day) I wasn't disturbed. There was an old hippo that had the bad habit of getting out on the bank and roaming at night over the station grounds. The pilgrims used to turn out in a body and empty every rifle they could lay hands on at him. Some even had sat up o' nights for him. All this energy was wasted, though. "That animal has a charmed life," he said; "but you can say this only of brutes in this country. No man – you apprehend me? – no man here bears a charmed life." He stood there for a moment in the moonlight with his delicate hooked nose set a little askew, and his mica eyes glittering without a wink, then, with a curt Good-night, he strode off. I could see he was disturbed and considerably puzzled, which made me feel more hopeful than I had been for days. It was a great comfort to turn from that chap to my influential friend, the battered, twisted, ruined, tin-pot steamboat. I clambered on board. She rang under my feet like an empty Huntley & Palmer biscuit-tin kicked along a gutter; she was nothing so solid in make, and rather less pretty in shape, but I had expended enough hard work on her to make me love her. No influential friend would have served me better. She had given me a chance to come out a bit – to find out what I could do. No, I don't like work. I had rather laze about and think of all the fine things that can be done. I don't like work – no man does – but I like what is in the work – the chance to find yourself. Your own reality – for yourself, not for others – what no other man can ever know. They can only see the mere show, and never can tell what it really means.

'I was not surprised to see somebody sitting aft, on the deck, with his legs dangling over the mud. You see I rather chummed with the few mechanics there were in that station, whom the other pilgrims naturally despised – on account of their imperfect manners, I suppose. This was the foreman – a boiler-maker by trade – a good worker. He was a lank, bony, yellow-faced man, with big intense eyes. His aspect was worried, and his head was as bald as the palm of my hand; but his hair in falling seemed to have stuck to his chin, and had prospered in the new locality, for his beard hung down to his waist. He was a widower with six young children (he had left them in charge of a sister of his to come out there), and the passion of his life was pigeon-flying. He was an enthusiast and a connoisseur. He would rave about pigeons. After work hours he used sometimes to come over from his hut for a talk about his children and his pigeons; at work, when he had to crawl in the mud under the bottom of the steamboat, he would tie up that beard of his in a kind of white serviette he brought for the purpose. It had loops to go over his ears. In the evening he could be seen squatted on the bank rinsing that wrapper in the creek with great care, then spreading it solemnly on a bush to dry.

'I slapped him on the back and shouted, "We shall have rivets!" He scrambled to his feet exclaiming, "No! Rivets!" as though he couldn't believe his ears. Then in a low voice, "You... eh?" I don't know why we behaved like lunatics. I put my finger to the side of my nose and nodded mysteriously. "Good for you!" he cried, snapped his fingers above his head, lifting one foot. I tried a jig. We capered on the iron deck. A frightful clatter came out of that hulk, and the virgin forest on the other bank of the creek sent it back in a thundering roll upon the sleeping station. It must have made some of the pilgrims sit up in their hovels. A dark figure obscured the lighted doorway of the manager's hut, vanished, then, a second or so after, the doorway itself vanished, too. We stopped, and the silence driven away by the stamping of our feet flowed back again from the recesses of the land. The great wall of vegetation, an exuberant and entangled mass of trunks, branches, leaves, boughs, festoons, motionless in the moonlight, was like a rioting invasion of soundless life, a rolling wave of plants, piled up, crested, ready to topple over the creek, to sweep every little man of us out of his little existence. And it moved not. A deadened burst of mighty splashes and snorts reached us from afar, as though an ichthyosaurus had been taking a bath of glitter in the great river. "After all," said the boiler-maker in a reasonable tone, "why shouldn't we get the rivets?" Why not, indeed! I did not know of any reason why we shouldn't. "They'll come in three weeks," I said confidently.

'But they didn't. Instead of rivets there came an invasion, an infliction, a visitation. It came in sections during the next three weeks, each section headed by a donkey carrying a white man in new clothes and tan shoes, bowing from that elevation right and left to the impressed pilgrims. A quarrelsome band of footsore sulky niggers trod on the heels of the donkey; a lot of tents, camp-stools, tin boxes, white cases, brown bales would be shot down in the courtyard, and the air of mystery would deepen a little over the muddle of the station. Five such instalments came, with their absurd air of disorderly flight with the loot of innumerable outfit shops and provision stores, that, one would think, they were lugging, after a raid, into the wilderness for equitable division. It was an inextricable mess of things decent in themselves but that human folly made look like the spoils of thieving.

'This devoted band called itself the Eldorado Exploring Expedition, and I believe they were sworn to secrecy. Their talk, however, was the talk of sordid buccaneers: it was reckless without hardihood, greedy without audacity, and cruel without courage; there was not an atom of foresight or of serious intention in the whole batch of them, and they did not seem aware these things are wanted for the work of the world. To tear treasure

out of the bowels of the land was their desire, with no more moral purpose
at the back of it than there is in burglars breaking into a safe. Who paid
the expenses of the noble enterprise I don't know; but the uncle of our
manager was leader of that lot.

'In exterior he resembled a butcher in a poor neighbourhood, and
his eyes had a look of sleepy cunning. He carried his fat paunch with
ostentation on his short legs, and during the time his gang infested the
station spoke to no one but his nephew. You could see these two roaming
about all day long with their heads close together in an everlasting
confab.

'I had given up worrying myself about the rivets. One's capacity for
that kind of folly is more limited than you would suppose. I said Hang! –
and let things slide. I had plenty of time for meditation, and now and then
I would give some thought to Kurtz. I wasn't very interested in him. No.
Still, I was curious to see whether this man, who had come out equipped
with moral ideas of some sort, would climb to the top after all, and how
he would set about his work when there.'

II

'One evening as I was lying flat on the deck of my steamboat, I heard
voices approaching – and there were the nephew and the uncle strolling
along the bank. I laid my head on my arm again, and had nearly lost myself
in a doze, when somebody said in my ear, as it were: "I am as harmless
as a little child, but I don't like to be dictated to. Am I the manager – or
am I not? I was ordered to send him there. It's incredible." . . . I became
aware that the two were standing on the shore alongside the forepart of
the steamboat, just below my head. I did not move; it did not occur to
me to move: I was sleepy. "It *is* unpleasant," grunted the uncle. "He has
asked the Administration to be sent there," said the other, "with the idea
of showing what he could do; and I was instructed accordingly. Look at
the influence that man must have. Is it not frightful?" They both agreed
it was frightful, then made several bizarre remarks: "Make rain and fine
weather – one man – the Council – by the nose" – bits of absurd sentences
that got the better of my drowsiness, so that I had pretty near the whole of
my wits about me when the uncle said, "The climate may do away with
this difficulty for you. Is he alone there?" "Yes," answered the manager;

"he sent his assistant down the river with a note to me in these terms:
'Clear this poor devil out of the country, and don't bother sending more
of that sort. I had rather be alone than have the kind of men you can
dispose of with me.' It was more than a year ago. Can you imagine such
impudence!" "Anything since then?" asked the other hoarsely. "Ivory,"
jerked the nephew; "lots of it – prime sort – lots – most annoying, from
him." "And with that?" questioned the heavy rumble. "Invoice," was
the reply fired out, so to speak. Then silence. They had been talking
about Kurtz.

'I was broad awake by this time, but, lying perfectly at ease, remained
still, having no inducement to change my position. "How did that ivory
come all this way?" growled the elder man, who seemed very vexed. The
other explained that it had come with a fleet of canoes in charge of an
English half-caste clerk Kurtz had with him; that Kurtz had apparently
intended to return himself, the station being by that time bare of goods
and stores, but after coming three hundred miles, had suddenly decided
to go back, which he started to do alone in a small dugout with four
paddlers, leaving the half-caste to continue down the river with the ivory.
The two fellows there seemed astounded at anybody attempting such a
thing. They were at a loss for an adequate motive. As to me, I seemed
to see Kurtz for the first time. It was a distinct glimpse: the dugout, four
paddling savages, and the lone white man turning his back suddenly
on the headquarters, on relief, on thoughts of home – perhaps; setting
his face towards the depths of the wilderness, towards his empty and
desolate station. I did not know the motive. Perhaps he was just simply
a fine fellow who stuck to his work for its own sake. His name, you
understand, had not been pronounced once. He was "that man". The half-
caste, who, as far as I could see, had conducted a difficult trip with great
prudence and pluck, was invariably alluded to as "that scoundrel". The
"scoundrel" had reported that the "man" had been very ill – had recovered
imperfectly . . . The two below me moved away then a few paces, and
strolled back and forth at some little distance. I heard: "Military post
– doctor – two hundred miles – quite alone now – unavoidable delays –
nine months – no news – strange rumours." They approached again, just
as the manager was saying, "No one, as far as I know, unless a species of
wandering trader – a pestilential fellow, snapping ivory from the natives."
Who was it they were talking about now? I gathered in snatches that

this was some man supposed to be in Kurtz's district, and of whom the manager did not approve. "We will not be free from unfair competition till one of these fellows is hanged for an example," he said. "Certainly," grunted the other; "get him hanged! Why not? Anything – anything can be done in this country. That's what I say; nobody here, you understand, *here*, can endanger your position. And why? You stand the climate – you outlast them all. The danger is in Europe; but there before I left I took care to – " They moved off and whispered, then their voices rose again. "The extraordinary series of delays is not my fault. I did my best." The fat man sighed. "Very sad." "And the pestiferous absurdity of his talk," continued the other; "he bothered me enough when he was here. 'Each station should be like a beacon on the road towards better things, a centre for trade of course, but also for humanizing, improving, instructing.' Conceive you – that ass! And he wants to be manager! No, it's —" Here he got choked by excessive indignation, and I lifted my head the least bit. I was surprised to see how near they were – right under me. I could have spat upon their hats. They were looking on the ground, absorbed in thought. The manager was switching his leg with a slender twig; his sagacious relative lifted his head. "You have been well since you came out this time?" he asked. The other gave a start. "Who? I? Oh! Like a charm – like a charm. But the rest – oh, my goodness! All sick. They die so quick, too, that I haven't the time to send them out of the country – it's incredible!" "Hm'm. Just so," grunted the uncle. "Ah! my boy, trust to this – I say, trust to this." I saw him extend his short flipper of an arm for a gesture that took in the forest, the creek, the mud, the river – seemed to beckon with a dishonouring flourish before the sunlit face of the land a treacherous appeal to the lurking death, to the hidden evil, to the profound darkness of its heart. It was so startling that I leaped to my feet and looked back at the edge of the forest, as though I had expected an answer of some sort to that black display of confidence. You know the foolish notions that come to one sometimes. The high stillness confronted these two figures with its ominous patience, waiting for the passing away of a fantastic invasion.

'They swore aloud together – out of sheer fright, I believe – then pretending not to know anything of my existence, turned back to the station. The sun was low; and leaning forward side by side, they seemed to be tugging painfully uphill their two ridiculous shadows of unequal length, that trailed behind them slowly over the tall grass without bending a single blade.

'In a few days the Eldorado Expedition went into the patient wilderness, that closed upon it as the sea closes over a diver. Long afterwards the news came that all the donkeys were dead. I know nothing as to the fate of the less valuable animals. They, no doubt, like the rest of us, found what they deserved. I did not inquire. I was then rather excited at the prospect of meeting Kurtz very soon. When I say very soon I mean it comparatively. It was just two months from the day we left the creek when we came to the bank below Kurtz's station.

'Going up that river was like travelling back to the earliest beginnings of the world, when vegetation rioted on the earth and the big trees were kings. An empty stream, a great silence, an impenetrable forest. The air was warm, thick, heavy, sluggish. There was no joy in the brilliance of sunshine. The long stretches of the waterway ran on, deserted, into the gloom of overshadowed distances. On silvery sand-banks hippos and alligators sunned themselves side by side. The broadening waters flowed through a mob of wooded islands; you lost your way on that river as you would in a desert, and butted all day long against shoals, trying to find the channel, till you thought yourself bewitched and cut off for ever from everything you had known once – somewhere – far away – in another existence perhaps. There were moments when one's past came back to one, as it will sometimes when you have not a moment to spare for yourself; but it came in the shape of an unrestful and noisy dream, remembered with wonder amongst the overwhelming realities of this strange world of plants, and water, and silence. And this stillness of life did not in the least resemble a peace. It was the stillness of an implacable force brooding over an inscrutable intention. It looked at you with a vengeful aspect. I got used to it afterwards; I did not see it any more; I had no time. I had to keep guessing at the channel; I had to discern, mostly by inspiration, the signs of hidden banks; I watched for sunken stones; I was learning to clap my teeth smartly before my heart flew out, when I shaved by a fluke some infernal sly old snag that would have ripped the life out of the tin-pot steamboat and drowned all the pilgrims; I had to keep a lookout for the signs of dead wood we could cut up in the night for next day's steaming. When you have to attend to things of that sort, to the mere incidents of the surface, the reality – the reality, I tell you – fades.

The inner truth is hidden – luckily, luckily. But I felt it all the same; I felt often its mysterious stillness watching me at my monkey tricks, just as it watches you fellows performing on your respective tight-ropes for – what is it? half-a-crown a tumble – '

'Try to be civil, Marlow,' growled a voice, and I knew there was at least one listener awake besides myself.

'I beg your pardon. I forgot the heartache which makes up the rest of the price. And indeed what does the price matter, if the trick be well done? You do your tricks very well. And I didn't do badly either, since I managed not to sink that steamboat on my first trip. It's a wonder to me yet. Imagine a blindfolded man set to drive a van over a bad road. I sweated and shivered over that business considerably, I can tell you. After all, for a seaman, to scrape the bottom of the thing that's supposed to float all the time under his care is the unpardonable sin. No one may know of it, but you never forget the thump – eh? A blow on the very heart. You remember it, you dream of it, you wake up at night and think of it – years after – and go hot and cold all over. I don't pretend to say that steamboat floated all the time. More than once she had to wade for a bit, with twenty cannibals splashing around and pushing. We had enlisted some of these chaps on the way for a crew. Fine fellows – cannibals – in their place. They were men one could work with, and I am grateful to them. And, after all, they did not eat each other before my face: they had brought along a provision of hippo–meat which went rotten, and made the mystery of the wilderness stink in my nostrils. Phoo! I can sniff it now. I had the manager on board and three or four pilgrims with their staves – all complete. Sometimes we came upon a station close by the bank, clinging to the skirts of the unknown, and the white men rushing out of a tumble-down hovel, with great gestures of joy and surprise and welcome, seemed very strange – had the appearance of being held there captive by a spell. The word ivory would ring in the air for a while – and on we went again into the silence, along empty reaches, round the still bends, between the high walls of our winding way, reverberating in hollow claps the ponderous beat of the stern-wheel. Trees, trees, millions of trees, massive, immense, running up high; and at their foot, hugging the bank against the stream, crept the little begrimed steamboat, like a sluggish beetle crawling on the floor of a lofty portico. It made you feel very small, very lost, and yet it was not altogether depressing, that feeling.

After all, if you were small, the grimy beetle crawled on – which was just what you wanted it to do. Where the pilgrims imagined it crawled to I don't know. To some place where they expected to get something. I bet! For me it crawled towards Kurtz – exclusively; but when the steam-pipes started leaking we crawled very slow. The reaches opened before us and closed behind, as if the forest had stepped leisurely across the water to bar the way for our return. We penetrated deeper and deeper into the heart of darkness. It was very quiet there. At night sometimes the roll of drums behind the curtain of trees would run up the river and remain sustained faintly, as if hovering in the air high over our heads, till the first break of day. Whether it meant war, peace, or prayer we could not tell. The dawns were heralded by the descent of a chill stillness; the wood-cutters slept, their fires burned low; the snapping of a twig would make you start. We were wanderers on a prehistoric earth, on an earth that wore the aspect of an unknown planet. We could have fancied ourselves the first of men taking possession of an accursed inheritance, to be subdued at the cost of profound anguish and of excessive toil. But suddenly, as we struggled round a bend, there would be a glimpse of rush walls, of peaked grass-roofs, a burst of yells, a whirl of black limbs, a mass of hands clapping. of feet stamping, of bodies swaying, of eyes rolling, under the droop of heavy and motionless foliage. The steamer toiled along slowly on the edge of a black and incomprehensible frenzy. The prehistoric man was cursing us, praying to us, welcoming us – who could tell? We were cut off from the comprehension of our surroundings; we glided past like phantoms, wondering and secretly appalled, as sane men would be before an enthusiastic outbreak in a madhouse. We could not understand because we were too far, and could not remember because we were travelling in the night of first ages, of those ages that are gone, leaving hardly a sign – and no memories.

'The earth seemed unearthly. We are accustomed to look upon the shackled form of a conquered monster, but there – there you could look at a thing monstrous and free. It was unearthly, and the men were – No, they were not inhuman. Well, you know, that was the worst of it – this suspicion of their not being inhuman. It would come slowly to one. They howled and leaped, and spun, and made horrid faces; but what thrilled you was just the thought of their humanity – like yours – the thought of your remote kinship with this wild and passionate uproar. Ugly. Yes, it was ugly enough; but if you were man enough you would admit to yourself that there was in you just the faintest trace of a response to the terrible frankness of that noise, a dim suspicion of there being a meaning in it which you – you so remote from the night of first ages – could comprehend. And why not? The mind of man is capable of anything – because everything is in it, all the past as well as all the future. What was there after all? Joy, fear, sorrow, devotion, valour, rage – who can tell? – but truth – truth stripped of its cloak of time. Let the fool gape and shudder – the man knows, and can look on without a wink. But he must at least be as much of a man as these on the shore. He must meet that truth with his own true stuff – with his own inborn strength. Principles? Principles won't do. Acquisitions, clothes, pretty rags – rags that would fly off at the first good shake. No; you want a deliberate belief. An appeal to me in this fiendish row – is there? Very well; I hear; I admit, but I have a voice, too, and for good or evil mine is the speech that cannot be silenced. Of course, a fool, what with sheer fright and fine sentiments, is always safe. Who's that grunting? You wonder I didn't go ashore for a howl and a dance? Well, no – I didn't. Fine sentiments, you say? Fine sentiments, be hanged! I had no time. I had to mess about with white-lead and strips of woollen blanket helping to put bandages on those leaky steam-pipes – I tell you. I had to watch the steering, and circumvent those snags, and get the tin-pot along by hook or by crook. There was surface-truth enough in these things to save a wiser man. And between whiles I had to look after the savage who was fireman. He was an improved specimen; he could fire up a vertical boiler. He was there below me, and, upon my word, to look at him was as edifying as seeing a dog in a parody of breeches and a feather hat, walking on his hind legs. A few months of training had done for that really fine chap. He squinted at the steam-gauge and at the water-gauge with an evident effort of intrepidity – and he had filed teeth, too, the poor devil, and the wool of his pate shaved into queer patterns, and three ornamental scars on each of his cheeks. He ought to have been clapping his hands and stamping his feet on the bank, instead of which he was hard at work, a thrall to strange witchcraft, full of improving knowledge. He was useful because he had been instructed; and what he knew was this – that should the water in that transparent thing disappear, the evil spirit inside the boiler would get angry through the greatness of his thirst and take a terrible vengeance. So he sweated and fired up and watched the glass fearfully (with an impromptu charm, made of rags, tied to his arm, and a piece of polished bone, as big as a watch, stuck flatways through his lower lip), while the wooded banks slipped past us slowly, the short noise was left behind, the interminable miles of silence – and we crept on, towards Kurtz. But the snags were thick, the water was treacherous and shallow, the boiler seemed indeed to have a sulky devil in it, and thus neither that fireman nor I had any time to peer into our creepy thoughts.

'Some fifty miles below the Inner Station we came upon a hut of reeds, an inclined and melancholy pole, with the unrecognizable tatters of what had been a flag of some sort flying from it, and a neatly stacked wood-pile. This was unexpected. We came to the bank, and on the stack of firewood found a flat piece of board with some faded pencil-writing on it. When deciphered it said: "Wood for you. Hurry up. Approach cautiously." There was a signature, but it was illegible – not Kurtz – a much longer word. "Hurry up." Where? Up the river? "Approach cautiously." We had not done so. But the warning could not have been meant for the place where it could be only found after approach. Something was wrong above. But what – and how much? That was the question. We commented adversely upon the imbecility of that telegraphic style. The bush around said nothing, and would not let us look very far, either. A torn curtain of red twill hung in the doorway of the hut, and flapped sadly in our faces. The dwelling was dismantled; but we could see a white man had lived there not very long ago. There remained a rude table – a plank on two posts; a heap of rubbish reposed in a dark corner, and by the door I picked up a book. It had lost its covers, and the pages had been thumbed into a state of extremely dirty softness; but the back had been lovingly stitched afresh with white cotton thread, which looked clean yet. It was an extraordinary find. Its title was, *An Inquiry into some Points of Seamanship*, by a man Tower, Towson – some such name – Master in his Majesty's Navy. The matter looked dreary reading enough, with illustrative diagrams and repulsive tables of figures, and the copy was sixty years old. I handled this amazing antiquity with the greatest possible tenderness, lest it should dissolve in my hands. Within, Towson or Towser was inquiring earnestly into the breaking strain of ships' chains and tackle, and other such matters. Not a very enthralling book; but at the first glance you could see there a singleness of intention, an honest concern for the right way of going to work, which made these humble pages, thought out so many years ago, luminous with another than a professional light. The simple old sailor, with his talk of chains and purchases, made me forget the jungle and the pilgrims in a delicious sensation of having come upon something unmistakably real. Such a book being there was wonderful enough; but still more astounding were the notes pencilled in the margin, and plainly referring to the text. I couldn't believe my eyes! They were in cipher! Yes, it looked like cipher. Fancy a man lugging with him a book of that description into this nowhere and studying it – and making notes – in cipher at that! It was an extravagant mystery.

'I had been dimly aware for some time of a worrying noise, and when I lifted my eyes I saw the wood-pile was gone, and the manager, aided by all the pilgrims, was shouting at me from the riverside. I slipped the book into my pocket. I assure you to leave off reading was like tearing myself away from the shelter of an old and solid friendship.

'I started the lame engine ahead. "It must be this miserable trader – this intruder," exclaimed the manager, looking back malevolently at the place we had left. "He must be English," I said. "It will not save him from getting into trouble if he is not careful," muttered the manager darkly. I observed with assumed innocence that no man was safe from trouble in this world.

'The current was more rapid now, the steamer seemed at her last gasp, the stern-wheel flopped languidly, and I caught myself listening on tiptoe for the next beat of the boat, for in sober truth I expected the wretched thing to give up every moment. It was like watching the last flickers of a life. But still we crawled. Sometimes I would pick out a tree a little way ahead to measure our progress towards Kurtz by, but I lost it invariably before we got abreast. To keep the eyes so long on one thing was too much for human patience. The manager displayed a beautiful resignation. I fretted and fumed and took to arguing with myself whether or no I would talk openly with Kurtz; but before I could come to any conclusion it occurred to me that my speech or my silence, indeed any action of mine, would be a mere futility. What did it matter what anyone knew or ignored? What did it matter who was manager? One gets sometimes such a flash of insight. The essentials of this affair lay deep under the surface, beyond my reach, and beyond my power of meddling.

'Towards the evening of the second day we judged ourselves about eight miles from Kurtz's station. I wanted to push on; but the manager looked grave, and told me the navigation up there was so dangerous that it would be advisable, the sun being very low already, to wait where we were till next morning. Moreover, he pointed out that if the warning to approach cautiously were to be followed, we must approach in daylight – not at dusk or in the dark. This was sensible enough. Eight miles meant nearly three hours' steaming for us, and I could also see suspicious ripples at the upper end of the reach. Nevertheless, I was annoyed beyond expression at the delay, and most unreasonably, too, since one night more could not matter much after so many months. As we had plenty of wood, and caution was the word, I brought up in the middle of the stream. The reach was narrow, straight, with high sides like a railway cutting. The dusk came gliding into it long before the sun had set. The current ran smooth and swift, but a dumb immobility sat on the banks. The living trees, lashed together by the creepers and every living bush of the undergrowth, might have been changed into stone, even to the slenderest twig, to the lightest leaf. It was not sleep – it seemed unnatural, like a state of trance. Not the faintest sound of any kind could be heard. You looked on amazed, and began to suspect yourself of being deaf – then the night came suddenly, and struck you blind as well. About three in the morning some large fish leaped, and the loud splash made me jump as though a gun had been fired. When the sun rose there was a white fog, very warm and clammy, and more blinding than the night. It did not shift or drive; it was just there, standing all round you like something solid. At eight or nine, perhaps, it lifted as a shutter lifts. We had a glimpse of the towering multitude of trees, of the immense matted jungle, with the blazing little ball of the sun hanging over it – all perfectly still – and then the white shutter came down again, smoothly, as if sliding in greased grooves. I ordered the chain, which we had begun to heave in, to be paid out again. Before it stopped running with a muffled rattle, a cry, a very loud cry, as of infinite desolation, soared slowly in the opaque air. It ceased. A complaining clamour, modulated in savage discords, filled our ears. The sheer unexpectedness of it made my hair stir under my cap. I don't know how it struck the others: to me it seemed as though the mist itself had screamed, so suddenly, and apparently from all sides at once, did this tumultuous and mournful uproar arise. It culminated in a hurried outbreak of almost intolerably excessive shrieking, which stopped short, leaving us stiffened in a variety of silly attitudes, and obstinately listening to the nearly as appalling and excessive silence. "Good God! What is the meaning – " stammered at my elbow one of the pilgrims – a little fat man, with sandy hair and red whiskers, who wore sidespring boots, and pink pyjamas tucked into his socks. Two others remained open-mouthed a whole minute, then dashed into the little cabin, to rush out incontinently and stand darting scared glances, with Winchesters at "ready" in their hands. What we could see was just the steamer we were on, her outlines blurred as though she had been on the point of dissolving, and a misty strip of water, perhaps two feet broad, around her – and that was all. The rest of the world was nowhere, as far as our eyes and ears were concerned. Just nowhere. Gone, disappeared; swept off without leaving a whisper or a shadow behind.

'I went forward, and ordered the chain to be hauled in short, so as to be ready to trip the anchor and move the steamboat at once if necessary. "Will they attack?" whispered an awed voice. "We will be all butchered in this fog," murmured another. The faces twitched with the strain, the hands trembled slightly, the eyes forgot to wink. It was very curious to see the contrast of expressions of the white men and of the black fellows of our crew, who were as much strangers to that part of the river as we, though their homes were only eight hundred miles away. The whites, of course greatly discomposed, had besides a curious look of being painfully shocked by such an outrageous row. The others had an alert, naturally interested expression; but their faces were essentially quiet, even those of the one or two who grinned as they hauled at the chain. Several exchanged short, grunting phrases, which seemed to settle the matter to their satisfaction. Their headman, a young, broad-chested black, severely draped in dark-blue fringed cloths, with fierce nostrils and his hair all done up artfully in oily ringlets, stood near me. "Aha!" I said, just for good fellowship's sake. "Catch 'im," he snapped, with a bloodshot widening of his eyes and a flash of sharp teeth – "catch 'im. Give 'im to us." "To you, eh?" I asked; "what would you do with them?" "Eat 'im!" he said curtly, and, leaning his elbow on the rail, looked out into the fog in a dignified and profoundly pensive attitude. I would no doubt have been properly horrified, had it not occurred to me that he and his chaps must be very hungry: that they must have been growing increasingly hungry for at least this month past. They had been engaged for six months (I don't think a single one of them had any clear idea of time, as we at the end of countless ages have. They still belonged to the beginnings of time – had no inherited experience to teach them as it were), and of course, as long as there was a piece of paper written over in accordance with some farcical law or other made down the river, it didn't enter anybody's head to trouble how they would live. Certainly they had brought with them some rotten hippo-meat, which couldn't have lasted very long, anyway, even if the pilgrims hadn't, in the midst of a shocking hullabaloo, thrown a considerable quantity of it overboard. It looked like a high-handed proceeding; but it was really a case of legitimate self-defence. You can't breathe dead hippo waking, sleeping, and eating, and at the same time keep your precarious grip on existence. Besides that, they had given them every week three pieces of brass wire, each about nine inches long; and the theory was they were to buy their provisions with that currency in river-side villages. You can see how *that* worked. There were either no villages, or the people were hostile, or the director, who like the rest of us fed out of tins, with an occasional old he-goat thrown in, didn't want to stop the steamer for some more or less recondite reason. So, unless they swallowed the wire itself, or made loops of it to snare the fishes with, I don't see what good their extravagant salary could be to them. I must say it was paid with a regularity worthy of a large and honourable trading company. For the rest, the only thing to eat – though it didn't look eatable in the least – I saw in their possession was a few lumps of some stuff like half-cooked dough, of a dirty lavender colour, they kept wrapped in leaves, and now and then swallowed a piece of, but so small that it seemed done more for the looks of the thing than for any serious purpose of sustenance. Why in the name of all the gnawing devils of hunger they didn't go for us – they were thirty to five – and have a good tuck-in for once, amazes me now when I think of it. They were big powerful men, with not much capacity to weigh the consequences, with courage, with strength, even yet, though their skins were no longer glossy and their muscles no longer hard. And I saw that something restraining, one of those human secrets that baffle probability, had come into play there. I looked at them with a swift quickening of interest – not because it occurred to me I might be eaten by them before very long, though I own to you that just then I perceived – in a new light, as it were – how unwholesome the pilgrims looked, and I hoped, yes, I positively hoped, that my aspect was not so – what shall I say? – so – unappetizing: a touch of fantastic vanity which fitted well with the dream-sensation that pervaded all my days at that time. Perhaps I had a little fever, too. One can't live with one's finger everlastingly on one's pulse. I had often "a little fever", or a little touch of other things – the playful paw-strokes of the wilderness, the preliminary trifling before the more serious onslaught which came in due course. Yes; I looked at them as you would on any human being, with a curiosity of their impulses, motives, capacities, weaknesses, when brought to the test of an inexorable physical necessity. Restraint! What possible restraint? Was it superstition, disgust, patience, fear – or some kind of primitive honour? No fear can stand up to hunger, no patience can wear it out, disgust simply does not exist where hunger is; and as to superstition, beliefs, and what you may call principles, they are less than chaff in a breeze. Don't you know the devilry of lingering starvation, its exasperating torment, its black thoughts, its sombre and brooding ferocity? Well, I do. It takes a man all his inborn strength to fight hunger properly. It's really easier to face bereavement, dishonour, and the perdition of one's soul – than this kind of prolonged hunger. Sad, but true. And these chaps, too, had no earthly reason for any kind of scruple. Restraint! I would just as soon have expected restraint from a hyena prowling amongst the corpses of a battlefield. But there was the fact facing me – the fact dazzling, to be seen, like the foam on the depths of the sea, like a ripple on an unfathomable enigma, a mystery greater – when I thought of it – than the curious, inexplicable note of desperate grief in this savage clamour that had swept by us on the river-bank, behind the blind whiteness of the fog.

'Two pilgrims were quarrelling in hurried whispers as to which bank. "Left." "No, no; how can you? Right, right, of course." "It is very serious," said the manager's voice behind me; "I would be desolated if anything should happen to Mr Kurtz before we came up." I looked at him, and had not the slightest doubt he was sincere. He was just the kind of man who would wish to preserve appearances. That was his restraint. But when he muttered something about going on at once, I did not even take the trouble to answer him. I knew, and he knew, that it was impossible. Were we to let go our hold of the bottom, we would be absolutely in the air – in space. We wouldn't be able to tell where we were going to – whether up or down stream, or across – till we fetched against one bank or the other – and then we wouldn't know at first which it was. Of course I made no move. I had no mind for a smash-up. You couldn't imagine a more deadly place for a shipwreck. Whether drowned at once or not, we were sure to perish speedily in one way or another. "I authorize you to take all the risks," he said, after a short silence. "I refuse to take any," I said shortly; which was just the answer he expected, though its tone might have surprised him. "Well, I must defer to your judgment. You are captain," he said with marked civility. I turned my shoulder to him in sign of my appreciation, and looked into the fog. How long would it last? It was the most hopeless lookout. The approach to this Kurtz grubbing for ivory in the wretched bush was beset by as many dangers as though he had been an enchanted princess sleeping in a fabulous castle. "Will they attack, do you think?" asked the manager, in a confidential tone.

'I did not think they would attack, for several obvious reasons. The thick fog was one. If they left the bank in their canoes they would get lost in it, as we would be if we attempted to move. Still, I had also judged the jungle of both banks quite impenetrable – and yet eyes were in it, eyes that had seen us. The river-side bushes were certainly very thick; but the undergrowth behind was evidently penetrable. However, during the short lift I had seen no canoes anywhere in the reach – certainly not abreast of the steamer. But what made the idea of attack inconceivable to me was the nature of the noise – of the cries we had heard. They had not the fierce character boding immediate hostile intention. Unexpected, wild, and violent as they had been, they had given me an irresistible impression of sorrow. The glimpse of the steamboat had for some reason filled those savages with unrestrained grief. The danger, if any, I expounded, was from our proximity to a great human passion let loose. Even extreme grief may ultimately vent itself in violence – but more generally takes the form of apathy…

'You should have seen the pilgrims stare! They had no heart to grin, or even to revile me; but I believe they thought me gone mad – with fright, maybe. I delivered a regular lecture. My dear boys, it was no good bothering. Keep a lookout? Well, you may guess I watched the fog for the signs of lifting as a cat watches a mouse; but for anything else our eyes were of no more use to us than if we had been buried miles deep in a heap of cotton-wool. It felt like it, too – choking, warm, stifling. Besides, all I said, though it sounded extravagant, was absolutely true to fact. What we afterwards alluded to as an attack was really an attempt at repulse. The action was very far from being aggressive – it was not even defensive, in the usual sense: it was undertaken under the stress of desperation, and in its essence was purely protective.

'It developed itself, I should say, two hours after the fog lifted, and its commencement was at a spot, roughly speaking, about a mile and a half below Kurtz's station. We had just floundered and flopped round a bend, when I saw an islet, a mere grassy hummock of bright green, in the middle of the stream. It was the only thing of the kind; but as we opened the reach more, I perceived it was the head of a long sandbank, or rather of a chain of shallow patches stretching down the middle of the river. They were discoloured, just awash, and the whole lot was seen just under the water, exactly as a man's backbone is seen running down the middle of his back under the skin. Now, as far as I did see, I could go to the right or to the left of this. I didn't know either channel, of course. The banks looked pretty well alike, the depth appeared the same; but as I had been informed the station was on the west side, I naturally headed for the western passage.

'No sooner had we fairly entered it than I became aware it was much narrower than I had supposed. To the left of us there was the long uninterrupted shoal, and to the right a high, steep bank heavily overgrown with bushes. Above the bush the trees stood in serried ranks. The twigs overhung the current thickly, and from distance to distance a large limb of some tree projected rigidly over the stream. It was then well on in the afternoon, the face of the forest was gloomy, and a broad strip of shadow had already fallen on the water. In this shadow we steamed up – very slowly, as you may imagine. I sheered her well inshore – the water being deepest near the bank, as the sounding-pole informed me.

'One of my hungry and forbearing friends was sounding in the bows just below me. This steamboat was exactly like a decked scow. On the deck there were two little teak-wood houses, with doors and windows. The boiler was in the fore-end, and the machinery right astern. Over the whole there was a light roof, supported on stanchions. The funnel projected through that roof, and in front of the funnel a small cabin built of light planks served for a pilot-house. It contained a couch, two camp-stools, a loaded Martini-Henry leaning in one corner, a tiny table, and the steering-wheel. It had a wide door in front and a broad shutter at each side. All these were always thrown open, of course. I spent my days perched up there on the extreme fore-end of that roof, before the door. At night

I slept, or tried to, on the couch. An athletic black belonging to some coast tribe and educated by my poor predecessor, was the helmsman. He sported a pair of brass earrings, wore a blue cloth wrapper from the waist to the ankles, and thought all the world of himself. He was the most unstable kind of fool I had ever seen. He steered with no end of a swagger while you were by; but if he lost sight of you, he became instantly the prey of an abject funk, and would let that cripple of a steamboat get the upper hand of him in a minute.

'I was looking down at the sounding-pole, and feeling much annoyed to see at each try a little more of it stick out of that river, when I saw my poleman give up on the business suddenly, and stretch himself flat on the deck, without even taking the trouble to haul his pole in. He kept hold on it though, and it trailed in the water. At the same time the fireman, whom I could also see below me, sat down abruptly before his furnace and ducked his head. I was amazed. Then I had to look at the river mighty quick, because there was a snag in the fairway. Sticks, little sticks, were flying about – thick: they were whizzing before my nose, dropping below me, striking behind me against my pilot-house. All this time the river, the shore, the woods, were very quiet – perfectly quiet. I could only hear the heavy splashing thump of the stern-wheel and the patter of these things. We cleared the snag clumsily. Arrows, by Jove! We were being shot at! I stepped in quickly to close the shutter on the landside. That fool-helmsman, his hands on the spokes, was lifting his knees high, stamping his feet, champing his mouth, like a reined-in horse. Confound him! And we were staggering within ten feet of the bank. I had to lean right out to swing the heavy shutter, and I saw a face amongst the leaves on the level with my own, looking at me very fierce and steady; and then suddenly, as though a veil had been removed from my eyes, I made out, deep in the tangled gloom, naked breasts, arms, legs, glaring eyes – the bush was swarming with human limbs in movement, glistening, of bronze colour. The twigs shook, swayed, and rustled, the arrows flew out of them, and then the shutter came to. "Steer her straight," I said to the helmsman. He held his head rigid, face forward; but his eyes rolled, he kept on lifting and setting down his feet gently, his mouth foamed a little. "Keep quiet!" I said in a fury. I might just as well have ordered a tree not to sway in the wind. I darted out. Below me there was a great scuffle of feet on the iron deck; confused exclamations; a voice screamed, "Can you turn back?"

I caught sight of a V-shaped ripple on the water ahead. What? Another snag! A fusillade burst out under my feet. The pilgrims had opened with their Winchesters, and were simply squirting lead into that bush. A deuce of a lot of smoke came up and drove slowly forward. I swore at it. Now I couldn't see the ripple or the snag either. I stood in the doorway, peering, and the arrows came in swarms. They might have been poisoned, but they looked as though they wouldn't kill a cat. The bush began to howl. Our wood-cutters raised a warlike whoop; the report of a rifle just at my back deafened me. I glanced over my shoulder, and the pilot-house was yet full of noise and smoke when I made a dash at the wheel. The fool-nigger had dropped everything, to throw the shutter open and let off that Martini-Henry. He stood before the wide opening, glaring, and I yelled at him to come back, while I straightened the sudden twist out of that steamboat. There was no room to turn even if I had wanted to, the snag was somewhere very near ahead in that confounded smoke, there was no time to lose, so I just crowded her into the bank – right into the bank, where I knew the water was deep.

'We tore slowly along the overhanging bushes in a whirl of broken twigs and flying leaves. The fusillade below stopped short, as I had foreseen it would when the squirts got empty. I threw my head back to a glinting whizz that traversed the pilot-house, in at one shutter-hole and out at the other. Looking past that mad helmsman, who was shaking the empty rifle and yelling at the shore, I saw vague forms of men running bent double, leaping, gliding, distinct, incomplete, evanescent. Something big appeared in the air before the shutter, the rifle went overboard, and the man stepped back swiftly, looked at me over his shoulder in an extraordinary, profound, familiar manner, and fell upon my feet. The side of his head hit the wheel twice, and the end of what appeared a long cane clattered round and knocked over a little camp-stool. It looked as though after wrenching that thing from somebody ashore he had lost his balance in the effort. The thin smoke had blown away, we were clear of the snag, and looking ahead I could see that in another hundred yards or so I would be free to sheer off, away from the bank; but my feet felt so very warm and wet that I had to look down. The man had rolled on his back and stared straight up at me; both his hands clutched that cane. It was the shaft of a spear that, either thrown or lunged through the opening, had caught him in the side, just below the ribs; the blade had gone in out of sight, after making a frightful gash; my shoes were full; a pool of blood lay very still, gleaming dark-red under the wheel; his eyes shone with an amazing lustre. The fusillade burst out again. He looked at me anxiously, gripping the spear like something precious, with an air of being afraid I would try to take it away from him. I had to make an effort to free my eyes from his gaze and attend to the steering. With one hand I felt above my head for the line of the steam whistle, and jerked out screech after screech hurriedly. The tumult of angry and warlike yells was checked instantly, and then from the depths of the woods went out such a tremulous and prolonged wail of mournful fear and utter despair as may be imagined to follow the flight of the last hope from the earth. There was a great commotion in the bush; the shower of arrows stopped, a few dropping shots rang out sharply – then silence, in which the languid beat of the stern-wheel came plainly to my ears. I put the helm hard a-starboard at the moment when the pilgrim in pink pyjamas, very hot and agitated, appeared in the doorway. "The manager sends me – " he began in an official tone, and stopped short. "Good God!" he said, glaring at the wounded man.

'We two whites stood over him, and his lustrous and inquiring glance enveloped us both. I declare it looked as though he would presently put to us some questions in an understandable language; but he died without uttering a sound, without moving a limb, without twitching a muscle. Only in the very last moment, as though in response to some sign we could not see, to some whisper we could not hear, he frowned heavily, and that frown gave to his black death-mask an inconceivably sombre, brooding, and menacing expression. The lustre of inquiring glance faded swiftly into vacant glassiness. "Can you steer?" I asked the agent eagerly. He looked very dubious; but I made a grab at his arm, and he understood at once I meant him to steer whether or no. To tell you the truth, I was morbidly anxious to change my shoes and socks. "He is dead," murmured the fellow, immensely impressed. "No doubt about it," said I, tugging like mad at the shoe-laces. "And by the way, I suppose Mr Kurtz is dead as well by this time."

'For the moment that was the dominant thought. There was a sense of extreme disappointment, as though I had found out I had been striving after something altogether without a substance. I couldn't have been more disgusted if I had travelled all this way for the sole purpose of talking with Mr Kurtz. Talking with... I flung one shoe overboard, and became aware that that was exactly what I had been looking forward to – a talk with Kurtz. I made the strange discovery that I had never imagined him as doing, you know, but as discoursing. I didn't say to myself, "Now I will never see him," or "Now I will never shake him by the hand," but, "Now I will never hear him." The man presented himself as a voice. Not of course that I did not connect him with some sort of action. Hadn't I been told in all the tones of jealousy and admiration that he had collected, bartered, swindled, or stolen more ivory than all the other agents together? That was not the point. The point was in his being a gifted creature, and that of all his gifts the one that stood out pre-eminently, that carried with it a sense of real presence, was his ability to talk, his words – the gift of expression, the bewildering, the illuminating, the most exalted and the most contemptible, the pulsating stream of light, or the deceitful flow from the heart of an impenetrable darkness.

'The other shoe went flying unto the devil-god of that river. I thought, "By Jove! It's all over. We are too late; he has vanished – the gift has vanished, by means of some spear, arrow, or club. I will never hear that chap speak after all" – and my sorrow had a startling extravagance of emotion, even such as I had noticed in the howling sorrow of these savages in the bush. I couldn't have felt more of lonely desolation somehow, had I been robbed of a belief or had missed my destiny in life…. Why do you sigh in this beastly way, somebody? Absurd? Well, absurd. Good Lord! mustn't a man ever – Here, give me some tobacco.' …

There was a pause of profound stillness, then a match flared, and Marlow's lean face appeared, worn, hollow, with downward folds and dropped eyelids, with an aspect of concentrated attention; and as he took vigorous draws at his pipe, it seemed to retreat and advance out of the night in the regular flicker of tiny flame. The match went out.

'Absurd!' he cried. 'This is the worst of trying to tell… Here you all are, each moored with two good addresses, like a hulk with two anchors, a butcher round one corner, a policeman round another, excellent appetites, and temperature normal – you hear – normal from year's end to year's end. And you say, Absurd! Absurd be – exploded! Absurd! My dear boys, what can you expect from a man who out of sheer nervousness had just flung overboard a pair of new shoes! Now I think of it, it is amazing I did not shed tears. I am, upon the whole, proud of my fortitude. I was cut to the quick at the idea of having lost the inestimable privilege of listening to the gifted Kurtz. Of course I was wrong. The privilege was waiting for me. Oh, yes, I heard more than enough. And I was right, too. A voice. He was very little more than a voice. And I heard – him – it – this voice – other voices – all of them were so little more than voices – and the memory of that time itself lingers around me, impalpable, like a dying vibration of one immense jabber, silly, atrocious, sordid, savage, or simply mean, without any kind of sense. Voices, voices – even the girl herself – now – '

He was silent for a long time.

'I laid the ghost of his gifts at last with a lie,' he began, suddenly. 'Girl! What? Did I mention a girl? Oh, she is out of it – completely. They – the women, I mean – are out of it – should be out of it. We must help them to stay in that beautiful world of their own, lest ours gets worse. Oh, she had to be out of it. You should have heard the disinterred body of Mr Kurtz saying, "My Intended." You would have perceived directly then how completely she was out of it. And the lofty frontal bone of Mr Kurtz! They say the hair goes on growing sometimes, but this – ah – specimen, was impressively bald. The wilderness had patted him on the head, and, behold, it was like a ball – an ivory ball; it had caressed him, and – lo! – he had withered; it had taken him, loved him, embraced him, got into his veins, consumed his flesh, and sealed his soul to its own by the inconceivable ceremonies of some devilish initiation. He was its spoiled and pampered favourite. Ivory? I should think so. Heaps of it, stacks of it. The old mud shanty was bursting with it. You would think there was not a single tusk left either above or below the ground in the whole country. "Mostly fossil," the manager had remarked, disparagingly. It was no more fossil than I am; but they call it fossil when it is dug up. It appears these niggers do bury the tusks sometimes – but evidently they couldn't bury this parcel deep enough to save the gifted Mr Kurtz from his fate. We filled the steamboat with it, and had to pile a lot on the deck. Thus he could see and enjoy as long as he could see, because the appreciation of this favour had remained with him to the last. You should have heard him say, "My ivory." Oh, yes, I heard him. "My Intended, my ivory, my station, my river, my – " everything belonged to him. It made me hold my breath in expectation of hearing the wilderness burst into a prodigious peal of laughter that would shake the fixed stars in their places. Everything belonged to him – but that was a trifle. The thing was to know what he belonged to, how many powers of darkness claimed him for their own. That was the reflection that made you creepy all over. It was impossible – it was not good for one either – trying to imagine. He had taken a high seat amongst the devils of the land – I mean literally. You can't understand. How could you? – with solid pavement under your feet, surrounded by kind neighbours ready to cheer you or to fall on you, stepping delicately between the butcher and the policeman, in the holy terror of scandal and gallows and lunatic asylums – how can you imagine what particular region of the first ages a man's untrammelled feet may take him into by the way of solitude – utter solitude without a policeman – by the way of silence – utter silence, where no warning voice of a kind neighbour can be heard whispering of public opinion? These little things make all the great difference. When they are gone you must fall back upon your own innate strength, upon your own capacity for faithfulness. Of course you may be too much of a fool to go wrong – too dull even to know you are being assaulted by the powers of darkness. I take it, no fool ever made a bargain for his soul with the devil; the fool is too much of a fool, or the devil too much of a devil – I don't know which. Or you may be such a thunderingly exalted creature as to be altogether deaf and blind to anything but heavenly sights and sounds. Then the earth for you is only a standing place – and whether to be like this is your loss or your gain I won't pretend to say. But most of us are neither one nor the other. The earth for us is a place to live in, where we must put up with sights, with sounds, with smells, too, by Jove! – breathe dead hippo, so to speak, and not be contaminated. And there, don't you see? Your strength comes in, the faith in your ability for the digging of unostentatious holes to bury the stuff in – your power of devotion, not to yourself, but to an obscure, back-breaking business. And that's difficult enough. Mind, I am not trying to excuse or even explain – I am trying to account to myself for – for – Mr Kurtz – for the shade of Mr Kurtz. This initiated wraith from the back of Nowhere honoured me with its amazing confidence before it vanished altogether. This was because it could speak English to me. The original Kurtz had been educated partly in England, and – as he was good enough to say himself – his sympathies were in the right place. His mother was half-English, his father was half-French. All Europe contributed to the making of Kurtz; and by-and-by I learned that, most appropriately, the International Society for the Suppression of Savage Customs had entrusted him with the making of a report, for its future guidance. And he had written it, too. I've seen it. I've read it. It was eloquent, vibrating with eloquence, but too highly strung, I think. Seventeen pages of close writing he had found time for! But this must have been before his – let us say – nerves, went wrong, and caused him to preside at certain midnight dances ending with unspeakable rites, which – as far as I reluctantly gathered from what I heard at various times – were offered up to him – do you understand? – to Mr Kurtz himself. But it was a beautiful piece of writing. The opening paragraph, however, in the light of later information, strikes me now as ominous. He began with the argument that we whites, from the point of development we had arrived at, "must necessarily appear to them [savages] in the nature of supernatural beings – we approach them with the might of a deity," and so on, and so on. "By the simple exercise of our will we can exert a power for good practically unbounded," etc., etc. From that point he soared and took me with him. The peroration was magnificent, though difficult to remember, you know. It gave me the notion of an exotic Immensity ruled by an august Benevolence. It made me tingle with enthusiasm. This was the unbounded power of eloquence – of words – of burning noble words. There were no practical hints to interrupt the magic current of phrases, unless a kind of note at the foot of the last page, scrawled evidently much later, in an unsteady hand, may be regarded as the exposition of a method. It was very simple, and at the end of that moving appeal to every altruistic sentiment it blazed at you, luminous and terrifying, like a flash of lightning in a serene sky: "Exterminate all the brutes!" The curious part was that he had apparently forgotten all about that valuable postscriptum, because, later on, when he in a sense came to himself, he repeatedly entreated me to take good care of "my pamphlet" (he called it), as it was sure to have in the future a good influence upon his career. I had full information about all these things, and, besides, as it turned out, I was to have the care of his memory. I've done enough for it to give me the indisputable right to lay it, if I choose, for an everlasting rest in the dustbin of progress, amongst all the sweepings and, figuratively speaking, all the dead cats of civilization. But then, you see, I can't choose. He won't be forgotten. Whatever he was, he was not common. He had the power to charm or frighten rudimentary souls into an aggravated witch-dance in his honour; he could also fill the small souls of the pilgrims with bitter misgivings: he had one devoted friend at least, and he had conquered one soul in the world that was neither rudimentary nor tainted with self-seeking. No; I can't forget him, though I am not prepared to affirm the fellow was exactly worth the life we lost in getting to him. I missed my late helmsman awfully – I missed him even while his body was still lying in the pilot-house. Perhaps you will think it passing strange, this regret for a savage who was no more account than a grain of sand in a black Sahara. Well, don't you see, he had done something, he had steered; for months I had him at my back – a help – an instrument. It was a kind of partnership. He steered for me – I had to look after him, I worried about his deficiencies, and thus a subtle bond had been created, of which I only became aware when it was suddenly broken. And the intimate profundity of that look he gave me when he received his hurt remains to this day in my memory – like a claim of distant kinship affirmed in a supreme moment.

'Poor fool! If he had only left that shutter alone. He had no restraint, no restraint – just like Kurtz – a tree swayed by the wind. As soon as I had put on a dry pair of slippers, I dragged him out, after first jerking the spear out of his side, which operation I confess I performed with my eyes shut tight. His heels leaped together over the little doorstep; his shoulders were pressed to my breast; I hugged him from behind desperately. Oh! he was heavy, heavy; heavier than any man on earth, I should imagine. Then without more ado I tipped him overboard. The current snatched him as though he had been a wisp of grass, and I saw the body roll over twice before I lost sight of it for ever. All the pilgrims and the manager were then congregated on the awning-deck about the pilot-house, chattering at each other like a flock of excited magpies, and there was a scandalized murmur at my heartless promptitude. What they wanted to keep that body hanging about for I can't guess. Embalm it, maybe. But I had also heard another, and a very ominous, murmur on the deck below. My friends the wood-cutters were likewise scandalized, and with a better show of reason – though I admit that the reason itself was quite inadmissible. Oh, quite! I had made up my mind that if my late helmsman was to be eaten, the fishes alone should have him. He had been a very second-rate helmsman while alive, but now he was dead he might have become a first-class temptation, and possibly cause some startling trouble. Besides, I was anxious to take the wheel, the man in pink pyjamas showing himself a hopeless duffer at the business.

'This I did directly the simple funeral was over. We were going half-

speed, keeping right in the middle of the stream, and I listened to the
talk about me. They had given up Kurtz, they had given up the station;
Kurtz was dead, and the station had been burnt – and so on – and so on.
The red-haired pilgrim was beside himself with the thought that at least
this poor Kurtz had been properly avenged. "Say! We must have made a
glorious slaughter of them in the bush. Eh? What do you think? Say?"
He positively danced, the bloodthirsty little gingery beggar. And he had
nearly fainted when he saw the wounded man! I could not help saying,
"You made a glorious lot of smoke, anyhow." I had seen, from the way
the tops of the bushes rustled and flew, that almost all the shots had gone
too high. You can't hit anything unless you take aim and fire from the
shoulder; but these chaps fired from the hip with their eyes shut. The
retreat, I maintained – and I was right – was caused by the screeching of
the steam whistle. Upon this they forgot Kurtz, and began to howl at me
with indignant protests.

'The manager stood by the wheel murmuring confidentially about the
necessity of getting well away down the river before dark at all events,
when I saw in the distance a clearing on the river-side and the outlines
of some sort of building. "What's this?" I asked. He clapped his hands in
wonder. "The station!" he cried. I edged in at once, still going half-speed.

'Through my glasses I saw the slope of a hill interspersed with rare
trees and perfectly free from undergrowth. A long decaying building on
the summit was half buried in the high grass; the large holes in the peaked
roof gaped black from afar; the jungle and the woods made a background.
There was no enclosure or fence of any kind; but there had been one
apparently, for near the house half a dozen slim posts remained in a row,
roughly trimmed, and with their upper ends ornamented with round carved
balls. The rails, or whatever there had been between, had disappeared. Of
course the forest surrounded all that. The river-bank was clear, and on
the water-side I saw a white man under a hat like a cart-wheel beckoning
persistently with his whole arm. Examining the edge of the forest above
and below, I was almost certain I could see movements – human forms
gliding here and there. I steamed past prudently, then stopped the engines
and let her drift down. The man on the shore began to shout, urging us to
land. "We have been attacked," screamed the manager. "I know – I know.
It's all right," yelled back the other, as cheerful as you please. "Come
along. It's all right. I am glad."

'His aspect reminded me of something I had seen – something funny
I had seen somewhere. As I manoeuvred to get alongside, I was asking
myself, "What does this fellow look like?" Suddenly I got it. He looked
like a harlequin. His clothes had been made of some stuff that was brown
holland probably, but it was covered with patches all over, with bright
patches, blue, red, and yellow – patches on the back, patches on the
front, patches on elbows, on knees; coloured binding around his jacket,
scarlet edging at the bottom of his trousers; and the sunshine made him
look extremely gay and wonderfully neat withal, because you could see
how beautifully all this patching had been done. A beardless, boyish
face, very fair, no features to speak of, nose peeling, little blue eyes,
smiles and frowns chasing each other over that open countenance like
sunshine and shadow on a wind-swept plain. "Look out, captain!" he
cried; "there's a snag lodged in here last night." What! Another snag? I
confess I swore shamefully. I had nearly holed my cripple, to finish off
that charming trip. The harlequin on the bank turned his little pug-nose
up to me. "You English?" he asked, all smiles. "Are you?" I shouted
from the wheel. The smiles vanished, and he shook his head as if sorry
for my disappointment. Then he brightened up. "Never mind!" he cried
encouragingly. "Are we in time?" I asked. "He is up there," he replied,
with a toss of the head up the hill, and becoming gloomy all of a sudden.
His face was like the autumn sky, overcast one moment and bright the
next.

'When the manager, escorted by the pilgrims, all of them armed to
the teeth, had gone to the house this chap came on board. "I say, I don't
like this. These natives are in the bush," I said. He assured me earnestly
it was all right. "They are simple people," he added; "well, I am glad
you came. It took me all my time to keep them off." "But you said it was
all right," I cried. "Oh, they meant no harm," he said; and as I stared he
corrected himself, "Not exactly." Then vivaciously, "My faith, your pilot-
house wants a clean-up!" In the next breath he advised me to keep enough
steam on the boiler to blow the whistle in case of any trouble. "One good
screech will do more for you than all your rifles. They are simple people,"
he repeated. He rattled away at such a rate he quite overwhelmed me. He
seemed to be trying to make up for lots of silence, and actually hinted,
laughing, that such was the case. "Don't you talk with Mr Kurtz?" I said.
"You don't talk with that man – you listen to him," he exclaimed with

severe exaltation. "But now – " He waved his arm, and in the twinkling of an eye was in the uttermost depths of despondency. In a moment he came up again with a jump, possessed himself of both my hands, shook them continuously, while he gabbled: "Brother sailor... honour... pleasure... delight... introduce myself... Russian... son of an arch-priest... Government of Tambov... What? Tobacco! English tobacco; the excellent English tobacco! Now, that's brotherly. Smoke? Where's a sailor that does not smoke?"

'The pipe soothed him, and gradually I made out he had run away from school, had gone to sea in a Russian ship; ran away again; served some time in English ships; was now reconciled with the arch-priest. He made a point of that. "But when one is young one must see things, gather experience, ideas; enlarge the mind." "Here!" I interrupted. "You can never tell! Here I met Mr Kurtz," he said, youthfully solemn and reproachful. I held my tongue after that. It appears he had persuaded a Dutch trading-house on the coast to fit him out with stores and goods, and had started for the interior with a light heart, and no more idea of what would happen to him than a baby. He had been wandering about that river for nearly two years alone, cut off from everybody and everything. "I am not so young as I look. I am twenty-five," he said. "At first old Van Shuyten would tell me to go to the devil," he narrated with keen enjoyment; "but I stuck to him, and talked and talked, till at last he got afraid I would talk the hind-leg off his favourite dog, so he gave me some cheap things and a few guns, and told me he hoped he would never see my face again. Good old Dutchman, Van Shuyten. I've sent him one small lot of ivory a year ago, so that he can't call me a little thief when I get back. I hope he got it. And for the rest I don't care. I had some wood stacked for you. That was my old house. Did you see?"

'I gave him Towson's book. He made as though he would kiss me, but restrained himself. "The only book I had left, and I thought I had lost it," he said, looking at it ecstatically. "So many accidents happen to a man going about alone, you know. Canoes get upset sometimes – and sometimes you've got to clear out so quick when the people get angry." He thumbed the pages. "You made notes in Russian?" I asked. He nodded. "I thought they were written in cipher," I said. He laughed, then became serious. "I had lots of trouble to keep these people off," he said. "Did they want to kill you?" I asked. "Oh, no!" he cried, and checked himself. "Why did they attack us?" I pursued. He hesitated, then said shamefacedly, "They don't want him to go." "Don't they?" I said curiously. He nodded a nod full of mystery and wisdom. "I tell you," he cried, "this man has enlarged my mind." He opened his arms wide, staring at me with his little blue eyes that were perfectly round.'

III

'I looked at him, lost in astonishment. There he was before me, in motley, as though he had absconded from a troupe of mimes, enthusiastic, fabulous. His very existence was improbable, inexplicable, and altogether bewildering. He was an insoluble problem. It was inconceivable how he had existed, how he had succeeded in getting so far, how he had managed to remain – why he did not instantly disappear. "I went a little farther," he said, "then still a little farther – till I had gone so far that I don't know how I'll ever get back. Never mind. Plenty time. I can manage. You take Kurtz away quick – quick – I tell you." The glamour of youth enveloped his particoloured rags, his destitution, his loneliness, the essential desolation of his futile wanderings. For months – for years – his life hadn't been worth a day's purchase; and there he was gallantly, thoughtlessly alive, to all appearance indestructible solely by the virtue of his few years and of his unreflecting audacity. I was seduced into something like admiration – like envy. Glamour urged him on, glamour kept him unscathed. He surely wanted nothing from the wilderness but space to breathe in and to push on through. His need was to exist, and to move onwards at the greatest possible risk, and with a maximum of privation. If the absolutely pure, uncalculating, unpractical spirit of adventure had ever ruled a human being, it ruled this be-patched youth. I almost envied him the possession of this modest and clear flame. It seemed to have consumed all thought of self so completely that, even while he was talking to you, you forgot that it was he – the man before your eyes – who had gone through these things. I did not envy him his devotion to Kurtz, though. He had not meditated over it. It came to him, and he accepted it with a sort of eager fatalism. I must say that to me it appeared about the most dangerous thing in every way he had come upon so far.

'They had come together unavoidably, like two ships becalmed near each other, and lay rubbing sides at last. I suppose Kurtz wanted an audience, because on a certain occasion, when encamped in the forest, they had talked all night, or more probably Kurtz had talked. "We talked of everything," he said, quite transported at the recollection. "I forgot there was such a thing as sleep. The night did not seem to last an hour. Everything! Everything!... Of love, too." "Ah, he talked to you of love!" I said, much amused. "It isn't what you think," he cried, almost passionately. "It was in general. He made me see things – things."

'He threw his arms up. We were on deck at the time, and the headman of my wood–cutters, lounging near by, turned upon him his heavy and glittering eyes. I looked around, and I don't know why, but I assure you that never, never before, did this land, this river, this jungle, the very arch of this blazing sky, appear to me so hopeless and so dark, so impenetrable to human thought, so pitiless to human weakness. "And, ever since, you have been with him, of course?" I said.

'On the contrary. It appears their intercourse had been very much broken by various causes. He had, as he informed me proudly, managed to nurse Kurtz through two illnesses (he alluded to it as you would to some risky feat), but as a rule Kurtz wandered alone, far in the depths of the forest. "Very often coming to this station, I had to wait days and days before he would turn up," he said. "Ah, it was worth waiting for! – sometimes." "What was he doing? exploring or what?" I asked. "Oh, yes, of course"; he had discovered lots of villages, a lake, too – he did not know exactly in what direction; it was dangerous to inquire too much – but mostly his expeditions had been for ivory. "But he had no goods to trade with by that time," I objected. "There's a good lot of cartridges left even yet," he answered, looking away. "To speak plainly, he raided the country," I said. He nodded. "Not alone, surely!" He muttered something about the villages round that lake. "Kurtz got the tribe to follow him, did he?" I suggested. He fidgeted a little. "They adored him," he said. The tone of these words was so extraordinary that I looked at him searchingly. It was curious to see his mingled eagerness and reluctance to speak of Kurtz. The man filled his life, occupied his thoughts, swayed his emotions. "What can you expect?" he burst out; "he came to them with thunder and lightning, you know – and they had never seen anything like it – and very terrible. He could be very terrible. You can't judge Mr Kurtz as you would an ordinary man. No, no, no! Now – just to give you an idea – I don't mind telling you, he wanted to shoot me, too, one day

– but I don't judge him." "Shoot you!" I cried. "What for?" "Well, I had a small lot of ivory the chief of that village near my house gave me. You see I used to shoot game for them. Well, he wanted it, and wouldn't hear reason. He declared he would shoot me unless I gave him the ivory and then cleared out of the country, because he could do so, and had a fancy for it, and there was nothing on earth to prevent him killing whom he jolly well pleased. And it was true, too. I gave him the ivory. What did I care! But I didn't clear out. No, no. I couldn't leave him. I had to be careful, of course, till we got friendly again for a time. He had his second illness then. Afterwards I had to keep out of the way; but I didn't mind. He was living for the most part in those villages on the lake. When he came down to the river, sometimes he would take to me, and sometimes it was better for me to be careful. This man suffered too much. He hated all this, and somehow he couldn't get away. When I had a chance I begged him to try and leave while there was time; I offered to go back with him. And he would say yes, and then he would remain; go off on another ivory hunt; disappear for weeks; forget himself amongst these people – forget himself – you know." "Why! he's mad," I said. He protested indignantly. Mr Kurtz couldn't be mad. If I had heard him talk, only two days ago, I wouldn't dare hint at such a thing . . . I had taken up my binoculars while we talked, and was looking at the shore, sweeping the limit of the forest at each side and at the back of the house. The consciousness of there being people in that bush, so silent, so quiet – as silent and quiet as the ruined house on the hill – made me uneasy. There was no sign on the face of nature of this amazing tale that was not so much told as suggested to me in desolate exclamations, completed by shrugs, in interrupted phrases, in hints ending in deep sighs. The woods were unmoved, like a mask – heavy, like the closed door of a prison – they looked with their air of hidden knowledge, of patient expectation, of unapproachable silence. The Russian was explaining to me that it was only lately that Mr Kurtz had come down to the river, bringing along with him all the fighting men of that lake tribe. He had been absent for several months – getting himself adored, I suppose – and had come down unexpectedly, with the intention to all appearance of making a raid either across the river or down stream. Evidently the appetite for more ivory had got the better of the – what shall I say? – less material aspirations. However he had got much worse suddenly. "I heard he was lying helpless, and so I came up – took my chance," said the Russian. "Oh, he is bad, very bad." I directed my glass to the house. There were no signs of life, but there was the ruined roof, the long mud wall peeping above the grass, with three little square window-holes, no two of the same size; all this brought within reach of my hand, as it were. And then I made a brusque movement, and one of the remaining posts of that vanished fence leaped up in the field of my glass. You remember I told you I had been struck at the distance by certain attempts at ornamentation, rather remarkable in the ruinous aspect of the place. Now I had suddenly a nearer view, and its first result was to make me throw my head back as if before a blow. Then I went carefully from post to post with my glass, and I saw my mistake. These round knobs were not ornamental but symbolic; they were expressive and puzzling, striking and disturbing – food for thought and also for the vultures if there had been any looking down from the sky; but at all events for such ants as were industrious enough to ascend the pole. They would have been even more impressive, those heads on the stakes, if their faces had not been turned to the house. Only one, the first I had made out, was facing my way. I was not so shocked as you may think. The start back I had given was really nothing but a movement of surprise. I had expected to see a knob of wood there, you know. I returned deliberately to the first I had seen – and there it was, black, dried, sunken, with closed eyelids – a head that seemed to sleep at the top of that pole, and, with the shrunken dry lips showing a narrow white line of the teeth, was smiling, too, smiling continuously at some endless and jocose dream of that eternal slumber.

'I am not disclosing any trade secrets. In fact, the manager said afterwards that Mr Kurtz's methods had ruined the district. I have no opinion on that point, but I want you clearly to understand that there was nothing exactly profitable in these heads being there. They only showed that Mr Kurtz lacked restraint in the gratification of his various lusts, that there was something wanting in him – some small matter which, when the pressing need arose, could not be found under his magnificent eloquence. Whether he knew of this deficiency himself I can't say. I think the knowledge came to him at last – only at the very last. But the wilderness had found him out early, and had taken on him a terrible vengeance for the fantastic invasion. I think it had whispered to him things about himself which he did not know, things of which he had no conception till he took counsel with this great solitude – and the whisper had proved irresistibly fascinating. It echoed loudly within him because he was hollow at the core… I put down the glass, and the head that had appeared near enough to be spoken to seemed at once to have leaped away from me into inaccessible distance.

'The admirer of Mr Kurtz was a bit crestfallen. In a hurried, indistinct voice he began to assure me he had not dared to take these – say, symbols – down. He was not afraid of the natives; they would not stir till Mr Kurtz gave the word. His ascendancy was extraordinary. The camps of these people surrounded the place, and the chiefs came every day to see him. They would crawl… "I don't want to know anything of the ceremonies used when approaching Mr Kurtz," I shouted. Curious, this feeling that came over me that such details would be more intolerable than those heads drying on the stakes under Mr Kurtz's windows. After all, that was only a savage sight, while I seemed at one bound to have been transported into some lightless region of subtle horrors, where pure, uncomplicated savagery was a positive relief, being something that had a right to exist – obviously – in the sunshine. The young man looked at me with surprise. I suppose it did not occur to him that Mr Kurtz was no idol of mine. He forgot I hadn't heard any of these splendid monologues on, what was it? on love, justice, conduct of life – or what not. If it had come to crawling before Mr Kurtz, he crawled as much as the veriest savage of them all. I had no idea of the conditions, he said: these heads were the heads of rebels. I shocked him excessively by laughing. Rebels! What would be the next definition I was to hear? There had been enemies, criminals, workers – and these were rebels. Those rebellious heads looked very subdued to me on their sticks. "You don't know how such a life tries a man like Kurtz," cried Kurtz's last disciple. "Well, and you?" I said. "I! I! I am a simple man. I have no great thoughts. I want nothing from anybody. How can you compare me to…?" His feelings were too much for speech, and suddenly he broke down. "I don't understand," he groaned. "I've been doing my best to keep him alive, and that's enough. I had no hand in all this. I have no abilities. There hasn't been a drop of medicine or a mouthful of invalid food for months here. He was shamefully abandoned. A man like this, with such ideas. Shamefully! Shamefully! I – I – haven't slept for the last ten nights…"

'His voice lost itself in the calm of the evening. The long shadows of the forest had slipped downhill while we talked, had gone far beyond the ruined hovel, beyond the symbolic row of stakes. All this was in the gloom, while we down there were yet in the sunshine, and the stretch of the river abreast of the clearing glittered in a still and dazzling splendour, with a murky and overshadowed bend above and below. Not a living soul was seen on the shore. The bushes did not rustle.

'Suddenly round the corner of the house a group of men appeared, as though they had come up from the ground. They waded waist-deep in the grass, in a compact body, bearing an improvised stretcher in their midst. Instantly, in the emptiness of the landscape, a cry arose whose shrillness pierced the still air like a sharp arrow flying straight to the very heart of the land; and, as if by enchantment, streams of human beings – of naked human beings – with spears in their hands, with bows, with shields, with wild glances and savage movements, were poured into the clearing by the dark-faced and pensive forest. The bushes shook, the grass swayed for a time, and then everything stood still in attentive immobility.

'"Now, if he does not say the right thing to them we are all done for," said the Russian at my elbow. The knot of men with the stretcher had stopped, too, half-way to the steamer, as if petrified. I saw the man on the stretcher sit up, lank and with an uplifted arm, above the shoulders of the bearers. "Let us hope that the man who can talk so well of love in general will find some particular reason to spare us this time," I said. I resented bitterly the absurd danger of our situation, as if to be at the mercy of that atrocious phantom had been a dishonouring necessity. I could not hear a sound, but through my glasses I saw the thin arm extended commandingly, the lower jaw moving, the eyes of that apparition shining darkly far in its bony head that nodded with grotesque jerks. Kurtz – Kurtz – that means short in German – don't it? Well, the name was as true as everything else in his life – and death. He looked at least seven feet long. His covering had fallen off, and his body emerged from it pitiful and appalling as from a winding-sheet. I could see the cage of his ribs all astir, the bones of his arm waving. It was as though an animated image of death carved out of old ivory had been shaking its hand with menaces at a motionless crowd of men made of dark and glittering bronze. I saw him open his mouth wide – it gave him a weirdly voracious aspect, as though he had wanted to swallow all the air, all the earth, all the men before him. A deep voice reached me faintly. He must have been shouting. He fell back suddenly. The stretcher shook as the bearers staggered forward again, and almost at the same time I noticed that the crowd of savages was vanishing without any perceptible movement of retreat, as if the forest that had ejected these beings so suddenly had drawn them in again as the breath is drawn in a long aspiration.

'Some of the pilgrims behind the stretcher carried his arms – two shot-guns, a heavy rifle, and a light revolver-carbine – the thunderbolts of that pitiful Jupiter. The manager bent over him murmuring as he walked beside his head. They laid him down in one of the little cabins – just a room for a bed-place and a camp-stool or two, you know. We had brought his belated correspondence, and a lot of torn envelopes and open letters littered his bed. His hand roamed feebly amongst these papers. I was struck by the fire of his eyes and the composed languor of his expression. It was not so much the exhaustion of disease. He did not seem in pain. This shadow looked satiated and calm, as though for the moment it had had its fill of all the emotions.

'He rustled one of the letters, and looking straight in my face said, "I am glad." Somebody had been writing to him about me. These special recommendations were turning up again. The volume of tone he emitted without effort, almost without the trouble of moving his lips, amazed me. A voice! a voice! It was grave, profound, vibrating, while the man did not seem capable of a whisper. However, he had enough strength in him – factitious no doubt – to very nearly make an end of us, as you shall hear directly.

'The manager appeared silently in the doorway; I stepped out at once and he drew the curtain after me. The Russian, eyed curiously by the pilgrims, was staring at the shore. I followed the direction of his glance.

'Dark human shapes could be made out in the distance, flitting indistinctly against the gloomy border of the forest, and near the river two bronze figures, leaning on tall spears, stood in the sunlight under fantastic head-dresses of spotted skins, warlike and still in statuesque repose. And from right to left along the lighted shore moved a wild and gorgeous apparition of a woman.

'She walked with measured steps, draped in striped and fringed cloths, treading the earth proudly, with a slight jingle and flash of barbarous ornaments. She carried her head high; her hair was done in the shape of a helmet; she had brass leggings to the knee, brass wire gauntlets to the elbow, a crimson spot on her tawny cheek, innumerable necklaces of glass beads on her neck; bizarre things, charms, gifts of witch-men, that hung about her, glittered and trembled at every step. She must have had the value of several elephant tusks upon her. She was savage and superb, wild-eyed and magnificent; there was something ominous and stately in her deliberate progress. And in the hush that had fallen suddenly upon the whole sorrowful land, the immense wilderness, the colossal body of the fecund and mysterious life seemed to look at her, pensive, as though it had been looking at the image of its own tenebrous and passionate soul.

'She came abreast of the steamer, stood still, and faced us. Her long shadow fell to the water's edge. Her face had a tragic and fierce aspect of wild sorrow and of dumb pain mingled with the fear of some struggling, half-shaped resolve. She stood looking at us without a stir, and like the wilderness itself, with an air of brooding over an inscrutable purpose. A whole minute passed, and then she made a step forward. There was a low jingle, a glint of yellow metal, a sway of fringed draperies, and she stopped as if her heart had failed her. The young fellow by my side growled. The pilgrims murmured at my back. She looked at us all as if her life had depended upon the unswerving steadiness of her glance. Suddenly she opened her bared arms and threw them up rigid above her head, as though in an uncontrollable desire to touch the sky, and at the same time the swift shadows darted out on the earth, swept around on the river, gathering the steamer into a shadowy embrace. A formidable silence hung over the scene.

'She turned away slowly, walked on, following the bank, and passed into the bushes to the left. Once only her eyes gleamed back at us in the dusk of the thickets before she disappeared.

'"If she had offered to come aboard I really think I would have tried to shoot her," said the man of patches, nervously. "I have been risking my life every day for the last fortnight to keep her out of the house. She got in one day and kicked up a row about those miserable rags I picked up in the storeroom to mend my clothes with. I wasn't decent. At least it must have been that, for she talked like a fury to Kurtz for an hour, pointing at me now and then. I don't understand the dialect of this tribe. Luckily for me, I fancy Kurtz felt too ill that day to care, or there would have been mischief. I don't understand… No – it's too much for me. Ah, well, it's all over now."

'At this moment I heard Kurtz's deep voice behind the curtain: "Save me! – save the ivory, you mean. Don't tell me. Save *me*! Why, I've had to save you. You are interrupting my plans now. Sick! Sick! Not so sick as you would like to believe. Never mind. I'll carry my ideas out yet – I will return. I'll show you what can be done. You with your little peddling notions – you are interfering with me. I will return. I..."

'The manager came out. He did me the honour to take me under the arm and lead me aside. "He is very low, very low," he said. He considered it necessary to sigh, but neglected to be consistently sorrowful. "We have done all we could for him – haven't we? But there is no disguising the fact, Mr Kurtz has done more harm than good to the Company. He did not see the time was not ripe for vigorous action. Cautiously, cautiously – that's my principle. We must be cautious yet. The district is closed to us for a time. Deplorable! Upon the whole, the trade will suffer. I don't deny there is a remarkable quantity of ivory – mostly fossil. We must save it, at all events – but look how precarious the position is – and why? Because the method is unsound." "Do you," said I, looking at the shore, "call it 'unsound method'?" "Without doubt," he exclaimed hotly. "Don't you?"... "No method at all," I murmured after a while. "Exactly," he exulted. "I anticipated this. Shows a complete want of judgment. It is my duty to point it out in the proper quarter." "Oh," said I, "that fellow – what's his name? – the brickmaker, will make a readable report for you." He appeared confounded for a moment. It seemed to me I had never breathed an atmosphere so vile, and I turned mentally to Kurtz for relief – positively for relief. "Nevertheless I think Mr Kurtz is a remarkable man," I said with emphasis. He started, dropped on me a cold heavy glance, said very quietly, "He *was*," and turned his back on me. My hour of favour was over; I found myself lumped along with Kurtz as a partisan of methods for which the time was not ripe: I was unsound! Ah! but it was something to have at least a choice of nightmares.

'I had turned to the wilderness really, not to Mr Kurtz, who, I was ready to admit, was as good as buried. And for a moment it seemed to me as if I also were buried in a vast grave full of unspeakable secrets. I felt an intolerable weight oppressing my breast, the smell of the damp earth, the unseen presence of victorious corruption, the darkness of an impenetrable night... The Russian tapped me on the shoulder. I heard him mumbling and stammering something about "brother seaman – couldn't conceal – knowledge of matters that would affect Mr Kurtz's reputation."

I waited. For him evidently Mr Kurtz was not in his grave; I suspect that for him Mr Kurtz was one of the immortals. "Well!" said I at last, "speak out. As it happens, I am Mr Kurtz's friend – in a way."

'He stated with a good deal of formality that, had we not been "of the same profession," he would have kept the matter to himself without regard to consequences. "He suspected there was an active ill-will towards him on the part of these white men that—" "You are right," I said, remembering a certain conversation I had overheard. "The manager thinks you ought to be hanged." He showed a concern at this intelligence which amused me at first. "I had better get out of the way quietly," he said earnestly. "I can do no more for Kurtz now, and they would soon find some excuse. What's to stop them? There's a military post three hundred miles from here." "Well, upon my word," said I, "perhaps you had better go if you have any friends amongst the savages near by." "Plenty," he said. "They are simple people – and I want nothing, you know." He stood biting his lip, then: "I don't want any harm to happen to these whites here, but of course I was thinking of Mr Kurtz's reputation – but you are a brother seaman and – " "All right," said I, after a time. "Mr Kurtz's reputation is safe with me." I did not know how truly I spoke.

'He informed me, lowering his voice, that it was Kurtz who had ordered the attack to be made on the steamer. "He hated sometimes the idea of being taken away – and then again... But I don't understand these matters. I am a simple man. He thought it would scare you away – that you would give it up, thinking him dead. I could not stop him. Oh, I had an awful time of it this last month." "Very well," I said. "He is all right now." "Ye–e–es," he muttered, not very convinced apparently. "Thanks," said I; "I shall keep my eyes open." "But quiet – eh?" he urged, anxiously. "It would be awful for his reputation if anybody here – " I promised a complete discretion with great gravity. "I have a canoe and three black fellows waiting not very far. I am off. Could you give me a few Martini-Henry cartridges?" I could, and did, with proper secrecy. He helped himself, with a wink at me, to a handful of my tobacco. "Between sailors – you know – good English tobacco." At the door of the pilot-house he turned round – "I say, haven't you a pair of shoes you could spare?" He raised one leg. "Look." The soles were tied with knotted strings sandal-wise under his bare feet. I rooted out an old pair, at which he looked with admiration before tucking it under his left arm. One of his pockets (bright red) was bulging with cartridges, from the other (dark blue) peeped "Towson's Inquiry," etc., etc. He seemed to think himself excellently well equipped for a renewed encounter with the wilderness. "Ah! I'll never, never meet such a man again. You ought to have heard him recite poetry – his own, too, it was, he told me. Poetry!" He rolled his eyes at the recollection of these delights. "Oh, he enlarged my mind!" "Goodbye," said I. He shook hands and vanished in the night. Sometimes I ask myself whether I had ever really seen him – whether it was possible to meet such a phenomenon!...

'When I woke up shortly after midnight his warning came to my mind with its hint of danger that seemed, in the starred darkness, real enough to make me get up for the purpose of having a look round. On the hill a big fire burned, illuminating fitfully a crooked corner of the station-house. One of the agents with a picket of a few of our blacks, armed for the purpose, was keeping guard over the ivory; but deep within the forest, red gleams that wavered, that seemed to sink and rise from the ground amongst confused columnar shapes of intense blackness, showed the exact position of the camp where Mr Kurtz's adorers were keeping their uneasy vigil. The monotonous beating of a big drum filled the air with muffled shocks and a lingering vibration. A steady droning sound of many men chanting each to himself some weird incantation came out from the black, flat wall of the woods as the humming of bees comes out of a hive, and had a strange narcotic effect upon my half-awake senses. I believe I dozed off leaning over the rail, till an abrupt burst of yells, an overwhelming outbreak of a pent-up and mysterious frenzy, woke me up in a bewildered wonder. It was cut short all at once, and the low droning went on with an effect of audible and soothing silence. I glanced casually into the little cabin. A light was burning within, but Mr Kurtz was not there.

'I think I would have raised an outcry if I had believed my eyes. But I didn't believe them at first – the thing seemed so impossible. The fact is I was completely unnerved by a sheer blank fright, pure abstract terror, unconnected with any distinct shape of physical danger. What made this emotion so overpowering was – how shall I define it? – the moral shock I received, as if something altogether monstrous, intolerable to thought and odious to the soul, had been thrust upon me unexpectedly. This lasted of course the merest fraction of a second, and then the usual sense of commonplace, deadly danger, the possibility of a sudden onslaught and massacre, or something of the kind, which I saw impending, was positively welcome and composing. It pacified me, in fact, so much that I did not raise an alarm.

'There was an agent buttoned up inside an ulster and sleeping on a chair on deck within three feet of me. The yells had not awakened him; he snored very slightly; I left him to his slumbers and leaped ashore. I did not betray Mr Kurtz – it was ordered I should never betray him – it was written I should be loyal to the nightmare of my choice. I was anxious to deal with this shadow by myself alone – and to this day I don't know why I was so jealous of sharing with anyone the peculiar blackness of that experience.

'As soon as I got on the bank I saw a trail – a broad trail through the grass. I remember the exultation with which I said to myself, "He can't walk – he is crawling on all-fours – I've got him." The grass was wet with dew. I strode rapidly with clenched fists. I fancy I had some vague notion of falling upon him and giving him a drubbing. I don't know. I had some imbecile thoughts. The knitting old woman with the cat obtruded herself upon my memory as a most improper person to be sitting at the other end of such an affair. I saw a row of pilgrims squirting lead in the air out of Winchesters held to the hip. I thought I would never get back to the steamer, and imagined myself living alone and unarmed in the woods to an advanced age. Such silly things – you know. And I remember I confounded the beat of the drum with the beating of my heart, and was pleased at its calm regularity.

'I kept to the track though – then stopped to listen. The night was very clear; a dark blue space, sparkling with dew and starlight, in which black things stood very still. I thought I could see a kind of motion ahead of me. I was strangely cocksure of everything that night. I actually left the track and ran in a wide semicircle (I verily believe chuckling to myself) so as to get in front of that stir, of that motion I had seen – if indeed I had seen anything. I was circumventing Kurtz as though it had been a boyish game.

'I came upon him, and, if he had not heard me coming, I would have fallen over him, too, but he got up in time. He rose, unsteady, long, pale, indistinct, like a vapour exhaled by the earth, and swayed slightly, misty and silent before me; while at my back the fires loomed between the trees, and the murmur of many voices issued from the forest. I had cut him off cleverly; but when actually confronting him I seemed to come to my senses, I saw the danger in its right proportion. It was by no means over yet. Suppose he began to shout? Though he could hardly stand, there was still plenty of vigour in his voice. "Go away – hide yourself," he said, in that profound tone. It was very awful. I glanced back. We were within thirty yards from the nearest fire. A black figure stood up, strode on long black legs, waving long black arms, across the glow. It had horns – antelope horns, I think – on its head. Some sorcerer, some witch-man, no doubt: it looked fiend-like enough. "Do you know what you are doing?" I whispered. "Perfectly," he answered, raising his voice for that single word: it sounded to me far off and yet loud, like a hail through a speaking-trumpet. If he makes a row we are lost, I thought to myself. This clearly was not a case for fisticuffs, even apart from the very natural aversion I had to beat that Shadow – this wandering and tormented thing. "You will be lost," I said – "utterly lost." One gets sometimes such a flash of inspiration, you know. I did say the right thing, though indeed he could not have been more irretrievably lost than he was at this very moment, when the foundations of our intimacy were being laid – to endure – to endure – even to the end – even beyond.

"'I had immense plans,' he muttered irresolutely. "Yes," said I; "but if you try to shout I'll smash your head with – " There was not a stick or a stone near. "I will throttle you for good," I corrected myself. "I was on the threshold of great things," he pleaded, in a voice of longing, with a wistfulness of tone that made my blood run cold. "And now for this stupid scoundrel – " "Your success in Europe is assured in any case," I affirmed steadily. I did not want to have the throttling of him, you understand – and indeed it would have been very little use for any practical purpose. I tried to break the spell – the heavy, mute spell of the wilderness – that seemed to draw him to its pitiless breast by the awakening of forgotten and brutal instincts, by the memory of gratified and monstrous passions. This alone, I was convinced, had driven him out to the edge of the forest, to the bush, towards the gleam of fires, the throb of drums, the drone of weird incantations; this alone had beguiled his unlawful soul beyond the bounds of permitted aspirations. And, don't you see, the terror of the position was not in being knocked on the head – though I had a very lively sense of that danger, too – but in this, that I had to deal with a being to whom I could not appeal in the name of anything high or low. I had, even like the niggers, to invoke him – himself – his own exalted and incredible degradation. There was nothing either above or below him, and I knew it. He had kicked himself loose of the earth. Confound the man! he had kicked the very earth to pieces. He was alone, and I before him did not know whether I stood on the ground or floated in the air. I've been telling you what we said – repeating the phrases we pronounced – but what's the good? They were common everyday words – the familiar, vague sounds exchanged on every waking day of life. But what of that? They had behind them, to my mind, the terrific suggestiveness of words heard in dreams, of phrases spoken in nightmares. Soul! If anybody had ever struggled with a soul, I am the man. And I wasn't arguing with a lunatic either. Believe me or not, his intelligence was perfectly clear – concentrated, it is true, upon himself with horrible intensity, yet clear; and therein was my only chance – barring, of course, the killing him there and then, which wasn't so good, on account of unavoidable noise. But his soul was mad. Being alone in the wilderness, it had looked within itself, and, by heavens! I tell you, it had gone mad. I had – for my sins, I suppose – to go through the ordeal of looking into it myself. No eloquence could have been so withering to one's belief in mankind as his final burst of sincerity. He struggled with himself, too. I saw it – I heard it. I saw the inconceivable mystery of a soul that knew no restraint, no faith, and no fear, yet struggling blindly with itself. I kept my head pretty well; but when I had him at last stretched on the couch, I wiped my forehead, while my legs shook under me as though I had carried half a ton on my back down that hill. And yet I had only supported him, his bony arm clasped round my neck – and he was not much heavier than a child.

'When next day we left at noon, the crowd, of whose presence behind the curtain of trees I had been acutely conscious all the time, flowed out of the woods again, filled the clearing, covered the slope with a mass of naked, breathing, quivering, bronze bodies. I steamed up a bit, then swung downstream, and two thousand eyes followed the evolutions of the splashing, thumping, fierce river-demon beating the water with its terrible tail and breathing black smoke into the air. In front of the first rank, along the river, three men, plastered with bright red earth from head to foot, strutted to and fro restlessly. When we came abreast again, they faced the river, stamped their feet, nodded their horned heads, swayed their scarlet bodies; they shook towards the fierce river-demon a bunch of black feathers, a mangy skin with a pendent tail – something that looked a dried gourd; they shouted periodically together strings of amazing words that resembled no sounds of human language; and the deep murmurs of the crowd, interrupted suddenly, were like the responses of some satanic litany.

'We had carried Kurtz into the pilot-house: there was more air there. Lying on the couch, he stared through the open shutter. There was an eddy in the mass of human bodies, and the woman with helmeted head and tawny cheeks rushed out to the very brink of the stream. She put out her hands, shouted something, and all that wild mob took up the shout in a roaring chorus of articulated, rapid, breathless utterance.

'"Do you understand this?" I asked.

'He kept on looking out past me with fiery, longing eyes, with a mingled expression of wistfulness and hate. He made no answer, but I saw a smile, a smile of indefinable meaning, appear on his colourless lips that a moment after twitched convulsively. "Do I not?" he said slowly, gasping, as if the words had been torn out of him by a supernatural power.

'I pulled the string of the whistle, and I did this because I saw the pilgrims on deck getting out their rifles with an air of anticipating a jolly lark. At the sudden screech there was a movement of abject terror through that wedged mass of bodies. "Don't! don't you frighten them away," cried some one on deck disconsolately. I pulled the string time after time. They broke and ran, they leaped, they crouched, they swerved, they dodged the flying terror of the sound. The three red chaps had fallen flat, face down on the shore, as though they had been shot dead. Only the barbarous and superb woman did not so much as flinch, and stretched tragically her bare arms after us over the sombre and glittering river.

'And then that imbecile crowd down on the deck started their little fun, and I could see nothing more for smoke.

'The brown current ran swiftly out of the heart of darkness, bearing us down towards the sea with twice the speed of our upward progress; and Kurtz's life was running swiftly, too, ebbing, ebbing out of his heart into the sea of inexorable time. The manager was very placid, he had no vital anxieties now, he took us both in with a comprehensive and satisfied glance: the "affair" had come off as well as could be wished. I saw the time approaching when I would be left alone of the party of "unsound method". The pilgrims looked upon me with disfavour. I was, so to speak, numbered with the dead. It is strange how I accepted this unforeseen partnership, this choice of nightmares forced upon me in the tenebrous land invaded by these mean and greedy phantoms.

'Kurtz discoursed. A voice! a voice! It rang deep to the very last. It survived his strength to hide in the magnificent folds of eloquence the barren darkness of his heart. Oh, he struggled! he struggled! The wastes of his weary brain were haunted by shadowy images now – images of wealth and fame revolving obsequiously round his inextinguishable gift of noble and lofty expression. My Intended, my station, my career, my ideas – these were the subjects for the occasional utterances of elevated sentiments. The shade of the original Kurtz frequented the bedside of the hollow sham, whose fate it was to be buried presently in the mould of primeval earth. But both the diabolic love and the unearthly hate of the mysteries it had penetrated fought for the possession of that soul satiated with primitive emotions, avid of lying fame, of sham distinction, of all the appearances of success and power.

'Sometimes he was contemptibly childish. He desired to have kings meet him at railway-stations on his return from some ghastly Nowhere, where he intended to accomplish great things. "You show them you have in you something that is really profitable, and then there will be no limits to the recognition of your ability," he would say. "Of course you must take care of the motives – right motives – always." The long reaches that were like one and the same reach, monotonous bends that were exactly alike, slipped past the steamer with their multitude of secular trees looking patiently after this grimy fragment of another world, the forerunner of change, of conquest, of trade, of massacres, of blessings. I looked ahead – piloting. "Close the shutter," said Kurtz suddenly one day; "I can't bear to look at this." I did so. There was a silence. "Oh, but I will wring your heart yet!" he cried at the invisible wilderness.

'We broke down – as I had expected – and had to lie up for repairs at the head of an island. This delay was the first thing that shook Kurtz's confidence. One morning he gave me a packet of papers and a photograph – the lot tied together with a shoe-string. "Keep this for me," he said. "This noxious fool" (meaning the manager) "is capable of prying into my boxes when I am not looking." In the afternoon I saw him. He was lying on his back with closed eyes, and I withdrew quietly, but I heard him mutter, "Live rightly, die, die…" I listened. There was nothing more. Was he rehearsing some speech in his sleep, or was it a fragment of a phrase from some newspaper article? He had been writing for the papers and meant to do so again, "for the furthering of my ideas. It's a duty."

'His was an impenetrable darkness. I looked at him as you peer down at a man who is lying at the bottom of a precipice where the sun never shines. But I had not much time to give him, because I was helping the engine-driver to take to pieces the leaky cylinders, to straighten a bent connecting-rod, and in other such matters. I lived in an infernal mess of rust, filings, nuts, bolts, spanners, hammers, ratchet-drills – things I abominate, because I don't get on with them. I tended the little forge we fortunately had aboard; I toiled wearily in a wretched scrap-heap – unless I had the shakes too bad to stand.

'One evening coming in with a candle I was startled to hear him say a little tremulously, "I am lying here in the dark waiting for death." The light was within a foot of his eyes. I forced myself to murmur, "Oh, nonsense!" and stood over him as if transfixed.

'Anything approaching the change that came over his features I have never seen before, and hope never to see again. Oh, I wasn't touched. I was fascinated. It was as though a veil had been rent. I saw on that ivory face the expression of sombre pride, of ruthless power, of craven terror – of an intense and hopeless despair. Did he live his life again in every detail of desire, temptation, and surrender during that supreme moment of complete knowledge? He cried in a whisper at some image, at some vision – he cried out twice, a cry that was no more than a breath:

'"The horror! The horror!"

'I blew the candle out and left the cabin. The pilgrims were dining in the mess-room, and I took my place opposite the manager, who lifted his eyes to give me a questioning glance, which I successfully ignored. He leaned back, serene, with that peculiar smile of his sealing the unexpressed depths of his meanness. A continuous shower of small flies streamed upon the lamp, upon the cloth, upon our hands and faces. Suddenly the manager's boy put his insolent black head in the doorway, and said in a tone of scathing contempt:

'"Mistah Kurtz – he dead."

'All the pilgrims rushed out to see. I remained, and went on with my dinner. I believe I was considered brutally callous. However, I did not eat much. There was a lamp in there – light, don't you know – and outside it was so beastly, beastly dark. I went no more near the remarkable man who had pronounced a judgment upon the adventures of his soul on this earth. The voice was gone. What else had been there? But I am of course aware that next day the pilgrims buried something in a muddy hole.

'And then they very nearly buried me.

'However, as you see, I did not go to join Kurtz there and then. I did not. I remained to dream the nightmare out to the end, and to show my loyalty to Kurtz once more. Destiny. My destiny! Droll thing life is – that mysterious arrangement of merciless logic for a futile purpose. The most you can hope from it is some knowledge of yourself – that comes too late – a crop of inextinguishable regrets. I have wrestled with death. It is the most unexciting contest you can imagine. It takes place in an impalpable greyness, with nothing underfoot, with nothing around, without spectators, without clamour, without glory, without the great desire of victory, without the great fear of defeat, in a sickly atmosphere of tepid scepticism, without much belief in your own right, and still less in that of your adversary. If such is the form of ultimate wisdom, then life is a greater riddle than some of us think it to be. I was within a hair's breadth of the last opportunity for pronouncement, and I found with humiliation that probably I would have nothing to say. This is the reason why I affirm that Kurtz was a remarkable man. He had something to say. He said it. Since I had peeped over the edge myself, I understand better the meaning of his stare, that could not see the flame of the candle, but was wide enough to embrace the whole universe, piercing enough to penetrate all the hearts that beat in the darkness. He had summed up – he had judged. "The horror!" He was a remarkable man. After all, this was the expression of some sort of belief; it had candour, it had conviction, it had a vibrating note of revolt in its whisper, it had the appalling face of a glimpsed truth – the strange commingling of desire and hate. And it is not my own extremity I remember best – a vision of greyness without form filled with physical pain, and a careless contempt for the evanescence of all things – even of this pain itself. No! It is his extremity that I seem to have lived through. True, he had made that last stride, he had stepped over the edge, while I had been permitted to draw back my hesitating foot. And perhaps in this is the whole difference; perhaps all the wisdom, and all truth, and all sincerity, are just compressed into that inappreciable moment of time in which we step over the threshold of the invisible. Perhaps! I like to think my summing-up would not have been a word of careless contempt. Better his cry – much better. It was an affirmation, a moral victory paid for by innumerable defeats, by abominable terrors, by abominable satisfactions. But it was a victory! That is why I have remained loyal to Kurtz to the last, and even beyond, when a long time after I heard once more, not his own voice, but the echo of his magnificent eloquence thrown to me from a soul as translucently pure as a cliff of crystal.

'No, they did not bury me, though there is a period of time which I remember mistily, with a shuddering wonder, like a passage through some inconceivable world that had no hope in it and no desire. I found myself back in the sepulchral city resenting the sight of people hurrying through the streets to filch a little money from each other, to devour their infamous cookery, to gulp their unwholesome beer, to dream their insignificant and silly dreams. They trespassed upon my thoughts. They were intruders whose knowledge of life was to me an irritating pretence, because I felt so sure they could not possibly know the things I knew. Their bearing, which was simply the bearing of commonplace individuals going about their business in the assurance of perfect safety, was offensive to me like the outrageous flauntings of folly in the face of a danger it is unable to comprehend. I had no particular desire to enlighten them, but I had some difficulty in restraining myself from laughing in their faces so full of stupid importance. I daresay I was not very well at that time. I tottered about the streets – there were various affairs to settle – grinning bitterly at perfectly respectable persons. I admit my behaviour was inexcusable, but then my temperature was seldom normal in these days. My dear aunt's endeavours to "nurse up my strength" seemed altogether beside the mark. It was not my strength that wanted nursing, it was my imagination that wanted soothing. I kept the bundle of papers given me by Kurtz, not knowing exactly what to do with it. His mother had died lately, watched over, as I was told, by his Intended. A clean-shaved man, with an official manner and wearing gold-rimmed spectacles, called on me one day and made inquiries, at first circuitous, afterwards suavely pressing, about what he was pleased to denominate certain "documents." I was not surprised, because I had had two rows with the manager on the subject out there. I had refused to give up the smallest scrap out of that package, and I took the same attitude with the spectacled man. He became darkly menacing at last, and with much heat argued that the Company had the right to every bit of information about its "territories". And said he, "Mr Kurtz's knowledge of unexplored regions must have been necessarily extensive and peculiar – owing to his great abilities and to the deplorable circumstances in which he had been placed: therefore – " I assured him Mr Kurtz's knowledge, however extensive, did not bear upon the problems of commerce or administration. He invoked then the name of science. "It would be an incalculable loss if," etc., etc. I offered him the report on the "Suppression of Savage Customs," with the postscriptum torn off. He took it up eagerly, but ended by sniffing at it with an air of contempt. "This is not what we had a right to expect," he remarked. "Expect nothing else," I said. "There are only private letters." He withdrew upon some threat of legal proceedings, and I saw him no more; but another fellow, calling himself Kurtz's cousin, appeared two days later, and was anxious to hear all the details about his dear relative's last moments. Incidentally he gave me to understand that Kurtz had been essentially a great musician. "There was the making of an immense success," said the man, who was an organist, I believe, with lank grey hair flowing over a greasy coat-collar. I had no reason to doubt his statement; and to this day I am unable to say what was Kurtz's profession, whether he ever had any – which was the greatest of his talents. I had taken him for a painter who wrote for the papers, or else for a journalist who could paint – but even the cousin (who took snuff during the interview) could not tell me what he had been – exactly. He was a universal genius – on that point I agreed with the old chap, who thereupon blew his nose noisily into a large cotton handkerchief and withdrew in senile agitation, bearing off some family letters and memoranda without importance. Ultimately a journalist anxious to know something of the fate of his "dear colleague" turned up. This visitor informed me Kurtz's proper sphere ought to have been politics "on the popular side". He had furry straight eyebrows, bristly hair cropped short, an eyeglass on a broad ribbon, and, becoming expansive, confessed his opinion that Kurtz really couldn't write a bit – "but heavens! how that man could talk. He electrified large meetings. He had faith – don't you see? – he had the faith. He could get himself to believe anything – anything. He would have been a splendid leader of an extreme party." "What party?" I asked. "Any party," answered the other. "He was an – an – extremist." Did I not think so? I assented. Did I know, he asked, with a sudden flash of curiosity, "what it was that had induced him to go out there?" "Yes," said I, and forthwith handed him the famous Report for publication, if he thought fit. He glanced through it hurriedly, mumbling all the time, judged "it would do," and took himself off with this plunder.

'Thus I was left at last with a slim packet of letters and the girl's portrait. She struck me as beautiful – I mean she had a beautiful expression. I know that the sunlight can be made to lie, too, yet one felt that no manipulation of light and pose could have conveyed the delicate shade of truthfulness upon those features. She seemed ready to listen without mental reservation, without suspicion, without a thought for herself. I concluded I would go and give her back her portrait and those letters myself. Curiosity? Yes; and also some other feeling perhaps. All that had been Kurtz's had passed out of my hands: his soul, his body, his station, his plans, his ivory, his career. There remained only his memory and his Intended – and I wanted to give that up, too, to the past, in a way – to surrender personally all that remained of him with me to that oblivion which is the last word of our common fate. I don't defend myself. I had no clear perception of what it was I really wanted. Perhaps it was an impulse of unconscious loyalty, or the fulfilment of one of those ironic necessities that lurk in the facts of human existence. I don't know. I can't tell. But I went.

'I thought his memory was like the other memories of the dead that accumulate in every man's life – a vague impress on the brain of shadows that had fallen on it in their swift and final passage; but before the high and ponderous door, between the tall houses of a street as still and decorous as a well-kept alley in a cemetery, I had a vision of him on the stretcher, opening his mouth voraciously, as if to devour all the earth with all its mankind. He lived then before me; he lived as much as he had ever lived – a shadow insatiable of splendid appearances, of frightful realities; a shadow darker than the shadow of the night, and draped nobly in the folds of a gorgeous eloquence. The vision seemed to enter the house with me – the stretcher, the phantom-bearers, the wild crowd of obedient worshippers, the gloom of the forests, the glitter of the reach between the murky bends, the beat of the drum, regular and muffled like the beating of a heart – the heart of a conquering darkness. It was a moment of triumph for the wilderness, an invading and vengeful rush which, it seemed to me, I would have to keep back alone for the salvation of another soul. And the memory of what I had heard him say afar there, with the horned shapes stirring at my back, in the glow of fires, within the patient woods, those broken phrases came back to me, were heard again in their ominous and terrifying simplicity. I remembered his abject pleading, his abject threats, the colossal scale of his vile desires, the meanness, the torment, the tempestuous anguish of his soul. And later on I seemed to see his collected languid manner, when he said one day, "This lot of ivory now is really mine. The Company did not pay for it. I collected it myself at a very great personal risk. I am afraid they will try to claim it as theirs though. H'm. It is a difficult case. What do you think I ought to do – resist? Eh? I want no more than justice."… He wanted no more than justice – no more than justice. I rang the bell before a mahogany door on the first floor, and while I waited he seemed to stare at me out of the glassy panel – stare with that wide and immense stare embracing, condemning, loathing all the universe. I seemed to hear the whispered cry, "The horror! The horror!"

'The dusk was falling. I had to wait in a lofty drawing-room with three long windows from floor to ceiling that were like three luminous and bedraped columns. The bent gilt legs and backs of the furniture shone in indistinct curves. The tall marble fireplace had a cold and monumental whiteness. A grand piano stood massively in a corner, with dark gleams on the flat surfaces like a sombre and polished sarcophagus. A high door opened – closed. I rose.

'She came forward, all in black, with a pale head, floating towards me in the dusk. She was in mourning. It was more than a year since his death, more than a year since the news came; she seemed as though she would remember and mourn forever. She took both my hands in hers and murmured, "I had heard you were coming." I noticed she was not very young – I mean not girlish. She had a mature capacity for fidelity, for belief, for suffering. The room seemed to have grown darker, as if all the sad light of the cloudy evening had taken refuge on her forehead. This fair hair, this pale visage, this pure brow, seemed surrounded by an ashy halo from which the dark eyes looked out at me. Their glance was guileless, profound, confident, and trustful. She carried her sorrowful head as though she were proud of that sorrow, as though she would say, "I – I alone know how to mourn for him as he deserves." But while we were still shaking hands, such a look of awful desolation came upon her face that I perceived she was one of those creatures that are not the playthings of Time. For her he had died only yesterday. And, by Jove! the impression was so powerful that for me, too, he seemed to have died only yesterday – nay, this very minute. I saw her and him in the same instant of time – his death and her sorrow – I saw her sorrow in the very moment of his death. Do you understand? I saw them together – I heard them together. She had said, with a deep catch of the breath, "I have survived," while my strained ears seemed to hear distinctly, mingled with her tone of despairing regret, the summing up whisper of his eternal condemnation. I asked myself what I was doing there, with a sensation of panic in my heart as though I had blundered into a place of cruel and absurd mysteries not fit for a human being to behold. She motioned me to a chair. We sat down. I laid the packet gently on the little table, and she put her hand over it… "You knew him well," she murmured, after a moment of mourning silence.

"'Intimacy grows quickly out there," I said. "I knew him as well as it is possible for one man to know another."

"'And you admired him," she said. "It was impossible to know him and not to admire him. Was it?"

"'He was a remarkable man," I said, unsteadily. Then before the appealing fixity of her gaze, that seemed to watch for more words on my lips, I went on, "It was impossible not to—"

"'Love him," she finished eagerly, silencing me into an appalled dumbness. "How true! how true! But when you think that no one knew him so well as I! I had all his noble confidence. I knew him best."

"'You knew him best," I repeated. And perhaps she did. But with every word spoken the room was growing darker, and only her forehead, smooth and white, remained illumined by the inextinguishable light of belief and love.

"'You were his friend," she went on. "His friend," she repeated, a little louder. "You must have been if he had given you this, and sent you to me. I feel I can speak to you – and oh! I must speak. I want you – you who have heard his last words – to know I have been worthy of him… It is not pride…Yes! I am proud to know I understood him better than anyone on earth – he told me so himself. And since his mother died I have had no one – no one – to – to – "

'I listened. The darkness deepened. I was not even sure whether he had given me the right bundle. I rather suspect he wanted me to take care of another batch of his papers which, after his death, I saw the manager examining under the lamp. And the girl talked, easing her pain in the certitude of my sympathy; she talked as thirsty men drink. I had heard that her engagement with Kurtz had been disapproved by her people. He wasn't rich enough or something. And indeed I don't know whether he had not been a pauper all his life. He had given me some reason to infer that it was his impatience of comparative poverty that drove him out there.

'"…Who was not his friend who had heard him speak once?" she was saying. "He drew men towards him by what was best in them." She looked at me with intensity. "It is the gift of the great," she went on, and the sound of her low voice seemed to have the accompaniment of all the other sounds, full of mystery, desolation, and sorrow, I had ever heard – the ripple of the river, the soughing of the trees swayed by the wind, the murmurs of the crowds, the faint ring of incomprehensible words cried from afar, the whisper of a voice speaking from beyond the threshold of an eternal darkness. "But you have heard him! You know!" she cried.

'"Yes, I know," I said with something like despair in my heart, but bowing my head before the faith that was in her, before that great and saving illusion that shone with an unearthly glow in the darkness, in the triumphant darkness from which I could not have defended her – from which I could not even defend myself.

'"What a loss to me – to us!" – she corrected herself with beautiful generosity; then added in a murmur, "To the world." By the last gleams of twilight I could see the glitter of her eyes, full of tears – of tears that would not fall.

'"I have been very happy – very fortunate – very proud," she went on. "Too fortunate. Too happy for a little while. And now I am unhappy for – for life."

'She stood up; her fair hair seemed to catch all the remaining light in a glimmer of gold. I rose, too.

'"And of all this," she went on mournfully, "of all his promise, and of all his greatness, of his generous mind, of his noble heart, nothing remains – nothing but a memory. You and I—"

"'We shall always remember him," I said hastily.

"'No!" she cried. "It is impossible that all this should be lost – that such a life should be sacrificed to leave nothing – but sorrow. You know what vast plans he had. I knew of them, too – I could not perhaps understand – but others knew of them. Something must remain. His words, at least, have not died."

"'His words will remain," I said.

"'And his example," she whispered to herself. "Men looked up to him – his goodness shone in every act. His example – "

"'True," I said; "his example, too. Yes, his example. I forgot that."

"'But I do not. I cannot – I cannot believe – not yet. I cannot believe that I shall never see him again, that nobody will see him again, never, never, never."

'She put out her arms as if after a retreating figure, stretching them back and with clasped pale hands across the fading and narrow sheen of the window. Never see him! I saw him clearly enough then. I shall see this eloquent phantom as long as I live, and I shall see her, too, a tragic and familiar Shade, resembling in this gesture another one, tragic also, and bedecked with powerless charms, stretching bare brown arms over the glitter of the infernal stream, the stream of darkness. She said suddenly very low, "He died as he lived."

"'His end," said I, with dull anger stirring in me; "was in every way worthy of his life."

"'And I was not with him," she murmured. My anger subsided before a feeling of infinite pity.

"'Everything that could be done—" I mumbled.

"'Ah, but I believed in him more than any one on earth – more than his own mother, more than – himself. He needed me! Me! I would have treasured every sigh, every word, every sign, every glance."

'I felt like a chill grip on my chest. "Don't," I said, in a muffled voice.

"'Forgive me. I – I have mourned so long in silence – in silence… You were with him – to the last? I think of his loneliness. Nobody near to understand him as I would have understood. Perhaps no one to hear…"

"'To the very end," I said, shakily. "I heard his very last words…" I stopped in a fright.

"'Repeat them," she murmured in a heart-broken tone. "I want – I want – something – something – to – to live with."

'I was on the point of crying at her, "Don't you hear them?" The dusk was repeating them in a persistent whisper all around us, in a whisper that seemed to swell menacingly like the first whisper of a rising wind. "The horror! The horror!"

"'His last word – to live with," she insisted. "Don't you understand I loved him – I loved him – I loved him!"

'I pulled myself together and spoke slowly.

"'The last word he pronounced was – your name."

'I heard a light sigh and then my heart stood still, stopped dead short by an exulting and terrible cry, by the cry of inconceivable triumph and of unspeakable pain. "I knew it – I was sure!"… She knew. She was sure. I heard her weeping; she had hidden her face in her hands. It seemed to me that the house would collapse before I could escape, that the heavens would fall upon my head. But nothing happened. The heavens do not fall for such a trifle. Would they have fallen, I wonder, if I had rendered Kurtz that justice which was his due? Hadn't he said he wanted only justice? But I couldn't. I could not tell her. It would have been too dark – too dark altogether…"

Marlow ceased, and sat apart, indistinct and silent, in the pose of a meditating Buddha. Nobody moved for a time. "We have lost the first of the ebb," said the Director suddenly. I raised my head. The offing was barred by a black bank of clouds, and the tranquil waterway leading to the uttermost ends of the earth flowed sombre under an overcast sky – seemed to lead into the heart of an immense darkness.

TALES OF UNREST

'Be it thy course to being giddy minds
With foreign quarrels.'

– SHAKESPEARE

TO ADOLF P. KRIEGER
FOR THE SAKE OF OLD DAYS

AUTHOR'S NOTE

Of the five stories in this volume, *The Lagoon*, the last in order, is the earliest in date. It is the first short story I ever wrote and marks, in a manner of speaking, the end of my first phase, the Malayan phase with its special subject and its verbal suggestions. Conceived in the same mood which produced *Almayer's Folly* and *An Outcast of the Islands*, it is told in the same breath (with what was left of it, that is, after the end of *An Outcast*), seen with the same vision, rendered in the same method – if such a thing as method did exist then in my conscious relation to this new adventure of writing for print. I doubt it very much. One does one's work first and theorizes about it afterwards. It is a very amusing and egotistical occupation of no use whatever to any one and just as likely as not to lead to false conclusions.

Anybody can see that between the last paragraph of *An Outcast* and the first of *The Lagoon* there has been no change of pen, figuratively speaking. It happens also to be literally true. It was the same pen: a common steel pen. Having been charged with a certain lack of emotional faculty I am glad to be able to say that on one occasion at least I did give way to a sentimental impulse. I thought the pen had been a good pen and that it had done enough for me, and so, with the idea of keeping it for a sort of memento on which I could look later with tender eyes, I put it into my waistcoat pocket. Afterwards it used to turn up in all sorts of places – at the bottom of small drawers, among my studs in cardboard boxes – till at last it found permanent rest in a large wooden bowl containing some loose keys, bits of sealing wax, bits of string, small broken chains, a few buttons, and similar minute wreckage that washes out of a man's life into such receptacles. I would catch sight of it from time to time with a distinct feeling of satisfaction till, one day, I perceived with horror that there were two old pens in there. How the other pen found its way into the bowl instead of the fireplace or wastepaper basket I can't imagine, but there the two were, lying side by side, both encrusted with ink and completely undistinguishable from each other. It was very distressing, but being determined not to share my sentiment between two pens or run the risk of sentimentalizing over a mere stranger, I threw them both out of the window into a flower bed – which strikes me now as a poetical grave for the remnants of one's past.

But the tale remained. It was first fixed in print in the 'Cornhill Magazine', being my first appearance in a serial of any kind; and I have lived long enough to see it most agreeably guyed by Mr Max Beerbohm in a volume of parodies entitled *A Christmas Garland*, where I found myself in very good company. I was immensely gratified. I began to believe in my public existence. I have much to thank *The Lagoon* for.

My next effort in short-story writing was a departure – I mean a departure from the Malay Archipelago. Without premeditation, without sorrow, without rejoicing, and almost without noticing it, I stepped into the very different atmosphere of *An Outpost of Progress*. I found there a different moral attitude. I seemed able to capture new reactions, new suggestions, and even new rhythms for my paragraphs. For a moment I fancied myself a new man – a most exciting illusion. It clung to me for some time, monstrous, half conviction and half hope as to its body, with an iridescent tail of dreams and with a changeable head like a plastic mask. It was only later that I perceived that in common with the rest of men nothing could deliver me from my fatal consistency. We cannot escape from ourselves.

An Outpost of Progress is the lightest part of the loot I carried off from Central Africa, the main portion being of course *The Heart of Darkness*. Other men have found a lot of quite different things there and I have the comfortable conviction that what I took would not have been of much use to anybody else. And it must be said that it was but a very small amount of plunder. All of it could go into one's breast pocket when folded neatly. As for the story itself it is true enough in its essentials. The sustained invention of a really telling lie demands a talent which I do not possess.

The Idiots is such an obviously derivative piece of work that it is impossible for me to say anything about it here. The suggestion of it was not mental but visual: the actual idiots. It was after an interval of long groping amongst vague impulses and hesitations which ended in the production of *The Nigger* that I turned to my third short story in the order of time, the first in this volume: *Karain: A Memory.*

Reading it after many years *Karain* produced on me the effect of something seen through a pair of glasses from a rather advantageous position. In that story I had not gone back to the Archipelago, I had only turned for another look at it. I admit that I was absorbed by the distant view, so absorbed that I didn't notice then that the motif of the story is almost identical with the motif of *The Lagoon*. However, the idea at the back is very different; but the story is mainly made memorable to me by the fact that it was my first contribution to 'Blackwood's Magazine' and that it led to my personal acquaintance with Mr William Blackwood whose guarded appreciation I felt nevertheless to be genuine, and prized accordingly. *Karain* was begun on a sudden impulse only three days after I wrote the last line of *The Nigger*, and the recollection of its difficulties is mixed up with the worries of the unfinished *Return*, the last pages of which I took up again at the time; the only instance in my life when I made an attempt to write with both hands at once as it were.

Indeed my innermost feeling, now, is that *The Return* is a left-handed production. Looking through that story lately I had the material impression of sitting under a large and expensive umbrella in the loud drumming of a furious rain-shower. It was very distracting. In the general uproar one could hear every individual drop strike on the stout and distended silk. Mentally, the reading rendered me dumb for the remainder of the day, not exactly with astonishment but with a sort of dismal wonder. I don't want to talk disrespectfully of any pages of mine. Psychologically there were no doubt good reasons for my attempt; and it was worthwhile, if only to see of what excesses I was capable in that sort of virtuosity. In this connection I should like to confess my surprise on finding that notwithstanding all its apparatus of analysis the story consists for the most part of physical impressions; impressions of sound and sight, railway station, streets, a trotting horse, reflections in mirrors and so on, rendered as if for their own sake and combined with a sublimated description of a desirable middle-class town-residence which somehow manages to produce a sinister effect. For the rest any kind word about *The Return* (and there have been such words said at different times) awakens in me the liveliest gratitude, for I know how much the writing of that fantasy has cost me in sheer toil, in temper, and in disillusion.

J. C.

KARAIN: A MEMORY

I

We knew him in those unprotected days when we were content to hold in our hands our lives and our property. None of us, I believe, has any property now, and I hear that many, negligently, have lost their lives; but I am sure that the few who survive are not yet so dim-eyed as to miss in the befogged respectability of their newspapers the intelligence of various native risings in the Eastern Archipelago. Sunshine gleams between the lines of those short paragraphs – sunshine and the glitter of the sea. A strange name wakes up memories; the printed words scent the smoky atmosphere of today faintly, with the subtle and penetrating perfume as of land breezes breathing through the starlight of bygone nights; a signal fire gleams like a jewel on the high brow of a sombre cliff; great trees, the advanced sentries of immense forests, stand watchful and still over sleeping stretches of open water; a line of white surf thunders on an empty beach, the shallow water foams on the reefs; and green islets scattered through the calm of noonday lie upon the level of a polished sea, like a handful of emeralds on a buckler of steel.

There are faces too – faces dark, truculent, and smiling; the frank audacious faces of men barefooted, well armed and noiseless. They thronged the narrow length of our schooner's decks with their ornamented and barbarous crowd, with the variegated colours of chequered sarongs, red turbans, white jackets, embroideries; with the gleam of scabbards, gold rings, charms, armlets, lance blades, and jewelled handles of their weapons. They had an independent bearing, resolute eyes, a restrained manner; and we seem yet to hear their soft voices speaking of battles, travels, and escapes; boasting with composure, joking quietly; sometimes in well-bred murmurs extolling their own valour, our generosity; or celebrating with loyal enthusiasm the virtues of their ruler. We remember the faces, the eyes, the voices, we see again the gleam of silk and metal; the murmuring stir of that crowd, brilliant, festive, and martial; and we seem to feel the touch of friendly brown hands that, after one short grasp, return to rest on a chased hilt. They were Karain's people – a devoted following. Their movements hung on his lips; they read their thoughts in

his eyes; he murmured to them nonchalantly of life and death, and they
accepted his words humbly, like gifts of fate. They were all free men, and
when speaking to him said, 'Your slave.' On his passage voices died out
as though he had walked guarded by silence; awed whispers followed
him. They called him their war-chief. He was the ruler of three villages on
a narrow plain; the master of an insignificant foothold on the earth – of a
conquered foothold that, shaped like a young moon, lay ignored between
the hills and the sea.

From the deck of our schooner, anchored in the middle of the bay, he
indicated by a theatrical sweep of his arm along the jagged outline of
the hills the whole of his domain; and the ample movement seemed to
drive back its limits, augmenting it suddenly into something so immense
and vague that for a moment it appeared to be bounded only by the sky.
And really, looking at that place, landlocked from the sea and shut off from
the land by the precipitous slopes of mountains, it was difficult to believe
in the existence of any neighbourhood. It was still, complete, unknown,
and full of a life that went on stealthily with a troubling effect of solitude;
of a life that seemed unaccountably empty of anything that would stir the
thought, touch the heart, give a hint of the ominous sequence of days. It
appeared to us a land without memories, regrets, and hopes; a land where
nothing could survive the coming of the night, and where each sunrise,
like a dazzling act of special creation, was disconnected from the eve and
the morrow.

Karain swept his hand over it. 'All mine!' He struck the deck with
his long staff; the gold head flashed like a falling star; very close behind
him a silent old fellow in a richly embroidered black jacket alone of all
the Malays around did not follow the masterful gesture with a look. He
did not even lift his eyelids. He bowed his head behind his master, and
without stirring held hilt up over his right shoulder a long blade in a silver
scabbard. He was there on duty, but without curiosity, and seemed weary,
not with age, but with the possession of a burdensome secret of existence.
Karain, heavy and proud, had a lofty pose and breathed calmly. It was our
first visit, and we looked about curiously.

The bay was like a bottomless pit of intense light. The circular sheet
of water reflected a luminous sky, and the shores enclosing it made an
opaque ring of earth floating in an emptiness of transparent blue. The
hills, purple and arid, stood out heavily on the sky: their summits seemed

to fade into a coloured tremble as of ascending vapour; their steep sides were streaked with the green of narrow ravines; at their foot lay rice-fields, plantain-patches, yellow sands. A torrent wound about like a dropped thread. Clumps of fruit-trees marked the villages; slim palms put their nodding heads together above the low houses; dried palm-leaf roofs shone afar, like roofs of gold, behind the dark colonnades of tree-trunks; figures passed vivid and vanishing; the smoke of fires stood upright above the masses of flowering bushes; bamboo fences glittered, running away in broken lines between the fields. A sudden cry on the shore sounded plaintive in the distance, and ceased abruptly, as if stifled in the downpour of sunshine. A puff of breeze made a flash of darkness on the smooth water, touched our faces, and became forgotten. Nothing moved. The sun blazed down into a shadowless hollow of colours and stillness.

It was the stage where, dressed splendidly for his part, he strutted, incomparably dignified, made important by the power he had to awaken an absurd expectation of something heroic going to take place – a burst of action or song – upon the vibrating tone of a wonderful sunshine. He was ornate and disturbing, for one could not imagine what depth of horrible void such an elaborate front could be worthy to hide. He was not masked – there was too much life in him, and a mask is only a lifeless thing; but he presented himself essentially as an actor, as a human being aggressively disguised. His smallest acts were prepared and unexpected, his speeches grave, his sentences ominous like hints and complicated like arabesques. He was treated with a solemn respect accorded in the irreverent West only to the monarchs of the stage, and he accepted the profound homage with a sustained dignity seen nowhere else but behind the footlights and in the condensed falseness of some grossly tragic situation. It was almost impossible to remember who he was – only a petty chief of a conveniently isolated corner of Mindanao, where he could in comparative safety break the law against the traffic in firearms and ammunition with the natives. What would happen should one of the moribund Spanish gun-boats be suddenly galvanized into a flicker of active life did not trouble us, once we were inside the bay – so completely did it appear out of the reach of a meddling world; and besides, in those days we were imaginative enough to look with a kind of joyous equanimity on any chance there was of being quietly hanged somewhere out of the way of diplomatic remonstrance. As to Karain, nothing could happen to him unless what happens to all – failure and death; but his quality was to appear clothed in the illusion of unavoidable success. He seemed too effective, too necessary there, too much of an essential condition for the existence of his land and his people, to be destroyed by anything short of an earthquake. He summed up his race, his country, the elemental force of ardent life, of tropical nature. He had its luxuriant strength, its fascination; and, like it, he carried the seed of peril within.

In many successive visits we came to know his stage well – the purple semicircle of hills, the slim trees leaning over houses, the yellow sands, the streaming green of ravines. All that had the crude and blended colouring, the appropriateness almost excessive, the suspicious immobility of a painted scene; and it enclosed so perfectly the accomplished acting of his amazing pretences that the rest of the world seemed shut out forever from the gorgeous spectacle. There could be nothing outside. It was as if the earth had gone on spinning, and had left that crumb of its surface alone in space. He appeared utterly cut off from everything but the sunshine, and that even seemed to be made for him alone. Once when asked what was on the other side of the hills, he said, with a meaning smile, 'Friends and enemies – many enemies; else why should I buy your rifles and powder?' He was always like this – word-perfect in his part, playing up faithfully to the mysteries and certitudes of his surroundings. 'Friends and enemies' – nothing else. It was impalpable and vast. The earth had indeed rolled away from under his land, and he, with his handful of people, stood surrounded by a silent tumult as of contending shades. Certainly no sound came from outside. 'Friends and enemies!' He might have added, 'and memories,' at least as far as he himself was concerned; but he neglected to make that point then. It made itself later on, though; but it was after the daily performance – in the wings, so to speak, and with the lights out. Meantime he filled the stage with barbarous dignity. Some ten years ago he had led his people – a scratch lot of wandering Bugis – to the conquest of the bay, and now in his august care they had forgotten all the past, and had lost all concern for the future. He gave them wisdom, advice, reward, punishment, life or death, with the same serenity of attitude and voice. He understood irrigation and the art of war – the qualities of weapons and the craft of boat-building. He could conceal his heart; had more endurance; he could swim longer, and steer a canoe better than any of his people; he could shoot straighter, and negotiate more tortuously than any man of his race I knew. He was an adventurer of the sea, an outcast, a ruler – and my very good friend. I wish him a quick death in a stand-up fight, a death in sunshine; for he had known remorse and power, and no man can demand more from life. Day after day he appeared before us, incomparably faithful to the illusions of the stage, and at sunset the night descended upon him quickly, like a falling curtain. The seamed hills became black shadows towering high upon a clear sky; above them the glittering confusion of stars resembled a mad turmoil stilled by a gesture; sounds ceased, men slept, forms vanished – and the reality of the universe alone remained – a marvellous thing of darkness and glimmers.

II

But it was at night that he talked openly, forgetting the exactions of his stage. In the daytime there were affairs to be discussed in state. There were at first between him and me his own splendour, my shabby suspicions, and the scenic landscape that intruded upon the reality of our lives by its motionless fantasy of outline and colour. His followers thronged round him; above his head the broad blades of their spears made a spiked halo of iron points, and they hedged him from humanity by the shimmer of silks, the gleam of weapons, the excited and respectful hum of eager voices. Before sunset he would take leave with ceremony, and go off sitting under a red umbrella, and escorted by a score of boats. All the paddles flashed and struck together with a mighty splash that reverberated loudly in the monumental amphitheatre of hills. A broad stream of dazzling foam trailed behind the flotilla. The canoes appeared very black on the white hiss of water; turbaned heads swayed back and forth; a multitude of arms in crimson and yellow rose and fell with one movement; the spearmen upright in the bows of canoes had variegated sarongs and gleaming shoulders like bronze statues; the muttered strophes of the paddlers' song ended periodically in a plaintive shout. They diminished in the distance; the song ceased; they swarmed on the beach in the long shadows of the western hills. The sunlight lingered on the purple crests, and we could see him leading the way to his stockade, a burly bareheaded figure walking far in advance of a straggling cortege, and swinging regularly an ebony staff taller than himself. The darkness deepened fast; torches gleamed fitfully, passing behind bushes; a long hail or two trailed in the silence of the evening; and at last the night stretched its smooth veil over the shore, the lights, and the voices.

Then, just as we were thinking of repose, the watchmen of the schooner would hail a splash of paddles away in the starlit gloom of the bay; a voice would respond in cautious tones, and our serang, putting his head down the open skylight, would inform us without surprise, 'That Rajah, he coming. He here now.' Karain appeared noiselessly in the doorway of the little cabin. He was simplicity itself then: all in white; muffled about his head; for arms only a kriss with a plain buffalo-horn handle, which he would politely conceal within a fold of his sarong before stepping over the threshold. The old sword-bearer's face, the worn-out and mournful face so covered with wrinkles that it seemed to look out through the meshes of a fine dark net, could be seen close above his shoulders. Karain never moved without that attendant, who stood or squatted close at his back. He had a dislike of an open space behind him. It was more than a dislike – it resembled fear, a nervous preoccupation of what went on where he could not see. This, in view of the evident and fierce loyalty that surrounded him, was inexplicable. He was there alone in the midst of devoted men; he was safe from neighbourly ambushes, from fraternal ambitions; and yet more than one of our visitors had assured us that their ruler could not bear to be alone. They said, 'Even when he eats and sleeps there is always one on the watch near him who has strength and weapons.' There was indeed always one near him, though our informants had no conception of that watcher's strength and weapons, which were both shadowy and terrible. We knew, but only later on, when we had heard the story. Meantime we noticed that, even during the most important interviews, Karain would often give a start, and interrupting his discourse, would sweep his arm back with a sudden movement, to feel whether the old fellow was there. The old fellow, impenetrable and weary, was always there. He shared his food, his repose, and his thoughts; he knew his plans, guarded his secrets; and, impassive behind his master's agitation, without stirring the least bit, murmured above his head in a soothing tone some words difficult to catch.

It was only on board the schooner, when surrounded by white faces, by unfamiliar sights and sounds, that Karain seemed to forget the strange obsession that wound like a black thread through the gorgeous pomp of his public life. At night we treated him in a free and easy manner, which just stopped short of slapping him on the back, for there are liberties one must not take with a Malay. He said himself that on such occasions he was only a private gentleman coming to see other gentlemen whom he supposed as well born as himself. I fancy that to the last he believed us to be emissaries of Government, darkly official persons furthering by our illegal traffic some dark scheme of high statecraft. Our denials and protestations were unavailing. He only smiled with discreet politeness and inquired about the queen. Every visit began with that inquiry; he was insatiable of details; he was fascinated by the holder of a sceptre the shadow of which, stretching from the westward over the earth and over the seas, passed far beyond his own hand's-breadth of conquered land. He multiplied questions; he could never know enough of the Monarch of whom he spoke with wonder and chivalrous respect – with a kind of affectionate awe! Afterwards, when we had learned that he was the son of a woman who had many years ago ruled a small Bugis state, we came to suspect that the memory of his mother (of whom he spoke with enthusiasm) mingled somehow in his mind with the image he tried to form for himself of the far-off queen whom he called Great, Invincible, Pious, and Fortunate. We had to invent details at last to satisfy his craving curiosity; and our loyalty must be pardoned, for we tried to make them fit for his august and resplendent ideal. We talked. The night slipped over us, over the still schooner, over the sleeping land, and over the sleepless sea that thundered amongst the reefs outside the bay. His paddlers, two trustworthy men, slept in the canoe at the foot of our side-ladder. The old confidant, relieved from duty, dozed on his heels, with his back against the companion-doorway; and Karain sat squarely in the ship's wooden armchair, under the slight sway of the cabin lamp, a cheroot between his dark fingers, and a glass of lemonade before him. He was amused by the fizz of the thing, but after a sip or two would let it get flat, and with a courteous wave of his hand ask for a fresh bottle. He decimated our slender stock; but we did not begrudge it to him, for, when he began, he talked well. He must have been a great Bugis dandy in his time, for even then (and when we knew him he was no longer young) his splendour was spotlessly neat, and he dyed his hair a light shade of brown. The quiet dignity of his bearing transformed the dim-lit cuddy of the schooner into an audience-hall. He talked of inter-island politics with an ironic and melancholy shrewdness. He had travelled much, suffered not a little, intrigued, fought. He knew native Courts, European Settlements, the forests, the sea, and, as he said himself, had spoken in his time to many great men. He liked to talk with me because I had known some of these men: he seemed to think that I could understand him, and, with a fine confidence, assumed that I, at least, could appreciate how much greater he was himself. But he preferred to talk of his native country – a small Bugis state on the island of Celebes. I had visited it some time before, and he asked eagerly for news. As men's names came up in conversation he would say, 'We swam against one another when we were boys,' or, 'We had hunted the deer together – he could use the noose and the spear as well as I.' Now and then his big dreamy eyes would roll restlessly; he frowned or smiled, or he would become pensive, and, staring in silence, would nod slightly for a time at some regretted vision of the past.

His mother had been the ruler of a small semi-independent state on the sea-coast at the head of the Gulf of Boni. He spoke of her with pride. She had been a woman resolute in affairs of state and of her own heart. After the death of her first husband, undismayed by the turbulent opposition of the chiefs, she married a rich trader, a Korinchi man of no family. Karain was her son by that second marriage, but his unfortunate descent had apparently nothing to do with his exile. He said nothing as to its cause, though once he let slip with a sigh, 'Ha! my land will not feel any more the weight of my body.' But he related willingly the story of his wanderings, and told us all about the conquest of the bay. Alluding to the people beyond the hills, he would murmur gently, with a careless wave of the hand, 'They came over the hills once to fight us, but those who got away never came again.' He thought for a while, smiling to himself. 'Very few got away,' he added, with proud serenity. He cherished the recollections of his successes; he had an exulting eagerness for endeavour; when he talked, his aspect was warlike, chivalrous, and uplifting. No wonder his people admired him. We saw him once walking in daylight amongst the houses of the settlement. At the doors of huts groups of women turned to look after him, warbling softly, and with gleaming eyes; armed men stood out of the way, submissive and erect; others approached from the side, bending their backs to address him humbly; an old woman stretched out a draped lean arm – 'Blessings on thy head!' she cried from a dark doorway; a fiery-eyed man showed above the low fence of a plantain-patch a streaming face, a bare breast scarred in two places, and bellowed out pantingly after him, 'God give victory to our master!' Karain walked fast, and with firm long strides; he answered greetings right and left by quick piercing glances. Children ran forward between the houses, peeped fearfully round corners; young boys kept up with him, gliding between bushes: their eyes gleamed through the dark leaves. The old sword-bearer, shouldering the silver scabbard, shuffled hastily at his heels with bowed head, and his eyes on the ground. And in the midst of a great stir they passed swift and absorbed, like two men hurrying through a great solitude.

In his council hall he was surrounded by the gravity of armed chiefs, while two long rows of old headmen dressed in cotton stuffs squatted on their heels, with idle arms hanging over their knees. Under the thatch roof supported by smooth columns, of which each one had cost the life of a straight-stemmed young palm, the scent of flowering hedges drifted in warm waves. The sun was sinking. In the open courtyard suppliants walked through the gate, raising, when yet far off, their joined hands above bowed heads, and bending low in the bright stream of sunlight. Young girls, with flowers in their laps, sat under the wide-spreading boughs of a big tree. The blue smoke of wood fires spread in a thin mist above the high-pitched roofs of houses that had glistening walls of woven reeds, and all round them rough wooden pillars under the sloping eaves. He dispensed justice in the shade; from a high seat he gave orders, advice, reproof. Now and then the hum of approbation rose louder, and idle spearmen that lounged listlessly against the posts, looking at the girls, would turn their heads slowly. To no man had been given the shelter of so much respect, confidence, and awe. Yet at times he would lean forward and appear to listen as for a far-off note of discord, as if expecting to hear some faint voice, the sound of light footsteps; or he would start half up in his seat, as though he had been familiarly touched on the shoulder. He glanced back with apprehension; his aged follower whispered inaudibly at his ear; the chiefs turned their eyes away in silence, for the old wizard, the man who could command ghosts and send evil spirits against enemies, was speaking low to their ruler. Around the short stillness of the open place the trees rustled faintly, the soft laughter of girls playing with the flowers rose in clear bursts of joyous sound. At the end of upright spear-shafts the long tufts of dyed horse-hair waved crimson and filmy in the gust of wind; and beyond the blaze of hedges the brook of limpid quick water ran invisible and loud under the drooping grass of the bank, with a great murmur, passionate and gentle.

After sunset, far across the fields and over the bay, clusters of torches could be seen burning under the high roofs of the council shed. Smoky red flames swayed on high poles, and the fiery blaze flickered over faces, clung to the smooth trunks of palm-trees, kindled bright sparks on the rims of metal dishes standing on fine floor-mats. That obscure adventurer feasted like a king. Small groups of men crouched in tight circles round the wooden platters; brown hands hovered over snowy heaps of rice. Sitting upon a rough couch apart from the others, he leaned on his elbow with inclined head; and near him a youth improvised in a high tone a song that celebrated his valour and wisdom. The singer rocked himself to and fro, rolling frenzied eyes; old women hobbled about with dishes, and men, squatting low, lifted their heads to listen gravely without ceasing to eat. The song of triumph vibrated in the night, and the stanzas rolled out mournful and fiery like the thoughts of a hermit. He silenced it with a sign, 'Enough!' An owl hooted far away, exulting in the delight of deep gloom in dense foliage; overhead lizards ran in the attap thatch, calling softly; the dry leaves of the roof rustled; the rumour of mingled voices grew louder suddenly. After a circular and startled glance, as of a man waking up abruptly to the sense of danger, he would throw himself back, and under the downward gaze of the old sorcerer take up, wide-eyed, the slender thread of his dream. They watched his moods; the swelling rumour of animated talk subsided like a wave on a sloping beach. The chief is pensive. And above the spreading whisper of lowered voices only a little rattle of weapons would be heard, a single louder word distinct and alone, or the grave ring of a big brass tray.

III

For two years at short intervals we visited him. We came to like him, to trust him, almost to admire him. He was plotting and preparing a war with patience, with foresight – with a fidelity to his purpose and with a steadfastness of which I would have thought him racially incapable. He seemed fearless of the future, and in his plans displayed a sagacity that was only limited by his profound ignorance of the rest of the world. We tried to enlighten him, but our attempts to make clear the irresistible nature of the forces which he desired to arrest failed to discourage his eagerness to strike a blow for his own primitive ideas. He did not understand us, and replied by arguments that almost drove one to desperation by their childish shrewdness. He was absurd and unanswerable. Sometimes we caught glimpses of a sombre, glowing fury within him – a brooding and vague sense of wrong, and a concentrated lust of violence which is dangerous in a native. He raved like one inspired. On one occasion, after we had been talking to him late in his campong, he jumped up. A great, clear fire blazed in the grove; lights and shadows danced together between the trees; in the still night bats flitted in and out of the boughs like fluttering flakes of denser darkness. He snatched the sword from the old man, whizzed it out of the scabbard, and thrust the point into the earth. Upon the thin, upright blade the silver hilt, released, swayed before him like something alive. He stepped back a pace, and in a deadened tone spoke fiercely to the vibrating steel: 'If there is virtue in the fire, in the iron, in the hand that forged thee, in the words spoken over thee, in the desire of my heart, and in the wisdom of thy makers, – then we shall be victorious together!' He drew it out, looked along the edge. 'Take,' he said over his shoulder to the old sword-bearer. The other, unmoved on his hams, wiped the point with a corner of his sarong, and returning the weapon to its scabbard, sat nursing it on his knees without a single look upwards. Karain, suddenly very calm, re-seated himself with dignity. We gave up remonstrating after this, and let him go his way to an honourable disaster. All we could do for him was to see to it that the powder was good for the money and the rifles serviceable, if old.

But the game was becoming at last too dangerous; and if we, who had faced it pretty often, thought little of the danger, it was decided for us by some very respectable people sitting safely in counting-houses that the risks were too great, and that only one more trip could be made. After giving in the usual way many misleading hints as to our destination, we slipped away quietly, and after a very quick passage entered the bay. It was early morning, and even before the anchor went to the bottom the schooner was surrounded by boats.

The first thing we heard was that Karain's mysterious sword-bearer had died a few days ago. We did not attach much importance to the news. It was certainly difficult to imagine Karain without his inseparable follower; but the fellow was old, he had never spoken to one of us, we hardly ever had heard the sound of his voice; and we had come to look upon him as upon something inanimate, as a part of our friend's trappings of state – like that sword he had carried, or the fringed red umbrella displayed during an official progress. Karain did not visit us in the afternoon as usual. A message of greeting and a present of fruit and vegetables came off for us before sunset. Our friend paid us like a banker, but treated us like a prince. We sat up for him till midnight. Under the stern awning bearded Jackson jingled an old guitar and sang, with an execrable accent, Spanish love-songs; while young Hollis and I, sprawling on the deck, had a game of chess by the light of a cargo lantern. Karain did not appear. Next day we were busy unloading, and heard that the Rajah was unwell. The expected invitation to visit him ashore did not come. We sent friendly messages, but, fearing to intrude upon some secret council, remained on board. Early on the third day we had landed all the powder and rifles, and also a six-pounder brass gun with its carriage which we had subscribed together for a present for our friend. The afternoon was sultry. Ragged edges of black clouds peeped over the hills, and invisible thunderstorms circled outside, growling like wild beasts. We got the schooner ready for sea, intending to leave next morning at daylight. All day a merciless sun blazed down into the bay, fierce and pale, as if at white heat. Nothing moved on the land. The beach was empty, the villages seemed deserted; the trees far off stood in unstirring clumps, as if painted; the white smoke of some invisible bush-fire spread itself low over the shores of the bay like a settling fog. Late in the day three of Karain's chief men, dressed in their best and armed to the teeth, came off in a canoe, bringing a case of dollars. They were gloomy and languid, and told us they had not seen their Rajah for five days. No one had seen him! We settled all accounts, and after shaking hands in turn and in profound silence, they descended one after another into their boat, and were paddled to the shore, sitting close together, clad in vivid colours, with hanging heads: the gold embroideries of their jackets flashed dazzlingly as they went away gliding on the smooth water, and not one of them looked back once. Before sunset the growling clouds carried with a rush the ridge of hills, and came tumbling down the inner slopes. Everything disappeared; black whirling vapours filled the bay, and in the midst of them the schooner swung here and there in the shifting gusts of wind. A single clap of thunder detonated in the hollow with a violence that seemed capable of bursting into small pieces the ring of high land, and a warm deluge descended. The wind died out. We panted in the close cabin; our faces streamed; the bay outside hissed as if boiling; the water fell in perpendicular shafts as heavy as lead; it swished about the deck, poured off the spars, gurgled, sobbed, splashed, murmured in the blind night. Our lamp burned low. Hollis, stripped to the waist, lay stretched out on the lockers, with closed eyes and motionless like a despoiled corpse; at his head Jackson twanged the guitar, and gasped out in sighs a mournful dirge about hopeless love and eyes like stars. Then we heard startled voices on deck crying in the rain, hurried footsteps overhead, and suddenly Karain appeared in the doorway of the cabin. His bare breast and his face glistened in the light; his sarong, soaked, clung about his legs; he had his sheathed kriss in his left hand; and wisps of wet hair, escaping from under his red kerchief, stuck over his eyes and down his cheeks. He stepped in with a headlong stride and looking over his shoulder like a man pursued. Hollis turned on his side quickly and opened his eyes. Jackson clapped his big hand over the strings and the jingling vibration died suddenly. I stood up.

'We did not hear your boat's hail!' I exclaimed.

'Boat! The man's swum off,' drawled out Hollis from the locker. 'Look at him!'

He breathed heavily, wild-eyed, while we looked at him in silence. Water dripped from him, made a dark pool, and ran crookedly across the cabin floor. We could hear Jackson, who had gone out to drive away our Malay seamen from the doorway of the companion; he swore menacingly in the patter of a heavy shower, and there was a great commotion on deck. The watchmen, scared out of their wits by the glimpse of a shadowy figure leaping over the rail, straight out of the night as it were, had alarmed all hands.

Then Jackson, with glittering drops of water on his hair and beard, came back looking angry, and Hollis, who, being the youngest of us, assumed an indolent superiority, said without stirring, 'Give him a dry sarong – give him mine; it's hanging up in the bathroom.' Karain laid the kriss on the table, hilt inwards, and murmured a few words in a strangled voice.

'What's that?' asked Hollis, who had not heard.

'He apologizes for coming in with a weapon in his hand,' I said, dazedly.

'Ceremonious beggar. Tell him we forgive a friend… on such a night,' drawled out Hollis. 'What's wrong?'

Karain slipped the dry sarong over his head, dropped the wet one at his feet, and stepped out of it. I pointed to the wooden armchair – his armchair. He sat down very straight, said 'Ha!' in a strong voice; a short shiver shook his broad frame. He looked over his shoulder uneasily, turned as if to speak to us, but only stared in a curious blind manner, and again looked back. Jackson bellowed out, 'Watch well on deck there!' heard a faint answer from above, and reaching out with his foot slammed-to the cabin door.

'All right now,' he said.

Karain's lips moved slightly. A vivid flash of lightning made the two round stern ports facing him glimmer like a pair of cruel and phosphorescent eyes. The flame of the lamp seemed to wither into brown dust for an instant, and the looking-glass over the little sideboard leaped out behind his back in a smooth sheet of livid light. The roll of thunder came near, crashed over us; the schooner trembled, and the great voice went on, threatening terribly, into the distance. For less than a minute a furious shower rattled on the decks. Karain looked slowly from face to face, and then the silence became so profound that we all could hear distinctly the two chronometers in my cabin ticking along with unflagging speed against one another.

And we three, strangely moved, could not take our eyes from him. He had become enigmatical and touching, in virtue of that mysterious cause that had driven him through the night and through the thunderstorm to the shelter of the schooner's cuddy. Not one of us doubted that we were looking at a fugitive, incredible as it appeared to us. He was haggard, as though he had not slept for weeks; he had become lean, as though he had not eaten for days. His cheeks were hollow, his eyes sunk, the muscles of his chest and arms twitched slightly as if after an exhausting contest. Of course it had been a long swim off to the schooner; but his face showed another kind of fatigue, the tormented weariness, the anger and the fear of a struggle against a thought, an idea – against something that cannot be grappled, that never rests – a shadow, a nothing, unconquerable and immortal, that preys upon life. We knew it as though he had shouted it at us. His chest expanded time after time, as if it could not contain the beating of his heart. For a moment he had the power of the possessed – the power to awaken in the beholders wonder, pain, pity, and a fearful near sense of things invisible, of things dark and mute, that surround the loneliness of mankind. His eyes roamed about aimlessly for a moment, then became still. He said with effort –

'I came here… I leaped out of my stockade as after a defeat. I ran in the night. The water was black. I left him calling on the edge of black water… I left him standing alone on the beach. I swam… he called out after me… I swam…'

He trembled from head to foot, sitting very upright and gazing straight before him. Left whom? Who called? We did not know. We could not understand. I said at all hazards –

'Be firm.'

The sound of my voice seemed to steady him into a sudden rigidity, but otherwise he took no notice. He seemed to listen, to expect something for a moment, then went on –

'He cannot come here – therefore I sought you. You men with white faces who despise the invisible voices. He cannot abide your unbelief and your strength.'

He was silent for a while, then exclaimed softly –

'Oh! the strength of unbelievers!'

'There's no one here but you – and we three,' said Hollis, quietly. He reclined with his head supported on elbow and did not budge.

'I know,' said Karain. 'He has never followed me here. Was not the wise man ever by my side? But since the old wise man, who knew of my trouble, has died, I have heard the voice every night. I shut myself up – for many days – in the dark. I can hear the sorrowful murmurs of women, the whisper of the wind, of the running waters; the clash of weapons in the hands of faithful men, their footsteps – and his voice!… Near… So! In my ear! I felt him near… His breath passed over my neck. I leaped out without a cry. All about me men slept quietly. I ran to the sea. He ran by my side without footsteps, whispering, whispering old words – whispering into my ear in his old voice. I ran into the sea; I swam off to you, with my kriss between my teeth. I, armed, I fled before a breath – to you. Take me away to your land. The wise old man has died, and with him is gone the power of his words and charms. And I can tell no one. No one. There is no one here faithful enough and wise enough to know. It is only near you, unbelievers, that my trouble fades like a mist under the eye of day.'

He turned to me.

'With you I go!' he cried in a contained voice. 'With you, who know so many of us. I want to leave this land – my people… and him – there!'

He pointed a shaking finger at random over his shoulder. It was hard for us to bear the intensity of that undisclosed distress. Hollis stared at him hard. I asked gently –

'Where is the danger?'

'Everywhere outside this place,' he answered, mournfully. 'In every place where I am. He waits for me on the paths, under the trees, in the place where I sleep – everywhere but here.'

He looked round the little cabin, at the painted beams, at the tarnished varnish of bulkheads; he looked round as if appealing to all its shabby strangeness, to the disorderly jumble of unfamiliar things that belong to an inconceivable life of stress, of power, of endeavour, of unbelief – to the strong life of white men, which rolls on irresistible and hard on the edge of outer darkness. He stretched out his arms as if to embrace it and us. We waited. The wind and rain had ceased, and the stillness of the night round the schooner was as dumb and complete as if a dead world had been laid to rest in a grave of clouds. We expected him to speak. The necessity within him tore at his lips. There are those who say that a native will not speak to a white man. Error. No man will speak to his master; but to a wanderer and a friend, to him who does not come to teach or to rule, to him who asks for nothing and accepts all things, words are spoken by the camp-fires, in the shared solitude of the sea, in riverside villages, in resting-places surrounded by forests – words are spoken that take no account of race or colour. One heart speaks – another one listens; and the earth, the sea, the sky, the passing wind and the stirring leaf, hear also the futile tale of the burden of life.

He spoke at last. It is impossible to convey the effect of his story. It is undying, it is but a memory, and its vividness cannot be made clear to another mind, any more than the vivid emotions of a dream. One must have seen his innate splendour, one must have known him before – looked at him then. The wavering gloom of the little cabin; the breathless stillness outside, through which only the lapping of water against the schooner's sides could be heard; Hollis's pale face, with steady dark eyes; the energetic head of Jackson held up between two big palms, and with the long yellow hair of his beard flowing over the strings of the guitar

lying on the table; Karain's upright and motionless pose, his tone – all
this made an impression that cannot be forgotten. He faced us across
the table. His dark head and bronze torso appeared above the tarnished
slab of wood, gleaming and still as if cast in metal. Only his lips moved,
and his eyes glowed, went out, blazed again, or stared mournfully. His
expressions came straight from his tormented heart. His words sounded
low, in a sad murmur as of running water; at times they rang loud like the
clash of a war-gong – or trailed slowly like weary travellers – or rushed
forward with the speed of fear.

IV

This is, imperfectly, what he said –

'It was after the great trouble that broke the alliance of the four states
of Wajo. We fought amongst ourselves, and the Dutch watched from afar
till we were weary. Then the smoke of their fire-ships was seen at the
mouth of our rivers, and their great men came in boats full of soldiers to
talk to us of protection and peace. We answered with caution and wisdom,
for our villages were burnt, our stockades weak, the people weary, and
the weapons blunt. They came and went; there had been much talk, but
after they went away everything seemed to be as before, only their ships
remained in sight from our coast, and very soon their traders came amongst
us under a promise of safety. My brother was a Ruler, and one of those
who had given the promise. I was young then, and had fought in the war,
and Pata Matara had fought by my side. We had shared hunger, danger,
fatigue, and victory. His eyes saw my danger quickly, and twice my arm
had preserved his life. It was his destiny. He was my friend. And he was
great amongst us – one of those who were near my brother, the Ruler. He
spoke in council, his courage was great, he was the chief of many villages
round the great lake that is in the middle of our country as the heart is in
the middle of a man's body. When his sword was carried into a campong
in advance of his coming, the maidens whispered wonderingly under the
fruit-trees, the rich men consulted together in the shade, and a feast was
made ready with rejoicing and songs. He had the favour of the Ruler and
the affection of the poor. He loved war, deer hunts, and the charms of
women. He was the possessor of jewels, of lucky weapons, and of men's
devotion. He was a fierce man; and I had no other friend.

'I was the chief of a stockade at the mouth of the river, and collected tolls for my brother from the passing boats. One day I saw a Dutch trader go up the river. He went up with three boats, and no toll was demanded from him, because the smoke of Dutch war-ships stood out from the open sea, and we were too weak to forget treaties. He went up under the promise of safety, and my brother gave him protection. He said he came to trade. He listened to our voices, for we are men who speak openly and without fear; he counted the number of our spears, he examined the trees, the running waters, the grasses of the bank, the slopes of our hills. He went up to Matara's country and obtained permission to build a house. He traded and planted. He despised our joys, our thoughts, and our sorrows. His face was red, his hair like flame, and his eyes pale, like a river mist; he moved heavily, and spoke with a deep voice; he laughed aloud like a fool, and knew no courtesy in his speech. He was a big, scornful man, who looked into women's faces and put his hand on the shoulders of free men as though he had been a noble-born chief. We bore with him. Time passed.

'Then Pata Matara's sister fled from the campong and went to live in the Dutchman's house. She was a great and wilful lady: I had seen her once carried high on slaves' shoulders amongst the people, with uncovered face, and I had heard all men say that her beauty was extreme, silencing the reason and ravishing the heart of the beholders. The people were dismayed; Matara's face was blackened with that disgrace, for she knew she had been promised to another man. Matara went to the Dutchman's house, and said, "Give her up to die – she is the daughter of chiefs." The white man refused and shut himself up, while his servants kept guard night and day with loaded guns. Matara raged. My brother called a council. But the Dutch ships were near, and watched our coast greedily. My brother said, "If he dies now our land will pay for his blood. Leave him alone till we grow stronger and the ships are gone." Matara was wise; he waited and watched. But the white man feared for her life and went away.

'He left his house, his plantations, and his goods! He departed, armed and menacing, and left all – for her! She had ravished his heart! From my stockade I saw him put out to sea in a big boat. Matara and I watched him from the fighting platform behind the pointed stakes. He sat cross-legged, with his gun in his hands, on the roof at the stern of his prau. The barrel of his rifle glinted aslant before his big red face. The broad river was stretched under him – level, smooth, shining, like a plain of silver; and his prau, looking very short and black from the shore, glided along the silver plain and over into the blue of the sea.

'Thrice Matara, standing by my side, called aloud her name with grief and imprecations. He stirred my heart. It leaped three times; and three times with the eyes of my mind I saw in the gloom within the enclosed space of the prau a woman with streaming hair going away from her land and her people. I was angry – and sorry. Why? And then I also cried out insults and threats. Matara said, "Now they have left our land their lives are mine. I shall follow and strike – and, alone, pay the price of blood." A great wind was sweeping towards the setting sun over the empty river. I cried, "By your side I will go!" He lowered his head in sign of assent. It was his destiny. The sun had set, and the trees swayed their boughs with a great noise above our heads.

'On the third night we two left our land together in a trading prau.

'The sea met us – the sea, wide, pathless, and without voice. A sailing prau leaves no track. We went south. The moon was full; and, looking up, we said to one another, "When the next moon shines as this one, we shall return and they will be dead." It was fifteen years ago. Many moons have grown full and withered and I have not seen my land since. We sailed south; we overtook many praus; we examined the creeks and the bays; we saw the end of our coast, of our island – a steep cape over a disturbed strait, where drift the shadows of shipwrecked praus and drowned men clamour in the night. The wide sea was all round us now. We saw a great mountain burning in the midst of water; we saw thousands of islets scattered like bits of iron fired from a big gun; we saw a long coast of mountain and lowlands stretching away in sunshine from west to east. It was Java. We said, "They are there; their time is near, and we shall return or die cleansed from dishonour."

'We landed. Is there anything good in that country? The paths run straight and hard and dusty. Stone campongs, full of white faces, are surrounded by fertile fields, but every man you meet is a slave. The rulers live under the edge of a foreign sword. We ascended mountains, we traversed valleys; at sunset we entered villages. We asked everyone, "Have you seen such a white man?" Some stared; others laughed; women gave us food, sometimes, with fear and respect, as though we had been distracted by the visitation of God; but some did not understand our language, and some cursed us, or, yawning, asked with contempt the reason of our quest. Once, as we were going away, an old man called after us, "Desist!"

'We went on. Concealing our weapons, we stood humbly aside before the horsemen on the road; we bowed low in the courtyards of chiefs who were no better than slaves. We lost ourselves in the fields, in the jungle; and one night, in a tangled forest, we came upon a place where crumbling old walls had fallen amongst the trees and where strange stone idols – carved images of devils with many arms and legs, with snakes twined round their bodies, with twenty heads and holding a hundred swords – seemed to live and threaten in the light of our camp fire. Nothing dismayed us. And on the road, by every fire, in resting-places, we always talked of her and of him. Their time was near. We spoke of nothing else. No! not of hunger, thirst, weariness, and faltering hearts. No! we spoke of him and her! Of her! And we thought of them – of her! Matara brooded by the fire. I sat and thought and thought, till suddenly I could see again the image of a woman, beautiful, and young, and great and proud, and tender, going away from her land and her people. Matara said, "When we find them we shall kill her first to cleanse the dishonour – then the man must die." I would say, "It shall be so; it is your vengeance." He stared long at me with his big sunken eyes.

'We came back to the coast. Our feet were bleeding, our bodies thin. We slept in rags under the shadow of stone enclosures; we prowled, soiled and lean, about the gateways of white men's courtyards. Their hairy dogs barked at us, and their servants shouted from afar, "Begone!" Low-born wretches, that keep watch over the streets of stone campongs, asked us who we were. We lied, we cringed, we smiled with hate in our hearts, and we kept looking here, looking there for them – for the white man with hair like flame, and for her, for the woman who had broken faith, and therefore must die. We looked. At last in every woman's face I thought I could see hers. We ran swiftly. No! Sometimes Matara would whisper, "Here is the man," and we waited, crouching. He came near. It was not the man – those Dutchmen are all alike. We suffered the anguish of deception. In my sleep I saw her face, and was both joyful and sorry... Why?... I seemed to hear a whisper near me. I turned swiftly. She was not there! And as we trudged wearily from stone city to stone city I seemed to hear a light footstep near me. A time came when I heard it always, and I was glad. I thought, walking dizzy and weary in sunshine on the hard paths of white men – I thought, She is there – with us!... Matara was sombre. We were often hungry.

'We sold the carved sheaths of our krisses – the ivory sheaths with golden ferules. We sold the jewelled hilts. But we kept the blades – for them. The blades that never touch but kill – we kept the blades for her... Why? She was always by our side... We starved. We begged. We left Java at last.

'We went West, we went East. We saw many lands, crowds of strange faces, men that live in trees and men who eat their old people. We cut rattans in the forest for a handful of rice, and for a living swept the decks of big ships and heard curses heaped upon our heads. We toiled in villages; we wandered upon the seas with the Bajow people, who have no country. We fought for pay; we hired ourselves to work for Goram men, and were cheated; and under the orders of rough white faces we dived for pearls in barren bays, dotted with black rocks, upon a coast of sand and desolation. And everywhere we watched, we listened, we asked. We asked traders, robbers, white men. We heard jeers, mockery, threats – words of wonder and words of contempt. We never knew rest; we never thought of home, for our work was not done. A year passed, then another. I ceased to count the number of nights, of moons, of years. I watched over Matara. He had my last handful of rice; if there was water enough for one he drank it; I covered him up when he shivered with cold; and when the hot sickness came upon him I sat sleepless through many nights and fanned his face. He was a fierce man, and my friend. He spoke of her with fury in the daytime, with sorrow in the dark; he remembered her in health, in sickness. I said nothing; but I saw her every day – always! At first I saw only her head, as of a woman walking in the low mist on a river bank. Then she sat by our fire. I saw her! I looked at her! She had tender eyes and a ravishing face. I murmured to her in the night. Matara said sleepily sometimes, "To whom are you talking? Who is there?" I answered quickly, "No one"... It was a lie! She never left me. She shared the warmth of our fire, she sat on my couch of leaves, she swam on the sea to follow me... I saw her! I tell you I saw her long black hair spread behind her upon the moonlit water as she struck out with bare arms by the side of a swift prau. She was beautiful, she was faithful, and in the silence of foreign countries she spoke to me very low in the language of my people. No one saw her; no one heard her; she was mine only! In daylight she moved with a swaying walk before me upon the weary paths; her figure was straight and flexible like the stem of a slender tree; the heels of her feet were round and polished like shells of eggs; with her round arm she made signs. At night she looked into my face. And she was sad! Her eyes were tender and frightened; her voice soft and pleading. Once I murmured to her, "You shall not die," and she smiled… ever after she smiled!… She gave me courage to bear weariness and hardships. Those were times of pain, and she soothed me. We wandered patient in our search. We knew deception, false hopes; we knew captivity, sickness, thirst, misery, despair… Enough! We found them…'

He cried out the last words and paused. His face was impassive, and he kept still like a man in a trance. Hollis sat up quickly, and spread his elbows on the table. Jackson made a brusque movement, and accidentally touched the guitar. A plaintive resonance filled the cabin with confused vibrations and died out slowly. Then Karain began to speak again. The restrained fierceness of his tone seemed to rise like a voice from outside, like a thing unspoken but heard; it filled the cabin and enveloped in its intense and deadened murmur the motionless figure in the chair.

'We were on our way to Atjeh, where there was war; but the vessel ran on a sandbank, and we had to land in Delli. We had earned a little money, and had bought a gun from some Selangore traders; only one gun, which was fired by the spark of a stone: Matara carried it. We landed. Many white men lived there, planting tobacco on conquered plains, and Matara… But no matter. He saw him!… The Dutchman!… At last!… We crept and watched. Two nights and a day we watched. He had a house – a big house in a clearing in the midst of his fields; flowers and bushes grew around; there were narrow paths of yellow earth between the cut grass, and thick hedges to keep people out. The third night we came armed, and lay behind a hedge.

'A heavy dew seemed to soak through our flesh and made our very entrails cold. The grass, the twigs, the leaves, covered with drops of water, were grey in the moonlight. Matara, curled up in the grass, shivered in his sleep. My teeth rattled in my head so loud that I was afraid the noise would wake up all the land. Afar, the watchmen of white men's houses struck wooden clappers and hooted in the darkness. And, as every night,

I saw her by my side. She smiled no more!…The fire of anguish burned in my breast, and she whispered to me with compassion, with pity, softly – as women will; she soothed the pain of my mind; she bent her face over me – the face of a woman who ravishes the hearts and silences the reason of men. She was all mine, and no one could see her – no one of living mankind! Stars shone through her bosom, through her floating hair. I was overcome with regret, with tenderness, with sorrow. Matara slept… Had I slept? Matara was shaking me by the shoulder, and the fire of the sun was drying the grass, the bushes, the leaves. It was day. Shreds of white mist hung between the branches of trees.

'Was it night or day? I saw nothing again till I heard Matara breathe quickly where he lay, and then outside the house I saw her. I saw them both. They had come out. She sat on a bench under the wall, and twigs laden with flowers crept high above her head, hung over her hair. She had a box on her lap, and gazed into it, counting the increase of her pearls. The Dutchman stood by looking on; he smiled down at her; his white teeth flashed; the hair on his lip was like two twisted flames. He was big and fat, and joyous, and without fear. Matara tipped fresh priming from the hollow of his palm, scraped the flint with his thumb-nail, and gave the gun to me. To me! I took it… O fate!

'He whispered into my ear, lying on his stomach, "I shall creep close and then amok… let her die by my hand. You take aim at the fat swine there. Let him see me strike my shame off the face of the earth – and then… you are my friend – kill with a sure shot." I said nothing; there was no air in my chest – there was no air in the world. Matara had gone suddenly from my side. The grass nodded. Then a bush rustled. She lifted her head.

'I saw her! The consoler of sleepless nights, of weary days; the companion of troubled years! I saw her! She looked straight at the place where I crouched. She was there as I had seen her for years – a faithful wanderer by my side. She looked with sad eyes and had smiling lips; she looked at me… Smiling lips! Had I not promised that she should not die!

'She was far off and I felt her near. Her touch caressed me, and her voice murmured, whispered above me, around me. "Who shall be thy companion, who shall console thee if I die?" I saw a flowering thicket to the left of her stir a little… Matara was ready… I cried aloud – "Return!"

'She leaped up; the box fell; the pearls streamed at her feet. The big Dutchman by her side rolled menacing eyes through the still sunshine. The gun went up to my shoulder. I was kneeling and I was firm – firmer than the trees, the rocks, the mountains. But in front of the steady long barrel the fields, the house, the earth, the sky swayed to and fro like shadows in a forest on a windy day. Matara burst out of the thicket; before him the petals of torn flowers whirled high as if driven by a tempest. I heard her cry; I saw her spring with open arms in front of the white man. She was a woman of my country and of noble blood. They are so! I heard her shriek of anguish and fear – and all stood still! The fields, the house, the earth, the sky stood still – while Matara leaped at her with uplifted arm. I pulled the trigger, saw a spark, heard nothing; the smoke drove back into my face, and then I could see Matara roll over head first and lie with stretched arms at her feet. Ha! A sure shot! The sunshine fell on my back colder than the running water. A sure shot! I flung the gun after the shot. Those two stood over the dead man as though they had been bewitched by a charm. I shouted at her, "Live and remember!" Then for a time I stumbled about in a cold darkness.

'Behind me there were great shouts, the running of many feet; strange men surrounded me, cried meaningless words into my face, pushed me, dragged me, supported me... I stood before the big Dutchman: he stared as if bereft of his reason. He wanted to know, he talked fast, he spoke of gratitude, he offered me food, shelter, gold – he asked many questions. I laughed in his face. I said, "I am a Korinchi traveller from Perak over there, and know nothing of that dead man. I was passing along the path when I heard a shot, and your senseless people rushed out and dragged me here." He lifted his arms, he wondered, he could not believe, he could not understand, he clamoured in his own tongue! She had her arms clasped round his neck, and over her shoulder stared back at me with wide eyes. I smiled and looked at her; I smiled and waited to hear the sound of her voice. The white man asked her suddenly. "Do you know him?" I listened – my life was in my ears! She looked at me long, she looked at me with unflinching eyes, and said aloud, "No! I never saw him before.".... What! Never before? Had she forgotten already? Was it possible? Forgotten already – after so many years – so many years of wandering, of companionship, of trouble, of tender words! Forgotten already!... I tore myself out from the hands that held me and went away without a word... They let me go.

'I was weary. Did I sleep? I do not know. I remember walking upon a broad path under a clear starlight; and that strange country seemed so big, the rice-fields so vast, that, as I looked around, my head swam with the fear of space. Then I saw a forest. The joyous starlight was heavy upon me. I turned off the path and entered the forest, which was very sombre and very sad.'

V

Karain's tone had been getting lower and lower, as though he had been going away from us, till the last words sounded faint but clear, as if shouted on a calm day from a very great distance. He moved not. He stared fixedly past the motionless head of Hollis, who faced him, as still as himself. Jackson had turned sideways, and with elbow on the table shaded his eyes with the palm of his hand. And I looked on, surprised and moved; I looked at that man, loyal to a vision, betrayed by his dream, spurned by his illusion, and coming to us unbelievers for help – against a thought. The silence was profound; but it seemed full of noiseless phantoms, of things sorrowful, shadowy, and mute, in whose invisible presence the firm, pulsating beat of the two ship's chronometers ticking off steadily the seconds of Greenwich Time seemed to me a protection and a relief. Karain stared stonily; and looking at his rigid figure, I thought of his wanderings, of that obscure Odyssey of revenge, of all the men that wander amongst illusions; of the illusions as restless as men; of the illusions faithful, faithless; of the illusions that give joy, that give sorrow, that give pain, that give peace; of the invincible illusions that can make life and death appear serene, inspiring, tormented, or ignoble.

A murmur was heard; that voice from outside seemed to flow out of a dreaming world into the lamplight of the cabin. Karain was speaking.

'I lived in the forest.

'She came no more. Never! Never once! I lived alone. She had forgotten. It was well. I did not want her; I wanted no one. I found an abandoned house in an old clearing. Nobody came near. Sometimes I heard in the distance the voices of people going along a path. I slept; I rested; there was wild rice, water from a running stream – and peace! Every night I sat alone by my small fire before the hut. Many nights passed over my head.

'Then, one evening, as I sat by my fire after having eaten, I looked down on the ground and began to remember my wanderings. I lifted my head. I had heard no sound, no rustle, no footsteps – but I lifted my head. A man was coming towards me across the small clearing. I waited. He came up without a greeting and squatted down into the firelight. Then he turned his face to me. It was Matara. He stared at me fiercely with his big sunken eyes. The night was cold; the heat died suddenly out of the fire, and he stared at me. I rose and went away from there, leaving him by the fire that had no heat.

'I walked all that night, all next day, and in the evening made up a big blaze and sat down – to wait for him. He had not come into the light. I heard him in the bushes here and there, whispering, whispering. I understood at last – I had heard the words before, "You are my friend – kill with a sure shot."

'I bore it as long as I could – then leaped away, as on this very night I leaped from my stockade and swam to you. I ran – I ran crying like a child left alone and far from the houses. He ran by my side, without footsteps, whispering, whispering – invisible and heard. I sought people – I wanted men around me! Men who had not died! And again we two wandered. I sought danger, violence, and death. I fought in the Atjeh war, and a brave people wondered at the valiance of a stranger. But we were two; he warded off the blows… Why? I wanted peace, not life. And no one could see him; no one knew – I dared tell no one. At times he would leave me, but not for long; then he would return and whisper or stare. My heart was torn with a strange fear, but could not die. Then I met an old man.

'You all knew him. People here called him my sorcerer, my servant and sword-bearer; but to me he was father, mother, protection, refuge and peace. When I met him he was returning from a pilgrimage, and I heard him intoning the prayer of sunset. He had gone to the holy place with his son, his son's wife, and a little child; and on their return, by the favour of the Most High, they all died: the strong man, the young mother, the little child – they died; and the old man reached his country alone. He was a pilgrim serene and pious, very wise and very lonely. I told him all. For a time we lived together. He said over me words of compassion, of wisdom, of prayer. He warded from me the shade of the dead. I begged him for a charm that would make me safe. For a long time he refused; but at last, with a sigh and a smile, he gave me one. Doubtless he could command a spirit stronger than the unrest of my dead friend, and again I had peace; but I had become restless, and a lover of turmoil and danger. The old man never left me. We travelled together. We were welcomed by the great; his wisdom and my courage are remembered where your strength, O white men, is forgotten! We served the Sultan of Sula. We fought the Spaniards. There were victories, hopes, defeats, sorrow, blood, women's tears... What for?... We fled. We collected wanderers of a warlike race and came here to fight again. The rest you know. I am the ruler of a conquered land, a lover of war and danger, a fighter and a plotter. But the old man has died, and I am again the slave of the dead. He is not here now to drive away the reproachful shade – to silence the lifeless voice! The power of his charm has died with him. And I know fear; and I hear the whisper, "Kill! kill! kill!"... Have I not killed enough?...'

For the first time that night a sudden convulsion of madness and rage passed over his face. His wavering glances darted here and there like scared birds in a thunderstorm. He jumped up, shouting –

'By the spirits that drink blood: by the spirits that cry in the night: by all the spirits of fury, misfortune, and death, I swear – some day I will strike into every heart I meet – I...'

He looked so dangerous that we all three leaped to our feet, and Hollis, with the back of his hand, sent the kriss flying off the table. I believe we shouted together. It was a short scare, and the next moment he was again composed in his chair, with three white men standing over him in rather foolish attitudes. We felt a little ashamed of ourselves. Jackson picked up the kriss, and, after an inquiring glance at me, gave it to him. He received it with a stately inclination of the head and stuck it in the twist of his sarong, with punctilious care to give his weapon a pacific position. Then he looked up at us with an austere smile. We were abashed and reproved. Hollis sat sideways on the table and, holding his chin in his hand, scrutinized him in pensive silence. I said –

'You must abide with your people. They need you. And there is forgetfulness in life. Even the dead cease to speak in time.'

'Am I a woman, to forget long years before an eyelid has had the time to beat twice?' he exclaimed, with bitter resentment. He startled me. It was amazing. To him his life – that cruel mirage of love and peace – seemed as real, as undeniable, as theirs would be to any saint, philosopher, or fool of us all. Hollis muttered –

'You won't soothe him with your platitudes.'

Karain spoke to me.

'You know us. You have lived with us. Why? – we cannot know; but you understand our sorrows and our thoughts. You have lived with my people, and you understand our desires and our fears. With you I will go. To your land – to your people. To your people, who live in unbelief; to whom day is day, and night is night – nothing more, because you understand all things seen, and despise all else! To your land of unbelief, where the dead do not speak, where every man is wise, and alone – and at peace!'

'Capital description,' murmured Hollis, with the flicker of a smile.

Karain hung his head.

'I can toil, and fight – and be faithful,' he whispered, in a weary tone, 'but I cannot go back to him who waits for me on the shore. No! Take me with you… Or else give me some of your strength – of your unbelief… A charm!…'

He seemed utterly exhausted.

'Yes, take him home,' said Hollis, very low, as if debating with himself. 'That would be one way. The ghosts there are in society, and talk affably to ladies and gentlemen, but would scorn a naked human being – like our princely friend… Naked… Flayed! I should say. I am sorry for him. Impossible – of course. The end of all this shall be,' he went on, looking up at us – 'the end of this shall be, that some day he will run amuck amongst his faithful subjects and send *ad patres* ever so many of them before they make up their minds to the disloyalty of knocking him on the head.'

I nodded. I thought it more than probable that such would be the end of Karain. It was evident that he had been hunted by his thought along the very limit of human endurance, and very little more pressing was needed to make him swerve over into the form of madness peculiar to his race. The respite he had during the old man's life made the return of the torment unbearable. That much was clear.

He lifted his head suddenly; we had imagined for a moment that he had been dozing.

'Give me your protection – or your strength!' he cried. 'A charm… a weapon!'

Again his chin fell on his breast. We looked at him, then looked at one another with suspicious awe in our eyes, like men who come unexpectedly upon the scene of some mysterious disaster. He had given himself up to us; he had thrust into our hands his errors and his torment, his life and his peace; and we did not know what to do with that problem from the outer darkness. We three white men, looking at the Malay, could not find one word to the purpose amongst us – if indeed there existed a word that could solve that problem. We pondered, and our hearts sank. We felt as though we three had been called to the very gate of Infernal Regions to judge, to decide the fate of a wanderer coming suddenly from a world of sunshine and illusions.

'By Jove, he seems to have a great idea of our power,' whispered Hollis, hopelessly. And then again there was a silence, the feeble plash of water, the steady tick of chronometers. Jackson, with bare arms crossed, leaned his shoulders against the bulkhead of the cabin. He was bending his head under the deck beam; his fair beard spread out magnificently over his chest; he looked colossal, ineffectual, and mild. There was something lugubrious in the aspect of the cabin; the air in it seemed to become slowly charged with the cruel chill of helplessness, with the pitiless anger of egoism against the incomprehensible form of an intruding pain. We had no idea what to do; we began to resent bitterly the hard necessity to get rid of him.

Hollis mused, muttered suddenly with a short laugh, 'Strength… Protection… Charm.' He slipped off the table and left the cuddy without a look at us. It seemed a base desertion. Jackson and I exchanged indignant glances. We could hear him rummaging in his pigeon-hole of a cabin. Was the fellow actually going to bed? Karain sighed. It was intolerable!

Then Hollis reappeared, holding in both hands a small leather box. He put it down gently on the table and looked at us with a queer gasp, we thought, as though he had from some cause become speechless for a moment, or were ethically uncertain about producing that box. But in an instant the insolent and unerring wisdom of his youth gave him the needed courage. He said, as he unlocked the box with a very small key, 'Look as solemn as you can, you fellows.'

Probably we looked only surprised and stupid, for he glanced over his shoulder, and said angrily –

'This is no play; I am going to do something for him. Look serious. Confound it!… Can't you lie a little… for a friend!'

Karain seemed to take no notice of us, but when Hollis threw open the lid of the box his eyes flew to it – and so did ours. The quilted crimson satin of the inside put a violent patch of colour into the sombre atmosphere; it was something positive to look at – it was fascinating.

VI

Hollis looked smiling into the box. He had lately made a dash home through the Canal. He had been away six months, and only joined us again just in time for this last trip. We had never seen the box before. His hands hovered above it; and he talked to us ironically, but his face became as grave as though he were pronouncing a powerful incantation over the things inside.

'Every one of us,' he said, with pauses that somehow were more offensive than his words – 'every one of us, you'll admit, has been haunted by some woman... And... as to friends... dropped by the way... Well!... ask yourselves...'

He paused. Karain stared. A deep rumble was heard high up under the deck. Jackson spoke seriously –

'Don't be so beastly cynical.'

'Ah! You are without guile,' said Hollis, sadly. 'You will learn... Meantime this Malay has been our friend...'

He repeated several times thoughtfully, 'Friend... Malay. Friend, Malay,' as though weighing the words against one another, then went on more briskly –

'A good fellow – a gentleman in his way. We can't, so to speak, turn our backs on his confidence and belief in us. Those Malays are easily impressed – all nerves, you know – therefore...'

He turned to me sharply.

'You know him best,' he said, in a practical tone. 'Do you think he is fanatical – I mean very strict in his faith?'

I stammered in profound amazement that 'I did not think so.'

'It's on account of its being a likeness – an engraved image,' muttered Hollis, enigmatically, turning to the box. He plunged his fingers into it. Karain's lips were parted and his eyes shone. We looked into the box.

There were there a couple of reels of cotton, a packet of needles, a bit of silk ribbon, dark blue; a cabinet photograph, at which Hollis stole a glance before laying it on the table face downwards. A girl's portrait, I could see. There were, amongst a lot of various small objects, a bunch of flowers, a narrow white glove with many buttons, a slim packet of letters carefully tied up. Amulets of white men! Charms and talismans! Charms that keep them straight, that drive them crooked, that have the power to make a young man sigh, an old man smile. Potent things that procure dreams of joy, thoughts of regret; that soften hard hearts, and can temper a soft one to the hardness of steel. Gifts of heaven – things of earth...

Hollis rummaged in the box.

And it seemed to me, during that moment of waiting, that the cabin of the schooner was becoming filled with a stir invisible and living as of subtle breaths. All the ghosts driven out of the unbelieving West by men who pretend to be wise and alone and at peace – all the homeless ghosts of an unbelieving world – appeared suddenly round the figure of Hollis bending over the box; all the exiled and charming shades of loved women; all the beautiful and tender ghosts of ideals, remembered, forgotten, cherished, execrated; all the cast-out and reproachful ghosts of friends admired, trusted, traduced, betrayed, left dead by the way – they all seemed to come from the inhospitable regions of the earth to crowd into the gloomy cabin, as though it had been a refuge and, in all the unbelieving world, the only place of avenging belief.... It lasted a second – all disappeared. Hollis was facing us alone with something small that glittered between his fingers. It looked like a coin.

'Ah! here it is,' he said.

He held it up. It was a sixpence – a Jubilee sixpence. It was gilt; it had a hole punched near the rim. Hollis looked towards Karain.

'A charm for our friend,' he said to us. 'The thing itself is of great power – money, you know – and his imagination is struck. A loyal vagabond; if only his puritanism doesn't shy at a likeness...'

We said nothing. We did not know whether to be scandalized, amused, or relieved. Hollis advanced towards Karain, who stood up as if startled, and then, holding the coin up, spoke in Malay.

'This is the image of the Great Queen, and the most powerful thing the white men know,' he said, solemnly.

Karain covered the handle of his kriss in sign of respect, and stared at the crowned head.

'The Invincible, the Pious,' he muttered.

'She is more powerful than Suleiman the Wise, who commanded the genii, as you know,' said Hollis, gravely. 'I shall give this to you.'

He held the sixpence in the palm of his hand, and looking at it thoughtfully, spoke to us in English.

'She commands a spirit, too – the spirit of her nation; a masterful, conscientious, unscrupulous, unconquerable devil... that does a lot of good – incidentally... a lot of good... at times – and wouldn't stand any fuss from the best ghost out for such a little thing as our friend's shot. Don't look thunderstruck, you fellows. Help me to make him believe – everything's in that.'

'His people will be shocked,' I murmured.

Hollis looked fixedly at Karain, who was the incarnation of the very essence of still excitement. He stood rigid, with head thrown back; his eyes rolled wildly, flashing; the dilated nostrils quivered.

'Hang it all!' said Hollis at last, 'he is a good fellow. I'll give him something that I shall really miss.'

He took the ribbon out of the box, smiled at it scornfully, then with a pair of scissors cut out a piece from the palm of the glove.

'I shall make him a thing like those Italian peasants wear, you know.'

He sewed the coin in the delicate leather, sewed the leather to the ribbon, tied the ends together. He worked with haste. Karain watched his fingers all the time.

'Now then,' he said – then stepped up to Karain. They looked close into one another's eyes. Those of Karain stared in a lost glance, but Hollis's seemed to grow darker and looked out masterful and compelling. They were in violent contrast together – one motionless and the colour of bronze, the other dazzling white and lifting his arms, where the powerful muscles rolled slightly under a skin that gleamed like satin. Jackson moved near with the air of a man closing up to a chum in a tight place. I said impressively, pointing to Hollis –

'He is young, but he is wise. Believe him!'

Karain bent his head: Hollis threw lightly over it the dark-blue ribbon and stepped back.

'Forget, and be at peace!' I cried.

Karain seemed to wake up from a dream. He said, 'Ha!' shook himself as if throwing off a burden. He looked round with assurance. Someone on deck dragged off the skylight cover, and a flood of light fell into the cabin. It was morning already.

'Time to go on deck,' said Jackson.

Hollis put on a coat, and we went up, Karain leading.

The sun had risen beyond the hills, and their long shadows stretched far over the bay in the pearly light. The air was clear, stainless, and cool. I pointed at the curved line of yellow sands.

'He is not there,' I said, emphatically, to Karain. 'He waits no more. He has departed forever.'

A shaft of bright hot rays darted into the bay between the summits of two hills, and the water all round broke out as if by magic into a dazzling sparkle.

'No! He is not there waiting,' said Karain, after a long look over the beach. 'I do not hear him,' he went on, slowly. 'No!'

He turned to us.

'He has departed again – forever!' he cried.

We assented vigorously, repeatedly, and without compunction. The great thing was to impress him powerfully; to suggest absolute safety – the end of all trouble. We did our best; and I hope we affirmed our faith in the power of Hollis's charm efficiently enough to put the matter beyond the shadow of a doubt. Our voices rang around him joyously in the still air, and above his head the sky, pellucid, pure, stainless, arched its tender blue from shore to shore and over the bay, as if to envelop the water, the earth, and the man in the caress of its light.

The anchor was up, the sails hung still, and half-a-dozen big boats were seen sweeping over the bay to give us a tow out. The paddlers in the first one that came alongside lifted their heads and saw their ruler standing amongst us. A low murmur of surprise arose – then a shout of greeting.

He left us, and seemed straightway to step into the glorious splendour of his stage, to wrap himself in the illusion of unavoidable success. For a moment he stood erect, one foot over the gangway, one hand on the hilt of his kriss, in a martial pose; and, relieved from the fear of outer darkness, he held his head high, he swept a serene look over his conquered foothold on the earth. The boats far off took up the cry of greeting; a great clamour rolled on the water; the hills echoed it, and seemed to toss back at him the words invoking long life and victories.

He descended into a canoe, and as soon as he was clear of the side we gave him three cheers. They sounded faint and orderly after the wild tumult of his loyal subjects, but it was the best we could do. He stood up in the boat, lifted up both his arms, then pointed to the infallible charm. We cheered again; and the Malays in the boats stared – very much puzzled and impressed. I wondered what they thought; what he thought... what the reader thinks?

We towed out slowly. We saw him land and watch us from the beach. A figure approached him humbly but openly – not at all like a ghost with a grievance. We could see other men running towards him. Perhaps he had been missed? At any rate there was a great stir. A group formed itself rapidly near him, and he walked along the sands, followed by a growing cortége and kept nearly abreast of the schooner. With our glasses we could see the blue ribbon on his neck and a patch of white on his brown chest. The bay was waking up. The smokes of morning fires stood in faint spirals higher than the heads of palms; people moved between the houses; a herd of buffaloes galloped clumsily across a green slope; the slender figures of boys brandishing sticks appeared black and leaping in the long grass; a coloured line of women, with water bamboos on their heads, moved swaying through a thin grove of fruit-trees. Karain stopped in the midst of his men and waved his hand; then, detaching himself from the splendid group, walked alone to the water's edge and waved his hand again. The schooner passed out to sea between the steep headlands that shut in the bay, and at the same instant Karain passed out of our life forever.

But the memory remains. Some years afterwards I met Jackson, in the Strand. He was magnificent as ever. His head was high above the crowd. His beard was gold, his face red, his eyes blue; he had a wide-brimmed grey hat and no collar or waistcoat; he was inspiring; he had just come home – had landed that very day! Our meeting caused an eddy in the current of humanity. Hurried people would run against us, then walk round us, and turn back to look at that giant. We tried to compress seven years of life into seven exclamations; then, suddenly appeased, walked sedately along, giving one another the news of yesterday. Jackson gazed about him, like a man who looks for landmarks, then stopped before Bland's window. He always had a passion for firearms; so he stopped short and contemplated the row of weapons, perfect and severe, drawn up in a line behind the black-framed panes. I stood by his side. Suddenly he said –

'Do you remember Karain?'

I nodded.

'The sight of all this made me think of him,' he went on, with his face near the glass… and I could see another man, powerful and bearded, peering at him intently from amongst the dark and polished tubes that can cure so many illusions. 'Yes; it made me think of him,' he continued, slowly. 'I saw a paper this morning; they are fighting over there again. He's sure to be in it. He will make it hot for the caballeros. Well, good luck to him, poor devil! He was perfectly stunning.'

We walked on.

'I wonder whether the charm worked – you remember Hollis's charm, of course. If it did… never was a sixpence wasted to better advantage! Poor devil! I wonder whether he got rid of that friend of his. Hope so… Do you know, I sometimes think that – '

I stood still and looked at him.

'Yes… I mean, whether the thing was so, you know… whether it really happened to him… What do you think?'

'My dear chap,' I cried, 'you have been too long away from home. What a question to ask! Only look at all this.'

A watery gleam of sunshine flashed from the West and went out between two long lines of walls; and then the broken confusion of roofs, the chimney-stacks, the gold letters sprawling over the fronts of houses, the sombre polish of windows, stood resigned and sullen under the falling gloom. The whole length of the street, deep as a well and narrow like a corridor, was full of a sombre and ceaseless stir. Our ears were filled by a headlong shuffle and beat of rapid footsteps and by an underlying rumour – a rumour vast, faint, pulsating, as of panting breaths, of beating hearts, of gasping voices. Innumerable eyes stared straight in front, feet moved hurriedly, blank faces flowed, arms swung. Over all, a narrow ragged strip of smoky sky wound about between the high roofs, extended and motionless, like a soiled streamer flying above the rout of a mob.

'Ye–e–e–s,' said Jackson, meditatively.

The big wheels of hansoms turned slowly along the edge of side-walks; a pale-faced youth strolled, overcome by weariness, by the side of his stick and with the tails of his overcoat flapping gently near his heels; horses stepped gingerly on the greasy pavement, tossing their heads; two young girls passed by, talking vivaciously and with shining eyes; a fine old fellow strutted, red-faced, stroking a white moustache; and a line of yellow boards with blue letters on them approached us slowly, tossing on high behind one another like some queer wreckage adrift upon a river of hats.

'Ye–e–es,' repeated Jackson. His clear blue eyes looked about, contemptuous, amused and hard, like the eyes of a boy. A clumsy string of red, yellow, and green omnibuses rolled swaying, monstrous and gaudy; two shabby children ran across the road; a knot of dirty men with red neckerchiefs round their bare throats lurched along, discussing filthily; a ragged old man with a face of despair yelled horribly in the mud the name of a paper; while far off, amongst the tossing heads of horses, the dull flash of harnesses, the jumble of lustrous panels and roofs of carriages, we could see a policeman, helmeted and dark, stretching out a rigid arm at the crossing of the streets.

'Yes; I see it,' said Jackson, slowly. 'It is there; it pants, it runs, it rolls; it is strong and alive; it would smash you if you didn't look out; but I'll be hanged if it is yet as real to me as… as the other thing… say, Karain's story.'

I think that, decidedly, he had been too long away from home.

THE IDIOTS

We were driving along the road from Treguier to Kervanda. We passed at a smart trot between the hedges topping an earth wall on each side of the road; then at the foot of the steep ascent before Ploumar the horse dropped into a walk, and the driver jumped down heavily from the box. He flicked his whip and climbed the incline, stepping clumsily uphill by the side of the carriage, one hand on the footboard, his eyes on the ground. After a while he lifted his head, pointed up the road with the end of the whip, and said –

'The idiot!'

The sun was shining violently upon the undulating surface of the land. The rises were topped by clumps of meagre trees, with their branches showing high on the sky as if they had been perched upon stilts. The small fields, cut up by hedges and stone walls that zigzagged over the slopes, lay in rectangular patches of vivid greens and yellows, resembling the unskilful daubs of a naive picture. And the landscape was divided in two by the white streak of a road stretching in long loops far away, like a river of dust crawling out of the hills on its way to the sea.

'Here he is,' said the driver again.

In the long grass bordering the road a face glided past the carriage at the level of the wheels as we drove slowly by. The imbecile face was red, and the bullet head with close-cropped hair seemed to lie alone, its chin in the dust. The body was lost in the bushes growing thick along the bottom of the deep ditch.

It was a boy's face. He might have been sixteen, judging from the size – perhaps less, perhaps more. Such creatures are forgotten by time, and live untouched by years till death gathers them up into its compassionate bosom; the faithful death that never forgets in the press of work the most insignificant of its children.

'Ah! there's another,' said the man, with a certain satisfaction in his tone, as if he had caught sight of something expected.

There was another. That one stood nearly in the middle of the road in the blaze of sunshine at the end of his own short shadow. And he stood with hands pushed into the opposite sleeves of his long coat, his head sunk between the shoulders, all hunched up in the flood of heat. From a distance he had the aspect of one suffering from intense cold.

'Those are twins,' explained the driver.

The idiot shuffled two paces out of the way and looked at us over his shoulder when we brushed past him. The glance was unseeing and staring, a fascinated glance; but he did not turn to look after us. Probably the image passed before the eyes without leaving any trace on the misshapen brain of the creature. When we had topped the ascent I looked over the hood. He stood in the road just where we had left him.

The driver clambered into his seat, clicked his tongue, and we went downhill. The brake squeaked horribly from time to time. At the foot he eased off the noisy mechanism and said, turning half round on his box –

'We shall see some more of them by-and-by.'

'More idiots? How many of them are there, then?' I asked.

'There's four of them – children of a farmer near Ploumar here… The parents are dead now,' he added, after a while. 'The grandmother lives on the farm. In the daytime they knock about on this road, and they come home at dusk along with the cattle… It's a good farm.'

We saw the other two: a boy and a girl, as the driver said. They were dressed exactly alike, in shapeless garments with petticoat-like skirts. The imperfect thing that lived within them moved those beings to howl at us from the top of the bank, where they sprawled amongst the tough stalks of furze. Their cropped black heads stuck out from the bright yellow wall of countless small blossoms. The faces were purple with the strain of yelling; the voices sounded blank and cracked like a mechanical imitation of old people's voices; and suddenly ceased when we turned into a lane.

I saw them many times in my wandering about the country. They lived on that road, drifting along its length here and there, according to the inexplicable impulses of their monstrous darkness. They were an offence to the sunshine, a reproach to empty heaven, a blight on the concentrated and purposeful vigour of the wild landscape. In time the story of their parents shaped itself before me out of the listless answers to my questions, out of the indifferent words heard in wayside inns or on the very road those idiots haunted. Some of it was told by an emaciated and sceptical old fellow with a tremendous whip, while we trudged together over the sands by the side of a two-wheeled cart loaded with dripping seaweed. Then at other times other people confirmed and completed the story: till it stood at last before me, a tale formidable and simple, as they always are, those disclosures of obscure trials endured by ignorant hearts.

When he returned from his military service Jean-Pierre Bacadou found the old people very much aged. He remarked with pain that the work of the farm was not satisfactorily done. The father had not the energy of old days. The hands did not feel over them the eye of the master. Jean-Pierre noted with sorrow that the heap of manure in the courtyard before the only entrance to the house was not so large as it should have been. The fences were out of repair, and the cattle suffered from neglect. At home the mother was practically bedridden, and the girls chattered loudly in the big kitchen, unrebuked, from morning to night. He said to himself: 'We must change all this.' He talked the matter over with his father one evening when the rays of the setting sun entering the yard between the outhouses ruled the heavy shadows with luminous streaks. Over the manure heap floated a mist, opal-tinted and odorous, and the marauding hens would stop in their scratching to examine with a sudden glance of their round eye the two men, both lean and tall, talking in hoarse tones. The old man, all twisted with rheumatism and bowed with years of work, the younger bony and straight, spoke without gestures in the indifferent manner of peasants, grave and slow. But before the sun had set the father had submitted to the sensible arguments of the son. 'It is not for me that I am speaking,' insisted Jean-Pierre. 'It is for the land. It's a pity to see it badly used. I am not impatient for myself.' The old fellow nodded over his stick. 'I dare say; I dare say,' he muttered. 'You may be right. Do what you like. It's the mother that will be pleased.'

The mother was pleased with her daughter-in-law. Jean-Pierre brought the two-wheeled spring-cart with a rush into the yard. The grey horse galloped clumsily, and the bride and bridegroom, sitting side by side, were jerked backwards and forwards by the up and down motion of the shafts, in a manner regular and brusque. On the road the distanced wedding guests straggled in pairs and groups. The men advanced with heavy steps, swinging their idle arms. They were clad in town clothes; jackets cut with clumsy smartness, hard black hats, immense boots, polished highly. Their women all in simple black, with white caps and shawls of faded tints folded triangularly on the back, strolled lightly by their side. In front the violin sang a strident tune, and the biniou snored and hummed, while the player capered solemnly, lifting high his heavy clogs. The sombre procession drifted in and out of the narrow lanes, through sunshine and through shade, between fields and hedgerows, scaring the little birds that darted away in troops right and left. In the yard of Bacadou's farm the dark ribbon wound itself up into a mass of men and women pushing at the door with cries and greetings. The wedding dinner was remembered for months. It was a splendid feast in the orchard. Farmers of considerable means and excellent repute were to be found sleeping in ditches, all along the road to Treguier, even as late as the afternoon of the next day. All the countryside participated in the happiness of Jean-Pierre. He remained sober, and, together with his quiet wife, kept out of the way, letting father and mother reap their due of honour and thanks. But the next day he took hold strongly, and the old folks felt a shadow – precursor of the grave – fall upon them finally. The world is to the young.

When the twins were born there was plenty of room in the house, for the mother of Jean-Pierre had gone away to dwell under a heavy stone in the cemetery of Ploumar. On that day, for the first time since his son's marriage, the elder Bacadou, neglected by the cackling lot of strange women who thronged the kitchen, left in the morning his seat under the mantel of the fireplace, and went into the empty cow-house, shaking his white locks dismally. Grandsons were all very well, but he wanted his soup at midday. When shown the babies, he stared at them with a fixed gaze, and muttered something like: 'It's too much.' Whether he meant too much happiness, or simply commented upon the number of his descendants, it is impossible to say. He looked offended – as far as his old wooden face could express anything; and for days afterwards he could be seen, almost any time of the day, sitting at the gate, with his nose over his knees, a pipe between his gums, and gathered up into a kind of raging concentrated sulkiness. Once he spoke to his son, alluding to the newcomers with a groan: 'They will quarrel over the land.' 'Don't bother about that, father,' answered Jean-Pierre, stolidly, and passed, bent double, towing a recalcitrant cow over his shoulder.

He was happy, and so was Susan, his wife. It was not an ethereal joy welcoming new souls to struggle, perchance to victory. In fourteen years both boys would be a help; and, later on, Jean-Pierre pictured two big sons striding over the land from patch to patch, wringing tribute from the earth beloved and fruitful. Susan was happy too, for she did not want to be spoken of as the unfortunate woman, and now she had children no one could call her that. Both herself and her husband had seen something of the larger world – he during the time of his service; while she had spent a year or so in Paris with a Breton family; but had been too home-sick to remain longer away from the hilly and green country, set in a barren circle of rocks and sands, where she had been born. She thought that one of the boys ought perhaps to be a priest, but said nothing to her husband, who was a republican, and hated the 'crows,' as he called the ministers of religion. The christening was a splendid affair. All the commune came to it, for the Bacadous were rich and influential, and, now and then, did not mind the expense. The grandfather had a new coat.

Some months afterwards, one evening when the kitchen had been swept, and the door locked, Jean-Pierre, looking at the cot, asked his wife: 'What's the matter with those children?' And, as if these words, spoken calmly, had been the portent of misfortune, she answered with a loud wail that must have been heard across the yard in the pig-sty; for the pigs (the Bacadous had the finest pigs in the country) stirred and grunted complainingly in the night. The husband went on grinding his bread and butter slowly, gazing at the wall, the soup-plate smoking under his chin. He had returned late from the market, where he had overheard (not for the first time) whispers behind his back. He revolved the words in his mind as he drove back. 'Simple! Both of them... Never any use!... Well! May be, may be. One must see. Would ask his wife.' This was her answer. He felt like a blow on his chest, but said only: 'Go, draw me some cider. I am thirsty!'

She went out moaning, an empty jug in her hand. Then he arose, took up the light, and moved slowly towards the cradle. They slept. He looked at them sideways, finished his mouthful there, went back heavily, and sat down before his plate. When his wife returned he never looked up, but swallowed a couple of spoonfuls noisily, and remarked, in a dull manner –

'When they sleep they are like other people's children.'

She sat down suddenly on a stool near by, and shook with a silent tempest of sobs, unable to speak. He finished his meal, and remained idly thrown back in his chair, his eyes lost amongst the black rafters of the ceiling. Before him the tallow candle flared red and straight, sending up a slender thread of smoke. The light lay on the rough, sunburnt skin of his throat; the sunk cheeks were like patches of darkness, and his aspect was mournfully stolid, as if he had ruminated with difficulty endless ideas. Then he said, deliberately –

'We must see... consult people. Don't cry... They won't all be like that... surely! We must sleep now.'

After the third child, also a boy, was born, Jean-Pierre went about his work with tense hopefulness. His lips seemed more narrow, more tightly compressed than before; as if for fear of letting the earth he tilled hear the voice of hope that murmured within his breast. He watched the child, stepping up to the cot with a heavy clang of sabots on the stone floor, and glanced in, along his shoulder, with that indifference which is like a deformity of peasant humanity. Like the earth they master and serve, those men, slow of eye and speech, do not show the inner fire; so that, at last, it becomes a question with them as with the earth, what there is in the core: heat, violence, a force mysterious and terrible – or nothing but a clod, a mass fertile and inert, cold and unfeeling, ready to bear a crop of plants that sustain life or give death.

The mother watched with other eyes; listened with otherwise expectant ears. Under the high hanging shelves supporting great sides of bacon overhead, her body was busy by the great fireplace, attentive to the pot swinging on iron gallows, scrubbing the long table where the field hands would sit down directly to their evening meal. Her mind remained by the cradle, night and day on the watch, to hope and suffer. That child, like the other two, never smiled, never stretched its hands to her, never spoke; never had a glance of recognition for her in its big black eyes, which could only stare fixedly at any glitter, but failed hopelessly to follow the brilliance of a sun-ray slipping slowly along the floor. When the men were at work she spent long days between her three idiot children and the childish grandfather, who sat grim, angular, and immovable, with his feet near the warm ashes of the fire. The feeble old fellow seemed to suspect that there was something wrong with his grandsons. Only once, moved either by affection or by the sense of proprieties, he attempted to nurse the youngest. He took the boy up from the floor, clicked his tongue at him, and essayed a shaky gallop of his bony knees. Then he looked closely with his misty eyes at the child's face and deposited him down gently on the floor again. And he sat, his lean shanks crossed, nodding at the steam escaping from the cooking-pot with a gaze senile and worried.

Then mute affliction dwelt in Bacadou's farmhouse, sharing the breath and the bread of its inhabitants; and the priest of the Ploumar parish had great cause for congratulation. He called upon the rich landowner, the Marquis de Chavanes, on purpose to deliver himself with joyful unction of solemn platitudes about the inscrutable ways of Providence. In the vast dimness of the curtained drawing-room, the little man, resembling a black bolster, leaned towards a couch, his hat on his knees, and gesticulated with a fat hand at the elongated, gracefully-flowing lines of the clear Parisian toilette from which the half-amused, half-bored marquis listened with gracious languor. He was exulting and humble, proud and awed. The impossible had come to pass. Jean-Pierre Bacadou, the enraged republican farmer, had been to mass last Sunday – had proposed to entertain the visiting priests at the next festival of Ploumar! It was a triumph for the Church and for the good cause. 'I thought I would come at once to tell Monsieur le Marquis. I know how anxious he is for the welfare of our country,' declared the priest, wiping his face. He was asked to stay to dinner.

The Chavanes returning that evening, after seeing their guest to the main gate of the park, discussed the matter while they strolled in the moonlight, trailing their long shadows up the straight avenue of chestnuts. The marquis, a royalist of course, had been mayor of the commune which includes Ploumar, the scattered hamlets of the coast, and the stony islands that fringe the yellow flatness of the sands. He had felt his position insecure, for there was a strong republican element in that part of the country; but now the conversion of Jean-Pierre made him safe. He was very pleased. 'You have no idea how influential those people are,' he explained to his wife. 'Now, I am sure, the next communal election will go all right. I shall be re-elected.' 'Your ambition is perfectly insatiable, Charles,' exclaimed the marquise, gaily. 'But, *ma chère amie*,' argued the husband, seriously, 'it's most important that the right man should be mayor this year, because of the elections to the Chamber. If you think it amuses me...'

Jean-Pierre had surrendered to his wife's mother. Madame Levaille was a woman of business, known and respected within a radius of at least fifteen miles. Thick-set and stout, she was seen about the country, on foot or in an acquaintance's cart, perpetually moving, in spite of her fifty-eight years, in steady pursuit of business. She had houses in all the hamlets, she worked quarries of granite, she freighted coasters with stone – even traded with the Channel Islands. She was broad-cheeked, wide-eyed, persuasive in speech: carrying her point with the placid and invincible obstinacy of an old woman who knows her own mind. She very seldom slept for two nights together in the same house; and the wayside inns were the best places to inquire in as to her whereabouts. She had either passed, or was expected to pass there at six; or somebody, coming in, had seen her in the morning, or expected to meet her that evening. After the inns that command the roads, the churches were the buildings she frequented most. Men of liberal opinions would induce small children to run into sacred edifices to see whether Madame Levaille was there, and to tell her that so-and-so was in the road waiting to speak to her – about potatoes, or flour, or stones, or houses; and she would curtail her devotions, come out blinking and crossing herself into the sunshine; ready to discuss business matters in a calm, sensible way across a table in the kitchen of the inn opposite. Latterly she had stayed for a few days several times with her son-in-law, arguing against sorrow and misfortune with composed face and gentle tones. Jean-Pierre felt the convictions imbibed in the regiment torn out of his breast – not by arguments, but by facts. Striding over his fields he thought it over. There were three of them. Three! All alike! Why? Such things did not happen to everybody – to nobody he ever heard of. One yet – might pass. But three! All three. Forever useless, to be fed while he lived and… What would become of the land when he died? This must be seen to. He would sacrifice his convictions. One day he told his wife –

'See what your God will do for us. Pay for some masses.'

Susan embraced her man. He stood unbending, then turned on his heels and went out. But afterwards, when a black soutane darkened his doorway, he did not object; even offered some cider himself to the priest. He listened to the talk meekly; went to mass between the two women; accomplished what the priest called 'his religious duties' at Easter. That morning he felt like a man who had sold his soul. In the afternoon he fought ferociously with an old friend and neighbour who had remarked that the priests had the best of it and were now going to eat the priest-eater. He came home dishevelled and bleeding, and happening to catch sight of his children (they were kept generally out of the way), cursed and swore incoherently, banging the table. Susan wept. Madame Levaille sat serenely unmoved. She assured her daughter that 'It will pass,' and taking up her thick umbrella, departed in haste to see after a schooner she was going to load with granite from her quarry.

A year or so afterwards the girl was born. A girl. Jean-Pierre heard of it in the fields, and was so upset by the news that he sat down on the boundary wall and remained there till the evening, instead of going home as he was urged to do. A girl! He felt half cheated. However, when he got home he was partly reconciled to his fate. One could marry her to a good fellow – not to a good for nothing, but to a fellow with some understanding and a good pair of arms. Besides, the next may be a boy, he thought. Of course they would be all right. His new credulity knew of no doubt. The ill luck was broken. He spoke cheerily to his wife. She was also hopeful. Three priests came to that christening, and Madame Levaille was godmother. The child turned out an idiot too.

Then on market days Jean-Pierre was seen bargaining bitterly, quarrelsome and greedy; then getting drunk with taciturn earnestness; then driving home in the dusk at a rate fit for a wedding, but with a face gloomy enough for a funeral. Sometimes he would insist on his wife coming with him; and they would drive in the early morning, shaking side by side on the narrow seat above the helpless pig, that, with tied legs, grunted a melancholy sigh at every rut. The morning drives were silent; but in the evening, coming home, Jean-Pierre, tipsy, was viciously muttering, and growled at the confounded woman who could not rear children that were like anybody else's. Susan, holding on against the erratic swayings of the cart, pretended not to hear. Once, as they were driving through Ploumar, some obscure and drunken impulse caused him to pull up sharply opposite the church. The moon swam amongst light white clouds. The tombstones gleamed pale under the fretted shadows of the trees in the churchyard. Even the village dogs slept. Only the nightingales, awake, spun out the thrill of their song above the silence of graves. Jean-Pierre said thickly to his wife –

'What do you think is there?'

He pointed his whip at the tower – in which the big dial of the clock appeared high in the moonlight like a pallid face without eyes – and getting out carefully, fell down at once by the wheel. He picked himself up and climbed one by one the few steps to the iron gate of the churchyard. He put his face to the bars and called out indistinctly –

'Hey there! Come out!'

'Jean! Return! Return!' entreated his wife in low tones.

He took no notice, and seemed to wait there. The song of nightingales beat on all sides against the high walls of the church, and flowed back between stone crosses and flat grey slabs, engraved with words of hope and sorrow.

'Hey! Come out!' shouted Jean-Pierre, loudly.

The nightingales ceased to sing.

'Nobody?' went on Jean-Pierre. 'Nobody there. A swindle of the crows. That's what this is. Nobody anywhere. I despise it. *Allez! Houp!*'

He shook the gate with all his strength, and the iron bars rattled with a frightful clanging, like a chain dragged over stone steps. A dog near by barked hurriedly. Jean-Pierre staggered back, and after three successive dashes got into his cart. Susan sat very quiet and still. He said to her with drunken severity –

'See? Nobody. I've been made a fool! *Malheur*! Somebody will pay for it. The next one I see near the house I will lay my whip on... on the black spine... I will. I don't want him in there... he only helps the carrion crows to rob poor folk. I am a man... We will see if I can't have children like anybody else... now you mind... They won't be all... all... we see...'

She burst out through the fingers that hid her face –

'Don't say that, Jean; don't say that, my man!'

He struck her a swinging blow on the head with the back of his hand and knocked her into the bottom of the cart, where she crouched, thrown about lamentably by every jolt. He drove furiously, standing up, brandishing his whip, shaking the reins over the grey horse that galloped ponderously, making the heavy harness leap upon his broad quarters. The country rang clamorous in the night with the irritated barking of farm dogs, that followed the rattle of wheels all along the road. A couple of belated wayfarers had only just time to step into the ditch. At his own gate he caught the post and was shot out of the cart head first. The horse went on slowly to the door. At Susan's piercing cries the farm hands rushed out. She thought him dead, but he was only sleeping where he fell, and cursed his men, who hastened to him, for disturbing his slumbers.

Autumn came. The clouded sky descended low upon the black contours of the hills; and the dead leaves danced in spiral whirls under naked trees, till the wind, sighing profoundly, laid them to rest in the hollows of bare valleys. And from morning till night one could see all over the land black denuded boughs, the boughs gnarled and twisted, as if contorted with pain, swaying sadly between the wet clouds and the soaked earth. The clear and gentle streams of summer days rushed discoloured and raging at the stones that barred the way to the sea, with the fury of madness bent upon suicide. From horizon to horizon the great road to the sands lay between the hills in a dull glitter of empty curves, resembling an unnavigable river of mud.

Jean-Pierre went from field to field, moving blurred and tall in the drizzle, or striding on the crests of rises, lonely and high upon the grey curtain of drifting clouds, as if he had been pacing along the very edge of the universe. He looked at the black earth, at the earth mute and promising, at the mysterious earth doing its work of life in death-like stillness under the veiled sorrow of the sky. And it seemed to him that to a man worse than childless there was no promise in the fertility of fields, that from him the earth escaped, defied him, frowned at him like the clouds, sombre and hurried above his head. Having to face alone his own fields, he felt the inferiority of man who passes away before the clod that remains. Must he give up the hope of having by his side a son who would look at the turned-up sods with a master's eye? A man that would think as he thought, that would feel as he felt; a man who would be part of himself, and yet remain to trample masterfully on that earth when he was gone? He thought of some distant relations, and felt savage enough to curse them aloud. They! Never! He turned homewards, going straight at the roof of his dwelling, visible between the enlaced skeletons of trees. As he swung his legs over the stile a cawing flock of birds settled slowly on the field; dropped down behind his back, noiseless and fluttering, like flakes of soot.

That day Madame Levaille had gone early in the afternoon to the house she had near Kervanion. She had to pay some of the men who worked in her granite quarry there, and she went in good time because her little house contained a shop where the workmen could spend their wages without the trouble of going to town. The house stood alone amongst rocks. A lane of mud and stones ended at the door. The sea-winds coming ashore on Stonecutter's point, fresh from the fierce turmoil of the waves, howled violently at the unmoved heaps of black boulders holding up steadily short-armed, high crosses against the tremendous rush of the invisible.

In the sweep of gales the sheltered dwelling stood in a calm resonant and disquieting, like the calm in the centre of a hurricane. On stormy nights, when the tide was out, the bay of Fougère, fifty feet below the house, resembled an immense black pit, from which ascended mutterings and sighs as if the sands down there had been alive and complaining. At high tide the returning water assaulted the ledges of rock in short rushes, ending in bursts of livid light and columns of spray, that flew inland, stinging to death the grass of pastures.

The darkness came from the hills, flowed over the coast, put out the red fires of sunset, and went on to seaward pursuing the retiring tide. The wind dropped with the sun, leaving a maddened sea and a devastated sky. The heavens above the house seemed to be draped in black rags, held up here and there by pins of fire. Madame Levaille, for this evening the servant of her own workmen, tried to induce them to depart. 'An old woman like me ought to be in bed at this late hour,' she good-humouredly repeated. The quarrymen drank, asked for more. They shouted over the table as if they had been talking across a field. At one end four of them played cards, banging the wood with their hard knuckles, and swearing at every lead. One sat with a lost gaze, humming a bar of some song, which he repeated endlessly. Two others, in a corner, were quarrelling confidentially and fiercely over some woman, looking close into one another's eyes as if they had wanted to tear them out, but speaking in whispers that promised violence and murder discreetly, in a venomous sibilation of subdued words. The atmosphere in there was thick enough to slice with a knife. Three candles burning about the long room glowed red and dull like sparks expiring in ashes.

The slight click of the iron latch was at that late hour as unexpected and startling as a thunder-clap. Madame Levaille put down a bottle she held above a liqueur glass; the players turned their heads; the whispered quarrel ceased; only the singer, after darting a glance at the door, went on humming with a stolid face. Susan appeared in the doorway, stepped in, flung the door to, and put her back against it, saying, half aloud –

'Mother!'

Madame Levaille, taking up the bottle again, said calmly: 'Here you are, my girl. What a state you are in!' The neck of the bottle rang on the rim of the glass, for the old woman was startled, and the idea that the farm had caught fire had entered her head. She could think of no other cause for her daughter's appearance.

Susan, soaked and muddy, stared the whole length of the room towards the men at the far end. Her mother asked –

'What has happened? God guard us from misfortune!'

Susan moved her lips. No sound came. Madame Levaille stepped up to her daughter, took her by the arm, looked into her face.

'In God's name,' she said, shakily, 'what's the matter? You have been rolling in mud... Why did you come?... Where's Jean?'

The men had all got up and approached slowly, staring with dull surprise. Madame Levaille jerked her daughter away from the door, swung her round upon a seat close to the wall. Then she turned fiercely to the men –

'Enough of this! Out you go – you others! I close.'

One of them observed, looking down at Susan collapsed on the seat: 'She is – one may say – half dead.'

Madame Levaille flung the door open.

'Get out! March!' she cried, shaking nervously.

They dropped out into the night, laughing stupidly. Outside, the two Lotharios broke out into loud shouts. The others tried to soothe them, all talking at once. The noise went away up the lane with the men, who staggered together in a tight knot, remonstrating with one another foolishly.

'Speak, Susan. What is it? Speak!' entreated Madame Levaille, as soon as the door was shut.

Susan pronounced some incomprehensible words, glaring at the table. The old woman clapped her hands above her head, let them drop, and stood looking at her daughter with disconsolate eyes. Her husband had been 'deranged in his head' for a few years before he died, and now she began to suspect her daughter was going mad. She asked, pressingly –

'Does Jean know where you are? Where is Jean?'

'He knows... he is dead.'

'What!' cried the old woman. She came up near, and peering at her daughter, repeated three times: 'What do you say? What do you say? What do you say?'

Susan sat dry-eyed and stony before Madame Levaille, who contemplated her, feeling a strange sense of inexplicable horror creep into the silence of the house. She had hardly realized the news, further than to understand that she had been brought in one short moment face to face with something unexpected and final. It did not even occur to her to ask for any explanation. She thought: accident – terrible accident – blood to the head – fell down a trap door in the loft … She remained there, distracted and mute, blinking her old eyes.

Suddenly, Susan said –

'I have killed him.'

For a moment the mother stood still, almost unbreathing, but with composed face. The next second she burst out into a shout –

'You miserable madwoman… they will cut your neck…'

She fancied the gendarmes entering the house, saying to her: 'We want your daughter; give her up': the gendarmes with the severe, hard faces of men on duty. She knew the brigadier well – an old friend, familiar and respectful, saying heartily, 'To your good health, Madame!' before lifting to his lips the small glass of cognac – out of the special bottle she kept for friends. And now!… She was losing her head. She rushed here and there, as if looking for something urgently needed – gave that up, stood stock still in the middle of the room, and screamed at her daughter –

'Why? Say! Say! Why?'

The other seemed to leap out of her strange apathy.

'Do you think I am made of stone?' she shouted back, striding towards her mother.

'No! It's impossible…' said Madame Levaille, in a convinced tone.

'You go and see, mother,' retorted Susan, looking at her with blazing eyes. 'There's no money in heaven – no justice. No!… I did not know… Do you think I have no heart? Do you think I have never heard people jeering at me, pitying me, wondering at me? Do you know how some of them were calling me? The mother of idiots – that was my nickname! And my children never would know me, never speak to me. They would know nothing; neither men – nor God. Haven't I prayed! But the Mother of God herself would not hear me. A mother!… Who is accursed – I, or the man who is dead? Eh? Tell me. I took care of myself. Do you think I would defy the anger of God and have my house full of those things – that are worse than animals who know the hand that feeds them? Who blasphemed in the night at the very church door? Was it I?… I only wept and prayed for mercy… and I feel the curse at every moment of the day – I see it round me from morning to night… I've got to keep them alive – to take care of my misfortune and shame. And he would come. I begged him and Heaven for mercy... No!... Then we shall see... He came this evening. I thought to myself: 'Ah! again!'... I had my long scissors. I heard him shouting...I saw him near... I must – must I?...Then take!... And I struck him in the throat above the breastbone... I never heard him even sigh... I left him standing... It was a minute ago. How did I come here?'

Madame Levaille shivered. A wave of cold ran down her back, down her fat arms under her tight sleeves, made her stamp gently where she stood. Quivers ran over the broad cheeks, across the thin lips, ran amongst the wrinkles at the corners of her steady old eyes. She stammered –

'You wicked woman – you disgrace me. But there! You always resembled your father. What do you think will become of you... in the other world? In this... Oh misery!'

She was very hot now. She felt burning inside. She wrung her perspiring hands – and suddenly, starting in great haste, began to look for her big shawl and umbrella, feverishly, never once glancing at her daughter, who stood in the middle of the room following her with a gaze distracted and cold.

'Nothing worse than in this,' said Susan.

Her mother, umbrella in hand and trailing the shawl over the floor, groaned profoundly.

'I must go to the priest,' she burst out passionately. 'I do not know whether you even speak the truth! You are a horrible woman. They will find you anywhere. You may stay here – or go. There is no room for you in this world.'

Ready now to depart, she yet wandered aimlessly about the room, putting the bottles on the shelf, trying to fit with trembling hands the covers on cardboard boxes. Whenever the real sense of what she had heard emerged for a second from the haze of her thoughts she would fancy that something had exploded in her brain without, unfortunately, bursting her head to pieces – which would have been a relief. She blew the candles out one by one without knowing it, and was horribly startled by the darkness. She fell on a bench and began to whimper. After a while she ceased, and sat listening to the breathing of her daughter, whom she could hardly see, still and upright, giving no other sign of life. She was becoming old rapidly at last, during those minutes. She spoke in tones unsteady, cut about by the rattle of teeth, like one shaken by a deadly cold fit of ague.

'I wish you had died little. I will never dare to show my old head in the sunshine again. There are worse misfortunes than idiot children. I wish you had been born to me simple – like your own…'

She saw the figure of her daughter pass before the faint and livid clearness of a window. Then it appeared in the doorway for a second, and the door swung to with a clang. Madame Levaille, as if awakened by the noise from a long nightmare, rushed out.

'Susan!' she shouted from the doorstep.

She heard a stone roll a long time down the declivity of the rocky beach above the sands. She stepped forward cautiously, one hand on the wall of the house, and peered down into the smooth darkness of the empty bay. Once again she cried –

'Susan! You will kill yourself there.'

The stone had taken its last leap in the dark, and she heard nothing now. A sudden thought seemed to strangle her, and she called no more. She turned her back upon the black silence of the pit and went up the lane towards Ploumar, stumbling along with sombre determination, as if she had started on a desperate journey that would last, perhaps, to the end of her life. A sullen and periodic clamour of waves rolling over reefs followed her far inland between the high hedges sheltering the gloomy solitude of the fields.

Susan had run out, swerving sharp to the left at the door, and on the edge of the slope crouched down behind a boulder. A dislodged stone went on downwards, rattling as it leaped. When Madame Levaille called out, Susan could have, by stretching her hand, touched her mother's skirt, had she had the courage to move a limb. She saw the old woman go away, and she remained still, closing her eyes and pressing her side to the hard and rugged surface of the rock. After a while a familiar face with fixed eyes and an open mouth became visible in the intense obscurity amongst the boulders. She uttered a low cry and stood up. The face vanished, leaving her to gasp and shiver alone in the wilderness of stone heaps. But as soon as she had crouched down again to rest, with her head against the rock, the face returned, came very near, appeared eager to finish the speech that had been cut short by death, only a moment ago. She scrambled quickly to her feet and said: 'Go away, or I will do it again.' The thing wavered, swung to the right, to the left. She moved this way and that, stepped back, fancied herself screaming at it, and was appalled by the unbroken stillness of the night. She tottered on the brink, felt the steep declivity under her feet, and rushed down blindly to save herself from a headlong fall. The shingle seemed to wake up; the pebbles began to roll before her, pursued her from above, raced down with her on both sides, rolling past with an increasing clatter. In the peace of the night the noise grew, deepening to a rumour, continuous and violent, as if the whole semicircle of the stony beach had started to tumble down into the bay. Susan's feet hardly touched the slope that seemed to run down with her. At the bottom she stumbled, shot forward, throwing her arms out, and fell heavily. She jumped up at once and turned swiftly to look back, her clenched hands full of sand she had clutched in her fall. The face was there, keeping its distance, visible in its own sheen that made a pale stain in the night. She shouted, 'Go away!' – she shouted at it with pain, with fear, with all the rage of that useless stab that could not keep him quiet, keep him out of her sight. What did he want now? He was dead. Dead men have no children. Would he never leave her alone? She shrieked at it – waved her outstretched hands. She seemed to feel the breath of parted lips, and, with a long cry of discouragement, fled across the level bottom of the bay.

She ran lightly, unaware of any effort of her body. High sharp rocks that, when the bay is full, show above the glittering plain of blue water like pointed towers of submerged churches, glided past her, rushing to the land at a tremendous pace. To the left, in the distance, she could see something shining: a broad disc of light in which narrow shadows pivoted round the centre like the spokes of a wheel. She heard a voice calling, 'Hey! There!' and answered with a wild scream. So, he could call yet! He was calling after her to stop. Never! . . . She tore through the night, past the startled group of seaweed-gatherers who stood round their lantern paralysed with fear at the unearthly screech coming from that fleeing shadow. The men leaned on their pitchforks staring fearfully. A woman fell on her knees, and, crossing herself, began to pray aloud. A little girl with her ragged skirt full of slimy seaweed began to sob despairingly, lugging her soaked burden close to the man who carried the light. Somebody said: 'The thing ran out towards the sea.' Another voice exclaimed: 'And the sea is coming back! Look at the spreading puddles. Do you hear –

you woman – there! Get up!' Several voices cried together. 'Yes, let us
be off! Let the accursed thing go to the sea!' They moved on, keeping
close round the light. Suddenly a man swore loudly. He would go and see
what was the matter. It had been a woman's voice. He would go. There
were shrill protests from women – but his high form detached itself from
the group and went off running. They sent a unanimous call of scared
voices after him. A word, insulting and mocking, came back, thrown at
them through the darkness. A woman moaned. An old man said gravely:
'Such things ought to be left alone.' They went on slower, shuffling in the
yielding sand and whispering to one another that Millot feared nothing,
having no religion, but that it would end badly some day.

Susan met the incoming tide by the Raven islet and stopped, panting,
with her feet in the water. She heard the murmur and felt the cold caress
of the sea, and, calmer now, could see the sombre and confused mass of
the Raven on one side and on the other the long white streak of Molène
sands that are left high above the dry bottom of Fougere Bay at every ebb.
She turned round and saw far away, along the starred background of the
sky, the ragged outline of the coast. Above it, nearly facing her, appeared
the tower of Ploumar Church; a slender and tall pyramid shooting up dark
and pointed into the clustered glitter of the stars. She felt strangely calm.
She knew where she was, and began to remember how she came there –
and why. She peered into the smooth obscurity near her. She was alone.
There was nothing there; nothing near her, either living or dead.

The tide was creeping in quietly, putting out long impatient arms of
strange rivulets that ran towards the land between ridges of sand. Under
the night the pools grew bigger with mysterious rapidity, while the great
sea, yet far off, thundered in a regular rhythm along the indistinct line of the
horizon. Susan splashed her way back for a few yards without being able
to get clear of the water that murmured tenderly all around and, suddenly,
with a spiteful gurgle, nearly took her off her feet. Her heart thumped
with fear. This place was too big and too empty to die in. Tomorrow they
would do with her what they liked. But before she died she must tell them
– tell the gentlemen in black clothes that there are things no woman can
bear. She must explain how it happened… She splashed through a pool,
getting wet to the waist, too preoccupied to care… She must explain.
'He came in the same way as ever and said, just so: "Do you think I
am going to leave the land to those people from Morbihan that I do not

know? Do you? We shall see! Come along, you creature of mischance!"
And he put his arms out. Then, Messieurs, I said: "Before God – never!"
And he said, striding at me with open palms: "There is no God to hold
me! Do you understand, you useless carcase. I will do what I like." And
he took me by the shoulders. Then I, Messieurs, called to God for help,
and next minute, while he was shaking me, I felt my long scissors in my
hand. His shirt was unbuttoned, and, by the candlelight, I saw the hollow
of his throat. I cried: "Let go!" He was crushing my shoulders. He was
strong, my man was! Then I thought: No!... Must I?... Then take! – and I
struck in the hollow place. I never saw him fall. Never! Never! Never saw
him fall... The old father never turned his head. He is deaf and childish,
gentlemen... Nobody saw him fall. I ran out... Nobody saw...'

She had been scrambling amongst the boulders of the Raven and now
found herself, all out of breath, standing amongst the heavy shadows of
the rocky islet. The Raven is connected with the main land by a natural
pier of immense and slippery stones. She intended to return home that
way. Was he still standing there? At home. Home! Four idiots and a
corpse. She must go back and explain. Anybody would understand . . .

Below her the night or the sea seemed to pronounce distinctly –

'Aha! I see you at last!'

She started, slipped, fell; and without attempting to rise, listened,
terrified. She heard heavy breathing, a clatter of wooden clogs. It
stopped.

'Where the devil did you pass?' said an invisible man, hoarsely.

She held her breath. She recognized the voice. She had not seen him
fall. Was he pursuing her there dead, or perhaps... alive?

She lost her head. She cried from the crevice where she lay huddled,
'Never, never!'

'Ah! You are still there. You led me a fine dance. Wait, my beauty, I
must see how you look after all this. You wait...'

Millot was stumbling, laughing, swearing meaninglessly out of pure
satisfaction, pleased with himself for having run down that fly-by-
night. 'As if there were such things as ghosts! Bah! It took an old African
soldier to show those clodhoppers... But it was curious. Who the devil
was she?'

Susan listened, crouching. He was coming for her, this dead man.
There was no escape. What a noise he made amongst the stones... She

saw his head rise up, then the shoulders. He was tall – her own man! His long arms waved about, and it was his own voice sounding a little strange… because of the scissors. She scrambled out quickly, rushed to the edge of the causeway, and turned round. The man stood still on a high stone, detaching himself in dead black on the glitter of the sky.

'Where are you going to?' he called, roughly.

She answered, 'Home!' and watched him intensely. He made a striding, clumsy leap on to another boulder, and stopped again, balancing himself, then said –

'Ha! ha! Well, I am going with you. It's the least I can do. Ha! ha! ha!'

She stared at him till her eyes seemed to become glowing coals that burned deep into her brain, and yet she was in mortal fear of making out the well-known features. Below her the sea lapped softly against the rock with a splash continuous and gentle.

The man said, advancing another step –

'I am coming for you. What do you think?'

She trembled. Coming for her! There was no escape, no peace, no hope. She looked round despairingly. Suddenly the whole shadowy coast, the blurred islets, the heaven itself, swayed about twice, then came to a rest. She closed her eyes and shouted –

'Can't you wait till I am dead!'

She was shaken by a furious hate for that shade that pursued her in this world, unappeased even by death in its longing for an heir that would be like other people's children.

'Hey! What?' said Millot, keeping his distance prudently. He was saying to himself: 'Look out! Some lunatic. An accident happens soon.'

She went on, wildly –

'I want to live. To live alone – for a week – for a day. I must explain to them… I would tear you to pieces, I would kill you twenty times over rather than let you touch me while I live. How many times must I kill you – you blasphemer! Satan sends you here. I am damned too!'

'Come,' said Millot, alarmed and conciliating. 'I am perfectly alive!… Oh, my God!'

She had screamed, 'Alive!' and at once vanished before his eyes, as if the islet itself had swerved aside from under her feet. Millot rushed forward, and fell flat with his chin over the edge. Far below he saw the water whitened by her struggles, and heard one shrill cry for help that seemed to dart upwards along the perpendicular face of the rock, and soar past, straight into the high and impassive heaven.

Madame Levaille sat, dry-eyed, on the short grass of the hillside, with her thick legs stretched out, and her old feet turned up in their black cloth shoes. Her clogs stood near by, and further off the umbrella lay on the withered sward like a weapon dropped from the grasp of a vanquished warrior. The Marquis of Chavanes, on horseback, one gloved hand on thigh, looked down at her as she got up laboriously, with groans. On the narrow track of the seaweed-carts four men were carrying inland Susan's body on a hand-barrow, while several others straggled listlessly behind. Madame Levaille looked after the procession. 'Yes, Monsieur le Marquis,' she said dispassionately, in her usual calm tone of a reasonable old woman. 'There are unfortunate people on this earth. I had only one child. Only one! And they won't bury her in consecrated ground!'

Her eyes filled suddenly, and a short shower of tears rolled down the broad cheeks. She pulled the shawl close about her. The Marquis leaned slightly over in his saddle, and said –

'It is very sad. You have all my sympathy. I shall speak to the Curé. She was unquestionably insane, and the fall was accidental. Millot says so distinctly. Good day, Madame.'

And he trotted off, thinking to himself: 'I must get this old woman appointed guardian of those idiots, and administrator of the farm. It would be much better than having here one of those other Bacadous, probably a red republican, corrupting my commune.'

AN OUTPOST OF PROGRESS

I

There were two white men in charge of the trading station. Kayerts, the chief, was short and fat; Carlier, the assistant, was tall, with a large head and a very broad trunk perched upon a long pair of thin legs. The third man on the staff was a Sierra Leone nigger, who maintained that his name was Henry Price. However, for some reason or other, the natives down the river had given him the name of Makola, and it stuck to him through all his wanderings about the country. He spoke English and French with a warbling accent, wrote a beautiful hand, understood bookkeeping, and cherished in his innermost heart the worship of evil spirits. His wife was a negress from Loanda, very large and very noisy. Three children rolled about in sunshine before the door of his low, shed-like dwelling. Makola, taciturn and impenetrable, despised the two white men. He had charge of a small clay storehouse with a dried-grass roof, and pretended to keep a correct account of beads, cotton cloth, red kerchiefs, brass wire, and other trade goods it contained. Besides the storehouse and Makola's hut, there was only one large building in the cleared ground of the station. It was built neatly of reeds, with a veranda on all the four sides. There were three rooms in it. The one in the middle was the living-room, and had two rough tables and a few stools in it. The other two were the bedrooms for the white men. Each had a bedstead and a mosquito net for all furniture. The plank floor was littered with the belongings of the white men; open half-empty boxes, torn wearing apparel, old boots; all the things dirty, and all the things broken, that accumulate mysteriously round untidy men. There was also another dwelling-place some distance away from the buildings. In it, under a tall cross much out of the perpendicular, slept the man who had seen the beginning of all this; who had planned and had watched the construction of this outpost of progress. He had been, at home, an unsuccessful painter who, weary of pursuing fame on an empty stomach, had gone out there through high protections. He had been the first chief of that station. Makola had watched the energetic artist die of fever in the just finished house with his usual kind of 'I told you so' indifference. Then, for a time, he dwelt alone with his family, his account books, and the Evil Spirit that rules the lands under the equator. He got on very well with his god. Perhaps he had propitiated him by a promise of more white men to play with, by and by. At any rate the director of the Great Trading Company, coming up in a steamer that resembled an enormous sardine box with a flat-roofed shed erected on it, found the station in good order, and Makola as usual quietly diligent. The director had the cross put up over the first agent's grave, and appointed Kayerts to the post. Carlier was told off as second in charge. The director was a man ruthless and efficient, who at times, but very imperceptibly, indulged in grim humour. He made a speech to Kayerts and Carlier, pointing out to them the promising aspect of their station. The nearest trading-post was about three hundred miles away. It was an exceptional opportunity for them to distinguish themselves and to earn percentages on the trade. This appointment was a favour done to beginners. Kayerts was moved almost to tears by his director's kindness. He would, he said, by doing his best, try to justify the flattering confidence, &c., &c. Kayerts had been in the Administration of the Telegraphs, and knew how to express himself correctly. Carlier, an ex-non-commissioned officer of cavalry in an army guaranteed from harm by several European Powers, was less impressed. If there were commissions to get, so much the better; and, trailing a sulky glance over the river, the forests, the impenetrable bush that seemed to cut off the station from the rest of the world, he muttered between his teeth, 'We shall see, very soon.'

Next day, some bales of cotton goods and a few cases of provisions having been thrown on shore, the sardine-box steamer went off, not to return for another six months. On the deck the director touched his cap to the two agents, who stood on the bank waving their hats, and turning to an old servant of the Company on his passage to headquarters, said, 'Look at those two imbeciles. They must be mad at home to send me such specimens. I told those fellows to plant a vegetable garden, build new storehouses and fences, and construct a landing-stage. I bet nothing will be done! They won't know how to begin. I always thought the station on this river useless, and they just fit the station!'

'They will form themselves there,' said the old stager with a quiet smile.

'At any rate, I am rid of them for six months,' retorted the director.

The two men watched the steamer round the bend, then, ascending arm in arm the slope of the bank, returned to the station. They had been in this vast and dark country only a very short time, and as yet always in the midst of other white men, under the eye and guidance of their superiors. And now, dull as they were to the subtle influences of surroundings, they felt themselves very much alone, when suddenly left unassisted to face the wilderness; a wilderness rendered more strange, more incomprehensible by the mysterious glimpses of the vigorous life it contained. They were two perfectly insignificant and incapable individuals, whose existence is only rendered possible through the high organization of civilized crowds. Few men realize that their life, the very essence of their character, their capabilities and their audacities, are only the expression of their belief in the safety of their surroundings. The courage, the composure, the confidence; the emotions and principles; every great and every insignificant thought belongs not to the individual but to the crowd: to the crowd that believes blindly in the irresistible force of its institutions and of its morals, in the power of its police and of its opinion. But the contact with pure unmitigated savagery, with primitive nature and primitive man, brings sudden and profound trouble into the heart. To the sentiment of being alone of one's kind, to the clear perception of the loneliness of one's thoughts, of one's sensations – to the negation of the habitual, which is safe, there is added the affirmation of the unusual, which is dangerous; a suggestion of things vague, uncontrollable, and repulsive, whose discomposing intrusion excites the imagination and tries the civilized nerves of the foolish and the wise alike.

Kayerts and Carlier walked arm in arm, drawing close to one another as children do in the dark; and they had the same, not altogether unpleasant, sense of danger which one half suspects to be imaginary. They chatted persistently in familiar tones. 'Our station is prettily situated,' said one. The other assented with enthusiasm, enlarging volubly on the beauties of the situation. Then they passed near the grave. 'Poor devil!' said Kayerts. 'He died of fever, didn't he?' muttered Carlier, stopping short. 'Why,' retorted Kayerts, with indignation, 'I've been told that the fellow exposed himself recklessly to the sun. The climate here, everybody says, is not at all worse than at home, as long as you keep out of the sun. Do you hear that, Carlier? I am chief here, and my orders are that you should not expose yourself to the sun!' He assumed his superiority jocularly, but his meaning was serious. The idea that he would, perhaps, have to bury

Carlier and remain alone, gave him an inward shiver. He felt suddenly that this Carlier was more precious to him here, in the centre of Africa, than a brother could be anywhere else. Carlier, entering into the spirit of the thing, made a military salute and answered in a brisk tone, 'Your orders shall be attended to, chief!' Then he burst out laughing, slapped Kayerts on the back and shouted, 'We shall let life run easily here! Just sit still and gather in the ivory those savages will bring. This country has its good points, after all!' They both laughed loudly while Carlier thought: 'That poor Kayerts; he is so fat and unhealthy. It would be awful if I had to bury him here. He is a man I respect.'… Before they reached the verandah of their house they called one another 'my dear fellow'.

The first day they were very active, pottering about with hammers and nails and red calico, to put up curtains, make their house habitable and pretty; resolved to settle down comfortably to their new life. For them an impossible task. To grapple effectually with even purely material problems requires more serenity of mind and more lofty courage than people generally imagine. No two beings could have been more unfitted for such a struggle. Society, not from any tenderness, but because of its strange needs, had taken care of those two men, forbidding them all independent thought, all initiative, all departure from routine; and forbidding it under pain of death. They could only live on condition of being machines. And now, released from the fostering care of men with pens behind the ears, or of men with gold lace on the sleeves, they were like those lifelong prisoners who, liberated after many years, do not know what use to make of their freedom. They did not know what use to make of their faculties, being both, through want of practice, incapable of independent thought.

At the end of two months Kayerts often would say, 'If it was not for my Melie, you wouldn't catch me here.' Melie was his daughter. He had thrown up his post in the Administration of the Telegraphs, though he had been for seventeen years perfectly happy there, to earn a dowry for his girl. His wife was dead, and the child was being brought up by his sisters. He regretted the streets, the pavements, the cafes, his friends of many years; all the things he used to see, day after day; all the thoughts suggested by familiar things – the thoughts effortless, monotonous, and soothing of a Government clerk; he regretted all the gossip, the small enmities, the mild venom, and the little jokes of Government offices. 'If I had had a decent brother-in-law,' Carlier would remark, 'a fellow with a heart, I would not be here.' He had left the army and had made himself so obnoxious to his family by his laziness and impudence, that an exasperated brother-in-law had made superhuman efforts to procure him an appointment in the Company as a second-class agent. Having not a penny in the world he was compelled to accept this means of livelihood as soon as it became quite clear to him that there was nothing more to squeeze out of his relations. He, like Kayerts, regretted his old life. He regretted the clink of sabre and spurs on a fine afternoon, the barrack-room witticisms, the girls of garrison towns; but, besides, he had also a sense of grievance. He was evidently a much ill-used man. This made him moody, at times. But the two men got on well together in the fellowship of their stupidity and laziness. Together they did nothing, absolutely nothing, and enjoyed the sense of the idleness for which they were paid. And in time they came to feel something resembling affection for one another.

They lived like blind men in a large room, aware only of what came in contact with them (and of that only imperfectly), but unable to see the general aspect of things. The river, the forest, all the great land throbbing with life, were like a great emptiness. Even the brilliant sunshine disclosed nothing intelligible. Things appeared and disappeared before their eyes in an unconnected and aimless kind of way. The river seemed to come from nowhere and flow nowhither. It flowed through a void. Out of that void, at times, came canoes, and men with spears in their hands would suddenly crowd the yard of the station. They were naked, glossy black, ornamented with snowy shells and glistening brass wire, perfect of limb. They made an uncouth babbling noise when they spoke, moved in a stately manner, and sent quick, wild glances out of their startled, never-resting eyes. Those warriors would squat in long rows, four or more deep, before the verandah, while their chiefs bargained for hours with Makola over an elephant tusk. Kayerts sat on his chair and looked down on the proceedings, understanding nothing. He stared at them with his round blue eyes, called out to Carlier, 'Here, look! look at that fellow there – and that other one, to the left. Did you ever such a face? Oh, the funny brute!'

Carlier, smoking native tobacco in a short wooden pipe, would swagger up twirling his moustaches, and surveying the warriors with haughty indulgence, would say –

'Fine animals. Brought any bone? Yes? It's not any too soon. Look at the muscles of that fellow third from the end. I wouldn't care to get a punch on the nose from him. Fine arms, but legs no good below the knee. Couldn't make cavalry men of them.' And after glancing down complacently at his own shanks, he always concluded: 'Pah! Don't they stink! You, Makola! Take that herd over to the fetish' (the storehouse was in every station called the fetish, perhaps because of the spirit of civilization it contained) 'and give them up some of the rubbish you keep there. I'd rather see it full of bone than full of rags.'

Kayerts approved.

'Yes, yes! Go and finish that palaver over there, Mr Makola. I will come round when you are ready, to weigh the tusk. We must be careful.' Then turning to his companion: 'This is the tribe that lives down the river; they are rather aromatic. I remember, they had been once before here. D'ye hear that row? What a fellow has got to put up with in this dog of a country! My head is split.'

Such profitable visits were rare. For days the two pioneers of trade and progress would look on their empty courtyard in the vibrating brilliance of vertical sunshine. Below the high bank, the silent river flowed on glittering and steady. On the sands in the middle of the stream, hippos and alligators sunned themselves side by side. And stretching away in all directions, surrounding the insignificant cleared spot of the trading post, immense forests, hiding fateful complications of fantastic life, lay in the eloquent silence of mute greatness. The two men understood nothing, cared for nothing but for the passage of days that separated them from the steamer's return. Their predecessor had left some torn books. They took up these wrecks of novels, and, as they had never read anything of the kind before, they were surprised and amused. Then during long days there were interminable and silly discussions about plots and personages. In the centre of Africa they made acquaintance of Richelieu and of d'Artagnan, of Hawk's Eye and of Father Goriot, and of many other people. All these imaginary personages became subjects for gossip as if they had been living friends. They discounted their virtues, suspected their motives, decried their successes; were scandalized at their duplicity or were doubtful about their courage. The accounts of crimes filled them with indignation, while tender or pathetic passages moved them deeply. Carlier cleared his throat and said in a soldierly voice, 'What nonsense!' Kayerts, his round eyes suffused with tears, his fat cheeks quivering, rubbed his bald head, and declared. 'This is a splendid book. I had no idea there were such clever fellows in the world.' They also found some old copies of a home paper. That print discussed what it was pleased to call 'Our Colonial Expansion' in high-flown language. It spoke much of the rights and duties of civilization, of the sacredness of the civilizing work, and extolled the merits of those who went about bringing light, and faith and commerce to the dark places of the earth. Carlier and Kayerts read, wondered, and began to think better of themselves. Carlier said one evening, waving his hand about, 'In a hundred years, there will be perhaps a town here. Quays, and warehouses, and barracks, and – and – billiard-rooms. Civilization, my boy, and virtue – and all. And then, chaps will read that two good fellows, Kayerts and Carlier, were the first civilized men to live in this very spot!' Kayerts nodded, 'Yes, it is a consolation to think of that.' They seemed to forget their dead predecessor; but, early one day, Carlier went out and replanted the cross firmly. 'It used to make me squint whenever I walked that way,' he explained to Kayerts over the morning coffee. 'It made me squint, leaning over so much. So I just planted it upright. And solid, I promise you! I suspended myself with both hands to the cross-piece. Not a move. Oh, I did that properly.'

At times Gobila came to see them. Gobila was the chief of the neighbouring villages. He was a grey-headed savage, thin and black, with a white cloth round his loins and a mangy panther skin hanging over his back. He came up with long strides of his skeleton legs, swinging a staff as tall as himself, and, entering the common room of the station, would squat on his heels to the left of the door. There he sat, watching Kayerts, and now and then making a speech which the other did not understand. Kayerts, without interrupting his occupation, would from time to time say in a friendly manner: 'How goes it, you old image?' and they would smile at one another. The two whites had a liking for that old and incomprehensible creature, and called him Father Gobila. Gobila's manner was paternal, and he seemed really to love all white men. They all appeared to him very young, indistinguishably alike (except for stature), and he knew that they were all brothers, and also immortal. The death of the artist, who was the first white man whom he knew intimately, did not disturb this belief, because he was firmly convinced that the white stranger had pretended to die and got himself buried for some mysterious purpose of his own, into which it was useless to inquire. Perhaps it was

his way of going home to his own country? At any rate, these were his
brothers, and he transferred his absurd affection to them. They returned
it in a way. Carlier slapped him on the back, and recklessly struck off
matches for his amusement. Kayerts was always ready to let him have
a sniff at the ammonia bottle. In short, they behaved just like that other
white creature that had hidden itself in a hole in the ground. Gobila
considered them attentively. Perhaps they were the same being with the
other – or one of them was. He couldn't decide – clear up that mystery;
but he remained always very friendly. In consequence of that friendship
the women of Gobila's village walked in single file through the reedy
grass, bringing every morning to the station, fowls, and sweet potatoes,
and palm wine, and sometimes a goat. The Company never provisions the
stations fully, and the agents required those local supplies to live. They
had them through the good-will of Gobila, and lived well. Now and then
one of them had a bout of fever, and the other nursed him with gentle
devotion. They did not think much of it. It left them weaker, and their
appearance changed for the worse. Carlier was hollow-eyed and irritable.
Kayerts showed a drawn, flabby face above the rotundity of his stomach,
which gave him a weird aspect. But being constantly together, they did
not notice the change that took place gradually in their appearance, and
also in their dispositions.

Five months passed in that way.

Then, one morning, as Kayerts and Carlier, lounging in their chairs
under the verandah, talked about the approaching visit of the steamer,
a knot of armed men came out of the forest and advanced towards the
station. They were strangers to that part of the country. They were tall,
slight, draped classically from neck to heel in blue-fringed cloths, and
carried percussion muskets over their bare right shoulders. Makola
showed signs of excitement, and ran out of the storehouse (where he
spent all his days) to meet these visitors. They came into the courtyard
and looked about them with steady, scornful glances. Their leader, a
powerful and determined-looking negro with bloodshot eyes, stood in
front of the verandah and made a long speech. He gesticulated much, and
ceased very suddenly.

There was something in his intonation, in the sounds of the long
sentences he used, that startled the two whites. It was like a reminiscence
of something not exactly familiar, and yet resembling the speech of

civilized men. It sounded like one of those impossible languages which sometimes we hear in our dreams.

'What lingo is that?' said the amazed Carlier. 'In the first moment I fancied the fellow was going to speak French. Anyway, it is a different kind of gibberish to what we ever heard.'

'Yes,' replied Kayerts. 'Hey, Makola, what does he say? Where do they come from? Who are they?'

But Makola, who seemed to be standing on hot bricks, answered hurriedly, 'I don't know. They come from very far. Perhaps Mrs Price will understand. They are perhaps bad men.'

The leader, after waiting for a while, said something sharply to Makola, who shook his head. Then the man, after looking round, noticed Makola's hut and walked over there. The next moment Mrs Makola was heard speaking with great volubility. The other strangers – they were six in all – strolled about with an air of ease, put their heads through the door of the storeroom, congregated round the grave, pointed understandingly at the cross, and generally made themselves at home.

'I don't like those chaps – and, I say, Kayerts, they must be from the coast; they've got firearms,' observed the sagacious Carlier.

Kayerts also did not like those chaps. They both, for the first time, became aware that they lived in conditions where the unusual may be dangerous, and that there was no power on earth outside of themselves to stand between them and the unusual. They became uneasy, went in and loaded their revolvers. Kayerts said, 'We must order Makola to tell them to go away before dark.'

The strangers left in the afternoon, after eating a meal prepared for them by Mrs Makola. The immense woman was excited, and talked much with the visitors. She rattled away shrilly, pointing here and there at the forests and at the river. Makola sat apart and watched. At times he got up and whispered to his wife. He accompanied the strangers across the ravine at the back of the station-ground, and returned slowly looking very thoughtful. When questioned by the white men he was very strange, seemed not to understand, seemed to have forgotten French – seemed to have forgotten how to speak altogether. Kayerts and Carlier agreed that the nigger had had too much palm wine.

There was some talk about keeping a watch in turn, but in the evening everything seemed so quiet and peaceful that they retired as usual.

All night they were disturbed by a lot of drumming in the villages. A deep, rapid roll near by would be followed by another far off – then all ceased. Soon short appeals would rattle out here and there, then all mingle together, increase, become vigorous and sustained, would spread out over the forest, roll through the night, unbroken and ceaseless, near and far, as if the whole land had been one immense drum booming out steadily an appeal to heaven. And through the deep and tremendous noise sudden yells that resembled snatches of songs from a madhouse darted shrill and high in discordant jets of sound which seemed to rush far above the earth and drive all peace from under the stars.

Carlier and Kayerts slept badly. They both thought they had heard shots fired during the night – but they could not agree as to the direction. In the morning Makola was gone somewhere. He returned about noon with one of yesterday's strangers, and eluded all Kayerts' attempts to close with him: had become deaf apparently. Kayerts wondered. Carlier, who had been fishing off the bank, came back and remarked while he showed his catch, 'The niggers seem to be in a deuce of a stir; I wonder what's up. I saw about fifteen canoes cross the river during the two hours I was there fishing.' Kayerts, worried, said, 'Isn't this Makola very queer today?' Carlier advised, 'Keep all our men together in case of some trouble.'

II

There were ten station men who had been left by the Director. Those fellows, having engaged themselves to the Company for six months (without having any idea of a month in particular and only a very faint notion of time in general), had been serving the cause of progress for upwards of two years. Belonging to a tribe from a very distant part of the land of darkness and sorrow, they did not run away, naturally supposing that as wandering strangers they would be killed by the inhabitants of the country; in which they were right. They lived in straw huts on the slope of a ravine overgrown with reedy grass, just behind the station buildings. They were not happy, regretting the festive incantations, the sorceries, the human sacrifices of their own land; where they also had parents, brothers, sisters, admired chiefs, respected magicians, loved friends, and other ties supposed generally to be human. Besides, the rice rations served out by the Company did not agree with them, being a food unknown to their land, and to which they could not get used. Consequently they were unhealthy and miserable. Had they been of any other tribe they would have made up their minds to die – for nothing is easier to certain savages than suicide – and so have escaped from the puzzling difficulties of existence. But belonging, as they did, to a warlike tribe with filed teeth, they had more grit, and went on stupidly living through disease and sorrow. They did very little work, and had lost their splendid physique. Carlier and Kayerts doctored them assiduously without being able to bring them back into condition again. They were mustered every morning and told off to different tasks – grass-cutting, fence-building, tree-felling, &c., &c., which no power on earth could induce them to execute efficiently. The two whites had practically very little control over them.

In the afternoon Makola came over to the big house and found Kayerts watching three heavy columns of smoke rising above the forests. 'What is that?' asked Kayerts. 'Some villages burn,' answered Makola, who seemed to have regained his wits. Then he said abruptly: 'We have got very little ivory; bad six months' trading. Do you like get a little more ivory?'

'Yes,' said Kayerts, eagerly. He thought of percentages which were low.

'Those men who came yesterday are traders from Loanda who have got more ivory than they can carry home. Shall I buy? I know their camp.'

'Certainly,' said Kayerts. 'What are those traders?'

'Bad fellows,' said Makola, indifferently. 'They fight with people, and catch women and children. They are bad men, and got guns. There is a great disturbance in the country. Do you want ivory?'

'Yes,' said Kayerts. Makola said nothing for a while. Then: 'Those workmen of ours are no good at all,' he muttered, looking round. 'Station in very bad order, sir. Director will growl. Better get a fine lot of ivory, then he say nothing.'

'I can't help it; the men won't work,' said Kayerts. 'When will you get that ivory?'

'Very soon,' said Makola. 'Perhaps to-night. You leave it to me, and keep indoors, sir. I think you had better give some palm wine to our men to make a dance this evening. Enjoy themselves. Work better to-morrow. There's plenty palm wine – gone a little sour.'

Kayerts said 'yes,' and Makola, with his own hands carried big calabashes to the door of his hut. They stood there till the evening, and

Mrs Makola looked into every one. The men got them at sunset. When Kayerts and Carlier retired, a big bonfire was flaring before the men's huts. They could hear their shouts and drumming. Some men from Gobila's village had joined the station hands, and the entertainment was a great success.

In the middle of the night, Carlier waking suddenly, heard a man shout loudly; then a shot was fired. Only one. Carlier ran out and met Kayerts on the veranda. They were both startled. As they went across the yard to call Makola, they saw shadows moving in the night. One of them cried, 'Don't shoot! It's me, Price.' Then Makola appeared close to them.'Go back, go back, please,' he urged, 'you spoil all.' 'There are strange men about,' said Carlier. 'Never mind; I know,' said Makola. Then he whispered, 'All right. Bring ivory. Say nothing! I know my business.' The two white men reluctantly went back to the house, but did not sleep. They heard footsteps, whispers, some groans. It seemed as if a lot of men came in, dumped heavy things on the ground, squabbled a long time, then went away. They lay on their hard beds and thought: 'This Makola is invaluable.' In the morning Carlier came out, very sleepy, and pulled at the cord of the big bell. The station hands mustered every morning to the sound of the bell. That morning nobody came. Kayerts turned out also, yawning. Across the yard they saw Makola come out of his hut, a tin basin of soapy water in his hand. Makola, a civilized nigger, was very neat in his person. He threw the soapsuds skilfully over a wretched little yellow cur he had, then turning his face to the agent's house, he shouted from the distance, 'All the men gone last night!'

They heard him plainly, but in their surprise they both yelled out together: 'What!' Then they stared at one another. 'We are in a proper fix now,' growled Carlier. 'It's incredible!' muttered Kayerts. 'I will go to the huts and see,' said Carlier, striding off. Makola coming up found Kayerts standing alone.

'I can hardly believe it,' said Kayerts, tearfully. 'We took care of them as if they had been our children.'

'They went with the coast people,' said Makola after a moment of hesitation.

'What do I care with whom they went – the ungrateful brutes!' exclaimed the other. Then with sudden suspicion, and looking hard at Makola, he added: 'What do you know about it?'

Makola moved his shoulders, looking down on the ground. 'What do I know? I think only. Will you come and look at the ivory I've got there? It is a fine lot. You never saw such.'

He moved towards the store. Kayerts followed him mechanically, thinking about the incredible desertion of the men. On the ground before the door of the fetish lay six splendid tusks.

'What did you give for it?' asked Kayerts, after surveying the lot with satisfaction.

'No regular trade,' said Makola. 'They brought the ivory and gave it to me. I told them to take what they most wanted in the station. It is a beautiful lot. No station can show such tusks. Those traders wanted carriers badly, and our men were no good here. No trade, no entry in books: all correct.'

Kayerts nearly burst with indignation. 'Why!' he shouted, 'I believe you have sold our men for these tusks!' Makola stood impassive and silent. 'I – I – will – I,' stuttered Kayerts. 'You fiend!' he yelled out.

'I did the best for you and the Company,' said Makola, imperturbably. 'Why you shout so much? Look at this tusk.'

'I dismiss you! I will report you – I won't look at the tusk. I forbid you to touch them. I order you to throw them into the river. You – you!'

'You very red, Mr Kayerts. If you are so irritable in the sun, you will get fever and die – like the first chief!' pronounced Makola impressively.

They stood still, contemplating one another with intense eyes, as if they had been looking with effort across immense distances. Kayerts shivered. Makola had meant no more than he said, but his words seemed to Kayerts full of ominous menace! He turned sharply and went away to the house. Makola retired into the bosom of his family; and the tusks, left lying before the store, looked very large and valuable in the sunshine.

Carlier came back on the veranda. 'They're all gone, hey?' asked Kayerts from the far end of the common room in a muffled voice. 'You did not find anybody?'

'Oh, yes,' said Carlier, 'I found one of Gobila's people lying dead before the huts – shot through the body. We heard that shot last night.'

Kayerts came out quickly. He found his companion staring grimly over the yard at the tusks, away by the store. They both sat in silence for a while. Then Kayerts related his conversation with Makola. Carlier said nothing. At the midday meal they ate very little. They hardly exchanged a word that day. A great silence seemed to lie heavily over the station and press on their lips. Makola did not open the store; he spent the day playing with his children. He lay full-length on a mat outside his door, and the youngsters sat on his chest and clambered all over him. It was a touching picture. Mrs Makola was busy cooking all day, as usual. The white men made a somewhat better meal in the evening. Afterwards, Carlier smoking his pipe strolled over to the store; he stood for a long time over the tusks, touched one or two with his foot, even tried to lift the largest one by its small end. He came back to his chief, who had not stirred from the verandah, threw himself in the chair and said –

'I can see it! They were pounced upon while they slept heavily after drinking all that palm wine you've allowed Makola to give them. A put-up job! See? The worst is, some of Gobila's people were there, and got carried off too, no doubt. The least drunk woke up, and got shot for his sobriety. This is a funny country. What will you do now?'

'We can't touch it, of course,' said Kayerts.

'Of course not,' assented Carlier.

'Slavery is an awful thing,' stammered out Kayerts in an unsteady voice.

'Frightful – the sufferings,' grunted Carlier with conviction.

They believed their words. Everybody shows a respectful deference to certain sounds that he and his fellows can make. But about feelings people really know nothing. We talk with indignation or enthusiasm; we talk about oppression, cruelty, crime, devotion, self-sacrifice, virtue, and we know nothing real beyond the words. Nobody knows what suffering or sacrifice mean – except, perhaps the victims of the mysterious purpose of these illusions.

Next morning they saw Makola very busy setting up in the yard the big scales used for weighing ivory. By and by Carlier said: 'What's that filthy scoundrel up to?' and lounged out into the yard. Kayerts followed. They stood watching. Makola took no notice. When the balance was swung true, he tried to lift a tusk into the scale. It was too heavy. He looked up helplessly without a word, and for a minute they stood round that balance as mute and still as three statues. Suddenly Carlier said: 'Catch hold of the other end, Makola – you beast!' and together they swung the tusk up. Kayerts trembled in every limb. He muttered, 'I say! O! I say!' and putting his hand in his pocket found there a dirty bit of paper and the stump of a pencil. He turned his back on the others, as if about to do something tricky, and noted stealthily the weights which Carlier shouted out to him with unnecessary loudness. When all was over Makola whispered to himself: 'The sun's very strong here for the tusks.' Carlier said to Kayerts in a careless tone: 'I say, chief, I might just as well give him a lift with this lot into the store.'

As they were going back to the house Kayerts observed with a sigh: 'It had to be done.' And Carlier said: 'It's deplorable, but, the men being Company's men the ivory is Company's ivory. We must look after it.' 'I will report to the Director, of course,' said Kayerts. 'Of course; let him decide,' approved Carlier.

At midday they made a hearty meal. Kayerts sighed from time to time. Whenever they mentioned Makola's name they always added to it an opprobrious epithet. It eased their conscience. Makola gave himself a half-holiday, and bathed his children in the river. No one from Gobila's villages came near the station that day. No one came the next day, and the next, nor for a whole week. Gobila's people might have been dead and buried for any sign of life they gave. But they were only mourning for those they had lost by the witchcraft of white men, who had brought wicked people into their country. The wicked people were gone, but fear remained. Fear always remains. A man may destroy everything within himself, love and hate and belief, and even doubt; but as long as he clings to life he cannot destroy fear: the fear, subtle, indestructible, and terrible, that pervades his being; that tinges his thoughts; that lurks in his heart; that watches on his lips the struggle of his last breath. In his fear, the mild old Gobila offered extra human sacrifices to all the Evil Spirits that had taken possession of his white friends. His heart was heavy. Some warriors spoke about burning and killing, but the cautious old savage dissuaded them. Who could foresee the woe those mysterious creatures, if irritated, might bring? They should be left alone. Perhaps in time they would disappear into the earth as the first one had disappeared. His people must keep away from them, and hope for the best.

Kayerts and Carlier did not disappear, but remained above on this earth, that, somehow, they fancied had become bigger and very empty. It was not the absolute and dumb solitude of the post that impressed them so much as an inarticulate feeling that something from within them was gone, something that worked for their safety, and had kept the wilderness from interfering with their hearts. The images of home; the memory of people like them, of men that thought and felt as they used to think and feel, receded into distances made indistinct by the glare of unclouded sunshine. And out of the great silence of the surrounding wilderness, its very hopelessness and savagery seemed to approach them nearer, to draw them gently, to look upon them, to envelop them with a solicitude irresistible, familiar, and disgusting.

Days lengthened into weeks, then into months. Gobila's people drummed and yelled to every new moon, as of yore, but kept away from the station. Makola and Carlier tried once in a canoe to open communications, but were received with a shower of arrows, and had to fly back to the station for dear life. That attempt set the country up and down the river into an uproar that could be very distinctly heard for days. The steamer was late. At first they spoke of delay jauntily, then anxiously, then gloomily. The matter was becoming serious. Stores were running short. Carlier cast his lines off the bank, but the river was low, and the fish kept out in the stream. They dared not stroll far away from the station to shoot. Moreover, there was no game in the impenetrable forest. Once Carlier shot a hippo in the river. They had no boat to secure it, and it sank. When it floated up it drifted away, and Gobila's people secured the carcase. It was the occasion for a national holiday, but Carlier had a fit of rage over it and talked about the necessity of exterminating all the niggers before the country could be made habitable. Kayerts mooned about silently; spent hours looking at the portrait of his Melie. It represented a little girl with long bleached tresses and a rather sour face. His legs were much swollen, and he could hardly walk. Carlier, undermined by fever, could not swagger any more, but kept tottering about, still with a devil-may-care air, as became a man who remembered his crack regiment. He had become hoarse, sarcastic, and inclined to say unpleasant things. He called it 'being frank with you'. They had long ago reckoned their percentages on trade, including in them that last deal of 'this infamous Makola'. They had also concluded not to say anything about it. Kayerts hesitated at first – was afraid of the Director.

'He has seen worse things done on the quiet,' maintained Carlier, with a hoarse laugh. 'Trust him! He won't thank you if you blab. He is no better than you or me. Who will talk if we hold our tongues? There is nobody here.'

That was the root of the trouble! There was nobody there; and being left there alone with their weakness, they became daily more like a pair of accomplices than like a couple of devoted friends. They had heard nothing from home for eight months. Every evening they said, 'To-morrow we shall see the steamer.' But one of the Company's steamers had been wrecked, and the Director was busy with the other, relieving very distant and important stations on the main river. He thought that the useless station, and the useless men, could wait. Meantime Kayerts and Carlier lived on rice boiled without salt, and cursed the Company, all Africa, and the day they were born. One must have lived on such diet to discover what ghastly trouble the necessity of swallowing one's food may become. There was literally nothing else in the station but rice and coffee; they drank the coffee without sugar. The last fifteen lumps Kayerts had solemnly locked away in his box, together with a half-bottle of Cognac, 'in case of sickness,' he explained. Carlier approved. 'When one is sick,' he said, 'any little extra like that is cheering.'

They waited. Rank grass began to sprout over the courtyard. The bell never rang now. Days passed, silent, exasperating, and slow. When the two men spoke, they snarled; and their silences were bitter, as if tinged by the bitterness of their thoughts.

One day after a lunch of boiled rice, Carlier put down his cup untasted, and said: 'Hang it all! Let's have a decent cup of coffee for once. Bring out that sugar, Kayerts!'

'For the sick,' muttered Kayerts, without looking up.

'For the sick,' mocked Carlier. 'Bosh!...Well! I am sick.'

'You are no more sick than I am, and I go without,' said Kayerts in a peaceful tone.

'Come! out with that sugar, you stingy old slave-dealer.'

Kayerts looked up quickly. Carlier was smiling with marked insolence. And suddenly it seemed to Kayerts that he had never seen that man before. Who was he? He knew nothing about him. What was he capable of? There was a surprising flash of violent emotion within him, as if in the presence of something undreamt-of, dangerous, and final. But he managed to pronounce with composure –

'That joke is in very bad taste. Don't repeat it.'

'Joke!' said Carlier, hitching himself forward on his seat. 'I am hungry – I am sick – I don't joke! I hate hypocrites. You are a hypocrite. You are a slave-dealer. I am a slave-dealer. There's nothing but slave-dealers in this cursed country. I mean to have sugar in my coffee today, anyhow!'

'I forbid you to speak to me in that way,' said Kayerts with a fair show of resolution.

'You! – What?' shouted Carlier, jumping up.

Kayerts stood up also. 'I am your chief,' he began, trying to master the shakiness of his voice.

'What?' yelled the other. 'Who's chief? There's no chief here. There's nothing here: there's nothing but you and I. Fetch the sugar – you potbellied ass.'

'Hold your tongue. Go out of this room,' screamed Kayerts. 'I dismiss you – you scoundrel!'

Carlier swung a stool. All at once he looked dangerously in earnest. 'You flabby, good-for-nothing civilian – take that!' he howled.

Kayerts dropped under the table, and the stool struck the grass inner wall of the room. Then, as Carlier was trying to upset the table, Kayerts in desperation made a blind rush, head low, like a cornered pig would do, and over-turning his friend, bolted along the verandah, and into his room. He locked the door, snatched his revolver, and stood panting. In less than a minute Carlier was kicking at the door furiously, howling, 'If you don't bring out that sugar, I will shoot you at sight, like a dog. Now then – one – two – three. You won't? I will show you who's the master.'

Kayerts thought the door would fall in, and scrambled through the square hole that served for a window in his room. There was then the whole breadth of the house between them. But the other was apparently not strong enough to break in the door, and Kayerts heard him running round. Then he also began to run laboriously on his swollen legs. He ran as quickly as he could, grasping the revolver, and unable yet to understand what was happening to him. He saw in succession Makola's house, the store, the river, the ravine, and the low bushes; and he saw all those things again as he ran for the second time round the house. Then again they flashed past him. That morning he could not have walked a yard without a groan.

And now he ran. He ran fast enough to keep out of sight of the other man.

Then as, weak and desperate, he thought, 'Before I finish the next round I shall die,' he heard the other man stumble heavily, then stop. He stopped also. He had the back and Carlier the front of the house, as before. He heard him drop into a chair cursing, and suddenly his own legs gave way, and he slid down into a sitting posture with his back to the wall. His mouth was as dry as a cinder, and his face was wet with perspiration – and tears. What was it all about? He thought it must be a horrible illusion; he thought he was dreaming; he thought he was going mad! After a while he collected his senses. What did they quarrel about? That sugar! How absurd! He would give it to him – didn't want it himself. And he began scrambling to his feet with a sudden feeling of security. But before he had fairly stood upright, a common-sense reflection occurred to him and drove him back into despair. He thought: 'If I give way now to that brute of a soldier, he will begin this horror again to-morrow – and the day after – every day – raise other pretensions, trample on me, torture me, make me his slave – and I will be lost! Lost! The steamer may not come for days – may never come.' He shook so that he had to sit down on the floor again. He shivered forlornly. He felt he could not, would not move any more. He was completely distracted by the sudden perception that the position was without issue – that death and life had in a moment become equally difficult and terrible.

All at once he heard the other push his chair back; and he leaped to his feet with extreme facility. He listened and got confused. Must run again! Right or left? He heard footsteps. He darted to the left, grasping his revolver, and at the very same instant, as it seemed to him, they came into violent collision. Both shouted with surprise. A loud explosion took place between them; a roar of red fire, thick smoke; and Kayerts, deafened and blinded, rushed back thinking: 'I am hit – it's all over.' He expected the other to come round – to gloat over his agony. He caught hold of an upright of the roof – 'All over!' Then he heard a crashing fall on the other side of the house, as if somebody had tumbled headlong over a chair – then silence. Nothing more happened. He did not die. Only his shoulder felt as if it had been badly wrenched, and he had lost his revolver. He was disarmed and helpless! He waited for his fate. The other man made no sound. It was a stratagem. He was stalking him now! Along what side? Perhaps he was taking aim this very minute!

After a few moments of an agony frightful and absurd, he decided to go and meet his doom. He was prepared for every surrender. He turned the corner, steadying himself with one hand on the wall; made a few paces, and nearly swooned. He had seen on the floor, protruding past the other corner, a pair of turned-up feet. A pair of white naked feet in red slippers. He felt deadly sick, and stood for a time in profound darkness. Then Makola appeared before him, saying quietly: 'Come along, Mr Kayerts. He is dead.' He burst into tears of gratitude; a loud, sobbing fit of crying. After a time he found himself sitting in a chair and looking at Carlier, who lay stretched on his back. Makola was kneeling over the body.

'Is this your revolver?' asked Makola, getting up.

'Yes,' said Kayerts; then he added very quickly, 'He ran after me to shoot me – you saw!'

'Yes, I saw,' said Makola. 'There is only one revolver; where's his?'

'Don't know,' whispered Kayerts in a voice that had become suddenly very faint.

'I will go and look for it,' said the other, gently. He made the round along the verandah, while Kayerts sat still and looked at the corpse. Makola came back empty-handed, stood in deep thought, then stepped quietly into the dead man's room, and came out directly with a revolver, which he held up before Kayerts. Kayerts shut his eyes. Everything was going round. He found life more terrible and difficult than death. He had shot an unarmed man.

After meditating for a while, Makola said softly, pointing at the dead man who lay there with his right eye blown out –

'He died of fever.' Kayerts looked at him with a stony stare. 'Yes,' repeated Makola, thoughtfully, stepping over the corpse, 'I think he died of fever. Bury him to-morrow.'

And he went away slowly to his expectant wife, leaving the two white men alone on the verandah.

Night came, and Kayerts sat unmoving on his chair. He sat quiet as if he had taken a dose of opium. The violence of the emotions he had passed through produced a feeling of exhausted serenity. He had plumbed in one short afternoon the depths of horror and despair, and now found repose in the conviction that life had no more secrets for him: neither had death! He sat by the corpse thinking; thinking very actively, thinking very new thoughts. He seemed to have broken loose from himself altogether. His old thoughts, convictions, likes and dislikes, things he respected and things he abhorred, appeared in their true light at last! Appeared contemptible and childish, false and ridiculous. He revelled in his new wisdom while he sat by the man he had killed. He argued with himself about all things under heaven with that kind of wrong-headed lucidity which may be observed in some lunatics. Incidentally he reflected that the fellow dead there had been a noxious beast anyway; that men died every day in thousands; perhaps in hundreds of thousands – who could tell? – and that in the number, that one death could not possibly make any difference; couldn't have any importance, at least to a thinking creature. He, Kayerts, was a thinking creature. He had been all his life, till that moment, a believer in a lot of nonsense like the rest of mankind – who are fools; but now he thought! He knew! He was at peace; he was familiar with the highest wisdom! Then he tried to imagine himself dead, and Carlier sitting in his chair watching him; and his attempt met with such unexpected success, that in a very few moments he became not at all sure who was dead and who was alive. This extraordinary achievement of his fancy startled him, however, and by a clever and timely effort of mind he saved himself just in time from becoming Carlier. His heart thumped, and he felt hot all over at the thought of that danger. Carlier! What a beastly thing! To compose his now disturbed nerves – and no wonder! – he tried to whistle a little. Then, suddenly, he fell asleep, or thought he had slept; but at any rate there was a fog, and somebody had whistled in the fog.

He stood up. The day had come, and a heavy mist had descended upon the land: the mist penetrating, enveloping, and silent; the morning mist of tropical lands; the mist that clings and kills; the mist white and deadly, immaculate and poisonous. He stood up, saw the body, and threw his arms above his head with a cry like that of a man who, waking from a trance, finds himself immured forever in a tomb. 'Help!... My God!'

A shriek inhuman, vibrating and sudden, pierced like a sharp dart the white shroud of that land of sorrow. Three short, impatient screeches followed, and then, for a time, the fog-wreaths rolled on, undisturbed, through a formidable silence. Then many more shrieks, rapid and piercing, like the yells of some exasperated and ruthless creature, rent the air. Progress was calling to Kayerts from the river. Progress and civilization and all the virtues. Society was calling to its accomplished child to come, to be taken care of, to be instructed, to be judged, to be condemned; it called him to return to that rubbish heap from which he had wandered away, so that justice could be done.

Kayerts heard and understood. He stumbled out of the verandah, leaving the other man quite alone for the first time since they had been thrown there together. He groped his way through the fog, calling in his ignorance upon the invisible heaven to undo its work. Makola flitted by in the mist, shouting as he ran –

'Steamer! Steamer! They can't see. They whistle for the station. I go ring the bell. Go down to the landing, sir. I ring.'

He disappeared. Kayerts stood still. He looked upwards; the fog rolled low over his head. He looked round like a man who has lost his way; and he saw a dark smudge, a cross-shaped stain, upon the shifting purity of the mist. As he began to stumble towards it, the station bell rang in a tumultuous peal its answer to the impatient clamour of the steamer.

The Managing Director of the Great Civilizing Company (since we know that civilization follows trade) landed first, and incontinently lost sight of the steamer. The fog down by the river was exceedingly dense; above, at the station, the bell rang unceasing and brazen.

The Director shouted loudly to the steamer:

'There is nobody down to meet us; there may be something wrong, though they are ringing. You had better come, too!'

And he began to toil up the steep bank. The captain and the engine-driver of the boat followed behind. As they scrambled up the fog thinned, and they could see their Director a good way ahead. Suddenly they saw him start forward, calling to them over his shoulder: – 'Run! Run to the house! I've found one of them. Run, look for the other!'

He had found one of them! And even he, the man of varied and startling experience, was somewhat discomposed by the manner of this finding. He stood and fumbled in his pockets (for a knife) while he faced Kayerts, who was hanging by a leather strap from the cross. He had evidently climbed the grave, which was high and narrow, and after tying the end of the strap to the arm, had swung himself off. His toes were only a couple of inches above the ground; his arms hung stiffly down; he seemed to be standing rigidly at attention, but with one purple cheek playfully posed on the shoulder. And, irreverently, he was putting out a swollen tongue at his Managing Director.

THE RETURN

The inner circle train from the City rushed impetuously out of a black hole and pulled up with a discordant, grinding racket in the smirched twilight of a West-End station. A line of doors flew open and a lot of men stepped out headlong. They had high hats, healthy pale faces, dark overcoats and shiny boots; they held in their gloved hands thin umbrellas and hastily folded evening papers that resembled stiff, dirty rags of greenish, pinkish, or whitish colour. Alvan Hervey stepped out with the rest, a smouldering cigar between his teeth. A disregarded little woman in rusty black, with both arms full of parcels, ran along in distress, bolted suddenly into a third-class compartment and the train went on. The slamming of carriage doors burst out sharp and spiteful like a fusillade; an icy draught mingled with acrid fumes swept the whole length of the platform and made a tottering old man, wrapped up to his ears in a woollen comforter, stop short in the moving throng to cough violently over his stick. No one spared him a glance.

Alvan Hervey passed through the ticket gate. Between the bare walls of a sordid staircase men clambered rapidly; their backs appeared alike – almost as if they had been wearing a uniform; their indifferent faces were varied but somehow suggested kinship, like the faces of a band of brothers who through prudence, dignity, disgust, or foresight would resolutely ignore each other; and their eyes, quick or slow; their eyes gazing up the dusty steps; their eyes brown, black, grey, blue, had all the same stare, concentrated and empty, satisfied and unthinking.

Outside the big doorway of the street they scattered in all directions, walking away fast from one another with the hurried air of men fleeing from something compromising; from familiarity or confidences; from something suspected and concealed – like truth or pestilence. Alvan Hervey hesitated, standing alone in the doorway for a moment; then decided to walk home.

He strode firmly. A misty rain settled like silvery dust on clothes, on moustaches; wetted the faces, varnished the flagstones, darkened the walls, dripped from umbrellas. And he moved on in the rain with careless serenity, with the tranquil ease of someone successful and disdainful, very sure of himself – a man with lots of money and friends. He was tall, well set-up, good-looking and healthy; and his clear pale face had under its commonplace refinement that slight tinge of overbearing brutality which is given by the possession of only partly difficult accomplishments; by excelling in games, or in the art of making money; by the easy mastery over animals and over needy men.

He was going home much earlier than usual, straight from the City and without calling at his club. He considered himself well connected, well educated and intelligent. Who doesn't? But his connections, education and intelligence were strictly on a par with those of the men with whom he did business or amused himself. He had married five years ago. At the time all his acquaintances had said he was very much in love; and he had said so himself, frankly, because it is very well understood that every man falls in love once in his life – unless his wife dies, when it may be quite praiseworthy to fall in love again. The girl was healthy, tall, fair, and in his opinion was well connected, well educated and intelligent. She was also intensely bored with her home where, as if packed in a tight box, her individuality – of which she was very conscious – had no play. She strode like a grenadier, was strong and upright like an obelisk, had a beautiful face, a candid brow, pure eyes, and not a thought of her own in her head. He surrendered quickly to all those charms, and she appeared to him so unquestionably of the right sort that he did not hesitate for a moment to declare himself in love. Under the cover of that sacred and poetical fiction he desired her masterfully, for various reasons; but principally for the satisfaction of having his own way. He was very dull and solemn about it – for no earthly reason, unless to conceal his feelings – which is an eminently proper thing to do. Nobody, however, would have been shocked had he neglected that duty, for the feeling he experienced really was a longing – a longing stronger and a little more complex no doubt, but no more reprehensible in its nature than a hungry man's appetite for his dinner.

After their marriage they busied themselves, with marked success, in enlarging the circle of their acquaintance. Thirty people knew them by sight; twenty more with smiling demonstrations tolerated their occasional presence within hospitable thresholds; at least fifty others became aware of their existence. They moved in their enlarged world amongst perfectly delightful men and women who feared emotion, enthusiasm, or failure, more than fire, war, or mortal disease; who tolerated only the commonest formulas of commonest thoughts, and recognized only profitable facts. It was an extremely charming sphere, the abode of all the virtues, where nothing is realized and where all joys and sorrows are cautiously toned down into pleasures and annoyances. In that serene region, then, where noble sentiments are cultivated in sufficient profusion to conceal the pitiless materialism of thoughts and aspirations Alvan Hervey and his wife spent five years of prudent bliss unclouded by any doubt as to the moral propriety of their existence. She, to give her individuality fair play, took up all manner of philanthropic work and became a member of various rescuing and reforming societies patronized or presided over by ladies of title. He took an active interest in politics; and having met quite by chance a literary man – who nevertheless was related to an earl – he was induced to finance a moribund society paper. It was a semi-political, and wholly scandalous publication, redeemed by excessive dullness; and as it was utterly faithless, as it contained no new thought, as it never by any chance had a flash of wit, satire, or indignation in its pages, he judged it respectable enough, at first sight. Afterwards, when it paid, he promptly perceived that upon the whole it was a virtuous undertaking. It paved the way of his ambition; and he enjoyed also the special kind of importance he derived from this connection with what he imagined to be literature.

This connection still further enlarged their world. Men who wrote or drew prettily for the public came at times to their house, and his editor came very often. He thought him rather an ass because he had such big front teeth (the proper thing is to have small, even teeth) and wore his hair a trifle longer than most men do. However, some dukes wear their hair long, and the fellow indubitably knew his business. The worst was that his gravity, though perfectly portentous, could not be trusted. He sat, elegant and bulky, in the drawing-room, the head of his stick hovering in front of his big teeth, and talked for hours with a thick-lipped smile (he said nothing that could be considered objectionable and not quite the thing) talked in an unusual manner – not obviously – irritatingly. His forehead was too lofty – unusually so – and under it there was a straight nose, lost between the hairless cheeks, that in a smooth curve ran into a chin shaped like the end of a snow-shoe. And in this face that resembled the face of a fat and fiendishly knowing baby there glittered a pair of clever, peering, unbelieving black eyes. He wrote verses too. Rather an ass. But the band of men who trailed at the skirts of his monumental frock-coat seemed to perceive wonderful things in what he said. Alvan Hervey put it down to affectation. Those artist chaps, upon the whole, were so affected. Still, all this was highly proper – very useful to him – and his wife seemed to like it – as if she also had derived some distinct and secret advantage from this intellectual connection. She received her mixed and decorous guests with a kind of tall, ponderous grace, peculiarly her own and which awakened in the mind of intimidated strangers incongruous and improper reminiscences of an elephant, a giraffe, a gazelle; of a gothic tower – of an overgrown angel. Her Thursdays were becoming famous in their world; and their world grew steadily, annexing street after street. It included also Somebody's Gardens, a Crescent – a couple of Squares.

Thus Alvan Hervey and his wife for five prosperous years lived by the side of one another. In time they came to know each other sufficiently well for all the practical purposes of such an existence, but they were no more capable of real intimacy than two animals feeding at the same manger, under the same roof, in a luxurious stable. His longing was appeased and became a habit; and she had her desire – the desire to get away from under the paternal roof, to assert her individuality, to move in her own set (so much smarter than the parental one); to have a home of her own, and her own share of the world's respect, envy, and applause. They understood each other warily, tacitly, like a pair of cautious conspirators in a profitable plot; because they were both unable to look at a fact, a sentiment, a principle, or a belief otherwise than in the light of their own dignity, of their own glorification, of their own advantage. They skimmed over the surface of life hand in hand, in a pure and frosty atmosphere – like two skilful skaters cutting figures on thick ice for the admiration of the beholders, and disdainfully ignoring the hidden stream, the stream restless and dark; the stream of life, profound and unfrozen.

Alvan Hervey turned twice to the left, once to the right, walked along two sides of a square, in the middle of which groups of tame-looking trees stood in respectable captivity behind iron railings, and rang at his door. A parlour maid opened. A fad of his wife's, this, to have only women servants. That girl, while she took his hat and overcoat, said something which made him look at his watch. It was five o'clock, and his wife not at home. There was nothing unusual in that. He said, 'No; no tea,' and went upstairs.

He ascended without footfalls. Brass rods glimmered all up the red carpet. On the first-floor landing a marble woman, decently covered from neck to instep with stone draperies, advanced a row of lifeless toes to the edge of the pedestal, and thrust out blindly a rigid white arm holding a cluster of lights. He had artistic tastes – at home. Heavy curtains caught back, half concealed dark corners. On the rich, stamped paper of the walls hung sketches, water-colours, engravings. His tastes were distinctly artistic. Old church towers peeped above green masses of foliage; the hills were purple, the sands yellow, the seas sunny, the skies blue. A young lady sprawled with dreamy eyes in a moored boat, in company of a lunch basket, a champagne bottle, and an enamoured man in a blazer. Bare-legged boys flirted sweetly with ragged maidens, slept on stone steps, gambolled with dogs. A pathetically lean girl flattened against a blank wall, turned up expiring eyes and tendered a flower for sale; while, near by, the large photographs of some famous and mutilated bas-reliefs seemed to represent a massacre turned into stone.

He looked, of course, at nothing, ascended another flight of stairs and went straight into the dressing room. A bronze dragon nailed by the tail to a bracket writhed away from the wall in calm convolutions, and held, between the conventional fury of its jaws, a crude gas flame that resembled a butterfly. The room was empty, of course; but, as he stepped in, it became filled all at once with a stir of many people; because the strips of glass on the doors of wardrobes and his wife's large pier-glass reflected him from head to foot, and multiplied his image into a crowd of gentlemanly and slavish imitators, who were dressed exactly like himself; had the same restrained and rare gestures; who moved when he moved, stood still with him in an obsequious immobility, and had just such appearances of life and feeling as he thought it dignified and safe for any man to manifest. And like real people who are slaves of common thoughts, that are not even their own, they affected a shadowy independence by the superficial variety of their movements. They moved together with him; but they either advanced to meet him, or walked away from him; they appeared, disappeared; they seemed to dodge behind walnut furniture, to be seen again, far within the polished panes, stepping about distinct and unreal in the convincing illusion of a room. And like the men he respected they could be trusted to do nothing individual, original, or startling – nothing unforeseen and nothing improper.

He moved for a time aimlessly in that good company, humming a popular but refined tune, and thinking vaguely of a business letter from abroad, which had to be answered on the morrow with cautious prevarication. Then, as he walked towards a wardrobe, he saw appearing at his back, in the high mirror, the corner of his wife's dressing-table, and amongst the glitter of silver-mounted objects on it, the square white patch of an envelope. It was such an unusual thing to be seen there that he spun round almost before he realized his surprise; and all the sham men about him pivoted on their heels; all appeared surprised; and all moved rapidly towards envelopes on dressing-tables.

He recognized his wife's handwriting and saw that the envelope was addressed to himself. He muttered, 'How very odd,' and felt annoyed. Apart from any odd action being essentially an indecent thing in itself, the fact of his wife indulging in it made it doubly offensive. That she should write to him at all, when she knew he would be home for dinner, was perfectly ridiculous; but that she should leave it like this – in evidence for chance discovery – struck him as so outrageous that, thinking of it, he experienced suddenly a staggering sense of insecurity, an absurd and bizarre flash of a notion that the house had moved a little under his feet. He tore the envelope open, glanced at the letter, and sat down in a chair near by.

He held the paper before his eyes and looked at half a dozen lines scrawled on the page, while he was stunned by a noise meaningless and violent, like the clash of gongs or the beating of drums; a great aimless uproar that, in a manner, prevented him from hearing himself think and made his mind an absolute blank. This absurd and distracting tumult seemed to ooze out of the written words, to issue from between his very fingers that trembled, holding the paper. And suddenly he dropped the letter as though it had been something hot, or venomous, or filthy; and rushing to the window with the unreflecting precipitation of a man anxious to raise an alarm of fire or murder, he threw it up and put his head out.

A chill gust of wind, wandering through the damp and sooty obscurity over the waste of roofs and chimney-pots, touched his face with a clammy flick. He saw an illimitable darkness, in which stood a black jumble of walls, and, between them, the many rows of gaslights stretched far away in long lines, like strung-up beads of fire. A sinister loom as of a hidden conflagration lit up faintly from below the mist, falling upon a billowy and motionless sea of tiles and bricks. At the rattle of the opened window the world seemed to leap out of the night and confront him, while floating up to his ears there came a sound vast and faint; the deep mutter of something immense and alive. It penetrated him with a feeling of dismay and he gasped silently. From the cab-stand in the square came distinct hoarse voices and a jeering laugh which sounded ominously harsh and cruel. It sounded threatening. He drew his head in, as if before an aimed blow, and flung the window down quickly. He made a few steps, stumbled against a chair, and with a great effort, pulled himself together to lay hold of a certain thought that was whizzing about loose in his head.

He got it at last, after more exertion than he expected; he was flushed and puffed a little as though he had been catching it with his hands, but his mental hold on it was weak, so weak that he judged it necessary to repeat it aloud – to hear it spoken firmly – in order to insure a perfect measure of possession. But he was unwilling to hear his own voice – to hear any sound whatever – owing to a vague belief, shaping itself slowly within him, that solitude and silence are the greatest felicities of mankind. The next moment it dawned upon him that they are perfectly unattainable – that faces must be seen, words spoken, thoughts heard. All the words – all the thoughts!

He said very distinctly, and looking at the carpet, 'She's gone.'

It was terrible – not the fact but the words; the words charged with the shadowy might of a meaning, that seemed to possess the tremendous power to call Fate down upon the earth, like those strange and appalling words that sometimes are heard in sleep. They vibrated round him in a metallic atmosphere, in a space that had the hardness of iron and the resonance of a bell of bronze. Looking down between the toes of his boots he seemed to listen thoughtfully to the receding wave of sound; to the wave spreading out in a widening circle, embracing streets, roofs, church-steeples, fields – and travelling away, widening endlessly, far, very far, where he could not hear – where he could not imagine anything – where…

'And – with that… ass,' he said again without stirring in the least. And there was nothing but humiliation. Nothing else. He could derive no moral solace from any aspect of the situation, which radiated pain only on every side. Pain. What kind of pain? It occurred to him that he ought to be heart-broken; but in an exceedingly short moment he perceived that his suffering was nothing of so trifling and dignified a kind. It was altogether a more serious matter, and partook rather of the nature of those subtle and cruel feelings which are awakened by a kick or a horse-whipping.

He felt very sick – physically sick – as though he had bitten through something nauseous. Life, that to a well-ordered mind should be a matter of congratulation, appeared to him, for a second or so, perfectly intolerable. He picked up the paper at his feet, and sat down with the wish to think it out, to understand why his wife – his wife! – should leave him, should throw away respect, comfort, peace, decency, position throw away everything for nothing! He set himself to think out the hidden logic of her action – a mental undertaking fit for the leisure hours of a madhouse, though he couldn't see it. And he thought of his wife in every relation except the only fundamental one. He thought of her as a well-bred girl, as a wife, as a cultured person, as the mistress of a house, as a lady; but he never for a moment thought of her simply as a woman.

Then a fresh wave, a raging wave of humiliation, swept through his mind, and left nothing there but a personal sense of undeserved abasement. Why should he be mixed up with such a horrid exposure! It annihilated all the advantages of his well-ordered past, by a truth effective and unjust like a calumny – and the past was wasted. Its failure was disclosed – a distinct failure, on his part, to see, to guard, to understand. It could not be denied; it could not be explained away, hustled out of sight. He could not sit on it and look solemn. Now – if she had only died!

If she had only died! He was driven to envy such a respectable bereavement, and one so perfectly free from any taint of misfortune that even his best friend or his best enemy would not have felt the slightest thrill of exultation. No one would have cared. He sought comfort in clinging to the contemplation of the only fact of life that the resolute efforts of mankind had never failed to disguise in the clatter and glamour of phrases. And nothing lends itself more to lies than death. If she had only died! Certain words would have been said to him in a sad tone, and he, with proper fortitude, would have made appropriate answers. There were precedents for such an occasion. And no one would have cared. If she had only died! The promises, the terrors, the hopes of eternity, are the concern of the corrupt dead; but the obvious sweetness of life belongs to living, healthy men. And life was his concern: that sane and gratifying existence untroubled by too much love or by too much regret. She had interfered with it; she had defaced it. And suddenly it occurred to him he must have been mad to marry. It was too much in the nature of giving yourself away, of wearing – if for a moment – your heart on your sleeve. But every one married. Was all mankind mad!

In the shock of that startling thought he looked up, and saw to the left, to the right, in front, men sitting far off in chairs and looking at him with wild eyes – emissaries of a distracted mankind intruding to spy upon his pain and his humiliation. It was not to be borne. He rose quickly, and the others jumped up, too, on all sides. He stood still in the middle of the room as if discouraged by their vigilance. No escape! He felt something akin to despair. Everybody must know. The servants must know tonight. He ground his teeth… And he had never noticed, never guessed anything. Everyone will know. He thought: 'The woman's a monster, but everybody will think me a fool'; and standing still in the midst of severe walnut-wood furniture, he felt such a tempest of anguish within him that he seemed to see himself rolling on the carpet, beating his head against the wall. He was disgusted with himself, with the loathsome rush of emotion breaking through all the reserves that guarded his manhood. Something unknown, withering and poisonous, had entered his life, passed near him, touched him, and he was deteriorating. He was appalled. What was it? She was gone. Why? His head was ready to burst with the endeavour to understand her act and his subtle horror of it. Everything was changed. Why? Only a woman gone, after all; and yet he had a vision, a vision quick and distinct as a dream: the vision of everything he had thought indestructible and safe in the world crashing down about him, like solid walls do before the fierce breath of a hurricane. He stared, shaking in every limb, while he felt the destructive breath, the mysterious breath, the breath of passion, stir the profound peace of the house. He looked round in fear. Yes. Crime may be forgiven; uncalculating sacrifice, blind trust, burning faith, other follies, may be turned to account; suffering, death itself, may with a grin or a frown be explained away; but passion is the unpardonable and secret infamy of our hearts, a thing to curse, to hide and to deny; a shameless and forlorn thing that tramples upon the smiling promises, that tears off the placid mask, that strips the body of life. And it had come to him! It had laid its unclean hand upon the spotless draperies of his existence, and he had to face it alone with all the world looking on. All the world! And he thought that even the bare suspicion of such an adversary within his house carried with it a taint and a condemnation.

He put both his hands out as if to ward off the reproach of a defiling truth; and, instantly, the appalled conclave of unreal men, standing about mutely beyond the clear lustre of mirrors, made at him the same gesture of rejection and horror.

He glanced vainly here and there, like a man looking in desperation for a weapon or for a hiding place, and understood at last that he was disarmed and cornered by the enemy that, without any squeamishness, would strike so as to lay open his heart. He could get help nowhere, or even take counsel with himself, because in the sudden shock of her desertion the sentiments which he knew that in fidelity to his bringing up, to his prejudices and his surroundings, he ought to experience, were so mixed up with the novelty of real feelings, of fundamental feelings that know nothing of creed, class, or education, that he was unable to distinguish clearly between what is and what ought to be; between the inexcusable truth and the valid pretences. And he knew instinctively that truth would be of no use to him. Some kind of concealment seemed a necessity because one cannot explain. Of course not! Who would listen? One had simply to be without stain and without reproach to keep one's place in the forefront of life.

He said to himself, 'I must get over it the best I can,' and began to walk up and down the room. What next? What ought to be done? He thought: 'I will travel – no I won't. I shall face it out.' And after that resolve he was greatly cheered by the reflection that it would be a mute and an easy part to play, for no one would be likely to converse with him about the abominable conduct of – that woman. He argued to himself that decent people – and he knew no others – did not care to talk about such indelicate affairs. She had gone off – with that unhealthy, fat ass of a journalist. Why? He had been all a husband ought to be. He had given her a good position – she shared his prospects – he had treated her invariably with great consideration. He reviewed his conduct with a kind of dismal pride. It had been irreproachable. Then, why? For love? Profanation! There could be no love there. A shameful impulse of passion. Yes, passion. His own wife! Good God!... And the indelicate aspect of his domestic misfortune struck him with such shame that, next moment, he caught himself in the act of pondering absurdly over the notion whether it would not be more dignified for him to induce a general belief that he had been in the habit of beating his wife. Some fellows do... and anything would be better than the filthy fact; for it was clear he had lived with the root of it for five years – and it was too shameful. Anything! Anything! Brutality . . . But he gave it up directly, and began to think of the Divorce Court. It did not present itself to him, notwithstanding his respect for law and usage, as a proper refuge for dignified grief. It appeared rather as an unclean and sinister cavern where men and women are haled by adverse fate to writhe ridiculously in the presence of uncompromising truth. It should not be allowed. That woman! Five... years... married five years... and never to see anything. Not to the very last day... not till she coolly went off. And he pictured to himself all the people he knew engaged in speculating as to whether all that time he had been blind, foolish, or infatuated. What a woman! Blind!... Not at all. Could a clean-minded man imagine such depravity? Evidently not. He drew a free breath. That was the attitude to take; it was dignified enough; it gave him the advantage, and he could not help perceiving that it was moral. He yearned unaffectedly to see morality (in his person) triumphant before the world. As to her she would be forgotten. Let her be forgotten – buried in oblivion – lost! No one would allude... Refined people – and every man and woman he knew could be so described – had, of course, a horror of such topics. Had they? Oh, yes. No one would allude to her... in his hearing. He stamped his foot, tore the letter across, then again and again. The thought of sympathizing friends excited in him a fury of mistrust. He flung down the small bits of paper. They settled, fluttering at his feet, and looked very white on the dark carpet, like a scattered handful of snow-flakes.

This fit of hot anger was succeeded by a sudden sadness, by the darkening passage of a thought that ran over the scorched surface of his heart, like upon a barren plain, and after a fiercer assault of sunrays, the melancholy and cooling shadow of a cloud. He realized that he had had a shock – not a violent or rending blow, that can be seen, resisted, returned, forgotten, but a thrust, insidious and penetrating, that had stirred all those feelings, concealed and cruel, which the arts of the devil, the fears of mankind – God's infinite compassion, perhaps – keep chained deep down in the inscrutable twilight of our breasts. A dark curtain seemed to rise before him, and for less than a second he looked upon the mysterious universe of moral suffering. As a landscape is seen complete, and vast, and vivid, under a flash of lightning, so he could see disclosed in a moment all the immensity of pain that can be contained in one short moment of human thought. Then the curtain fell again, but his rapid vision left in Alvan Hervey's mind a trail of invincible sadness, a sense of loss and bitter solitude, as though he had been robbed and exiled. For a moment he ceased to be a member of society with a position, a career, and a name attached to all this, like a descriptive label of some complicated compound. He was a simple human being removed from the delightful world of crescents and squares. He stood alone, naked and afraid, like the first man on the first day of evil. There are in life events, contacts, glimpses, that seem brutally to bring all the past to a close. There is a shock and a crash, as of a gate flung to behind one by the perfidious hand of fate. Go and seek another paradise, fool or sage. There is a moment of dumb dismay, and the wanderings must begin again; the painful explaining away of facts, the feverish raking up of illusions, the cultivation of a fresh crop of lies in the sweat of one's brow, to sustain life, to make it supportable, to make it fair, so as to hand intact to another generation of blind wanderers the charming legend of a heartless country, of a promised land, all flowers and blessings…

He came to himself with a slight start, and became aware of an oppressive, crushing desolation. It was only a feeling, it is true, but it produced on him a physical effect, as though his chest had been squeezed in a vice. He perceived himself so extremely forlorn and lamentable, and was moved so deeply by the oppressive sorrow, that another turn of the screw, he felt, would bring tears out of his eyes. He was deteriorating. Five years of life in common had appeased his longing. Yes, long-time ago. The first five months did that – but… There was the habit – the habit of her person, of her smile, of her gestures, of her voice, of her silence. She had a pure brow and good hair. How utterly wretched all this was. Good hair and fine eyes – remarkably fine. He was surprised by the number of details that intruded upon his unwilling memory. He could not help remembering her footsteps, the rustle of her dress, her way of holding her head, her decisive manner of saying 'Alvan,' the quiver of her nostrils when she was annoyed. All that had been so much his property, so intimately and specially his! He raged in a mournful, silent way, as he took stock of his losses. He was like a man counting the cost of an unlucky speculation – irritated, depressed – exasperated with himself and with others, with the fortunate, with the indifferent, with the callous;

yet the wrong done him appeared so cruel that he would perhaps have dropped a tear over that spoliation if it had not been for his conviction that men do not weep. Foreigners do; they also kill sometimes in such circumstances. And to his horror he felt himself driven to regret almost that the usages of a society ready to forgive the shooting of a burglar forbade him, under the circumstances, even as much as a thought of murder. Nevertheless, he clenched his fists and set his teeth hard. And he was afraid at the same time. He was afraid with that penetrating faltering fear that seems, in the very middle of a beat, to turn one's heart into a handful of dust. The contamination of her crime spread out, tainted the universe, tainted himself; woke up all the dormant infamies of the world; caused a ghastly kind of clairvoyance in which he could see the towns and fields of the earth, its sacred places, its temples and its houses, peopled by monsters – by monsters of duplicity, lust, and murder. She was a monster – he himself was thinking monstrous thoughts... and yet he was like other people. How many men and women at this very moment were plunged in abominations – meditated crimes. It was frightful to think of. He remembered all the streets – the well-to-do streets he had passed on his way home; all the innumerable houses with closed doors and curtained windows. Each seemed now an abode of anguish and folly. And his thought, as if appalled, stood still, recalling with dismay the decorous and frightful silence that was like a conspiracy; the grim, impenetrable silence of miles of walls concealing passions, misery, thoughts of crime. Surely he was not the only man; his was not the only house... and yet no one knew – no one guessed. But he knew. He knew with unerring certitude that could not be deceived by the correct silence of walls, of closed doors, of curtained windows. He was beside himself with a despairing agitation, like a man informed of a deadly secret – the secret of a calamity threatening the safety of mankind – the sacredness, the peace of life.

He caught sight of himself in one of the looking-glasses. It was a relief. The anguish of his feeling had been so powerful that he more than half expected to see some distorted wild face there, and he was pleasantly surprised to see nothing of the kind. His aspect, at any rate, would let no one into the secret of his pain. He examined himself with attention. His trousers were turned up, and his boots a little muddy, but he looked very much as usual. Only his hair was slightly ruffled, and that disorder,

somehow, was so suggestive of trouble that he went quickly to the
table, and began to use the brushes, in an anxious desire to obliterate
the compromising trace, that only vestige of his emotion. He brushed
with care, watching the effect of his smoothing; and another face, slightly
pale and more tense than was perhaps desirable, peered back at him
from the toilet glass. He laid the brushes down, and was not satisfied.
He took them up again and brushed, brushed mechanically – forgot
himself in that occupation. The tumult of his thoughts ended in a sluggish
flow of reflection, such as, after the outburst of a volcano, the almost
imperceptible progress of a stream of lava, creeping languidly over a
convulsed land and pitilessly obliterating any landmark left by the shock
of the earthquake. It is a destructive but, by comparison, it is a peaceful
phenomenon. Alvan Hervey was almost soothed by the deliberate pace
of his thoughts. His moral landmarks were going one by one, consumed
in the fire of his experience, buried in hot mud, in ashes. He was cooling
– on the surface; but there was enough heat left somewhere to make him
slap the brushes on the table, and turning away, say in a fierce whisper: 'I
wish him joy… Damn the woman.'

He felt himself utterly corrupted by her wickedness, and the most
significant symptom of his moral downfall was the bitter, acrid satisfaction
with which he recognized it. He, deliberately, swore in his thoughts; he
meditated sneers; he shaped in profound silence words of cynical unbelief,
and his most cherished convictions stood revealed finally as the narrow
prejudices of fools. A crowd of shapeless, unclean thoughts crossed his
mind in a stealthy rush, like a band of veiled malefactors hastening to a
crime. He put his hands deep into his pockets. He heard a faint ringing
somewhere, and muttered to himself: 'I am not the only one… not the
only one.' There was another ring. Front door!

His heart leaped up into his throat, and forthwith descended as low as
his boots. A call! Who? Why? He wanted to rush out on the landing and
shout to the servant: 'Not at home! Gone away abroad!'… Any excuse.
He could not face a visitor. Not this evening. No. Tomorrow… Before
he could break out of the numbness that enveloped him like a sheet of
lead, he heard far below, as if in the entrails of the earth, a door close
heavily. The house vibrated to it more than to a clap of thunder. He stood
still, wishing himself invisible. The room was very chilly. He did not
think he would ever feel like that. But people must be met – they must be

faced – talked to – smiled at. He heard another door, much nearer – the door of the drawing-room – being opened and flung to again. He imagined for a moment he would faint. How absurd! That kind of thing had to be gone through. A voice spoke. He could not catch the words. Then the voice spoke again, and footsteps were heard on the first floor landing. Hang it all! Was he to hear that voice and those footsteps whenever any one spoke or moved? He thought: 'This is like being haunted – I suppose it will last for a week or so, at least. Till I forget. Forget! Forget!' Someone was coming up the second flight of stairs. Servant? He listened, then, suddenly, as though an incredible, frightful revelation had been shouted to him from a distance, he bellowed out in the empty room: 'What! What!' in such a fiendish tone as to astonish himself. The footsteps stopped outside the door. He stood open-mouthed, maddened and still, as if in the midst of a catastrophe. The door-handle rattled lightly. It seemed to him that the walls were coming apart, that the furniture swayed at him; the ceiling slanted queerly for a moment, a tall wardrobe tried to topple over. He caught hold of something and it was the back of a chair. So he had reeled against a chair! Oh! Confound it! He gripped hard.

The flaming butterfly poised between the jaws of the bronze dragon radiated a glare, a glare that seemed to leap up all at once into a crude, blinding fierceness, and made it difficult for him to distinguish plainly the figure of his wife standing upright with her back to the closed door. He looked at her and could not detect her breathing. The harsh and violent light was beating on her, and he was amazed to see her preserve so well the composure of her upright attitude in that scorching brilliance which, to his eyes, enveloped her like a hot and consuming mist. He would not have been surprised if she had vanished in it as suddenly as she had appeared. He stared and listened; listened for some sound, but the silence round him was absolute – as though he had in a moment grown completely deaf as well as dim-eyed. Then his hearing returned, preternaturally sharp. He heard the patter of a rain-shower on the window panes behind the lowered blinds, and below, far below, in the artificial abyss of the square, the deadened roll of wheels and the splashy trotting of a horse. He heard a groan also – very distinct – in the room – close to his ear.

He thought with alarm: 'I must have made that noise myself;' and at the same instant the woman left the door, stepped firmly across the floor before him, and sat down in a chair. He knew that step. There was no doubt about it. She had come back! And he very nearly said aloud 'Of course!' – such was his sudden and masterful perception of the indestructible character of her being. Nothing could destroy her – and nothing but his own destruction could keep her away. She was the incarnation of all the short moments which every man spares out of his life for dreams, for precious dreams that concrete the most cherished, the most profitable of his illusions. He peered at her with inward trepidation. She was mysterious, significant, full of obscure meaning – like a symbol. He peered, bending forward, as though he had been discovering about her things he had never seen before. Unconsciously he made a step towards her – then another. He saw her arm make an ample, decided movement and he stopped. She had lifted her veil. It was like the lifting of a visor.

The spell was broken. He experienced a shock as though he had been called out of a trance by the sudden noise of an explosion. It was even more startling and more distinct; it was an infinitely more intimate change, for he had the sensation of having come into this room only that very moment; of having returned from very far; he was made aware that some essential part of himself had in a flash returned into his body, returned finally from a fierce and lamentable region, from the dwelling-place of unveiled hearts. He woke up to an amazing infinity of contempt, to a droll bitterness of wonder, to a disenchanted conviction of safety. He had a glimpse of the irresistible force, and he saw also the barrenness of his convictions – of her convictions. It seemed to him that he could never make a mistake as long as he lived. It was morally impossible to go wrong. He was not elated by that certitude; he was dimly uneasy about its price; there was a chill as of death in this triumph of sound principles, in this victory snatched under the very shadow of disaster.

The last trace of his previous state of mind vanished, as the instantaneous and elusive trail of a bursting meteor vanishes on the profound blackness of the sky; it was the faint flicker of a painful thought, gone as soon as perceived, that nothing but her presence – after all – had the power to recall him to himself. He stared at her. She sat with her hands on her lap, looking down; and he noticed that her boots were dirty, her skirts wet and splashed, as though she had been driven back there by a blind fear through a waste of mud. He was indignant, amazed and shocked, but in a natural, healthy way now; so that he could control those unprofitable sentiments by the dictates of cautious self-restraint. The light in the room had no unusual brilliance now; it was a good light in which he could easily observe the expression of her face. It was that of dull fatigue. And the silence that surrounded them was the normal silence of any quiet house, hardly disturbed by the faint noises of a respectable quarter of the town. He was very cool – and it was quite coolly that he thought how much better it would be if neither of them ever spoke again. She sat with closed lips, with an air of lassitude in the stony forgetfulness of her pose, but after a moment she lifted her drooping eyelids and met his tense and inquisitive stare by a look that had all the formless eloquence of a cry. It penetrated, it stirred without informing; it was the very essence of anguish stripped of words that can be smiled at, argued away, shouted down, disdained. It was anguish naked and unashamed, the bare pain of existence let loose upon the world in the fleeting unreserve of a look that had in it an immensity of fatigue, the scornful sincerity, the black impudence of an extorted confession. Alvan Hervey was seized with wonder, as though he had seen something inconceivable; and some obscure part of his being was ready to exclaim with him: 'I would never have believed it!' but an instantaneous revulsion of wounded susceptibilities checked the unfinished thought.

He felt full of rancorous indignation against the woman who could look like this at one. This look probed him; it tampered with him. It was dangerous to one as would be a hint of unbelief whispered by a priest in the august decorum of a temple; and at the same time it was impure, it was disturbing, like a cynical consolation muttered in the dark, tainting the sorrow, corroding the thought, poisoning the heart. He wanted to ask her furiously: 'Who do you take me for? How dare you look at me like this?' He felt himself helpless before the hidden meaning of that look; he resented it with pained and futile violence as an injury so secret that it could never, never be redressed. His wish was to crush her by a single sentence. He was stainless. Opinion was on his side; morality, men and gods were on his side; law, conscience – all the world! She had nothing but that look. And he could only say:

'How long do you intend to stay here?'

Her eyes did not waver, her lips remained closed; and for any effect of his words he might have spoken to a dead woman, only that this one breathed quickly. He was profoundly disappointed by what he had said. It was a great deception, something in the nature of treason. He had deceived himself. It should have been altogether different – other words – another sensation. And before his eyes, so fixed that at times they saw nothing, she sat apparently as unconscious as though she had been alone, sending that look of brazen confession straight at him – with an air of staring into empty space. He said significantly:

'Must I go then?' And he knew he meant nothing of what he implied.

One of her hands on her lap moved slightly as though his words had fallen there and she had thrown them off on the floor. But her silence encouraged him. Possibly it meant remorse – perhaps fear. Was she thunderstruck by his attitude?... Her eyelids dropped. He seemed to understand ever so much – everything! Very well – but she must be made to suffer. It was due to him. He understood everything, yet he judged it indispensable to say with an obvious affectation of civility:

'I don't understand – be so good as to...'

She stood up. For a second he believed she intended to go away, and it was as though someone had jerked a string attached to his heart. It hurt. He remained open-mouthed and silent. But she made an irresolute step towards him, and instinctively he moved aside. They stood before one another, and the fragments of the torn letter lay between them – at their feet – like an insurmountable obstacle, like a sign of eternal separation! Around them three other couples stood still and face to face, as if waiting for a signal to begin some action – a struggle, a dispute, or a dance.

She said: 'Don't – Alvan!' and there was something that resembled a warning in the pain of her tone. He narrowed his eyes as if trying to pierce her with his gaze. Her voice touched him. He had aspirations after magnanimity, generosity, superiority – interrupted, however, by flashes of indignation and anxiety – frightful anxiety to know how far she had gone. She looked down at the torn paper. Then she looked up, and their eyes met again, remained fastened together, like an unbreakable bond, like a clasp of eternal complicity; and the decorous silence, the pervading quietude of the house which enveloped this meeting of their glances became for a moment inexpressibly vile, for he was afraid she would say too much and make magnanimity impossible, while behind the profound mournfulness of her face there was a regret – a regret of things done – the regret of delay – the thought that if she had only turned back a week sooner – a day sooner – only an hour sooner... They were afraid to hear again the sound of their voices; they did not know what they might say – perhaps something that could not be recalled; and words are more terrible than facts. But the tricky fatality that lurks in obscure impulses spoke through Alvan Hervey's lips suddenly; and he heard his own voice with the excited and sceptical curiosity with which one listens to actors' voices speaking on the stage in the strain of a poignant situation.

'If you have forgotten anything... of course... I...'

Her eyes blazed at him for an instant; her lips trembled – and then she also became the mouth-piece of the mysterious force forever hovering near us; of that perverse inspiration, wandering capricious and uncontrollable, like a gust of wind.

'What is the good of this, Alvan?... You know why I came back... You know that I could not...'

He interrupted her with irritation.

'Then! what's this?' he asked, pointing downwards at the torn letter.

'That's a mistake,' she said hurriedly, in a muffled voice.

This answer amazed him. He remained speechless, staring at her. He had half a mind to burst into a laugh. It ended in a smile as involuntary as a grimace of pain.

'A mistake...' he began, slowly, and then found himself unable to say another word.

'Yes... it was honest,' she said very low, as if speaking to the memory of a feeling in a remote past.

He exploded.

'Curse your honesty!... Is there any honesty in all this!... When did you begin to be honest? Why are you here? What are you now?... Still honest?...'

He walked at her, raging, as if blind; during these three quick strides he lost touch of the material world and was whirled interminably through a kind of empty universe made up of nothing but fury and anguish, till he came suddenly upon her face – very close to his. He stopped short, and all at once seemed to remember something heard ages ago.

'You don't know the meaning of the word,' he shouted.

She did not flinch. He perceived with fear that everything around him was still. She did not move a hair's breadth; his own body did not stir. An imperturbable calm enveloped their two motionless figures, the house, the town, all the world – and the trifling tempest of his feelings. The violence of the short tumult within him had been such as could well have shattered all creation; and yet nothing was changed. He faced his wife in the familiar room in his own house. It had not fallen. And right and left all the innumerable dwellings, standing shoulder to shoulder, had resisted the shock of his passion, had presented, unmoved, to the loneliness of his trouble, the grim silence of walls, the impenetrable and polished discretion of closed doors and curtained windows. Immobility and silence pressed on him, assailed him, like two accomplices of the immovable and mute woman before his eyes. He was suddenly vanquished. He was shown his impotence. He was soothed by the breath of a corrupt resignation coming to him through the subtle irony of the surrounding peace.

He said with villainous composure:

'At any rate it isn't enough for me. I want to know more – if you're going to stay.'

'There is nothing more to tell,' she answered, sadly.

It struck him as so very true that he did not say anything. She went on:

'You wouldn't understand…'

'No?' he said, quietly. He held himself tight not to burst into howls and imprecations.

'I tried to be faithful…' she began again.

'And this?' he exclaimed, pointing at the fragments of her letter.

'This – this is a failure,' she said.

'I should think so,' he muttered, bitterly.

'I tried to be faithful to myself – Alvan – and… and honest to you…'

'If you had tried to be faithful to me it would have been more to the purpose,' he interrupted, angrily. 'I've been faithful to you – and you have spoiled my life – both our lives…' Then after a pause the unconquerable preoccupation of self came out, and he raised his voice to ask resentfully, 'And, pray, for how long have you been making a fool of me?'

She seemed horribly shocked by that question. He did not wait for an answer, but went on moving about all the time; now and then coming up to her, then wandering off restlessly to the other end of the room.

'I want to know. Everybody knows, I suppose, but myself – and that's your honesty!'

'I have told you there is nothing to know,' she said, speaking unsteadily as if in pain. 'Nothing of what you suppose. You don't understand me. This letter is the beginning – and the end.'

'The end – this thing has no end,' he clamoured, unexpectedly. 'Can't you understand that? I can… The beginning…'

He stopped and looked into her eyes with concentrated intensity, with a desire to see, to penetrate, to understand, that made him positively hold his breath till he gasped.

'By Heavens!' he said, standing perfectly still in a peering attitude and within less than a foot from her.

'By Heavens!' he repeated, slowly, and in a tone whose involuntary strangeness was a complete mystery to himself. 'By Heavens – I could believe you – I could believe anything – now!'

He turned short on his heel and began to walk up and down the room with an air of having disburdened himself of the final pronouncement of his life – of having said something on which he would not go back, even if he could. She remained as if rooted to the carpet. Her eyes followed the restless movements of the man, who avoided looking at her. Her wide stare clung to him, inquiring, wondering and doubtful.

'But the fellow was forever sticking in here,' he burst out, distractedly. 'He made love to you, I suppose – and, and...' He lowered his voice. 'And – you let him.'

'And I let him,' she murmured, catching his intonation, so that her voice sounded unconscious, sounded far off and slavish, like an echo.

He said twice, 'You! You!' violently, then calmed down. 'What could you see in the fellow?' he asked, with unaffected wonder. 'An effeminate, fat ass. What could you... Weren't you happy? Didn't you have all you wanted? Now – frankly; did I deceive your expectations in any way? Were you disappointed with our position – or with our prospects – perhaps? You know you couldn't be – they are much better than you could hope for when you married me...'

He forgot himself so far as to gesticulate a little while he went on with animation:

'What could you expect from such a fellow? He's an outsider – a rank outsider... If it hadn't been for my money... do you hear?... for my money, he wouldn't know where to turn. His people won't have anything to do with him. The fellow's no class – no class at all. He's useful, certainly, that's why I... I thought you had enough intelligence to see it... And you... No! It's incredible! What did he tell you? Do you care for no one's opinion – is there no restraining influence in the world for you – women? Did you ever give me a thought? I tried to be a good husband. Did I fail? Tell me – what have I done?'

Carried away by his feelings he took his head in both his hands and repeated wildly:

'What have I done?… Tell me! What?…'

'Nothing,' she said.

'Ah! You see… you can't…' he began, triumphantly, walking away; then suddenly, as though he had been flung back at her by something invisible he had met, he spun round and shouted with exasperation:

'What on earth did you expect me to do?'

Without a word she moved slowly towards the table, and, sitting down, leaned on her elbow, shading her eyes with her hand. All that time he glared at her watchfully as if expecting every moment to find in her deliberate movements an answer to his question. But he could not read anything, he could gather no hint of her thought. He tried to suppress his desire to shout, and after waiting awhile, said with incisive scorn:

'Did you want me to write absurd verses; to sit and look at you for hours – to talk to you about your soul? You ought to have known I wasn't that sort… I had something better to do. But if you think I was totally blind…'

He perceived in a flash that he could remember an infinity of enlightening occurrences. He could recall ever so many distinct occasions when he came upon them; he remembered the absurdly interrupted gesture of his fat, white hand, the rapt expression of her face, the glitter of unbelieving eyes; snatches of incomprehensible conversations not worth listening to, silences that had meant nothing at the time and seemed now illuminating like a burst of sunshine. He remembered all that. He had not been blind. Oh! No! And to know this was an exquisite relief: it brought back all his composure.

'I thought it beneath me to suspect you,' he said, loftily.

The sound of that sentence evidently possessed some magical power, because, as soon as he had spoken, he felt wonderfully at ease; and directly afterwards he experienced a flash of joyful amazement at the discovery that he could be inspired to such noble and truthful utterance. He watched the effect of his words. They caused her to glance to him quickly over her shoulder. He caught a glimpse of wet eyelashes, of a red cheek with a tear running down swiftly; and then she turned away again and sat as before, covering her face with her hands.

'You ought to be perfectly frank with me,' he said, slowly.

'You know everything,' she answered, indistinctly, through her fingers.
'This letter... Yes... but...'

'And I came back,' she exclaimed in a stifled voice; 'you know everything.'

'I am glad of it – for your sake,' he said with impressive gravity. He listened to himself with solemn emotion. It seemed to him that something inexpressibly momentous was in progress within the room, that every word and every gesture had the importance of events preordained from the beginning of all things, and summing up in their finality the whole purpose of creation.

'For your sake,' he repeated.

Her shoulders shook as though she had been sobbing, and he forgot himself in the contemplation of her hair. Suddenly he gave a start, as if waking up, and asked very gently and not much above a whisper –

'Have you been meeting him often?'

'Never!' she cried into the palms of her hands.

This answer seemed for a moment to take from him the power of speech. His lips moved for some time before any sound came.

'You preferred to make love here – under my very nose,' he said, furiously. He calmed down instantly, and felt regretfully uneasy, as though he had let himself down in her estimation by that outburst. She rose, and with her hand on the back of the chair confronted him with eyes that were perfectly dry now. There was a red spot on each of her cheeks.

'When I made up my mind to go to him – I wrote,' she said.

'But you didn't go to him,' he took up in the same tone. 'How far did you go? What made you come back?'

'I didn't know myself,' she murmured. Nothing of her moved but her lips. He fixed her sternly.

'Did he expect this? Was he waiting for you?' he asked.

She answered him by an almost imperceptible nod, and he continued to look at her for a good while without making a sound. Then, at last –

'And I suppose he is waiting yet?' he asked, quickly.

Again she seemed to nod at him. For some reason he felt he must know the time. He consulted his watch gloomily. Half-past seven.

'Is he?' he muttered, putting the watch in his pocket. He looked up at her, and, as if suddenly overcome by a sense of sinister fun, gave a short, harsh laugh, directly repressed.

'No! It's the most unheard!…' he mumbled while she stood before him biting her lower lip, as if plunged in deep thought. He laughed again in one low burst that was as spiteful as an imprecation. He did not know why he felt such an overpowering and sudden distaste for the facts of existence – for facts in general – such an immense disgust at the thought of all the many days already lived through. He was wearied. Thinking seemed a labour beyond his strength. He said –

'You deceived me – now you make a fool of him… It's awful! Why?'

'I deceived myself!' she exclaimed.

'Oh! Nonsense!' he said, impatiently.

'I am ready to go if you wish it,' she went on, quickly. 'It was due to you – to be told – to know. No! I could not!' she cried, and stood still wringing her hands stealthily.

'I am glad you repented before it was too late,' he said in a dull tone and looking at his boots. 'I am glad… some spark of better feeling,' he muttered, as if to himself. He lifted up his head after a moment of brooding silence. 'I am glad to see that there is some sense of decency left in you,' he added a little louder. Looking at her he appeared to hesitate, as if estimating the possible consequences of what he wished to say, and at last blurted out –

'After all, I loved you…'

'I did not know,' she whispered.

'Good God!' he cried. 'Why do you imagine I married you?'

The indelicacy of his obtuseness angered her.

'Ah – why?' she said through her teeth.

He appeared overcome with horror, and watched her lips intently as though in fear.

'I imagined many things,' she said, slowly, and paused. He watched, holding his breath. At last she went on musingly, as if thinking aloud, 'I tried to understand. I tried honestly… Why?… To do the usual thing – I suppose… To please yourself.'

He walked away smartly, and when he came back, close to her, he had a flushed face.

'You seemed pretty well pleased, too – at the time,' he hissed, with scathing fury. 'I needn't ask whether you loved me.'

'I know now I was perfectly incapable of such a thing,' she said, calmly, 'If I had, perhaps you would not have married me.'

'It's very clear I would not have done it if I had known you – as I know you now.'

He seemed to see himself proposing to her – ages ago. They were strolling up the slope of a lawn. Groups of people were scattered in sunshine. The shadows of leafy boughs lay still on the short grass. The coloured sunshades far off, passing between trees, resembled deliberate and brilliant butterflies moving without a flutter. Men smiling amiably, or else very grave, within the impeccable shelter of their black coats, stood by the side of women who, clustered in clear summer toilettes, recalled all the fabulous tales of enchanted gardens where animated flowers smile at bewitched knights. There was a sumptuous serenity in it all, a thin, vibrating excitement, the perfect security, as of an invincible ignorance, that evoked within him a transcendent belief in felicity as the lot of all mankind, a recklessly picturesque desire to get promptly something for himself only, out of that splendour unmarred by any shadow of a thought. The girl walked by his side across an open space; no one was near, and suddenly he stood still, as if inspired, and spoke. He remembered looking at her pure eyes, at her candid brow; he remembered glancing about quickly to see if they were being observed, and thinking that nothing could go wrong in a world of so much charm, purity, and distinction. He was proud of it. He was one of its makers, of its possessors, of its guardians, of its extollers. He wanted to grasp it solidly, to get as much gratification as he could out of it; and in view of its incomparable quality, of its unstained atmosphere, of its nearness to the heaven of its choice, this gust of brutal desire seemed the most noble of aspirations. In a second he lived again through all these moments, and then all the pathos of his failure presented itself to him with such vividness that there was a suspicion of tears in his tone when he said almost unthinkingly, 'My God! I did love you!'

She seemed touched by the emotion of his voice. Her lips quivered a little, and she made one faltering step towards him, putting out her hands in a beseeching gesture, when she perceived, just in time, that being absorbed by the tragedy of his life he had absolutely forgotten her very existence. She stopped, and her outstretched arms fell slowly. He, with his features distorted by the bitterness of his thought, saw neither her movement nor her gesture. He stamped his foot in vexation, rubbed his head – then exploded.

'What the devil am I to do now?'

He was still again. She seemed to understand, and moved to the door firmly.

'It's very simple – I'm going,' she said aloud.

At the sound of her voice he gave a start of surprise, looked at her wildly, and asked in a piercing tone –

'You… Where? To him?'

'No – alone – goodbye.'

The door-handle rattled under her groping hand as though she had been trying to get out of some dark place.

'No – stay!' he cried.

She heard him faintly. He saw her shoulder touch the lintel of the door. She swayed as if dazed. There was less than a second of suspense while they both felt as if poised on the very edge of moral annihilation, ready to fall into some devouring nowhere. Then, almost simultaneously, he shouted, 'Come back!' and she let go the handle of the door. She turned round in peaceful desperation like one who deliberately has thrown away the last chance of life; and, for a moment, the room she faced appeared terrible, and dark, and safe – like a grave.

He said, very hoarse and abrupt: 'It can't end like this… Sit down;' and while she crossed the room again to the low-backed chair before the dressing-table, he opened the door and put his head out to look and listen. The house was quiet. He came back pacified, and asked –

'Do you speak the truth?'

She nodded.

'You have lived a lie, though,' he said, suspiciously.

'Ah! You made it so easy,' she answered.

'You reproach me – me!'

'How could I?' she said; 'I would have you no other – now.'

'What do you mean by…' he began, then checked himself, and without waiting for an answer went on, 'I won't ask any questions. Is this letter the worst of it?'

She had a nervous movement of her hands.

'I must have a plain answer,' he said, hotly.

'Then, no! The worst is my coming back.'

There followed a period of dead silence, during which they exchanged searching glances.

He said authoritatively –

'You don't know what you are saying. Your mind is unhinged. You are beside yourself, or you would not say such things. You can't control yourself. Even in your remorse...' He paused a moment, then said with a doctoral air: 'Self-restraint is everything in life, you know. It's happiness, it's dignity... it's everything.'

She was pulling nervously at her handkerchief while he went on watching anxiously to see the effect of his words. Nothing satisfactory happened. Only, as he began to speak again, she covered her face with both her hands.

'You see where the want of self-restraint leads to. Pain – humiliation – loss of respect – of friends, of everything that ennobles life, that... All kinds of horrors,' he concluded, abruptly.

She made no stir. He looked at her pensively for some time as though he had been concentrating the melancholy thoughts evoked by the sight of that abased woman. His eyes became fixed and dull. He was profoundly penetrated by the solemnity of the moment; he felt deeply the greatness of the occasion. And more than ever the walls of his house seemed to enclose the sacredness of ideals to which he was about to offer a magnificent sacrifice. He was the high priest of that temple, the severe guardian of formulas, of rites, of the pure ceremonial concealing the black doubts of life. And he was not alone. Other men, too – the best of them – kept watch and ward by the hearthstones that were the altars of that profitable persuasion. He understood confusedly that he was part of an immense and beneficent power, which had a reward ready for every discretion. He dwelt within the invincible wisdom of silence; he was protected by an indestructible faith that would last forever, that would withstand unshaken all the assaults – the loud execrations of apostates, and the secret weariness of its confessors! He was in league with a universe of untold advantages. He represented the moral strength of a beautiful reticence that could vanquish all the deplorable crudities of life – fear, disaster, sin – even death itself. It seemed to him he was on the point of sweeping triumphantly away all the illusory mysteries of existence. It was simplicity itself.

'I hope you see now the folly – the utter folly of wickedness,' he began in a dull, solemn manner. 'You must respect the conditions of your life or lose all it can give you. All! Everything!'

He waved his arm once, and three exact replicas of his face, of his clothes, of his dull severity, of his solemn grief, repeated the wide gesture that in its comprehensive sweep indicated an infinity of moral sweetness, embraced the walls, the hangings, the whole house, all the crowd of houses outside, all the flimsy and inscrutable graves of the living with their doors numbered like the doors of prison-cells, and as impenetrable as the granite of tombstones.

'Yes! Restraint, duty, fidelity – unswerving fidelity to what is expected of you. This – only this – secures the reward, the peace. Everything else we should labour to subdue – to destroy. It's misfortune; it's disease. It is terrible – terrible. We must not know anything about it – we needn't. It is our duty to ourselves – to others. You do not live all alone in the world – and if you have no respect for the dignity of life, others have. Life is a serious matter. If you don't conform to the highest standards you are no one – it's a kind of death. Didn't this occur to you? You've only to look round you to see the truth of what I am saying. Did you live without noticing anything, without understanding anything? From a child you had examples before your eyes – you could see daily the beauty, the blessings of morality, of principles...'

His voice rose and fell pompously in a strange chant. His eyes were still, his stare exalted and sullen; his face was set, was hard, was woodenly exulting over the grim inspiration that secretly possessed him, seethed within him, lifted him up into a stealthy frenzy of belief. Now and then he would stretch out his right arm over her head, as it were, and he spoke down at that sinner from a height, and with a sense of avenging virtue, with a profound and pure joy as though he could from his steep pinnacle see every weighty word strike and hurt like a punishing stone.

'Rigid principles – adherence to what is right,' he finished after a pause.

'What is right?' she said, distinctly, without uncovering her face.

'Your mind is diseased!' he cried, upright and austere. 'Such a question is rot – utter rot. Look round you – there's your answer, if you only care to see. Nothing that outrages the received beliefs can be right. Your conscience tells you that. They are the received beliefs because they are the best, the noblest, the only possible. They survive...'

He could not help noticing with pleasure the philosophic breadth of his view, but he could not pause to enjoy it, for his inspiration, the call of august truth, carried him on.

'You must respect the moral foundations of a society that has made you what you are. Be true to it. That's duty – that's honour – that's honesty.'

He felt a great glow within him, as though he had swallowed something hot. He made a step nearer. She sat up and looked at him with an ardour of expectation that stimulated his sense of the supreme importance of that moment. And as if forgetting himself he raised his voice very much.

"What's right?' you ask me. Think only. What would you have been if you had gone off with that infernal vagabond?…What would you have been?… You! My wife!…'

He caught sight of himself in the pier glass, drawn up to his full height, and with a face so white that his eyes, at the distance, resembled the black cavities in a skull. He saw himself as if about to launch imprecations, with arms uplifted above her bowed head. He was ashamed of that unseemly posture, and put his hands in his pockets hurriedly. She murmured faintly, as if to herself –

'Ah! What am I now?'

'As it happens you are still Mrs Alvan Hervey – uncommonly lucky for you, let me tell you,' he said in a conversational tone. He walked up to the furthest corner of the room, and, turning back, saw her sitting very upright, her hands clasped on her lap, and with a lost, unswerving gaze of her eyes which stared unwinking like the eyes of the blind, at the crude gas flame, blazing and still, between the jaws of the bronze dragon.

He came up quite close to her, and straddling his legs a little, stood looking down at her face for some time without taking his hands out of his pockets. He seemed to be turning over in his mind a heap of words, piecing his next speech out of an overpowering abundance of thoughts.

'You've tried me to the utmost,' he said at last; and as soon as he said these words he lost his moral footing, and felt himself swept away from his pinnacle by a flood of passionate resentment against the bungling creature that had come so near to spoiling his life. 'Yes; I've been tried more than any man ought to be,' he went on with righteous bitterness. 'It was unfair. What possessed you to?… What possessed you?…Write such a… After five years of perfect happiness! 'Pon my word, no one would believe… Didn't you feel you couldn't? Because you couldn't… it was impossible – you know. Wasn't it? Think. Wasn't it?'

'It was impossible,' she whispered, obediently.

This submissive assent given with such readiness did not soothe

him, did not elate him; it gave him, inexplicably, that sense of terror
we experience when in the midst of conditions we had learned to think
absolutely safe we discover all at once the presence of a near and
unsuspected danger. It was impossible, of course! He knew it. She knew
it. She confessed it. It was impossible! That man knew it, too – as well as
any one; couldn't help knowing it. And yet those two had been engaged
in a conspiracy against his peace – in a criminal enterprise for which
there could be no sanction of belief within themselves. There could
not be! There could not be! And yet how near to… With a short thrill
he saw himself an exiled forlorn figure in a realm of ungovernable, of
unrestrained folly. Nothing could be foreseen, foretold – guarded against.
And the sensation was intolerable, had something of the withering horror
that may be conceived as following upon the utter extinction of all hope.
In the flash of thought the dishonouring episode seemed to disengage
itself from everything actual, from earthly conditions, and even from
earthly suffering; it became purely a terrifying knowledge, an annihilating
knowledge of a blind and infernal force. Something desperate and vague,
a flicker of an insane desire to abase himself before the mysterious
impulses of evil, to ask for mercy in some way, passed through his mind;
and then came the idea, the persuasion, the certitude, that the evil must
be forgotten – must be resolutely ignored to make life possible; that the
knowledge must be kept out of mind, out of sight, like the knowledge
of certain death is kept out of the daily existence of men. He stiffened
himself inwardly for the effort, and next moment it appeared very easy,
amazingly feasible, if one only kept strictly to facts, gave one's mind to
their perplexities and not to their meaning. Becoming conscious of a long
silence, he cleared his throat warningly, and said in a steady voice –

'I am glad you feel this… uncommonly glad… you felt this in time.
For, don't you see…' Unexpectedly he hesitated.

'Yes… I see,' she murmured.

'Of course you would,' he said, looking at the carpet and speaking like
one who thinks of something else. He lifted his head. 'I cannot believe –
even after this – even after this – that you are altogether – altogether… other
than what I thought you. It seems impossible – to me.'

'And to me,' she breathed out.

'Now – yes,' he said, 'but this morning? And tomorrow?… This is
what…'

He started at the drift of his words and broke off abruptly. Every train of thought seemed to lead into the hopeless realm of ungovernable folly, to recall the knowledge and the terror of forces that must be ignored. He said rapidly –

'My position is very painful – difficult… I feel…'

He looked at her fixedly with a pained air, as though frightfully oppressed by a sudden inability to express his pent-up ideas.

'I am ready to go,' she said very low. 'I have forfeited everything… to learn… to learn…'

Her chin fell on her breast; her voice died out in a sigh. He made a slight gesture of impatient assent.

'Yes! Yes! It's all very well… of course. Forfeited – ah! Morally forfeited – only morally forfeited… if I am to believe you…'

She startled him by jumping up.

'Oh! I believe, I believe,' he said, hastily, and she sat down as suddenly as she had got up. He went on gloomily –

'I've suffered – I suffer now. You can't understand how much. So much that when you propose a parting I almost think… But no. There is duty. You've forgotten it; I never did. Before heaven, I never did. But in a horrid exposure like this the judgment of mankind goes astray – at least for a time. You see, you and I – at least I feel that – you and I are one before the world. It is as it should be. The world is right – in the main – or else it couldn't be – couldn't be – what it is. And we are part of it. We have our duty to – to our fellow beings who don't want to… to… er.'

He stammered. She looked up at him with wide eyes, and her lips were slightly parted. He went on mumbling.

'…Pain… Indignation… Sure to misunderstand. I've suffered enough. And if there has been nothing irreparable – as you assure me… then…'

'Alvan!' she cried.

'What?' he said, morosely. He gazed down at her for a moment with a sombre stare, as one looks at ruins, at the devastation of some natural disaster.

'Then,' he continued after a short pause, 'the best thing is… the best for us… for every one… Yes… least pain – most unselfish…' His voice faltered, and she heard only detached words. '…Duty… Burden… Ourselves… Silence.'

A moment of perfect stillness ensued.

'This is an appeal I am making to your conscience,' he said, suddenly, in an explanatory tone, 'not to add to the wretchedness of all this: to try loyally and help me to live it down somehow. Without any reservations – you know. Loyally! You can't deny I've been cruelly wronged and – after all – my affection deserves…' He paused with evident anxiety to hear her speak.

'I make no reservations,' she said, mournfully. 'How could I? I found myself out and came back to…' her eyes flashed scornfully for an instant '…to what – to what you propose. You see… I… I can be trusted… now.'

He listened to every word with profound attention, and when she ceased seemed to wait for more.

'Is that all you've got to say?' he asked.

She was startled by his tone, and said faintly –

'I spoke the truth. What more can I say?'

'Confound it! You might say something human,' he burst out. 'It isn't being truthful; it's being brazen – if you want to know. Not a word to show you feel your position, and – and mine. Not a single word of acknowledgment, or regret – or remorse… or… something.'

'Words!' she whispered in a tone that irritated him. He stamped his foot.

'This is awful!' he exclaimed. 'Words? Yes, words. Words mean something – yes – they do – for all this infernal affectation. They mean something to me – to everybody – to you. What the devil did you use to express those sentiments – sentiments – pah! – which made you forget me, duty, shame!' …He foamed at the mouth while she stared at him, appalled by this sudden fury. 'Did you two talk only with your eyes?' he spluttered savagely. She rose.

'I can't bear this,' she said, trembling from head to foot. 'I am going.'

They stood facing one another for a moment.

'Not you,' he said, with conscious roughness, and began to walk up and down the room. She remained very still with an air of listening anxiously to her own heart-beats, then sank down on the chair slowly, and sighed, as if giving up a task beyond her strength.

'You misunderstand everything I say,' he began quietly, 'but I prefer to think that – just now – you are not accountable for your actions.'

He stopped again before her. 'Your mind is unhinged,' he said, with unction. 'To go now would be adding crime – yes, crime – to folly. I'll have no scandal in my life, no matter what's the cost. And why? You are sure to misunderstand me – but I'll tell you. As a matter of duty. Yes. But you're sure to misunderstand me – recklessly. Women always do – they are too – too narrow-minded.'

He waited for a while, but she made no sound, didn't even look at him; he felt uneasy, painfully uneasy, like a man who suspects he is unreasonably mistrusted. To combat that exasperating sensation he recommenced talking very fast. The sound of his words excited his thoughts, and in the play of darting thoughts he had glimpses now and then of the inexpugnable rock of his convictions, towering in solitary grandeur above the unprofitable waste of errors and passions.

'For it is self-evident,' he went on with anxious vivacity, 'it is self-evident that, on the highest ground we haven't the right – no, we haven't the right to intrude our miseries upon those who – who naturally expect better things from us. Every one wishes his own life and the life around him to be beautiful and pure. Now, a scandal amongst people of our position is disastrous for the morality – a fatal influence – don't you see – upon the general tone of the class – very important – the most important, I verily believe, in – in the community. I feel this – profoundly. This is the broad view. In time you'll give me... when you become again the woman I loved – and trusted...'

He stopped short, as though unexpectedly suffocated, then in a completely changed voice said, 'For I did love and trust you' – and again was silent for a moment. She put her handkerchief to her eyes.

'You'll give me credit for – for – my motives. It's mainly loyalty to – to the larger conditions of our life – where you – you! of all women – failed. One doesn't usually talk like this – of course – but in this case you'll admit... And consider – the innocent suffer with the guilty. The world is pitiless in its judgments. Unfortunately there are always those in it who are only too eager to misunderstand. Before you and before my conscience I am guiltless, but any – any disclosure would impair my usefulness in the sphere – in the larger sphere in which I hope soon to... I believe you fully shared my views in that matter – I don't want to say any more... on – on that point – but, believe me, true unselfishness is to bear one's burdens in – in silence. The ideal must – must be preserved – for others, at least.

It's clear as daylight. If I've a – a loathsome sore, to gratuitously display it would be abominable – abominable! And often in life – in the highest conception of life – outspokenness in certain circumstances is nothing less than criminal. Temptation, you know, excuses no one. There is no such thing really if one looks steadily to one's welfare – which is grounded in duty. But there are the weak.'... His tone became ferocious for an instant... 'And there are the fools and the envious – especially for people in our position. I am guiltless of this terrible – terrible... estrangement; but if there has been nothing irreparable.'... Something gloomy, like a deep shadow passed over his face... 'Nothing irreparable – you see even now I am ready to trust you implicitly – then our duty is clear.'

He looked down. A change came over his expression and straightway from the outward impetus of his loquacity he passed into the dull contemplation of all the appeasing truths that, not without some wonder, he had so recently been able to discover within himself. During this profound and soothing communion with his innermost beliefs he remained staring at the carpet, with a portentously solemn face and with a dull vacuity of eyes that seemed to gaze into the blankness of an empty hole. Then, without stirring in the least, he continued:

'Yes. Perfectly clear. I've been tried to the utmost, and I can't pretend that, for a time, the old feelings – the old feelings are not...' He sighed... 'But I forgive you...'

She made a slight movement without uncovering her eyes. In his profound scrutiny of the carpet he noticed nothing. And there was silence, silence within and silence without, as though his words had stilled the beat and tremor of all the surrounding life, and the house had stood alone – the only dwelling upon a deserted earth.

He lifted his head and repeated solemnly:

'I forgive you... from a sense of duty – and in the hope...'

He heard a laugh, and it not only interrupted his words but also destroyed the peace of his self-absorption with the vile pain of a reality intruding upon the beauty of a dream. He couldn't understand whence the sound came. He could see, foreshortened, the tear-stained, dolorous face of the woman stretched out, and with her head thrown over the back of the seat. He thought the piercing noise was a delusion. But another shrill peal followed by a deep sob and succeeded by another shriek of mirth positively seemed to tear him out from where he stood. He bounded to the door. It was closed. He turned the key and thought: that's no good... 'Stop this!' he cried, and perceived with alarm that he could hardly hear his own voice in the midst of her screaming. He darted back with the idea of stifling that unbearable noise with his hands, but stood still distracted, finding himself as unable to touch her as though she had been on fire. He shouted, 'Enough of this!' like men shout in the tumult of a riot, with a red face and starting eyes; then, as if swept away before another burst of laughter, he disappeared in a flash out of three looking-glasses, vanished suddenly from before her. For a time the woman gasped and laughed at no one in the luminous stillness of the empty room.

He reappeared, striding at her, and with a tumbler of water in his hand. He stammered: 'Hysterics – Stop – They will hear – Drink this.' She laughed at the ceiling. 'Stop this!' he cried. 'Ah!'

He flung the water in her face, putting into the action all the secret brutality of his spite, yet still felt that it would have been perfectly excusable – in any one – to send the tumbler after the water. He restrained himself, but at the same time was so convinced nothing could stop the horror of those mad shrieks that, when the first sensation of relief came, it did not even occur to him to doubt the impression of having become suddenly deaf. When, next moment, he became sure that she was sitting up, and really very quiet, it was as though everything – men, things, sensations, had come to a rest. He was prepared to be grateful. He could not take his eyes off her, fearing, yet unwilling to admit, the possibility of her beginning again; for, the experience, however contemptuously he tried to think of it, had left the bewilderment of a mysterious terror. Her face was streaming with water and tears; there was a wisp of hair on her forehead, another stuck to her cheek; her hat was on one side, undecorously tilted; her soaked veil resembled a sordid rag festooning her forehead. There was an utter unreserve in her aspect, an abandonment of safeguards, that ugliness of truth which can only be kept out of daily life by unremitting care for appearances. He did not know why, looking at her, he thought suddenly of tomorrow, and why the thought called out a deep feeling of unutterable, discouraged weariness – a fear of facing the succession of days. Tomorrow! It was as far as yesterday. Ages elapsed between sunrises – sometimes. He scanned her features like one looks at a forgotten country. They were not distorted – he recognized landmarks, so to speak; but it was only a resemblance that he could see, not the woman of yesterday – or was it, perhaps, more than the woman of yesterday? Who could tell? Was it something new? A new expression – or a new shade of expression? or something deep – an old truth unveiled, a fundamental and hidden truth – some unnecessary, accursed certitude? He became aware that he was trembling very much, that he had an empty tumbler in his hand – that time was passing. Still looking at her with lingering mistrust he reached towards the table to put the glass down and was startled to feel it apparently go through the wood. He had missed the edge. The surprise, the slight jingling noise of the accident annoyed him beyond expression. He turned to her, irritated.

'What's the meaning of this?' he asked, grimly.

She passed her hand over her face and made an attempt to get up.

'You're not going to be absurd again,' he said. ''Pon my soul, I did not know you could forget yourself to that extent.' He didn't try to conceal his physical disgust, because he believed it to be a purely moral reprobation of every unreserve, of anything in the nature of a scene. 'I assure you – it was revolting,' he went on. He stared for a moment at her. 'Positively degrading,' he added with insistence.

She stood up quickly, as if moved by a spring, and tottered. He started forward instinctively. She caught hold of the back of the chair and steadied herself. This arrested him, and they faced each other wide-eyed, uncertain, and yet coming back slowly to the reality of things with relief and wonder, as though just awakened after tossing through a long night of fevered dreams.

'Pray, don't begin again,' he said, hurriedly, seeing her open her lips. 'I deserve some little consideration – and such unaccountable behaviour is painful to me. I expect better things… I have the right…'

She pressed both her hands to her temples.

'Oh, nonsense!' he said, sharply. 'You are perfectly capable of coming down to dinner. No one should even suspect; not even the servants. No one! No one!… I am sure you can.'

She dropped her arms; her face twitched. She looked straight into his eyes and seemed incapable of pronouncing a word. He frowned at her.

'I – wish – it,' he said, tyrannically. 'For your own sake also…' He meant to carry that point without any pity. Why didn't she speak? He feared passive resistance. She must… Make her come. His frown deepened, and he began to think of some effectual violence, when most unexpectedly she said in a firm voice, 'Yes, I can,' and clutched the chair-back again. He was relieved, and all at once her attitude ceased to interest him. The important thing was that their life would begin again with an every-day act – with something that could not be misunderstood, that, thank God, had no moral meaning, no perplexity – and yet was symbolic of their uninterrupted communion in the past – in all the future. That morning, at that table, they had breakfast together; and now they would dine. It was all over! What had happened between could be forgotten – must be forgotten, like things that can only happen once – death for instance.

'I will wait for you,' he said, going to the door. He had some difficulty with it, for he did not remember he had turned the key. He hated that delay, and his checked impatience to be gone out of the room made him feel quite ill as, with the consciousness of her presence behind his back, he fumbled at the lock. He managed it at last; then in the doorway he glanced over his shoulder to say, 'It's rather late – you know –' and saw her standing where he had left her, with a face white as alabaster and perfectly still, like a woman in a trance.

He was afraid she would keep him waiting, but without any breathing time, he hardly knew how, he found himself sitting at table with her. He had made up his mind to eat, to talk, to be natural. It seemed to him necessary that deception should begin at home. The servants must not know – must not suspect. This intense desire of secrecy; of secrecy dark, destroying, profound, discreet like a grave, possessed him with the strength of a hallucination – seemed to spread itself to inanimate objects that had been the daily companions of his life, affected with a taint of enmity every single thing within the faithful walls that would stand forever between the shamelessness of facts and the indignation of mankind. Even when – as it happened once or twice – both the servants left the room together he remained carefully natural, industriously hungry, laboriously at his ease, as though he had wanted to cheat the black oak sideboard, the heavy curtains, the stiff-backed chairs, into the belief of an unstained happiness. He was mistrustful of his wife's self-control, unwilling to look at her and reluctant to speak, for it seemed to him inconceivable that she should not betray herself by the slightest movement, by the very first word spoken. Then he thought the silence in the room was becoming dangerous, and so excessive as to produce the effect of an intolerable uproar. He wanted to end it, as one is anxious to interrupt an indiscreet confession; but with the memory of that laugh upstairs he dared not give her an occasion to open her lips. Presently he heard her voice pronouncing in a calm tone some unimportant remark. He detached his eyes from the centre of his plate and felt excited as if on the point of looking at a wonder. And nothing could be more wonderful than her composure. He was looking at the candid eyes, at the pure brow, at what he had seen every evening for years in that place; he listened to the voice that for five years he had heard every day. Perhaps she was a little pale – but a healthy pallor had always been for him one of her chief attractions. Perhaps her face was rigidly set – but that marmoreal impassiveness, that magnificent stolidity, as of a wonderful statue by some great sculptor working under the curse of the gods; that imposing, unthinking stillness of her features, had till then mirrored for him the tranquil dignity of a soul of which he had thought himself – as a matter of course – the inexpugnable possessor. Those were the outward signs of her difference from the ignoble herd that feels, suffers, fails, errs – but has no distinct value in the world except as a moral contrast to the prosperity of the elect. He had been proud of her appearance. It had the perfectly proper frankness of perfection – and now he was shocked to see it unchanged. She looked like this, spoke like this, exactly like this, a year ago, a month ago – only yesterday when she… What went on within made no difference. What did she think? What meant the pallor, the placid face, the candid brow, the pure eyes? What did she think during all these years? What did she think yesterday – today; what would she think to-morrow? He must find out… And yet how could he get to know? She had been false to him, to that man, to herself; she was ready to be false – for him. Always false. She looked lies, breathed lies, lived lies – would tell lies – always – to the end of life! And he would never know what she meant. Never! Never! No one could. Impossible to know.

He dropped his knife and fork, brusquely, as though by the virtue of a sudden illumination he had been made aware of poison in his plate, and became positive in his mind that he could never swallow another morsel of food as long as he lived. The dinner went on in a room that had been steadily growing, from some cause, hotter than a furnace. He had to drink. He drank time after time, and, at last, recollecting himself, was frightened at the quantity, till he perceived that what he had been drinking was water – out of two different wine glasses; and the discovered unconsciousness of his actions affected him painfully. He was disturbed to find himself in such an unhealthy state of mind. Excess of feeling – excess of feeling; and it was part of his creed that any excess of feeling was unhealthy – morally unprofitable; a taint on practical manhood. Her fault. Entirely her fault. Her sinful self-forgetfulness was contagious. It made him think thoughts he had never had before; thoughts disintegrating, tormenting, sapping to the very core of life – like mortal disease; thoughts that bred the fear of air, of sunshine, of men – like the whispered news of a pestilence.

The maids served without noise; and to avoid looking at his wife and looking within himself, he followed with his eyes first one and then the other without being able to distinguish between them. They moved silently about, without one being able to see by what means, for their skirts touched the carpet all round; they glided here and there, receded, approached, rigid in black and white, with precise gestures, and no life in their faces, like a pair of marionettes in mourning; and their air of wooden unconcern struck him as unnatural, suspicious, irremediably hostile. That such people's feelings or judgment could affect one in any way, had never occurred to him before. He understood they had no prospects, no principles – no refinement and no power. But now he had become so debased that he could not even attempt to disguise from himself his yearning to know the secret thoughts of his servants. Several times he looked up covertly at the faces of those girls. Impossible to know. They changed his plates and utterly ignored his existence. What impenetrable duplicity. Women – nothing but women round him. Impossible to know. He experienced that heart-probing, fiery sense of dangerous loneliness, which sometimes assails the courage of a solitary adventurer in an unexplored country. The sight of a man's face – he felt – of any man's face, would have been a profound relief. One would know then – something – could understand… He decided he must have men servants. He would engage a butler as soon as possible. And then the end of that dinner – which had seemed to have been going on for hours – the end came, taking him violently by surprise, as though he had expected in the natural course of events to sit at that table for ever and ever.

But upstairs in the drawing-room he became the victim of a restless fate, that would, on no account, permit him to sit down. She had sunk on a low easy-chair, and taking up from a small table at her elbow a fan with ivory leaves, shaded her face from the fire. The coals glowed without a flame; and upon the red glow the vertical bars of the grate stood out at her feet, black and curved, like the charred ribs of a consumed sacrifice. Far off, a lamp perched on a slim brass rod, burned under a wide shade of crimson silk: the centre, within the shadows of the large room, of a fiery twilight that had in the warm quality of its tint something delicate, refined and infernal. His soft footfalls and the subdued beat of the clock on the high mantel-piece answered each other regularly – as if time and himself, engaged in a measured contest, had been pacing together through the infernal delicacy of twilight towards a mysterious goal.

He walked from one end of the room to the other without a pause, like a traveller who, at night, hastens doggedly upon an interminable journey. Now and then he glanced at her. Impossible to know. The gross precision of that thought expressed to his practical mind something illimitable and infinitely profound, the all-embracing subtlety of a feeling, the eternal origin of his pain. This woman had accepted him, had abandoned him – had returned to him. And of all this he would never know the truth. Never. Not till death – not after – not on judgment day when all shall be disclosed, thoughts and deeds, rewards and punishments, but the secret of hearts alone shall return, forever unknown, to the Inscrutable Creator of good and evil, to the Master of doubts and impulses.

He stood still to look at her. Thrown back and with her face turned away from him, she did not stir – as if asleep. What did she think? What did she feel? And in the presence of her perfect stillness, in the breathless silence, he felt himself insignificant and powerless before her, like a prisoner in chains. The fury of his impotence called out sinister images, that faculty of tormenting vision, which in a moment of anguishing sense of wrong induces a man to mutter threats or make a menacing gesture in the solitude of an empty room. But the gust of passion passed at once, left him trembling a little, with the wondering, reflective fear of a man who has paused on the very verge of suicide. The serenity of truth and the peace of death can be only secured through a largeness of contempt embracing all the profitable servitudes of life. He found he did not want to know. Better not. It was all over. It was as if it hadn't been. And it was very necessary for both of them, it was morally right, that nobody should know.

He spoke suddenly, as if concluding a discussion.

'The best thing for us is to forget all this.'

She started a little and shut the fan with a click.

'Yes, forgive – and forget,' he repeated, as if to himself.

'I'll never forget,' she said in a vibrating voice. 'And I'll never forgive myself…'

'But I, who have nothing to reproach myself…' He began, making a step towards her. She jumped up.

'I did not come back for your forgiveness,' she exclaimed, passionately, as if clamouring against an unjust aspersion.

He only said 'oh!' and became silent. He could not understand this unprovoked aggressiveness of her attitude, and certainly was very far from thinking that an unpremeditated hint of something resembling emotion in the tone of his last words had caused that uncontrollable burst of sincerity. It completed his bewilderment, but he was not at all angry now. He was as if benumbed by the fascination of the incomprehensible. She stood before him, tall and indistinct, like a black phantom in the red twilight. At last poignantly uncertain as to what would happen if he opened his lips, he muttered:

'But if my love is strong enough…' and hesitated.

He heard something snap loudly in the fiery stillness. She had broken her fan. Two thin pieces of ivory fell, one after another, without a sound, on the thick carpet, and instinctively he stooped to pick them up. While he groped at her feet it occurred to him that the woman there had in her hands an indispensable gift which nothing else on earth could give; and when he stood up he was penetrated by an irresistible belief in an enigma, by the conviction that within his reach and passing away from him was the very secret of existence – its certitude, immaterial and precious! She moved to the door, and he followed at her elbow, casting about for a magic word that would make the enigma clear, that would compel the surrender of the gift. And there is no such word! The enigma is only made clear by sacrifice, and the gift of heaven is in the hands of every man. But they had lived in a world that abhors enigmas, and cares for no gifts but such as can be obtained in the street. She was nearing the door. He said hurriedly:

''Pon my word, I loved you – I love you now.'

She stopped for an almost imperceptible moment to give him an indignant glance, and then moved on. That feminine penetration – so clever and so tainted by the eternal instinct of self-defence, so ready to see an obvious evil in everything it cannot understand – filled her with bitter resentment against both the men who could offer to the spiritual and tragic strife of her feelings nothing but the coarseness of their abominable materialism. In her anger against her own ineffectual self-deception she found hate enough for them both. What did they want? What more did this one want? And as her husband faced her again, with his hand on the door-handle, she asked herself whether he was unpardonably stupid, or simply ignoble.

She said nervously, and very fast:

'You are deceiving yourself. You never loved me. You wanted a wife – some woman – any woman that would think, speak, and behave in a certain way – in a way you approved. You loved yourself.'

'You won't believe me?' he asked, slowly.

'If I had believed you loved me,' she began, passionately, then drew in a long breath; and during that pause he heard the steady beat of blood in his ears. 'If I had believed it… I would never have come back,' she finished, recklessly.

He stood looking down as though he had not heard. She waited. After a moment he opened the door, and, on the landing, the sightless woman of marble appeared, draped to the chin, thrusting blindly at them a cluster of lights.

He seemed to have forgotten himself in a meditation so deep that on the point of going out she stopped to look at him in surprise. While she had been speaking he had wandered on the track of the enigma, out of the world of senses into the region of feeling. What did it matter what she had done, what she had said, if through the pain of her acts and words he had obtained the word of the enigma! There can be no life without faith and love – faith in a human heart, love of a human being! That touch of grace, whose help once in life is the privilege of the most undeserving, flung open for him the portals of beyond, and in contemplating there the certitude immaterial and precious he forgot all the meaningless accidents of existence: the bliss of getting, the delight of enjoying; all the protean and enticing forms of the cupidity that rules a material world of foolish joys, of contemptible sorrows. Faith! – Love! – the undoubting, clear faith in the truth of a soul – the great tenderness, deep as the ocean, serene and eternal, like the infinite peace of space above the short tempests of the earth. It was what he had wanted all his life – but he understood it only then for the first time. It was through the pain of losing her that the knowledge had come. She had the gift! She had the gift! And in all the world she was the only human being that could surrender it to his immense desire. He made a step forward, putting his arms out, as if to take her to his breast, and, lifting his head, was met by such a look of blank consternation that his arms fell as though they had been struck down by a blow. She started away from him, stumbled over the threshold, and once on the landing turned, swift and crouching. The train of her gown swished as it flew round her feet. It was an undisguised panic. She panted, showing her teeth, and the hate of strength, the disdain of weakness, the eternal preoccupation of sex came out like a toy demon out of a box.

'This is odious,' she screamed.

He did not stir; but her look, her agitated movements, the sound of her voice were like a mist of facts thickening between him and the vision of love and faith. It vanished; and looking at that face triumphant and scornful, at that white face, stealthy and unexpected, as if discovered staring from an ambush, he was coming back slowly to the world of senses. His first clear thought was: I am married to that woman; and the next: she will give nothing but what I see. He felt the need not to see. But the memory of the vision, the memory that abides forever within the seer made him say to her with the naive austerity of a convert awed by the touch of a new creed, 'You haven't the gift.' He turned his back on her, leaving her completely mystified. And she went upstairs slowly, struggling with a distasteful suspicion of having been confronted by something more subtle than herself – more profound than the misunderstood and tragic contest of her feelings.

He shut the door of the drawing-room and moved at hazard, alone amongst the heavy shadows and in the fiery twilight as of an elegant place of perdition. She hadn't the gift – no one had... He stepped on a book that had fallen off one of the crowded little tables. He picked up the slender volume, and holding it, approached the crimson-shaded lamp. The fiery tint deepened on the cover, and contorted gold letters sprawling all over it in an intricate maze, came out, gleaming redly. 'Thorns and Arabesques.' He read it twice, 'Thorns and Ar...' The other's book of verses. He dropped it at his feet, but did not feel the slightest pang of jealousy or indignation. What did he know?... What?... The mass of hot coals tumbled down in the grate, and he turned to look at them... Ah! That one was ready to give up everything he had for that woman – who did not come – who had not the faith, the love, the courage to come. What did that man expect, what did he hope, what did he want? The woman – or the certitude immaterial and precious! The first unselfish thought he had ever given to any human being was for that man who had tried to do him a terrible wrong. He was not angry. He was saddened by an impersonal sorrow, by a vast melancholy as of all mankind longing for what cannot be attained. He felt his fellowship with every man – even with that man – especially with that man. What did he think now? Had he ceased to wait – and hope? Would he ever cease to wait and hope? Would he understand that the woman, who had no courage, had not the gift – had not the gift!

The clock began to strike, and the deep-toned vibration filled the room as though with the sound of an enormous bell tolling far away. He counted the strokes. Twelve. Another day had begun. Tomorrow had come; the mysterious and lying tomorrow that lures men, disdainful of love and faith, on and on through the poignant futilities of life to the fitting reward of a grave. He counted the strokes, and gazing at the grate seemed to wait for more. Then, as if called out, left the room, walking firmly.

When outside he heard footsteps in the hall and stood still. A bolt was shot – then another. They were locking up – shutting out his desire and his deception from the indignant criticism of a world full of noble gifts for those who proclaim themselves without stain and without reproach. He was safe; and on all sides of his dwelling servile fears and servile hopes slept, dreaming of success, behind the severe discretion of doors as impenetrable to the truth within as the granite of tombstones. A lock snapped – a short chain rattled. Nobody shall know!

Why was this assurance of safety heavier than a burden of fear, and why the day that began presented itself obstinately like the last day of all – like a today without a tomorrow? Yet nothing was changed, for nobody would know; and all would go on as before – the getting, the enjoying, the blessing of hunger that is appeased every day; the noble incentives of unappeasable ambitions. All – all the blessings of life. All – but the certitude immaterial and precious – the certitude of love and faith. He believed the shadow of it had been with him as long as he could remember; that invisible presence had ruled his life. And now the shadow had appeared and faded he could not extinguish his longing for the truth of its substance. His desire of it was naive; it was masterful like the material aspirations that are the groundwork of existence, but, unlike these, it was unconquerable. It was the subtle despotism of an idea that suffers no rivals, that is lonely, inconsolable, and dangerous. He went slowly up the stairs. Nobody shall know. The days would go on and he would go far – very far. If the idea could not be mastered, fortune could be, man could be – the whole world. He was dazzled by the greatness of the prospect; the brutality of a practical instinct shouted to him that only that which could be had was worth having. He lingered on the steps. The lights were out in the hall, and a small yellow flame flitted about down there. He felt a sudden contempt for himself which braced him up. He went on, but at the door of their room and with his arm advanced to open it, he faltered. On the flight of stairs below the head of the girl who had been locking up appeared. His arm fell. He thought, 'I'll wait till she is gone' – and stepped back within the perpendicular folds of a portière.

He saw her come up gradually, as if ascending from a well. At every step the feeble flame of the candle swayed before her tired, young face, and the darkness of the hall seemed to cling to her black skirt, followed her, rising like a silent flood, as though the great night of the world had broken through the discreet reserve of walls, of closed doors, of curtained windows. It rose over the steps, it leaped up the walls like an angry wave, it flowed over the blue skies, over the yellow sands, over the sunshine of landscapes, and over the pretty pathos of ragged innocence and of meek starvation. It swallowed up the delicious idyll in a boat and the mutilated immortality of famous bas-reliefs. It flowed from outside – it rose higher, in a destructive silence. And, above it, the woman of marble, composed and blind on the high pedestal, seemed to ward off the devouring night with a cluster of lights.

He watched the rising tide of impenetrable gloom with impatience, as if anxious for the coming of a darkness black enough to conceal a shameful surrender. It came nearer. The cluster of lights went out. The girl ascended facing him. Behind her the shadow of a colossal woman danced lightly on the wall. He held his breath while she passed by, noiseless and with heavy eyelids. And on her track the flowing tide of a tenebrous sea filled the house, seemed to swirl about his feet, and rising unchecked, closed silently above his head.

The time had come but he did not open the door. All was still; and instead of surrendering to the reasonable exigencies of life he stepped out, with a rebelling heart, into the darkness of the house. It was the abode of an impenetrable night; as though indeed the last day had come and gone, leaving him alone in a darkness that has no tomorrow. And looming vaguely below the woman of marble, livid and still like a patient phantom, held out in the night a cluster of extinguished lights.

His obedient thought traced for him the image of an uninterrupted life, the dignity and the advantages of an uninterrupted success; while his rebellious heart beat violently within his breast, as if maddened by the desire of a certitude immaterial and precious – the certitude of love and faith. What of the night within his dwelling if outside he could find the sunshine in which men sow, in which men reap! Nobody would know. The days, the years would pass, and… He remembered that he had loved her. The years would pass… And then he thought of her as we think of the dead – in a tender immensity of regret, in a passionate longing for the return of idealized perfections. He had loved her – he had loved her – and he never knew the truth… The years would pass in the anguish of doubt… He remembered her smile, her eyes, her voice, her silence, as though he had lost her forever. The years would pass and he would always mistrust her smile, suspect her eyes; he would always misbelieve her voice, he would never have faith in her silence. She had no gift – she had no gift! What was she? Who was she?… The years would pass; the memory of this hour would grow faint – and she would share the material serenity of an unblemished life. She had no love and no faith for any one. To give her your thought, your belief, was like whispering your confession over the edge of the world. Nothing came back – not even an echo.

In the pain of that thought was born his conscience; not that fear of remorse which grows slowly, and slowly decays amongst the complicated facts of life, but a Divine wisdom springing full-grown, armed and severe out of a tried heart, to combat the secret baseness of motives. It came to him in a flash that morality is not a method of happiness. The revelation was terrible. He saw at once that nothing of what he knew mattered in the least. The acts of men and women, success, humiliation, dignity, failure – nothing mattered. It was not a question of more or less pain, of this joy, of that sorrow. It was a question of truth or falsehood – it was a question of life or death.

He stood in the revealing night – in the darkness that tries the hearts, in the night useless for the work of men, but in which their gaze, undazzled by the sunshine of covetous days, wanders sometimes as far as the stars.

The perfect stillness around him had something solemn in it, but he felt it was the lying solemnity of a temple devoted to the rites of a debasing persuasion. The silence within the discreet walls was eloquent of safety but it appeared to him exciting and sinister, like the discretion of a profitable infamy; it was the prudent peace of a den of coiners – of a house of ill-fame! The years would pass – and nobody would know. Never! Not till death – not after…

'Never!' he said aloud to the revealing night.

And he hesitated. The secret of hearts, too terrible for the timid eyes of men, shall return, veiled forever, to the Inscrutable Creator of good and evil, to the Master of doubts and impulses. His conscience was born – he heard its voice, and he hesitated, ignoring the strength within, the fateful power, the secret of his heart! It was an awful sacrifice to cast all one's life into the flame of a new belief. He wanted help against himself, against the cruel decree of salvation. The need of tacit complicity, where it had never failed him, the habit of years affirmed itself. Perhaps she would help… He flung the door open and rushed in like a fugitive.

He was in the middle of the room before he could see anything but the dazzling brilliance of the light; and then, as if detached and floating in it on the level of his eyes, appeared the head of a woman. She had jumped up when he burst into the room.

For a moment they contemplated each other as if struck dumb with amazement. Her hair streaming on her shoulders glinted like burnished gold. He looked into the unfathomable candour of her eyes. Nothing within – nothing – nothing.

He stammered distractedly.

'I want…I want… to… to… know…'

On the candid light of the eyes flitted shadows; shadows of doubt, of suspicion, the ready suspicion of an unquenchable antagonism, the pitiless mistrust of an eternal instinct of defence; the hate, the profound, frightened hate of an incomprehensible – of an abominable emotion intruding its coarse materialism upon the spiritual and tragic contest of her feelings.

'Alvan… I won't bear this…' She began to pant suddenly, 'I've a right – a right to – to – myself…'

He lifted one arm, and appeared so menacing that she stopped in a fright and shrank back a little.

He stood with uplifted hand… The years would pass – and he would have to live with that unfathomable candour where flit shadows of suspicions and hate… The years would pass – and he would never know – never trust… The years would pass without faith and love…

'Can you stand it?' he shouted, as though she could have heard all his thoughts.

He looked menacing. She thought of violence, of danger – and, just for an instant, she doubted whether there were splendours enough on earth to pay the price of such a brutal experience. He cried again:

'Can you stand it?' and glared as if insane. Her eyes blazed, too. She could not hear the appalling clamour of his thoughts. She suspected in him a sudden regret, a fresh fit of jealousy, a dishonest desire of evasion. She shouted back angrily –

'Yes!'

He was shaken where he stood as if by a struggle to break out of invisible bonds. She trembled from head to foot.

'Well, I can't!' He flung both his arms out, as if to push her away, and strode from the room. The door swung to with a click. She made three quick steps towards it and stood still, looking at the white and gold panels. No sound came from beyond, not a whisper, not a sigh; not even a footstep was heard outside on the thick carpet. It was as though no sooner gone he had suddenly expired – as though he had died there and his body had vanished on the instant together with his soul. She listened, with parted lips and irresolute eyes. Then below, far below her, as if in the entrails of the earth, a door slammed heavily; and the quiet house vibrated to it from roof to foundations, more than to a clap of thunder.

He never returned.

THE LAGOON

The white man, leaning with both arms over the roof of the little house in the stern of the boat, said to the steersman –

'We will pass the night in Arsat's clearing. It is late.'

The Malay only grunted, and went on looking fixedly at the river. The white man rested his chin on his crossed arms and gazed at the wake of the boat. At the end of the straight avenue of forests cut by the intense glitter of the river, the sun appeared unclouded and dazzling, poised low over the water that shone smoothly like a band of metal. The forests, sombre and dull, stood motionless and silent on each side of the broad stream. At the foot of big, towering trees, trunkless nipa palms rose from the mud of the bank, in bunches of leaves enormous and heavy, that hung unstirring over the brown swirl of eddies. In the stillness of the air every tree, every leaf, every bough, every tendril of creeper and every petal of minute blossoms seemed to have been bewitched into an immobility perfect and final. Nothing moved on the river but the eight paddles that rose flashing regularly, dipped together with a single splash; while the steersman swept right and left with a periodic and sudden flourish of his blade describing a glinting semicircle above his head. The churned-up water frothed alongside with a confused murmur. And the white man's canoe, advancing upstream in the short-lived disturbance of its own making, seemed to enter the portals of a land from which the very memory of motion had forever departed.

The white man, turning his back upon the setting sun, looked along the empty and broad expanse of the sea-reach. For the last three miles of its course the wandering, hesitating river, as if enticed irresistibly by the freedom of an open horizon, flows straight into the sea, flows straight to the east – to the east that harbours both light and darkness. Astern of the boat the repeated call of some bird, a cry discordant and feeble, skipped along over the smooth water and lost itself, before it could reach the other shore, in the breathless silence of the world.

The steersman dug his paddle into the stream, and held hard with stiffened arms, his body thrown forward. The water gurgled aloud; and suddenly the long straight reach seemed to pivot on its centre, the forests swung in a semicircle, and the slanting beams of sunset touched the broadside of the canoe with a fiery glow, throwing the slender and distorted shadows of its crew upon the streaked glitter of the river. The white man turned to look ahead. The course of the boat had been altered at right-angles to the stream, and the carved dragon-head of its prow was pointing now at a gap in the fringing bushes of the bank. It glided through, brushing the overhanging twigs, and disappeared from the river like some slim and amphibious creature leaving the water for its lair in the forests.

The narrow creek was like a ditch: tortuous, fabulously deep; filled with gloom under the thin strip of pure and shining blue of the heaven. Immense trees soared up, invisible behind the festooned draperies of creepers. Here and there, near the glistening blackness of the water, a twisted root of some tall tree showed amongst the tracery of small ferns, black and dull, writhing and motionless, like an arrested snake. The short words of the paddlers reverberated loudly between the thick and sombre walls of vegetation. Darkness oozed out from between the trees, through the tangled maze of the creepers, from behind the great fantastic and unstirring leaves; the darkness mysterious and invincible; the darkness scented and poisonous of impenetrable forests.

The men poled in the shoaling water. The creek broadened, opening out into a wide sweep of a stagnant lagoon. The forests receded from the marshy bank, leaving a level strip of bright green, reedy grass to frame the reflected blueness of the sky. A fleecy pink cloud drifted high above, trailing the delicate colouring of its image under the floating leaves and the silvery blossoms of the lotus. A little house, perched on high piles, appeared black in the distance. Near it, two tall nibong palms, that seemed to have come out of the forests in the background, leaned slightly over the ragged roof, with a suggestion of sad tenderness and care in the droop of their leafy and soaring heads.

The steersman, pointing with his paddle, said, 'Arsat is there. I see his canoe fast between the piles.'

The polers ran along the sides of the boat glancing over their shoulders at the end of the day's journey. They would have preferred to spend the night somewhere else than on this lagoon of weird aspect and ghostly reputation. Moreover, they disliked Arsat, first as a stranger, and also because he who repairs a ruined house, and dwells in it, proclaims that he is not afraid to live amongst the spirits that haunt the places abandoned by mankind. Such a man can disturb the course of fate by glances or words;

while his familiar ghosts are not easy to propitiate by casual wayfarers upon whom they long to wreak the malice of their human master. White men care not for such things, being unbelievers and in league with the Father of Evil, who leads them unharmed through the invisible dangers of this world. To the warnings of the righteous they oppose an offensive pretence of disbelief. What is there to be done?

So they thought, throwing their weight on the end of their long poles. The big canoe glided on swiftly, noiselessly, and smoothly, towards Arsat's clearing, till, in a great rattling of poles thrown down, and the loud murmurs of 'Allah be praised!' it came with a gentle knock against the crooked piles below the house.

The boatmen with uplifted faces shouted discordantly, 'Arsat! O Arsat!' Nobody came. The white man began to climb the rude ladder giving access to the bamboo platform before the house. The juragan of the boat said sulkily, 'We will cook in the sampan, and sleep on the water.'

'Pass my blankets and the basket,' said the white man, curtly.

He knelt on the edge of the platform to receive the bundle. Then the boat shoved off, and the white man, standing up, confronted Arsat, who had come out through the low door of his hut. He was a man young, powerful, with broad chest and muscular arms. He had nothing on but his sarong. His head was bare. His big, soft eyes stared eagerly at the white man, but his voice and demeanour were composed as he asked, without any words of greeting –

'Have you medicine, Tuan?'

'No,' said the visitor in a startled tone. 'No. Why? Is there sickness in the house?'

'Enter and see,' replied Arsat, in the same calm manner, and turning short round, passed again through the small doorway. The white man, dropping his bundles, followed.

In the dim light of the dwelling he made out on a couch of bamboos a woman stretched on her back under a broad sheet of red cotton cloth. She lay still, as if dead; but her big eyes, wide open, glittered in the gloom, staring upwards at the slender rafters, motionless and unseeing. She was in a high fever, and evidently unconscious. Her cheeks were sunk slightly, her lips were partly open, and on the young face there was the ominous and fixed expression – the absorbed, contemplating expression of the unconscious who are going to die. The two men stood looking down at her in silence.

'Has she been long ill?' asked the traveller.

'I have not slept for five nights,' answered the Malay, in a deliberate tone. 'At first she heard voices calling her from the water and struggled against me who held her. But since the sun of today rose she hears nothing – she hears not me. She sees nothing. She sees not me – me!'

He remained silent for a minute, then asked softly –

'Tuan, will she die?'

'I fear so,' said the white man, sorrowfully. He had known Arsat years ago, in a far country in times of trouble and danger, when no friendship is to be despised. And since his Malay friend had come unexpectedly to dwell in the hut on the lagoon with a strange woman, he had slept many times there, in his journeys up and down the river. He liked the man who knew how to keep faith in council and how to fight without fear by the side of his white friend. He liked him – not so much perhaps as a man likes his favourite dog – but still he liked him well enough to help and ask no questions, to think sometimes vaguely and hazily in the midst of his own pursuits, about the lonely man and the long-haired woman with audacious face and triumphant eyes, who lived together hidden by the forests – alone and feared.

The white man came out of the hut in time to see the enormous conflagration of sunset put out by the swift and stealthy shadows that, rising like a black and impalpable vapour above the tree-tops, spread over the heaven, extinguishing the crimson glow of floating clouds and the red brilliance of departing daylight. In a few moments all the stars came out above the intense blackness of the earth and the great lagoon gleaming suddenly with reflected lights resembled an oval patch of night sky flung down into the hopeless and abysmal night of the wilderness. The white man had some supper out of the basket, then collecting a few sticks that lay about the platform, made up a small fire, not for warmth, but for the sake of the smoke, which would keep off the mosquitoes. He wrapped himself in the blankets and sat with his back against the reed wall of the house, smoking thoughtfully.

Arsat came through the doorway with noiseless steps and squatted down by the fire. The white man moved his outstretched legs a little.

'She breathes,' said Arsat in a low voice, anticipating the expected question. 'She breathes and burns as if with a great fire. She speaks not; she hears not – and burns!'

He paused for a moment, then asked in a quiet, incurious tone –

'Tuan… will she die?'

The white man moved his shoulders uneasily and muttered in a hesitating manner –

'If such is her fate.'

'No, Tuan,' said Arsat, calmly. 'If such is my fate. I hear, I see, I wait. I remember… Tuan, do you remember the old days? Do you remember my brother?'

'Yes,' said the white man. The Malay rose suddenly and went in. The other, sitting still outside, could hear the voice in the hut. Arsat said: 'Hear me! Speak!' His words were succeeded by a complete silence. 'O Diamelen!' he cried, suddenly. After that cry there was a deep sigh. Arsat came out and sank down again in his old place.

They sat in silence before the fire. There was no sound within the house, there was no sound near them; but far away on the lagoon they could hear the voices of the boatmen ringing fitful and distinct on the calm water. The fire in the bows of the sampan shone faintly in the distance with a hazy red glow. Then it died out. The voices ceased. The land and the water slept invisible, unstirring and mute. It was as though there had been nothing left in the world but the glitter of stars streaming, ceaseless and vain, through the black stillness of the night.

The white man gazed straight before him into the darkness with wide-open eyes. The fear and fascination, the inspiration and the wonder of death – of death near, unavoidable, and unseen, soothed the unrest of his race and stirred the most indistinct, the most intimate of his thoughts. The ever-ready suspicion of evil, the gnawing suspicion that lurks in our hearts, flowed out into the stillness round him – into the stillness profound and dumb, and made it appear untrustworthy and infamous, like the placid and impenetrable mask of an unjustifiable violence. In that fleeting and powerful disturbance of his being, the earth enfolded in the starlight peace became a shadowy country of inhuman strife, a battle-field of phantoms terrible and charming, august or ignoble, struggling ardently for the possession of our helpless hearts. An unquiet and mysterious country of inextinguishable desires and fears.

A plaintive murmur rose in the night; a murmur saddening and startling, as if the great solitudes of surrounding woods had tried to whisper into his ear the wisdom of their immense and lofty indifference. Sounds hesitating and vague floated in the air round him, shaped themselves slowly into words; and at last flowed on gently in a murmuring stream of soft and monotonous sentences. He stirred like a man waking up and changed his position slightly. Arsat, motionless and shadowy, sitting with bowed head under the stars, was speaking in a low and dreamy tone –

'...for where can we lay down the heaviness of our trouble but in a friend's heart? A man must speak of war and of love. You, Tuan, know what war is, and you have seen me in time of danger seek death as other men seek life! A writing may be lost; a lie may be written; but what the eye has seen is truth and remains in the mind!'

'I remember,' said the white man, quietly. Arsat went on with mournful composure –

'Therefore I shall speak to you of love. Speak in the night. Speak before both night and love are gone – and the eye of day looks upon my sorrow and my shame; upon my blackened face; upon my burnt-up heart.'

A sigh, short and faint, marked an almost imperceptible pause, and then his words flowed on, without a stir, without a gesture.

'After the time of trouble and war was over and you went away from my country in the pursuit of your desires, which we, men of the islands, cannot understand, I and my brother became again, as we had been before, the sword-bearers of the Ruler. You know we were men of family, belonging to a ruling race, and more fit than any to carry on our right shoulder the emblem of power. And in the time of prosperity Si Dendring showed us favour, as we, in time of sorrow, had showed to him the faithfulness of our courage. It was a time of peace. A time of deer-hunts and cock-fights; of idle talks and foolish squabbles between men whose bellies are full and weapons are rusty. But the sower watched the young rice-shoots grow up without fear, and the traders came and went, departed lean and returned fat into the river of peace. They brought news, too. Brought lies and truth mixed together, so that no man knew when to rejoice and when to be sorry. We heard from them about you also. They had seen you here and had seen you there. And I was glad to hear, for I remembered the stirring times, and I always remembered you, Tuan, till the time came when my eyes could see nothing in the past, because they had looked upon the one who is dying there – in the house.'

He stopped to exclaim in an intense whisper, 'O *Mara bahia*! O Calamity!' then went on speaking a little louder:

'There's no worse enemy and no better friend than a brother, Tuan, for one brother knows another, and in perfect knowledge is strength for good or evil. I loved my brother. I went to him and told him that I could see nothing but one face, hear nothing but one voice. He told me: "Open your heart so that she can see what is in it – and wait. Patience is wisdom. Inchi Midah may die or our Ruler may throw off his fear of a woman!"... I waited!... You remember the lady with the veiled face, Tuan, and the fear of our Ruler before her cunning and temper. And if she wanted her servant, what could I do? But I fed the hunger of my heart on short glances and stealthy words. I loitered on the path to the bath-houses in the daytime, and when the sun had fallen behind the forest I crept along the jasmine hedges of the women's courtyard. Unseeing, we spoke to one another through the scent of flowers, through the veil of leaves, through the blades of long grass that stood still before our lips; so great was our prudence, so faint was the murmur of our great longing. The time passed swiftly... and there were whispers amongst women – and our enemies watched – my brother was gloomy, and I began to think of killing and of a fierce death... We are of a people who take what they want – like you whites. There is a time when a man should forget loyalty and respect. Might and authority are given to rulers, but to all men is given love and strength and courage. My brother said, "You shall take her from their midst. We are two who are like one." And I answered, "Let it be soon, for I find no warmth in sunlight that does not shine upon her." Our time came when the Ruler and all the great people went to the mouth of the river to fish by torchlight. There were hundreds of boats, and on the white sand, between the water and the forests, dwellings of leaves were built for the households of the Rajahs. The smoke of cooking-fires was like a blue mist of the evening, and many voices rang in it joyfully. While they were making the boats ready to beat up the fish, my brother came to me and said, "Tonight!" I looked to my weapons, and when the time came our canoe took its place in the circle of boats carrying the torches. The lights blazed on the water, but behind the boats there was darkness. When the shouting began and the excitement made them like mad we dropped out. The water swallowed our fire, and we floated back to the shore that was dark with only here and there the glimmer of embers. We could hear the talk of slave-girls amongst the sheds. Then we found a place deserted and silent. We waited there. She came. She came running along the shore, rapid and leaving no trace, like a leaf driven by the wind into the sea. My brother said gloomily, "Go and take her; carry her into our boat." I lifted her in my arms. She panted. Her heart was beating against my breast. I said, "I take you from those people. You came to the cry of my heart, but my arms take you into my boat against the will of the great!" "It is right," said my brother. "We are men who take what we want and can hold it against many. We should have taken her in daylight." I said, "Let us be off;" for since she was in my boat I began to think of our Ruler's many men. "Yes. Let us be off," said my brother. "We are cast out and this boat is our country now – and the sea is our refuge." He lingered with his foot on the shore, and I entreated him to hasten, for I remembered the strokes of her heart against my breast and thought that two men cannot withstand a hundred. We left, paddling downstream close to the bank; and as we passed by the creek where they were fishing, the great shouting had ceased, but the murmur of voices was loud like the humming of insects flying at noonday. The boats floated, clustered together, in the red light of torches, under a black roof of smoke; and men talked of their sport. Men that boasted, and praised, and jeered – men that would have been our friends in the morning, but on that night were already our enemies. We paddled swiftly past. We had no more friends in the country of our birth. She sat in the middle of the canoe with covered face; silent as she is now; unseeing as she is now – and I had no regret at what I was leaving because I could hear her breathing close to me – as I can hear her now.'

He paused, listened with his ear turned to the doorway, then shook his head and went on:

'My brother wanted to shout the cry of challenge – one cry only – to let the people know we were freeborn robbers who trusted our arms and the great sea. And again I begged him in the name of our love to be silent. Could I not hear her breathing close to me? I knew the pursuit would come quick enough. My brother loved me. He dipped his paddle without a splash. He only said, "There is half a man in you now – the other half is in that woman. I can wait. When you are a whole man again, you will come back with me here to shout defiance. We are sons of the same mother." I made no answer. All my strength and all my spirit were in my hands that held the paddle – for I longed to be with her in a safe place beyond the reach of men's anger and of women's spite. My love was so great, that I thought it could guide me to a country where death was unknown, if I could only escape from Inchi Midah's fury and from our Ruler's sword. We paddled with haste, breathing through our teeth. The blades bit deep into the smooth water. We passed out of the river; we flew in clear channels amongst the shallows. We skirted the black coast; we skirted the sand beaches where the sea speaks in whispers to the land; and the gleam of white sand flashed back past our boat, so swiftly she ran upon the water. We spoke not. Only once I said, "Sleep, Diamelen, for soon you may want all your strength." I heard the sweetness of her voice, but I never turned my head. The sun rose and still we went on. Water fell from my face like rain from a cloud. We flew in the light and heat. I never looked back, but I knew that my brother's eyes, behind me, were looking steadily ahead, for the boat went as straight as a bushman's dart, when it leaves the end of the sumpitan. There was no better paddler, no better steersman than my brother. Many times, together, we had won races in that canoe. But we never had put out our strength as we did then – then, when for the last time we paddled together! There was no braver or stronger man in our country than my brother. I could not spare the strength to turn my head and look at him, but every moment I heard the hiss of his breath getting louder behind me. Still he did not speak. The sun was high. The heat clung to my back like a flame of fire. My ribs were ready to burst, but I could no longer get enough air into my chest. And then I felt I must cry out with my last breath, "Let us rest!"… "Good!" he answered; and his voice was firm. He was strong. He was brave. He knew not fear and no fatigue… My brother!'

A murmur powerful and gentle, a murmur vast and faint; the murmur of trembling leaves, of stirring boughs, ran through the tangled depths of the forests, ran over the starry smoothness of the lagoon, and the water between the piles lapped the slimy timber once with a sudden splash. A breath of warm air touched the two men's faces and passed on with a mournful sound – a breath loud and short like an uneasy sigh of the dreaming earth.

Arsat went on in an even, low voice.

'We ran our canoe on the white beach of a little bay close to a long tongue of land that seemed to bar our road; a long wooded cape going far into the sea. My brother knew that place. Beyond the cape a river has its entrance, and through the jungle of that land there is a narrow path. We made a fire and cooked rice. Then we lay down to sleep on the soft sand

in the shade of our canoe, while she watched. No sooner had I closed my
eyes than I heard her cry of alarm. We leaped up. The sun was halfway
down the sky already, and coming in sight in the opening of the bay we
saw a prau manned by many paddlers. We knew it at once; it was one of
our Rajah's praus. They were watching the shore, and saw us. They beat
the gong, and turned the head of the prau into the bay. I felt my heart
become weak within my breast. Diamelen sat on the sand and covered
her face. There was no escape by sea. My brother laughed. He had the
gun you had given him, Tuan, before you went away, but there was only a
handful of powder. He spoke to me quickly: "Run with her along the path.
I shall keep them back, for they have no firearms, and landing in the face
of a man with a gun is certain death for some. Run with her. On the other
side of that wood there is a fisherman's house – and a canoe. When I
have fired all the shots I will follow. I am a great runner, and before they
can come up we shall be gone. I will hold out as long as I can, for she
is but a woman – that can neither run nor fight, but she has your heart in
her weak hands." He dropped behind the canoe. The prau was coming.
She and I ran, and as we rushed along the path I heard shots. My brother
fired – once – twice – and the booming of the gong ceased. There was
silence behind us. That neck of land is narrow. Before I heard my brother
fire the third shot I saw the shelving shore, and I saw the water again; the
mouth of a broad river. We crossed a grassy glade. We ran down to the
water. I saw a low hut above the black mud, and a small canoe hauled
up. I heard another shot behind me. I thought, "That is his last charge."
We rushed down to the canoe; a man came running from the hut, but I
leaped on him, and we rolled together in the mud. Then I got up, and he
lay still at my feet. I don't know whether I had killed him or not. I and
Diamelen pushed the canoe afloat. I heard yells behind me, and I saw
my brother run across the glade. Many men were bounding after him, I
took her in my arms and threw her into the boat, then leaped in myself.
When I looked back I saw that my brother had fallen. He fell and was up
again, but the men were closing round him. He shouted, "I am coming!"
The men were close to him. I looked. Many men. Then I looked at her.
Tuan, I pushed the canoe! I pushed it into deep water. She was kneeling
forward looking at me, and I said, "Take your paddle," while I struck
the water with mine. Tuan, I heard him cry. I heard him cry my name
twice; and I heard voices shouting, "Kill! Strike!" I never turned back.

I heard him calling my name again with a great shriek, as when life is going out together with the voice – and I never turned my head. My own name!… My brother! Three times he called – but I was not afraid of life. Was she not there in that canoe? And could I not with her find a country where death is forgotten – where death is unknown!'

The white man sat up. Arsat rose and stood, an indistinct and silent figure above the dying embers of the fire. Over the lagoon a mist drifting and low had crept, erasing slowly the glittering images of the stars. And now a great expanse of white vapour covered the land: it flowed cold and grey in the darkness, eddied in noiseless whirls round the tree-trunks and about the platform of the house, which seemed to float upon a restless and impalpable illusion of a sea. Only far away the tops of the trees stood outlined on the twinkle of heaven, like a sombre and forbidding shore – a coast deceptive, pitiless and black.

Arsat's voice vibrated loudly in the profound peace.

'I had her there! I had her! To get her I would have faced all mankind. But I had her – and –'

His words went out ringing into the empty distances. He paused, and seemed to listen to them dying away very far – beyond help and beyond recall. Then he said quietly –

'Tuan, I loved my brother.'

A breath of wind made him shiver. High above his head, high above the silent sea of mist the drooping leaves of the palms rattled together with a mournful and expiring sound. The white man stretched his legs. His chin rested on his chest, and he murmured sadly without lifting his head –

'We all love our brothers.'

Arsat burst out with an intense whispering violence –

'What did I care who died? I wanted peace in my own heart.'

He seemed to hear a stir in the house – listened – then stepped in noiselessly. The white man stood up. A breeze was coming in fitful puffs. The stars shone paler as if they had retreated into the frozen depths of immense space. After a chill gust of wind there were a few seconds of perfect calm and absolute silence. Then from behind the black and wavy line of the forests a column of golden light shot up into the heavens and spread over the semicircle of the eastern horizon. The sun had risen. The mist lifted, broke into drifting patches, vanished into thin flying wreaths;

and the unveiled lagoon lay, polished and black, in the heavy shadows at the foot of the wall of trees. A white eagle rose over it with a slanting and ponderous flight, reached the clear sunshine and appeared dazzlingly brilliant for a moment, then soaring higher, became a dark and motionless speck before it vanished into the blue as if it had left the earth forever. The white man, standing gazing upwards before the doorway, heard in the hut a confused and broken murmur of distracted words ending with a loud groan. Suddenly Arsat stumbled out with outstretched hands, shivered, and stood still for some time with fixed eyes. Then he said –

'She burns no more.'

Before his face the sun showed its edge above the tree-tops rising steadily. The breeze freshened; a great brilliance burst upon the lagoon, sparkled on the rippling water. The forests came out of the clear shadows of the morning, became distinct, as if they had rushed nearer – to stop short in a great stir of leaves, of nodding boughs, of swaying branches. In the merciless sunshine the whisper of unconscious life grew louder, speaking in an incomprehensible voice round the dumb darkness of that human sorrow. Arsat's eyes wandered slowly, then stared at the rising sun.

'I can see nothing,' he said half aloud to himself.

'There is nothing,' said the white man, moving to the edge of the platform and waving his hand to his boat. A shout came faintly over the lagoon and the sampan began to glide towards the abode of the friend of ghosts.

'If you want to come with me, I will wait all the morning,' said the white man, looking away upon the water.

'No, Tuan,' said Arsat, softly. 'I shall not eat or sleep in this house, but I must first see my road. Now I can see nothing – see nothing! There is no light and no peace in the world; but there is death – death for many. We are sons of the same mother – and I left him in the midst of enemies; but I am going back now.'

He drew a long breath and went on in a dreamy tone:

'In a little while I shall see clear enough to strike – to strike. But she has died, and… now… darkness.'

He flung his arms wide open, let them fall along his body, then stood still with unmoved face and stony eyes, staring at the sun. The white man got down into his canoe. The polers ran smartly along the sides of the boat, looking over their shoulders at the beginning of a weary journey. High in the stern, his head muffled up in white rags, the juragan sat moody, letting his paddle trail in the water. The white man, leaning with both arms over the grass roof of the little cabin, looked back at the shining ripple of the boat's wake. Before the sampan passed out of the lagoon into the creek he lifted his eyes. Arsat had not moved. He stood lonely in the searching sunshine; and he looked beyond the great light of a cloudless day into the darkness of a world of illusions.